VANGO

VANGO

BETWEEN SKY AND EARTH

Timothée de Fombelle

translated by Sarah Ardizzone

CANDLEWICK PRESS

Text and cover design © 2010 Gallimard Jeunesse
English translation © 2013 Sarah Ardizzone

Picture of Graf Zeppelin: property of the author, all rights reserved.
Section of the gondola of the Graf Zeppelin: illustrations by McMaster, in *Dirigeables* © Gallimard 1997, all rights reserved.
Map of the Aeolian Islands: illustrations by Vincent Brunot.

First U.S. edition 2014

Library of Congress Catalog Card Number 2013955696
ISBN 978-0-7636-7196-9

15 16 17 18 19 BVG 10 9 8 7 6 5 4 3

Printed in Berryville, VA, U.S.A.

This book was typeset in Perpetua.

Candlewick Press
99 Dover Street
Somerville, Massachusetts 02144

visit us at www.candlewick.com

*I have hung ropes from steeple to steeple; garlands
from window to window; golden chains from star to star, and I dance.*

—Arthur Rimbaud

CONTENTS

PART ONE

I

THE WAY OF THE ANGELS

Paris, April 1934

Forty men in white were lying facedown on the cobbled square.

It looked like a giant snowfield. Swallows whistled as they brushed past the bodies. Thousands of people were watching the spectacle. The cathedral of Notre Dame in Paris spread her shadow over the assembled crowd.

All around, the city seemed to be gathering its thoughts.

Vango's forehead was pressed against the stone. He was listening to the sound of his own breathing and thinking about the life that had brought him here. But for once, he wasn't frightened.

He was remembering the sea, the briny air, a few special voices, a few special faces, and the warm tears of the woman who had raised him.

Rain started falling on the square in front of the cathedral, but Vango didn't notice. Lying on the ground in the midst of his companions, he wasn't aware of the umbrellas bursting into bloom one after another.

Vango didn't see the crowd of Parisians, the families dressed in their Sunday best, the devotion of the old ladies, the children squeezing between people's legs, the pigeons numb with cold, the dance of the swallows, the onlookers standing up in their carriages. Nor did he see the pair of green eyes, over there, to the side, watching only him.

Two green eyes brimming with tears, behind a veil.

Vango kept his own eyes tightly shut. He hadn't turned twenty yet. This was the biggest day of his life. A solemn feeling of happiness welled up inside him.

He was about to become a priest.

"Sweet madness!"

The bell ringer of Notre Dame, high above, muttered these words as he glanced down at the square below. He was waiting. He had invited a young lady by the name of Clara to dine with him on boiled eggs in his tower.

He knew she wouldn't come: she'd be just like all the others. And while the water was simmering in the pan beneath the giant clock, the bell ringer took a good look at the young seminarians down below who were about to be ordained as priests. They would lie on the ground for a few minutes more before making their commitment for life. From his perch fifty meters above the crowd, it wasn't the sheer drop that made Simon the bell ringer's head spin but the leap into the unknown that these prostrated lives on the ground were, of their own accord, about to make.

"Madness," he said again. "Madness!"

He made the sign of the cross, because you never know, and went back to his eggs.

The green eyes were still fixed on Vango.

They belonged to a girl of sixteen or seventeen who was wearing a charcoal-colored velvet coat. She rummaged in her pocket but couldn't find the handkerchief she was looking for. The back of that white hand ventured under the veil and wiped away the tears on her cheeks. The rain was starting to come in through her coat.

The girl shivered and glanced across to the other side of the cathedral square.

A man looked away abruptly. He had been watching her. She felt sure of that. It was the second time she had noticed him this morning, but she knew, far back in her memory, that she had already seen him somewhere. A waxen face, white hair, a thin mustache, and small wire glasses. Where had she met him before?

The thunder of the organ brought her back to Vango.

The ceremony was about to begin. The elderly cardinal stood up and made his way toward the young men in white. He brushed aside the umbrella held out to keep him dry, just as he brushed aside all the hands that offered to help him down the steps.

"Leave me be!"

He was carrying his heavy crosier, and every step was a small miracle.

The cardinal was old and sick. That same morning, his doctor, Esquirol, had banned him from celebrating mass. The cardinal had laughed, sent everybody away, and heaved himself out of bed to get dressed. As soon as he was alone, he could groan freely with every gesture. In public, he was a rock.

Now he was walking down the steps in the rain.

Two hours earlier, with the black clouds thickening, everyone had begged him to move the ceremony inside the cathedral. Once again, he'd held firm. He wanted it to take place outside, facing the world these young men would engage with for their whole lives.

"If they're worried about catching a cold, let them choose another job. They'll live through other storms."

On the final step, the cardinal came to a stop.

He was the first to detect something afoot in the square.

Up above, Simon the bell ringer didn't suspect a thing. He dropped his eggs into the water and started counting.

Who could have predicted what would happen in the time it takes to boil an egg?

Three minutes to change the course of destiny.

While the water was coming to a boil, the crowd was simmering in a similar state of excitement, starting from the back row. The girl gave another shudder. Something was going on in the square. The cardinal raised his head.

Twenty individuals were beating a path through the crowd. The murmuring swelled. Shouts could be heard.

"Make way!"

But the forty seminarians didn't move. Only Vango turned his head to the side, putting his ear to the ground. He could see the shadows closing in.

The voices were becoming clearer now.

"What's going on?"

"Move back!"

People were distrustful. Two months earlier, riots had led to fatalities and hundreds wounded in the Place de la Concorde.

"It's the police!" a woman called out to reassure the crowd.

They were looking for somebody. The faithful tried to quell the hubbub.

"Shhhh . . . be quiet!"

Fifty-nine seconds.

Under his clock, the bell ringer was still counting. He was thinking about young Clara, who had promised him she would come. He looked at the wooden crate set with two places. He could hear the saucepan humming on the embers.

A cleric wearing a white robe went over to the cardinal and whispered something in his ear. Just behind them stood a short, rotund man, holding his hat in his hand: Superintendent Boulard. There was no mistaking his drooping eyelids, like those of an old dog, his big snout, his ruddy cheeks, and his eyes, which twinkled with a zest for life. Auguste Boulard. Unflappable under the April shower, he was on the lookout for the slightest sign of movement from the young men lying on the ground.

One minute and twenty seconds.

Just then, one of the seminarians stood up. He wasn't very tall. His robe was weighed down with the rain. His face was streaming. He turned full circle in the midst of so many bodies, none of which moved. On every side, plainclothes policemen emerged from the crowd and began to advance toward him. The young man brought his hands together as if in prayer, then let them fall to his sides. The clouds in the sky were reflected in his eyes.

"Vango Romano?" the superintendent called out.

The boy nodded.

In the crowd, somewhere, a pair of green eyes was flitting, like butterflies in a net. What did these people want from Vango?

The young man started moving. He stepped over his fellow

seminarians and walked toward the superintendent. The police officers were edging forward.

As he advanced, Vango pulled off his white robe to reveal the black clothes underneath. He stopped in front of the cardinal and dropped to his knees.

"Forgive me, Father."

"What have you done, Vango?"

"I don't know, Your Grace. Please believe me. I don't know."

One minute and fifty seconds.

The old cardinal gripped the cross with both hands. He leaned on it with his full weight, his arm and shoulder wrapped around the gilded wood like ivy on a tree. He looked sadly around him. He knew every one of these forty young men by name.

"I believe you, little one, but I fear I may be the only one here who does."

"That already means a great deal, if you really do believe me."

"But it won't be enough," whispered the cardinal.

He was right. Boulard and his comrades were only a few paces away now.

"Forgive me," Vango begged again.

"What do you want me to forgive you for, if you haven't done anything?"

Superintendent Boulard, who was now standing right behind him, put his hand on the boy's shoulder, and Vango gave the cardinal his answer: "For this . . ."

Vango grabbed hold of the superintendent's hand, stood up, and twisted Boulard's arm behind his back. Then he flung him toward one of his men.

In a few leaps, the young man had escaped the two police officers who rushed toward him. A third brandished his gun.

"Don't shoot!" ordered Boulard from the ground.

A great clamor rose up from the crowd, but with a simple hand gesture, the cardinal silenced it.

Vango had made his way up the platform steps. A group of choristers scattered noisily as he ran through them. The police officers looked like they were crossing a school play-ground. With every step, they tripped on a child or were head-butted in the stomach.

"Tell them to stand aside! Who is in charge of them?"

The cardinal raised his finger in the air, delighted.

"God alone, Superintendent."

Two minutes and thirty seconds.

Vango had reached the central portal of the cathedral. He saw a small, pale, plump woman disappear behind one side of the double doors and close it after her. He threw himself against the wooden door.

On the other side, the lock turned.

"Open up!" shouted Vango. "Open up for me!"

"I knew I shouldn't have," a trembling voice answered him. "I'm sorry. I didn't mean any harm. It was the bell ringer who told me to come here."

Behind the door, the woman was crying.

"Open up!" Vango called out again. "I don't even know what you're talking about. I'm just asking you to open the door."

"He seemed a nice person. . . . Please. My name is Clara. I'm not a bad girl."

Vango could hear the policemen's voices behind him. He felt his legs buckle.

"I'm not blaming you for anything. I just need your help. Open the door for me."

"No . . . I can't . . . I'm frightened."

Vango turned around.

There were ten men in a semicircle around the carved cathedral gates.

"Don't move," said one of them.

Vango pinned his back against the door that shone with brass. "It's too late now," he whispered. "Whatever you do, don't open up. I'll have to go another way."

He took a step toward the men, then turned around and looked up. Above him was the Portal of the Last Judgment. He knew every detail by heart. There was carved stone fili-gree around the door. To the right, in relief, the damned of hell were depicted. To the left, paradise and its angels.

Vango chose the way of the angels.

Just then, Superintendent Boulard reached the scene. He nearly passed out when he saw what was happening. In less than a second, Vango Romano had scaled the first rows of statues. He was five meters above the ground now.

Three minutes.

Simon the bell ringer, who hadn't seen anything, removed the eggs with a spoon.

Vango wasn't so much climbing as gliding gently across the cathedral facade. His fingers were able to get a grip on the tiniest piece of relief. His arms and legs moved effortlessly. He looked like he was swimming vertically.

The crowd watched him, openmouthed. A lady fainted and slid off her chair like a scrap of cloth. Down at the foot of the great wall, police officers were moving around in every direction. As for the superintendent, he was frozen to the spot.

A first shot rang out. Boulard managed to find enough breath to bellow, "Stop! I told you not to open fire!"

But none of the policemen had used a weapon. One officer was pointlessly giving a leg up to his colleague. The poor devil was all of eighty centimeters off the cobbles. Others were trying to open the two-ton door with their nails.

A fresh burst of gunfire.

"Who is shooting?" roared Boulard, grabbing one of his men by the collar. "Instead of wrestling with that door, find me the person who's shooting. What do you want to get in there for, anyway? To light a candle?"

"We thought we'd catch him in the towers, Superintendent."

"There's a staircase on the north side," an irritable Boulard informed them, pointing to the left. "I'm keeping Remi and Avignon with me. I want to know who's trying to shoot my target."

Vango had already made it to the level of the Kings' Gallery. He drew himself up to his full height and hung on to a column. He was breathing calmly. Determination and despair were both visible on his face. He was looking down at the square below. Thousands of eyes stared up at him. A bullet caused a stone crown to shatter into smithereens, just by his ear, blowing showers of white powder onto his cheek. Far down below, he could see the superintendent pacing in circles like a madman.

"Who did that?" boomed Boulard.

It wasn't the police firing at him. Vango soon realized that. He had other enemies in the vicinity.

He continued his ascent and in a few moves had reached the foot of the Rose Window. He was now climbing the most beautiful stained-glass window in the world, much as a spider glides over its web.

Down below, a hush had fallen on the crowd. The onlookers stood there, captivated by the vision of this boy hanging on to the West Rose Window of Notre Dame.

The swallows flew in a tightly packed flotilla around Vango, as if to protect him with their tiny feathery bodies.

Below his bell, and with a tear in his eye, Simon took the top off the first egg with his knife. Once again, she hadn't come.

"It's a sad world," he mumbled.

When he heard the squeaking of the wooden staircase that led to the bell, he stopped.

"Clara?" he called.

He looked at his second egg. Confused, Simon thought for a split second that happiness was knocking at his door.

"Clara? Is that you?"

"She's waiting for you downstairs."

It was Vango. A bullet had grazed him while he was regaining his footing in the Grand Gallery.

"She needs you," he told the bell ringer.

Simon felt a flicker of joy. Nobody had ever needed him.

"And you? Who are you? What are you doing here?"

"I don't know," said Vango. "I've got no idea. I need you too."

* * *

Out in the square, the other girl, the one with green eyes and the charcoal-colored coat, was battling against the crowd. At the precise moment when Vango had made a run for it, she had seen the man with the waxen face taking out a gun from his coat. She had rushed toward him, but the crowd prevented her from making any progress. When she finally got to the other side, he was no longer there.

Earlier, she had looked as forlorn as a bedraggled cat. Now she was a fierce lion clearing everything in her path.

And then she heard the shot. Strangely, she knew at once that Vango was the target. With the second shot, her eyes turned toward the Hôtel-Dieu Hospital, on the north side of the square. That was when she saw the man. He was on the first floor. The pistol was protruding from a broken window, and in the gloom, it was possible to make out the icy reflection of the shooter. It was him.

She glanced upward. Vango was doing his balancing act on high. Heaven had wrenched him from his destiny at the last moment. But for her, everything had become possible again. As long as he was alive.

The girl with green eyes strode toward the hospital.

Suddenly, in the sky above Notre Dame, a gigantic monster rose up, almost making the crowd forget everything at ground level. As tall and majestic as the cathedral itself and gleaming with rain, the zeppelin appeared. It filled the sky.

At the front of the cockpit, Hugo Eckener, the elderly commander of the *Graf Zeppelin,* was peering through his telescope in search of his friend down in the cathedral square

13

below. Returning from Brazil and heading for Lake Constance, he had made the balloon take a detour via Paris so that the shadow of the zeppelin would play a small part in this important moment of Vango's life.

At the third shot, Eckener realized something was wrong.

"We have to leave, Commander," urged Lehmann, his captain.

A stray bullet risked puncturing the balloon, which held sixty passengers and crew members in its gleaming body.

There was a final explosion at ground level.

"Quickly, Commander . . ."

Eckener lowered his telescope and agreed reluctantly: "Yes, let's go."

Down below, a dead swallow fell at Superintendent Boulard's feet.

And the bells of Notre Dame began to ring.

THE SMOKING WILD BOAR

Paris, the same evening

Superintendent Boulard was sitting in a smoke-filled room with a large steak in front of him and a checked napkin tucked in at his neck while his troops stood around him. He had some choice words for the men who were watching him eat.

"If my steak wasn't up to scratch, I would ask for it to be taken away and I'd order a fresh one. But as for you, you bunch of spineless good-for-nothings, you're breathing down my neck and I can't trade you in. You're putting me off my food. . . ."

The superintendent was eating rather heartily, as it happened. In the course of his forty-three years on the job, he had learned how to keep his morale up when the going got tough.

They were on the second floor of the Smoking Wild Boar, the famous brasserie in Les Halles.

"He made fools of you! A kid managed to get away from you in front of two thousand people!"

Boulard picked at a sautéed potato, stopped, rolled his eyes, and summed up the evidence: "You're a bunch of incompetents!"

Incredibly, not one of the strapping men would have dreamed of casting doubt on this declaration. When Boulard said something, it was always true. If he had said, "You're a troupe of ballet dancers from the opera house!" they would all have gone up on tiptoes with their arms in the air.

Superintendent Boulard was worshipped by his men. He let them cry on his shoulder when they were feeling low, he knew the names of all their children, he gave their wives flowers on their birthdays, but when he felt let down, when he felt really let down, he didn't even recognize them in the street and deliberately avoided them as if they were stray dogs.

The second floor of the Smoking Wild Boar had been closed to the public so that this meeting could take place. Only two lightbulbs had been left on, and they drew attention to a large wild boar's head just above Boulard. The kitchen lay behind them. A stream of waiters came in and out, loaded up with plates.

In a corner, some distance from the superintendent's men, a kitchen porter, a boy, was sitting with his back to them at a lone table, peeling vegetables.

Boulard preferred this atmosphere to the one at the police headquarters at the Quai des Orfèvres. He held his meetings here whenever he could. He loved the smell of the sauces and the flapping of the kitchen doors. He had been brought up in a small family-run hotel in the Aveyron.

"And what about that zeppelin?" railed Boulard. "Does anybody know what it was doing there? Don't tell me it was by chance!"

Nobody answered.

A man entered the room. He whispered something in the ear of the superintendent, who raised his eyebrows.

"Who is it?"

The man didn't know.

"All right. Tell her to come up."

The messenger disappeared.

Boulard tore off a piece of bread to mop up what was left on his plate. He gestured vaguely toward the kitchen porter in the corner.

"I want people like that," he grumbled. "You ask him for something, he does it. As for you lot, there are twenty-five of you, but you let the kid escape. If that fellow was in this room right now, one of you would even open the window for him."

"Superintendent . . ."

Boulard looked up to see who had dared answer him back. It was Augustin Avignon, his faithful lieutenant for twenty years. Boulard squinted at him, as if his face was vaguely familiar.

"Superintendent, there's no explanation for what happened. Even the bell ringer, all that way up, says he didn't see him. That kid is the devil himself. I swear we did everything in our power."

Boulard gently rubbed his earlobe. Whenever he did this, you had to be on your guard.

He answered Avignon slowly: "I'm sorry. . . . What are you doing here? Do I know you? At the end of the street, on the left, there is a snail seller who would be more competent at your job than you are."

Boulard dived back into his sauce. Avignon's nose twitched a bit. His eyes were smarting. He turned away to wipe them with his sleeve. Luckily, nobody was looking.

As if a trembling antelope had suddenly appeared on the

second floor of the Smoking Wild Boar, the troops turned in one breath toward the young woman who had just emerged at the top of the stairs.

It was the girl with green eyes.

Boulard wiped his mouth with the corner of his napkin, gently pushed himself away from the table, and stood up.

"Good evening, Mademoiselle."

The young woman stared at her feet before this regiment of police officers.

"You wish to speak with me?" asked Boulard.

He took a few steps in her direction, grabbed the hat from one of his lieutenants who had neglected to take it off, and thrust it discreetly into a half-empty soup tureen, which a waiter promptly cleared away. The hat headed off toward the kitchen.

The young lady looked up. She seemed hesitant to talk in front of this gathering.

"Just pretend they aren't here," Boulard reassured her. "As far as I'm concerned, they no longer exist."

"I was there this morning," she said.

Every man in the room gently drew himself up to his full height. She had a very faint accent, and there was a misty quality to her voice, which made everybody want to show off his best side. Even the boy with the vegetables finally stopped peeling, although he didn't turn around.

"I saw something," she added.

"You're not the only one," quipped Boulard. "These gentlemen put on a fine show for us."

"No, I saw something else, Officer."

There were a few smirks. She was addressing the renowned superintendent as if he were a low-ranking policeman.

"I saw the man who opened fire."

The smiles vanished. Boulard clutched his table napkin in his fist.

"He was at the window of the Hôtel-Dieu," she went on. "I got there too late. He'd already gone. That's all I know."

She held out a piece of paper that was folded in half. The superintendent opened it to reveal a portrait sketched in black pencil: a mustache and thin glasses.

"That's the man's face," she said. "Try to find him."

Boulard was struggling to hide his surprise. Now he had a lead. For him, the man who had opened fire counted as much as the boy who had gotten away. "Follow us, Mademoiselle," he said. "I'd like to get some more details."

"There are no more details. It's all there."

Then she walked over to the blackboard where the menu was chalked up and used her elbow to rub out the black pudding and the pig's trotters. She wrote down an address instead, adding, "I've got to catch a boat that leaves from Calais tomorrow morning at five o'clock. I'll be driving all night. My car is down in the street. But you can pay me a visit over there, if you really want to."

All the men had silly grins on their faces. They had sudden urges to go to sea.

Superintendent Boulard looked at the address she had written in chalk. Above it, she had put her first name and the initials of her surname.

Ethel B. H.
Everland Castle
Inverness

For the first time in his life, Boulard was at a loss for words. And in front of his men, he felt embarrassed about being embarrassed.

"Right," he said. "England it is."

"No. Not at all. It's not in England," replied Ethel, tucking her brown hair into a leather helmet with large goggles on the front.

"It's . . ."

"It's in Scotland, Officer."

"Of course," said Boulard briskly, instinctively imitating a bagpipe player with his elbows.

He was toying with the idea of adding a few touristic touches to prove to the young lady that he was perfectly well aware of the existence of Scotland, its whiskey, and its kilts. But she got in there first with a question: "What's Vango done for you to be hunting him down like this?"

"I'm not at liberty to disclose," replied Boulard, delighted to be able to exert his authority again. "Does he interest you?"

"I like the idea of a priest who climbs cathedrals to escape the police."

"He hadn't yet been ordained a priest," Boulard pointed out.

"Thank God."

She uttered these words even more mistily and mysteriously. The superintendent could hear their double meaning. Ethel intimated that she was reassured it wasn't an ordained priest who had behaved in such an unorthodox way. But there was something else. . . . Boulard sensed her secret joy that this young man, this young man in particular, had not become a priest after all.

"Did you know him?" inquired Boulard, taking a step toward her.

"No."

This time, he noticed a hidden sadness in her voice. And Boulard, who couldn't help analyzing everything, could tell that she wasn't lying. She didn't know this cathedral-climbing seminarian—she no longer recognized the Vango who had revealed himself that day—but Boulard guessed that she had certainly known him in the past.

The superintendent also noticed that she had called Vango by his first name. He was almost sure about that. How did she know his first name? Boulard had only used it once in the crowd at the cathedral square. The evening newspapers hadn't made any mention. He tried to delay her a little longer.

"Why were you there this morning?"

"I enjoy romantic ceremonies."

She pulled on a pair of gloves, which only emphasized the slenderness of her hands.

Boulard found his manners again.

"Shall I ask one of my men to drive you?"

"I'm a perfectly good driver. Good night, Monsieur."

She ran down the stairs.

Boulard saw his men rush over to the windows. They watched Ethel make her way over to a tiny mud-splattered Napier-Railton, an ultra-powerful gem of an automobile that the workshops of Thomson and Taylor had just created at Brooklands. It boasted a real airplane engine in tempered steel.

She started the car, pulled down her goggles, and disappeared off into the night.

The atmosphere in the dining room of the Smoking Wild Boar suddenly became much more relaxed. Everybody started laughing and patting one another on the back as if they'd just survived the aftershock of an earthquake.

Boulard remained at the window. He was watching a boy in a claret-colored apron, alone under the street lamp. He had seen him go down to the street just as the automobile was pulling off, run for a moment in the same direction, then stop and lean against the gaslight.

The exhaust fumes made it impossible to see his face. But when they cleared, Superintendent Boulard let out a roar and rushed downstairs.

Five seconds later, the superintendent was on the opposite sidewalk.

Nobody.

Boulard gave the lamppost a kick and hobbled back toward the brasserie. He made his way up to the second floor, went into the kitchens, grabbed the chef by the collar, dragged him into the main room, and showed him the pile of perfectly peeled potatoes that had been left on the table.

The chef straightened his toque, picked up a potato, which he held between his thumb and index finger, and examined it slowly but expertly, looking for something to complain about, but he could find nothing.

"Impressive. Eight sides, the eight-sided peeled potato. You don't get better than that. A true talent."

"Where is the person who produced that?" asked Boulard.

"I . . . I don't know. But I'd be happy to see him again. Don't worry—he won't go without being paid. You can tell him then what you think of his potatoes. . . ."

Boulard forced a smile.

"Oh, yes? And have you known this artist long?"

"No. When it's busy on Saturdays, we take day workers from Les Halles market, in front of Saint-Eustache. I got him at nine o'clock this evening. I don't know his name."

Boulard knocked over the table and its precious pyramid of eight-sided potatoes.

"I'll tell you his name. His name is Vango Romano. And he killed a man last night."

PARANOIA

Sochi, by the Black Sea,
the same night, April 1934

A small conservatory radiates light, like a crystal lantern, on the side of a large house. The rest is darkness. Armed guards, positioned on the roof and in the trees, are invisible. A sea breeze rises up from the valley.

In the conservatory, three spirit lamps suspended between orchids shine down on a man. A gardener perhaps. He is pruning the potted orange trees.

"Go to bed, Setanka, my Setanotchka."

He has a soft voice. Setanka pretends not to hear him. She is eight years old. Sitting on the floor in her nightie, she is making long seeds float in the water from a watering can: they look like miniature dugout canoes.

Outside, a lamp sways. A worried face appears at the door. Someone raps on one of the thick glass panes.

The gardener's mustache twitches. He carries on pruning but doesn't answer.

The visitor enters and makes his way over to the orange trees.

"There's news from Paris," he announces.

The gardener hasn't so much as glanced his way. The hint of a smile can be guessed at in the crease of his eyes.

"It's not good news," the man adds.

This time the gardener's gaze meets his, and it is as blue as the ice of Lake Baikal.

"The Bird," announces the messenger, taking a step back. "The Bird has flown. Nobody can understand what's happened."

The gardener sucks his finger, which is bleeding a little. He has just snagged the skin with his copper scissors.

At his feet, the little girl has stopped playing. She is listening.

She's heard mention of the Bird for several years now.

Out of all the unfathomable conversations she's heard between her father and people who come to talk to him, this mention of the Bird is the only thing that has ever attracted her attention.

She's even made up stories about him. In the evenings, she dreams that he's flying in her bedroom; she hides him in her hands, or in her sheets.

"Boris fired but just missed the target," the man explains. "But Boris says he'll find him again. Otherwise, the French police will take matters into their own hands. . . ."

The messenger stands there in silence. He can feel the cold air on his back. When the gardener finally turns away, the messenger makes to leave, looking very pale. Carefully, he closes the glass door behind him and heads off.

The lamp disappears into the night.

"What bird was he talking about?" asks a small voice.

Still the gardener doesn't move.

"Go to bed, Setanka."

This time, she stands up and kisses her father's thick mustache just as she does every evening. She whispers something in his ear.

Setanka wanders off in her white nightgown, spreading her arms like wings. The gardener slams his scissors into the table. He has already forgotten what his daughter has just told him.

"You should never shoot birds."

That's what she said.

If she only knew.

Paris, at exactly the same time

Vango is walking on the rooftops of Paris. He knows the aerial path between the Jardin du Luxembourg and the Carmelites by heart. He barely needs to touch the ground when he's making this journey. He's aware that the police are stationed in front of the seminary and that they're waiting for him.

Vango crosses the stretches of zinc, slides over the slates, and leaps between chimneys. He knows where to find the cables to cross the streets. He doesn't even disturb the romantic April pigeons cooing in the gutters. He flies over the attic dwellers: the students, maids, and artists. He doesn't wake the cats, and he doesn't so much as brush against the laundry hanging out to dry on the terraces. Occasionally, at an open window, a woman wrapped in a blanket is breathing in the springtime night air.

Jumping from roof to roof, he passes just above them all, without a sound.

A few days earlier, Vango had taken this route in the opposite direction, to escape from the seminary in the middle of the night in order to reach the snow-covered park.

From the last gutter, he had leaped into an old chestnut tree that straddled the park fence with its spikes, before sliding down the tree trunk.

It had snowed during the first few days of April. Vango had kept walking until dawn, making his way through the snow, across lawns and deserted pathways. He had stared at the ice in the lakes. Then, again by way of the rooftops, he had returned to the Carmelite Chapel for morning mass.

Father Jean had given him a mild telling-off for being a few seconds late.

"You sleep too much, little one."

He had said this while looking at Vango's shoes, which were soaked through with snow and mud. There was no hiding anything from Father Jean.

But this time, as he walked over the rooftops of Paris, Vango knew what would be waiting for him at the seminary, and it wouldn't be the gentle reproaches of Father Jean, or even the fury of old Bastide, the canon, who ran the house like an army barracks.

What was waiting for him was the police, handcuffs, and perhaps prison.

Why had he fled, that same morning, from Notre Dame? Why had he run away, if he had nothing to reproach himself for? Doing so meant that the finger was now firmly pointed at him. But then again, for reasons that he didn't quite understand, Vango always felt compelled to be suspicious of everything, with the result that he believed himself to be a target for all sorts of enemies.

Vango firmly believed he was under threat. Since the age of fourteen, he had been told he suffered from something that a psychiatrist had written in capital letters on his file: PARANOIA. Because of those eight letters, he had nearly been thrown out of the seminary. Father Jean had done everything in his power to defend him. He had personally undertaken to guarantee Vango's mental well-being.

"You're taking risks," Canon Bastide had told Father Jean. "You'll regret it."

Father Jean took risks every day, and he never regretted them.

This time, however, he was worried.

Deep down, he felt responsible for what was happening to Vango. He had betrayed the secrecy of confession by revealing Vango's fears to Bastide.

The young seminarian had told him everything. He was convinced that he was being hunted down: cars following him in the street, his room being searched when he was out, scaffolding collapsing just behind him, as if by chance, and his nighttime struggle in the Carmelite cloisters against a shadow with a knife.

Somebody wanted his skin.

Paranoid confusion, persecution complex. Father Jean knew all about these matters. He had been a military doctor during the Great War. He knew how to gauge the effects of an illness that could lead to madness. At the beginning, people just felt they were being spied on or harassed, but then they started suspecting those close to them, and everyone became a potential threat.

*   *   *

Vango stopped, with tears in his eyes. He was balancing on a steel girder linking two buildings. He had just heard the seminary clock strike three in the morning. His whole life could be played out to the sound of church bells. Others, far away, chimed too, both across Paris and in his memories.

By the time the peal of bells was over, Vango had decided. He was going to make his way to Father Jean's bedroom and turn himself in.

The priest would take him to the police and be his advocate. Vango would explain his flight. At last they would find out what he was being blamed for. This was the decision that he had reached. He would be able to explain himself because he hadn't done anything wrong.

A few minutes later, he caught sight of the rooftops of the Carmelite seminary. There was just one more street left to cross. A black Citroën Rosalie was parked by the sidewalk. Red cigarette tips flickered inside it. It must have been hard to breathe in there. There was probably an entire police station, two or three rows deep, crammed into the smoky van. Even the metal bodywork seemed to be coughing.

The scene made Vango smile. And it gave him an idea.

Moments later, Vango found himself on the roof of the building opposite the seminary, on the other side of the street. Against his back, he could feel the warm flue of a chimney, and he could see the wreaths of smoke escaping above him.

He pulled a few badly pointed bricks out of the wall and placed them on top of each terra-cotta chimney pot. Now the smoke was being held prisoner. He positioned himself close to the gutter and waited.

It didn't take long.

Windows could be seen lighting up and opening, and people were coming outside to catch their breath on the balconies. A few first shouts were heard, then came the stampede down the staircase. Because the smoke couldn't get out up above, it was spreading through the apartments.

Vango slid in through a skylight, landed in a stairwell now heaving with people, and carefully started combing the smoke-filled apartments. He didn't want to put anybody in danger. He made sure that everywhere was empty. While he was moving about, he deliberately put his hand in some fireplace soot and rubbed it on his face. It would be impossible to recognize Vango in the middle of these shadowy figures rushing down the stairs, their cheeks blackened with smoke.

On the second floor, he went up to a woman carrying two children. He grabbed hold of the little one, who was crying.

"I'll help you."

He hurried down into the street, caught up in a crowd of people in pajamas. The police officers had come out of their car. They were as surprised as everyone else.

Vango crossed the street to join those waiting on the sidewalk. He was just a few paces away from the seminary door. He turned toward a police officer and placed the screaming baby in his arms.

"Are you the police?" asked Vango.

"Yes . . ."

"Right, well, tell your friends that my grandmother is up on the top floor. She's looking for her cat. She won't come out without it."

The police officer was holding the baby as if it were a

bomb about to explode. He handed it over to the first person who came along, signaled to his colleagues, and ran toward the building. The bell on the fire engine was getting closer.

"There's a grandmother on the fifth floor!"

Vango disappeared into the crowd.

Small miracles can accompany great misfortune. He had always thought that. You just need the confidence to believe it.

Vango arrived in front of the seminary door and pushed against it with his shoulder. Bad luck—it was closed. He took a step backward but didn't even have time to try it again. By a miracle, it opened straight away. Bad luck, it revealed Weber, the seminary caretaker. By a miracle . . . no. Weber froze.

For a moment they stared at each other.

Was it possible that he might not recognize Vango? The latter was counting the seconds and waiting for the miracle to happen. Weber's face lit up. He opened his mouth wide and had to restrain himself from calling out.

Vango had stopped breathing.

"Nina Bienvenue," said Weber.

"I beg your pardon?" mumbled Vango.

"It's Nina Bienvenue."

"Who?"

"I'm a girl from out of town . . ."

"Come again?"

"Look, my loverboy . . ."

Spoken by a Capuchin monk in his dressing gown, these words were surprising to say the least. His cheeks had turned bright red.

"Take me in your arms, my tender one, my handsome one, take me in your arms, my pet. . . ."

Weber had indeed opened his arms wide. Vango took a step to the side.

"Look," said the caretaker solemnly. "Nina Bienvenue, the singer from La Lune Rousse!"

Vango turned around. On the opposite sidewalk, barefoot and breathtaking in a nightgown that didn't cover her knees, with a pink fur collar and a pink flannel knot tied at the hip, not to mention the face to match, was Nina Bienvenue, the cabaret star from La Lune Rousse nightclub in Montmartre. She was twenty-five and had already captured all the hearts in Paris.

She was the final miracle. The ideal diversion. She had found herself as smoked as a kipper in her spacious second-floor apartment.

Weber was seeing stars. He knew every song.

It helps to know that Raimundo Weber was a Capuchin monk from Perpignan who had been allowed to retire to the capital and who played the foxtrot at night on the chapel organ. He was less than five feet tall, but each hand spanned two octaves.

He threw back his shoulders, undid his dressing gown, and twirled it around him like a bullfighter. He was wearing checked pajamas. He took one step toward the singer, then another, then another, as if inviting her to dance the tango in the street. He ended up giving a bow that, given his lack of height, brought him level with the cobbles. Then, with another bullfighting swish of his dressing gown, he covered the bare shoulders of the beauty.

"Allow me, Mademoiselle. From an admirer."

Nina Bienvenue smiled.

Vango was already in the courtyard. He crept down a long corridor and entered another courtyard. Hearing voices draw near, he threw himself into a dark corner, then climbed lizard-like up a pipe attached to the wall. He was back on the roof. He could breathe again.

He had always felt better closer to the sky. He was instinctively drawn to heights. Take yesterday's bad luck, for example, which had threatened to shatter his life—hadn't it occurred just as he was lying on the ground for the first time?

He had spent his childhood on cliff tops, directly above the sea, among the birds. He had learned to tame the vertical.

Vango took a few steps along a narrow ledge. Father Jean's bedroom was just there, in the small wing, at the back of the cobbled courtyard.

Father Jean, his only hope.

Two men were standing on the steps, guarding the door.

These guards weren't in Vango's way, because he wasn't the kind of person who entered boringly via the doors, but their presence alarmed him. He hoped they hadn't caused Father Jean any bother on his account. Above all, he hoped that nobody thought Father Jean was involved in his escape or in whatever misdeed he stood accused of. Misdeed. What misdeed?

When he had slipped into the Smoking Wild Boar, as a last-minute hire to peel potatoes, Vango was trying to find out about his crime. He had discovered the superintendent's hideout and had listened in on him, but he hadn't learned anything. The only revelation had come from another voice, as gentle as the summer rain, which had stirred up emotions inside him, making him capsize under the weight of tears.

Ethel.

He had heard Ethel's voice for the first time in five years. So she had come.

In the restaurant, he hadn't even been able to turn around to take a look at her. But he could tell that she hadn't changed. Vango had met Ethel in 1929, when she was twelve and he was fourteen. That meeting had changed a lot of things in his life. From that day on, the world had seemed more wonderful to him, and a bit more complicated too.

A candle was shining in Father Jean's window. He must be at home. Vango climbed over the gutter, lowered himself so that he was hanging over the void, dropped to the window ledge on the top floor, and then performed the same set of acrobatics to descend another floor. Just below him, on the steps, the guards were lighting a cigarette. Vango glued his face to the windowpane. A single candle, almost burned to the quick, illuminated the room. He could see Father Jean asleep in bed.

He must have dropped off during his evening meditation. Vango smiled. That was just like him. Father Jean was still fully clothed and holding his rosary.

The window was open. Vango simply had to push it. He entered the room.

He was almost safe. With Father Jean by his side, nothing more could happen to him.

Vango was worried about frightening the priest.

"It's me, Father. Vango," he called out very softly.

Because the window had been left half open, the temperature in the bedroom was glacial. Vango didn't dare get too close to the bed. He decided to wait for the priest to wake up.

Looking for a chair, he noticed that one section of the room was cordoned off with tape a meter off the floor.

Vango slid underneath the tape and got as far as the small desk where he had spent many hours at the side of his old friend.

"A desk is a boat," Father Jean had told him one day as he sat down at it. "This is how you should work. Lean over your book and hoist the sails."

Out in the corridor, a door slammed. Vango waited for some time before taking another step.

The desktop was in disarray. Fountain pens lay in a sea of ink half soaked up by the wood. A large notebook was open. Strangest of all, a line of white chalk had been drawn around each object as if to mark its place.

Vango shivered and leaned over the notebook. On the page he saw a dark stain and two words, in Latin, scribbled feverishly in the hand of Father Jean:

Fugere Vango

It only took a second.

He understood everything. The stain was a bloodstain. The room had been left in the state in which it had been discovered. The man lying on the bed was dead.

Now Vango understood his crime.

Father Jean was dead.

And the two words written on the notebook were accusing him:

Flee Vango

In everyone's eyes, he was Father Jean's murderer.

He was being hunted down for this crime, which must have been committed the previous night, just before the ordination.

Vango collapsed on his knees in front of his friend's bed. He took the dead man's frozen hand and pressed it against his forehead.

The worst. The worst had just happened. A spiky ball of nails was spinning around in the pit of his stomach. He could feel his heart and his skin being turned inside out, the way the hunters of his childhood skinned rabbits in Sicily.

But by the time he stood up, a moment later, he was convinced that the two words written by Father Jean weren't an accusation.

They were an alarm cry, an order telling Vango what to do.

Flee.

4

THE FIRST MORNING IN THE WORLD

Salina, Aeolian Islands, Sicily,
sixteen years earlier, October 1918

They pushed open the door, and the storm entered too.

There were four of them. Four men carrying a lifeless-looking woman wrapped in the red sail of a boat. Everybody stood up. Tonino the innkeeper cleared a table in front of the bread oven and called to his daughters. They put the body down on the wooden tabletop.

"Is she still alive?" asked Tonino.

His oldest daughter unwrapped the red cloth, ripped open the soaking-wet dress, and put her ear to the woman's heart. The customers at the inn, the owner, the fisherman who had brought the body in—the whole room held its breath.

Carla listened for a long time.

"Well? Carlotta!" Tonino shouted impatiently.

"Shhhh," came her reply.

She couldn't be sure. The wind was whistling outside. A bougainvillea branch was knocking against the shutters. Nothing is quieter than a heartbeat. And when it's up against a storm, it's like the tinkling of a tiny bell against a brass band.

Carla finally drew herself up to her full height and smiled. "She's alive."

Her little sister was already bringing over sheets to dry the body off. She took two large stones that were warming up near the fire, wrapped them in a piece of fabric, and slid them like hot-water bottles against the woman's damp skin. The girls waved their arms to shoo away the men, who were entranced by the pair of naked shoulders.

"Ciao, signori! Ciao!"

They held up a sheet as a partition so they could undress her. Tonino declared that the drinks were on the house. There were twenty people at his inn here at the small port of Malfa.

Bad weather's good for business, the innkeeper had thought earlier in the day as the sky turned black. And sure enough, that morning the inn at Malfa was full.

Not that there were many inhabitants left on the island. In just a few decades, the population had been decimated. People had set off in boatloads to seek their fortunes in America or Australia. They left ghost villages in their wake.

"Where did she come from?" he asked.

"We found her on the stone path above Scario Beach."

So spoke Pippo Troisi. He wasn't a fisherman. He grew capers and had a vineyard, but he was a plump man who was hired to help make the boats heavier on days when the wind was up.

Pippo had been the first to see the woman and he felt personally responsible. This was a very proud moment in his life. From time to time he would glance proprietarily at the shadow-play being acted out behind the sheet.

"But where does she come from?" Tonino asked again.

"Nobody knows her," Pippo replied.

This news resulted in a lengthy silence. Everybody knows everybody on an island. And although a few foreign sailors turned up occasionally in the ports, no one had ever brought back an unknown and extremely beautiful woman from a cliff-top path.

"She was soaked to the bone," added Pippo. "She must have been out there in the rain for a long time."

"But where does she come from?" the innkeeper repeated, staring into his glass.

The wind was now playing notes down the chimney as if it were a flute.

"She comes from the sea," answered a voice from behind the sheet.

It was Carla. She stuck her head out to say, "This woman is as salty as a barrel of your capers, Pippo Troisi!"

They all stared at one another in silence. The sea had given them everything. They lived by it, and sometimes they died by it. The Tyrrhenian Sea delivered surprises to them: a washed-up whale calf, pieces of wreckage, and even seven crates of bananas that had fallen off a boat the previous summer. But it had never flung out a woman like a flying fish, halfway up the cliff on Scario Beach.

"She's opening her eyes!"

They rushed over. But Carla and her sister kept everyone at a respectful distance, and they didn't dare come any closer.

The woman was now covered in a thick layer of shawls and blankets. The girls had done a good job. She was more decent than a nun. Even her hair was covered with a piece of cloth. All you could see was her face, and her neck leaning against a cushion.

She wasn't nearly as young as they'd initially thought. But it was as if the cold had applied makeup to her face: pale complexion, dark lips, eye shadow. As she warmed up, her cheeks became powdered with pink. She kept her eyes open for a long time before uttering a single word:

"Vango."

They found the little boy an hour later, between two rocks on the beach. He was two or three years old. His name was Vango. He was wearing blue silk pajamas. His curls fell over his eyes. He didn't seem to be afraid. In his hand he held an embroidered handkerchief scrunched into a ball. He stared at everybody around him.

Vango.

The woman had described the exact place where he was hidden. They had brought in the doctor to translate her instructions. He leaned over and listened to her as she whispered a few words.

"She speaks French," he said, sounding very serious, as if diagnosing tonsillitis.

There was a ripple of satisfaction. Everybody knew that the doctor, who liked to recount his past travels, could talk forever about France.

"What's she saying?"

Dr. Basilio seemed a bit embarrassed. The truth was, he had never been farther than Naples. His knowledge of the French language was rather hazy, even if he always walked around with an old copy of *L'Aurore* newspaper and liked to sigh, "Ah! Paris, Paris!" while staring at fashion photos.

He was trying to piece together everything he knew in a bid to understand her.

"She speaks other languages as well. It's all mixed up like the Tower of Babel."

This time, he wasn't lying. In her state of extreme fatigue, the woman kept switching languages.

"That's Greek," said the doctor.

"But what does it mean?"

"It means that she speaks Greek."

His logic was met with general admiration.

Eventually they found out that she spoke Italian too. Feeling relieved, the doctor led the interrogation. He repeated in Sicilian everything she mumbled in near perfect Italian, which everybody understood anyway.

The woman and child had been washed up onto the pebble beach along with a makeshift raft of planks and beams. She had put the little one in a sheltered place before setting off in search of help, climbing the path to the left of the stream. She had collapsed along the way.

She was sitting in an armchair now, and Vango was burying his face in her chest.

"Is he your child?" asked the doctor, deliberately over-pronouncing his words.

She attempted a smile. She was too old to have a three-year-old son.

The doctor nodded, rather ashamed of his question. He had always been a bachelor, but given his line of work, he should have known about biological clocks.

As a diversion, and because they were getting to the end of what she could remember, Dr. Basilio started repeating the only two French words he knew: *"Souvenez-vous, souvenez-vous . . ."*

He said these words imploringly, leaning over her.

Other people's languages sound like strange songs, whose music we can hum long before we can understand the lyrics. On hearing French being spoken, the audience in the inn was amused. They didn't know what these words meant, but everyone turned to one another and said, *"Souvenez-vous,"* like old chatterboxes.

From these two words, everyone set off on a flight of fantasy.

"Souvenez-vous," said a woman to her husband as she batted her eyelids.

"Souvenez-vous!"

The brouhaha got louder.

"Souvenez-vous!" shouted Pippo Troisi as he raised his glass.

The doctor sharply interrupted this game:

"Be quiet!"

A classroom silence settled on the inn.

Once again the doctor translated into Sicilian what everybody had already understood.

"She doesn't know anything. She doesn't know where she's come from or where she's going. She says she's called Mademoiselle. All she knows is that the child is called Vango. That's it. She's the little boy's nurse."

"What's she going to do?" asked one of the innkeeper's daughters.

The rescued woman answered with a few words, and tears in her eyes.

"She doesn't know," the doctor repeated. "She wants to stay here. She's frightened."

"But what's she going to do here? The little one's parents

must be somewhere. She should catch a boat back to her own country!"

"What country?" asked the doctor, getting angry now.

"You say that she speaks French."

"She also speaks English. And she said something in Greek. So where is her country?"

As if to confuse things further, the woman made a few noises.

"And that's German," the doctor pointed out.

She said something else again.

"And that's Russian."

The little boy clutched his handkerchief between his fingers. Against the midnight-blue background, a large *V* embroidered in gold was visible. *V* for *Vango*.

Gently taking that little hand in his, the doctor managed to borrow the precious handkerchief for a few seconds. Above the golden *V,* the letters of what was presumably the little boy's family name could be made out: ROMANO.

"That's a local surname," declared Carla.

"Vango Romano," said her sister.

And, higher up, on the edge of the handkerchief, the doctor spotted the following mysterious French words, embroidered in small red letters, although he couldn't understand them:

Combien de royaumes nous ignorent.

He read them again as slowly as a child learning the alphabet: *"Combien . . . de royaumes . . . nous ignorent."*

Nobody at the inn said a word.

Like a miniature bird of prey, Vango's hand dived for the tiny square of handkerchief and made it vanish.

"My God," a woman sighed.

"We're not out of the woods yet," concluded Tonino.

A man had just walked in. He tucked himself into a corner and took off his leather jacket, which was soaked through, before ordering a glass of fortified wine and some biscuits. His long hair, which he wore in a ponytail, had been slicked back by the rain.

"You've got to pay first," the innkeeper insisted suspiciously.

The man was named Mazzetta. Everybody knew him. He lived with his donkey and didn't have the means to buy wine and biscuits for himself except at Christmas and Easter. Tonino didn't trust him.

"You've got to pay first!"

The man looked at him. He slid a brand-new coin onto the bar. The innkeeper picked it up and looked at it.

"Have you sold your donkey, Mazzetta?"

Mazzetta was tempted to smash the counter. He wanted to string Tonino up from the beam in his kitchen, along with the garlic and the hams.

But he saw the little boy in the blue pajamas.

The little boy was watching him. His cheek was squashed against his nurse's shoulder, and he was watching Mazzetta as if he knew him.

Mazzetta let the innkeeper carry on with his business. He couldn't hold Vango's stare for long. He looked down, then stood up again slowly. That was when he saw Mademoiselle.

When Mazzetta saw the nurse, and his bloodshot eyes met her blue eyes, he froze.

He turned into a block of stone.

It was like the lava of Stromboli making contact with the sea.

For the first time since she had been carried there, Mademoiselle started crying.

Mazzetta pushed his chair away and turned to face the wall.

Apart from Vango, nobody had noticed this odd exchange of looks. All they could see were the tears on Mademoiselle's cheeks. What were they going to do with this woman and this child? It was the only question that mattered.

"Can you take them to your place, Pippo Troisi?"

Pippo was busy eating a large piece of fried ravioli, as thick as his hand, which he had removed from a napkin. He nearly choked.

"My place?"

"Until we have a better idea . . ."

Pippo would have loved to say yes. It should have been his role, since he was the one who had spotted them first. A glimmer of pride shone for a moment in his eye. But then he remembered how things really were. Pippo Troisi was not the master of his own home.

"The trouble is . . ."

Giuseppina. He didn't need to finish his sentence. Everybody knew what the trouble was. It was his wife.

Giuseppina watched over her husband to the point of squeezing the lifeblood out of him. When it came to other people, she was about as welcoming as a goose defending her egg. She would never let a stray woman and a child near her nest.

Perhaps it was because of his wife that Pippo the farmer dreamed of becoming a sailor. There are certain people on this earth who make you want to sail very far away, and above all for a very long time.

Nobody could remember exactly how Vango and Mademoiselle ended up going to live in Mazzetta's gloomy house.

But when Mazzetta got up to say, "I can take them," everybody looked surprised. Mademoiselle had clutched the little boy tightly in her arms. She had shaken her head without being able to utter a word.

Mazzetta's house consisted of two white cubes located in the crater at Pollara, which was crumbling into the sea. An olive tree grew up between the two cubes. The other houses in the hamlet of Pollara had long since been abandoned.

Vango and Mademoiselle set up home there.

Mazzetta and his donkey had moved into a hut a hundred meters away. It was more like a hole in the rock, carpeted with straw and closed off by a stone wall. As if to thank his donkey for accommodating their guests, Mazzetta made him a beautiful collar out of wood and leather that was so heavy the beast had to hang his head.

From that day on, until his death, Mazzetta never once set foot again in his former home. From that day on, miserable Mazzetta managed to support his two wards by placing a silver coin on the threshold of their door every new moon. From that day on, violent Mazzetta became more gentle than his donkey, whom he renamed Tesoro, and several people were surprised to find him weeping as he looked out to the sea.

In all the years that followed, he never once got a word or a glance out of Mademoiselle.

An incomprehensible pact linked these two beings. But it was a pact that no word had sealed. A pact of silence.

Vango grew up on the slopes of the extinct volcano. There he found all he needed.

He was raised by three nurses: freedom, solitude, and Mademoiselle. Together, the three of them provided him with an education. From them, he learned everything he believed it was possible to learn.

At the age of five, he understood five languages, but he didn't speak to anybody. At seven, he could scale the cliffs without needing to use his feet. At nine, he could feed the falcons that swooped down to eat out of his hand. He slept bare-chested on the rocks with a lizard lying on his heart. He called to the swallows by whistling to them. He read the French novels that his nurse bought him in Lipari. He climbed to the top of the volcano to wet his hair in the clouds. He sang Russian lullabies to the beetles. He watched Mademoiselle chopping vegetables until they were perfect diamonds. And then he hungrily devoured all her fairy-tale cooking.

For seven years, Vango didn't think he needed anything other than Mademoiselle's tenderness, the wilderness of the island, the sun and shadow of his volcano.

But what happened when he was ten would transform

his life forever. Because of this discovery, his fragment of an island suddenly seemed tiny in his eyes. What was taking place in him was like a fire beneath the sea.

The world changed color before his eyes.

And when he set foot on his little paradise again, he couldn't help looking beyond the cliffs and the last rock, toward the horizon and the sky.

ON THE OTHER SIDE OF THE MIST

Aeolian Islands, September 1925

The adventure began at night.

He heard the cries before he heard the sea.

And yet the sea was strongest of all. Violent as thunder, it was hurling itself against the foot of the cliff. Then tucking in again, turning on itself, attacking from different angles to explode all over again. Vango opened his eyes and realized that he had fallen asleep in a hole. He was just ten years old. He couldn't even remember why he'd gone up to the top of the cliff that evening.

It was the middle of the night.

He strained his ears and heard another cry. You had to be very familiar with the sea to detect that feeble call in the middle of the storm.

Vango got up and leaned over the edge of his shelter. There was still a glimmer in the sky despite the darkness. Perhaps the evening wasn't so long past or else the dawn wasn't so far off. The crests of the waves were like an army of bayonets attacking the island. In the crashing of the storm, Vango sometimes thought he could make out the sound of bells. And there was the wind too, above it all, making the spray fly up.

Vango remembered now that he had come to see the falcons hovering at dusk. And, as he often did, he had fallen asleep there. There was no pressure to go home. Mademoiselle wouldn't be fretting. They had an arrangement that she shouldn't worry unless he was away for a second night.

For someone barely ten years old, this was an unimaginable freedom, irresponsible even, but for Vango his island was like a child's bedroom. He felt as safe and at home there as another little boy would have been playing between his bed, the chest of drawers, and the toy box.

The shouting had stopped now. Vango hesitated for a moment, then decided to go and investigate. He slid out of his hole, his belly against the cliff.

He began his descent.

He had to lower himself a little less than one meter of sheer slippery cliff face jutting out above the raging sea, but the boy moved confidently with his arms and legs in a star shape. By living like this, Vango had gradually altered the relationship between his own weight and strength. He could support himself for several minutes with just two or three fingers clinging on to a hole, the rest of his body dangling in the void until he managed to touch, with the other hand, the downy feathers of a nest in the rock.

Only the flatness of the sea gave him vertigo these days. He had never been on board a boat, and he would never dip a toe in the sea.

From autumn onward, when the rain was generous, the cliff started to be shot through with green. But for now, it was completely bare and seemed to light up the sea with its whiteness. Vango stopped five meters above the waves. He listened.

This time, the cries had cut out altogether. He tried to

reassure himself that it was just a passing bird. He recognized all the cries of the birds on the island, but sometimes a few migrating birds would take a detour and come to sound their strange songs at nighttime.

Nothing surprised Vango anymore: Sicily was on the way to Africa, and if elephants could fly, he might have seen squadrons of them overhead.

As long as he was holding on to the rock, his body swinging in thin air, the gusts of wind didn't frighten Vango. But as he got closer to the water, he stopped. The movement of the sea did scare him.

He started climbing up the cliff, and already the thought of Mademoiselle's white bread was enticing him home, sucking him back toward the top. If he hurried, he would be at the kitchen table in less than an hour.

A little lower down, at the bottom of his boat, big Pippo Troisi was crying.

Pippo Troisi, the caper farmer, the man who, several years earlier, had found Vango and his nurse on the pebbles of Scario Beach.

Now he was holding on to his suitcase as if it were a life preserver. He clung to it a bit more tightly with each crack of the hull.

The little boat was caught between two black rocks above the waves. He had called out three or four times but without much hope. This was the deserted side of the island. Nobody would be able to hear him on this stretch of wild coast. He had left everything for the adventure of a lifetime, and it was all over already.

Pippo Troisi had just had time to toss his entire existence into this boat and push out for the open sea.

His sail had ripped immediately. An oar had broken. His bag of provisions had fallen into the water. He had drifted for a few hours along the coast before getting pushed against the rocks. In the end, his hand had been crushed between the hull and the rock as he tried to push the boat off again. He couldn't feel anything from his elbow down, and his fingers were hanging limply, like the shreds of a bloody handkerchief.

It was all over before it had even begun.

To escape his life, to sail away . . . in fifteen minutes the dream of escape, which he'd been harboring for ten years, was in tatters.

Pippo Troisi was waiting for the final wave now. He was begging for it to come.

And, if his hand hadn't been injured, he would have turned his thumb downward, demanding that he be put to death. But nothing happened. The waves coldly rolled around the boat and looked the other way, like passersby before a dying person.

It was Pippo's frustration that saved him. All he asked for was a quick ending. Nothing more. Couldn't he at least be granted that? A wave! A single wave that would turn the last foamy page on his life!

So he let out a final cry.

A few seconds later, the boy appeared just above him in the darkness. Vango stared at the boat for a long time, and at this man who couldn't see him.

"Signor . . ."

Hearing the voice, Pippo Troisi clung to his suitcase even more tightly.

"Signor Troisi . . ."

The man rolled over and saw the child against the cliff face. He immediately recognized Vango, the wild boy from Pollara.

"I can't feel my hand anymore," said Troisi.

That was when Vango realized he was going to have to do something he didn't want to. Jump into the boat. Help Pippo Troisi to save his skin.

"Go and find someone, little one."

Vango knew there was no time to go in search of help. He had to free the boat, which each wave risked smashing to pieces. Pippo was staring up at the bat-boy who was hanging off a deserted cliff top in the storm. How had he come to be there at this exact moment?

Vango relaxed the grip that was maintaining his position on the rock. This single gesture determined his destiny. By allowing himself to fall into Pippo Troisi's hull, Vango was embarking on a stormy life ahead.

When Pippo Troisi woke up, he could feel that the sea had calmed. He saw Vango standing at the stern of the boat with the single oar. The wind had given way to fog. The water was as flat as a lake. The day was refusing to rise under the thick layer of mist.

"Thank you," he said to Vango.

The dark-eyed boy stared at him. The boat was heading nowhere. They couldn't see beyond the oval shape of the hull as it sliced through the water. The end of the oar disappeared before coming into contact with the sea.

It was cold. But Vango wasn't shivering. He had been doing battle all night.

It had taken two hours to bail out the water, using the only remaining oar, and to set the boat free. Another hour to leave the coast behind them in the middle of the eddying waves. The fine line of the beach had been eaten up by the storm. There was no suitable place for them to rejoin land.

Then the mist lifted.

"I wanted to leave. I'd got everything ready," said Pippo Troisi. "I know about the sea."

Pippo knew the sea from a distance, but he loved it with all his heart. Up until then, he had only served as a ballast for the fishermen of Salina when the weather was bad, but his natural habitat was his vineyard and his field full of stones and caper bushes. He lived on his land, childless, under the empire of his wife.

It took him a while to admit to his rescuer what he had tried to do. Vango hadn't asked any questions. And he listened without looking at the old man.

Pippo Troisi had spent a long time preparing his escape. He wanted to get to Lipari, from where he planned to take the boat to Milazzo in order to reach Palermo. He knew that in Palermo there were ships leaving for Egypt and that he would be able to make it to Port Said, the Suez Canal, and then the Red Sea. His dream could be spelled out in three syllables: Zanzibar. He had heard this name being sung by a sailor in a tavern in Rinella.

Zanzibar.

He couldn't remember the words of the song exactly, but

there was something about the sea breeze in Zanzibar leaving a sugary taste on your tongue.

That was enough to make him pack his bags.

"I don't want to go back home," said Pippo Troisi.

Vango was scanning the horizon. He couldn't even hear his passenger's sobs anymore. He was tired, but he was also excited to be discovering unknown worlds. It was the same joy he had experienced when he had first explored his island, finding a forest of chestnut trees at the bottom of the south volcano or unearthing a hot spring under a rock . . .

Now, more than anything else, he was steering a course over his fear. The sea was becoming a pathway. He was proud of this victory.

When Vango spotted land, he almost regretted their voyage coming to an end. They were back already. The mist revealed only a few scraps of the coast. Pippo was using his left elbow to push himself up and kept saying over and over again, "I don't want to go back home."

He knew that Pina, his wife, would screech like a turkey and impose a raft of punishments, but his greatest cause for despair was that he would no longer have, deep down inside him, the dream that had sustained him. Zanzibar . . .

In one night, Zanzibar, along with its palm trees and sugary taste, had been swallowed up by the waves.

Vango didn't recognize the beach where he landed the boat. As it rolled over the first large pebbles, the hull creaked one final time before splitting from fore to aft. You could get a whole arm into the gap.

Vango wanted to help Pippo Troisi stand up, but the latter gently pushed him away.

"Leave me here for a bit. I'm out of danger now."

"Signor Troisi . . ."

"Please, little one. Leave me in my own boat for a while. Afterward, I'll go back home."

Vango hesitated. But when he remembered the terrifying figure of Giuseppina, he felt sorry for Pippo. He could perfectly well spend a few more hours in his wreck. He was out of danger now. A little imaginary voyage on the spot toward Zanzibar wouldn't do any harm. Vango crouched down and looked Pippo in the eyes.

"I swear I won't do anything silly," insisted Pippo.

He watched Vango head off; he had hardly heard him speak all night. He was a strange boy, he really was.

Ever since Vango had arrived in Salina, seven years earlier, nobody had approached him. You saw his shadow sometimes, in the evening, on the island's craters. Some people said that he fed the swallows from his hand. But surely that was a myth.

A steep wall rose up above the creek. The mist was still there. Vango didn't yet recognize the place where he had landed the boat. Behind the curtain of fog, he couldn't even locate the sun. And so he climbed without asking himself any questions, always picking the most vertical path ahead. High up, he would be able to see more clearly—he always did.

The more he climbed, the thicker the air became and the more it soaked his face. He thought of Mademoiselle's breakfast, waiting for him somewhere behind these clouds.

* * *

Mademoiselle was a magician in the kitchen.

On her little stone stove, on the edge of this forgotten island in the Mediterranean, she created fresh miracles every day that would have brought tears to the eyes of food lovers in the world's greatest gastronomic capitals. At the bottom of her deep pots, vegetables performed a dance in sauces whose aromas cast a spell on your mind and your soul. A simple thyme tart became a magic carpet that transported you to far-away lands. Cheese gratins made you weep even before you'd stepped across the threshold. And as for her soufflés . . . my God. Those soufflés could have floated up to the ceiling they were so light, so barely there, so fluffy. But Vango pounced on them before they melted away.

Mademoiselle would prepare impossible soups and pastries. She made mousses with forbidden flavors rise by hand. She served up fish in black juices flavored with mysterious herbs.

For a long time Vango thought everybody ate like that at home. He had never eaten in anyone else's kitchen. But ever since the day they'd sent for the doctor because the little boy had pneumonia, when he was five or six years old, he had understood that Mademoiselle was no ordinary cook.

Dr. Basilio had invited himself to lunch. This normally talkative man was unable to utter a single word throughout the meal. He ate with his eyes closed. He had kissed Mademoiselle four times on both cheeks before leaving.

He had returned that same evening, by chance at suppertime, to take Vango's pulse again. And the next day at midday. By chance. Each time, he had sat down at the table, a little embarrassed at first, then less and less so.

When Vango returned to full health, the doctor had appeared so traumatized by his recovery that Mademoiselle had suggested he join them for lunch every Monday.

It became a little custom. The doctor was the only outsider who entered the house in Pollara.

Over in the hut with his donkey, Mazzetta watched him pass by.

"Did you use to do this professionally?" the doctor asked Mademoiselle one day.

"I'm sorry?"

Between his fingers he held a sliver of translucent potato in which a sage leaf was held prisoner.

"Were you a cook, before . . . ?"

"Before? I can't remember anything about before."

"Were you a cook?"

"Is that what you think?"

She seemed sad.

"How do you do it?" he inquired, biting into the crusty mirage of potato.

"It just comes to me," she answered.

One morning, when the doctor had once again refused to receive payment for treating them, Mademoiselle had confided in Vango, "I think the doctor is courting me."

She seemed a bit embarrassed.

Courting . . . Vango had never really understood what that activity really involved, but he had worked out from different situations that it meant wanting to help someone out, doing someone a favor. Yes, the doctor was certainly courting them.

But this didn't explain why he looked at Mademoiselle in

that strange way or why, when she smiled back at him, he turned pale at first and then as red as his scarf. He was like a flashing beacon.

Climbing through the mist in a regular rhythm, Vango was dreaming of Mademoiselle's delicacies.

The moment came when he couldn't go any higher. He stopped and bent down to pick a little blue flower right by his foot. He stared at it and then turned around. Still that wall of fog. But the flower had just delicately confirmed something he'd sensed ever since setting foot on dry land.

He didn't recognize this flower.

This wasn't his island.

"I was expecting you later on. Which way did you come?"

Vango couldn't see the person who was speaking just behind him.

"I went straight ahead," he instinctively replied. "I don't know."

"You climb quickly."

Vango almost felt he should apologize for being early for an unknown appointment.

"Hello."

A hand was being held out toward him and a face rose up from the fog.

Vango shook the hand.

"Come with me. I was told to collect you from here."

It was an old man with a long goatskin coat and a gun.

Vango stopped thinking. He followed him blindly through a maze of exploded rock. He was surprised by the scent of flowers assailing their nostrils. They could hear a gentle babbling noise. Where were they?

Minutes later, they reached a door. Before pushing it open, the man took off his coat. Underneath he was wearing a black cape and a rope belt around his waist. He propped the gun against the wall.

They walked into a long, low-ceilinged room that was dimly lit by a fire. At the far end, by the flames, the shadow of a plump man sitting on a stool could be made out. He gave Vango a delighted look and waved a slice of bread dripping with olive oil in his left hand.

"You've got a treat in store," the man said. "They really know how to put on a good welcome!"

How had Pippo Troisi gotten here already? They had tended to his hand. He was a different man.

Vango turned toward the old man with the gun, who said very softly, "The problem isn't welcoming you. The real problem will be letting you leave Arkudah. We'll have to ask Zefiro."

Arkudah. Vango had heard that name before, in the old pirate stories people told on the islands.

"It's time," said somebody.

At which point, Vango saw the darkness of the room suddenly come alive. Shadows rose up all around him. He hadn't seen them until now. But since the moment he had walked in, dozens of men dressed in black, sitting on stone benches, had not taken their eyes off him for a second.

THE MYSTERY ISLAND

The same place, the following day

Vango felt as if he'd dropped off to sleep in the bowels of the earth, but when he woke up, he was close to the sun. A thick ray slid across his face like warm oil.

"I'm not sure what to do with you, little one."

The speaker was standing in front of the window ledge. There was a wide horizontal window, which the man didn't altogether obscure. It was impossible to see his face because he was backlit, and the ray of sunlight over his shoulder was blinding Vango.

"Your friend over there, what's he called?"

"Pippo Troisi," said Vango. "He's not my friend."

"Yes, Troisi. That's it. He's going to stay here. But as for you . . . How old are you?"

"Mademoiselle is waiting for me."

"Mademoiselle?"

Vango didn't answer. He didn't really know who he was talking to. And he didn't like that.

"These days, I'm not very good at telling how old children are," said the man. "I can tell you the exact age of a bee or a vine. But I haven't met any children for a long time now."

"I'm fifteen years old," said Vango, seizing the opportunity to grow up by five years in a single breath.

This was his first lie. It had never occurred to him to lie before, and he'd never needed to either. It was quite fun.

"Have a little drink."

A tumbler was put in front of Vango. He stood up to drink.

The man watched him putting down the tumbler. He moved away from the window and headed over to the door.

Vango had a strange taste on his tongue. What had he just drunk? His head was spinning.

"If you'd been ten, for example," said the man, "I'd happily have let you go. A child of ten is no danger. But at fifteen . . ."

He slammed the door and turned the lock. Vango lost consciousness.

This time, Vango woke up in a haze of familiar smells.

He was lying on a blue tiled bench, near the table where Basilio and Mademoiselle were sitting. The doctor was eating almond cookies, which he enjoyed dipping in his hot chocolate. Mademoiselle smiled at Vango.

"Where are they?" he croaked through dry lips.

"Here they are," said the doctor, holding out the basket of little cookies. "We've left some for you."

Vango shook his head. He wasn't talking about cookies.

"The people, where are they?"

"What people?" Mademoiselle inquired gently.

"The pirates."

Dr. Basilio smiled, made a reassuring sign to Mademoiselle, and said to Vango, "You were found by Mazzetta, the neighbor. You must have had a fall and fainted on the wild coast."

"I don't fall," replied the boy.

"He found you by chance. He's a brave man."

What none of them realized was that Mazzetta hadn't found Vango by chance. He had searched for him day and night in every corner of the island as soon as he'd seen how worried Mademoiselle was.

In the end, he had found him lying inert in a place he could have sworn he'd passed by at least three times. For years now, Mazzetta had felt responsible for Vango.

"I took the boat," said Vango. "I was on the island of men in black."

"Yes, you've been somewhere very far away," said the doctor, flashing a big smile. "But you didn't take the boat, Vango. You fell. You're already much better."

"I don't fall," the boy repeated.

"Well, have a feel of that bump just above your neck. . . . I'm going to leave you to get some rest now, and I'll be back this evening," said the doctor, over the moon at being able to keep Mademoiselle company outside of the regular Monday lunchtime slot.

"Thank you, Doctor," said the nurse, shaking his hand.

He was always begging her to call him by his first name, Basilio, but she didn't want to raise any false hopes. He held her hand a little too long.

She escaped to open the door.

"And you? Won't you tell me your first name, Mademoiselle?" asked the doctor.

"I don't even know it myself. I'm sorry."

She was wearing a short shawl over her neck and shoulders. Before closing the door again, she noticed Mazzetta watching them at a distance.

The doctor saw him as well and let Mademoiselle know:

"I'll tell him that Vango is doing better. Mazzetta saved his life by finding him just in time."

"Tell him what you like."

"What have you got against him, Mademoiselle? That man has given you everything he has."

She didn't answer.

"Did you know that he calls his donkey 'my treasure'?" The doctor laughed.

"I didn't know that."

She shut the door.

I don't know. I can't remember. Always the same turns of phrase.

Mademoiselle was fully aware that one day she would have to stop running away from what she knew perfectly well, from what she spent every minute of the day remembering.

She went to kneel down next to Vango. His heavy eyelids had closed again.

It was for the sake of this little one that she had chosen to forget everything. So that he could live.

Vango, in his drowsy state, was trying to remember what had happened to him in those final hours.

His memories were fuzzy. The sequence of events had become muddled in his mind. He could recall the boat, the journey in the mist, some men in black, but already he couldn't remember whether there was just one or several of them, if it had taken place at night or in broad daylight. Above these hazy images floated a single voice that resonated clearly. A deep voice in the light.

A voice that made this strange remark: *I haven't met any children for a long time now.*

But a few hours later, when he was able to get up and sit at the table with Mademoiselle, he decided to draw a line. His adventure seemed too much like a dream that was already dissolving.

All he had left was a big bump and a strange sense of nostalgia.

He ate heartily. The doctor turned up just as it was time for dessert. He started off by feeling the back of Vango's head.

"It's almost gone now."

Yes, for Vango, it had almost gone.

"Would you like some soup?" asked Mademoiselle, as if the matter were in question. "There's a big bowl left."

"Oh, I wouldn't like to impose," declared the doctor, already tying a napkin around his neck. "I really shouldn't."

The doctor sat down. It was hard to tell whether it was the scent of the soup or Mademoiselle's smile that most made his eyes shine.

And then, at the end, after some *vin d'orange,* which he had gotten Vango to taste, when they had all laughed at the stories Basilio always carried in his doctor's bag, and when Vango had almost put that bizarre experience out of his mind for once and for all, the doctor said one sentence that changed everything:

"Something very sad has happened, which is that Pippo Troisi—you know who I mean, the man with the capers—has disappeared."

Vango thought he couldn't have heard properly.

"What did you just say?"

"Pippo Troisi. His wife, Pina, has been crying for three days now. He's disappeared."

Vango closed his eyes.

"I'd never have thought Giuseppina would be so upset about it," the doctor went on. "To tell you the truth, she's such a force to be reckoned with that when it first happened, some people even claimed she'd eaten him."

The doctor smiled. Vango got up suddenly and slipped outside.

He took a few steps in the fading sunlight and stared into the distance. Behind a long and bumpy island lying like a pregnant woman in the water, he could make out another island. This island was called Alicudi. Its last inhabitants had long since abandoned it. People said it had been deserted for at least twenty years.

"Vango?"

Concerned, the doctor had followed the boy outside.

"You must rest for two or three days more."

"All right. I'll rest. I'm coming. . . ."

The doctor started to go back inside the house.

"Doctor . . ."

"Yes?"

"What's that island called?"

"Over there, the farthest one?"

The doctor squinted as he stared out to sea.

"Alicudi."

"Just that?"

"Yes, just that."

"Before, a long time ago, it had another name . . . in the time of the pirates."

"Yes, that's true. It had an Arabic name."

"And what was it?"

"Arkudah."

Arkudah, seven days later

Vango climbed the final ten meters.

If he approached from this side, nobody would be expecting him. He could explore on the sly.

The swallows were practicing their final arrow formations around him, before the great migration. Like a magnet, Vango attracted the swallows and all the other birds too.

One winter, when he was six or seven years old, he had rescued a swallow that had crashed into the windows of a deserted house. He had looked after it for six months, keeping its wing in a splint made out of a vine shoot. It had spent the winter without traveling, fed on crushed midges and butter. And then it had flown off in April, when its companions returned from exile.

Since that time, all swallows seemed to feel a mysterious gratitude toward Vango. A dancing gratitude that brushed against him at a hundred miles an hour, whipping up breezes in his direction.

Sometimes Vango found them a bit too close for comfort. "All right, all right," he would say to them when they flew between his legs. Swallows grow to a ripe old age—much older than the oldest horse—and their affection for the boy showed no signs of abating.

Vango turned back toward the sea. In the middle of the huge expanse, he could make out a sail in the distance. It was the big merchant ship on its way to Palermo, the same ship that had dropped him off when it passed close to the island of Arkudah.

Just as the vessel was leaving the port of Malfa, Vango had jumped aboard. The captain was a Frenchman. He had been taken aback by this boy who spoke to him in his own language, with no trace of an accent and a refined way of speaking that seemed to date back to another era. Vango explained that his uncle lived on the island they could see across the way and that he'd missed the fisherman who usually took him there every Sunday.

"But it's not Sunday today," the captain had pointed out, "it's Wednesday."

Vango had confidently stared him out.

"Wednesday is called Sunday over here," he had explained very seriously. "You're not in France now, remember!"

In just a few days, Vango had caught up in the game of lying. He was enjoying beginner's luck.

He spent the few hours of the crossing explaining to the crew that his uncle lived on the island with a bear and a small monkey. Vango had never been so talkative in all his life. When a Russian sailor inquired where the monkey came from, Vango told him, in Russian, that the monkey had been found in a barrel that had washed up on the pebbles.

"You speak Russian?"

Vango hadn't replied, as he was too busy explaining how the bear had swum to the island. It was hard for him to resist the thrill of talking complete and utter nonsense.

He had left a note for Mademoiselle, letting her know that he would be away for a few days because he was going to "court somebody." He still believed this meant he was going to give a hand, which, for once, wasn't far from the truth. Pippo Troisi was in danger.

Above all, his real goal was to understand if what he thought he'd seen on this island really existed.

But when he got to the top, there was nothing.

He looked around and couldn't see any sign of human life. He'd been expecting to find a dirty encampment, a few caves: the pirates' hideout he had imagined as he had repeated the name of Arkudah over and over again.

As far as he was concerned, the man he had talked to in the dazzling light of that morning back then was the pirate chief, and Pippo Troisi was their prisoner.

But there wasn't a single three-cornered pirate's or corsair's hat on the island, no black flag with a skull and crossbones, no rude loud parrot, no human skull carved into an ashtray.

There were just stones and shrubs.

He couldn't quite admit it to himself, but Vango felt let down.

"Of course, I knew it."

He kept repeating those words over and over again, and for once in his life, he sounded just like any other ten-year-old boy.

He headed off down the gentle slope. A single tree had sprung up among the rocks. He decided to establish his base there and to draw up his plan to leave this island and get back home to Mademoiselle. He leaned against the trunk and stared out to sea.

The green terrace where he was sitting was in perfect

contrast to the glassy mirror of the sea. Suddenly, in the distance, along the line separating the grass from the water, Vango saw a burst of color. He thought it must be a sail on the waves. Screwing up his eyes, he recognized a flower. A blue flower just like the one he had picked last time, the flower that proved he wasn't on his island. He stood up, strode the five paces that separated him from the flower, and crouched over it.

Down on his knees, he found a lot more than he had bargained for.

ZEFIRO

It wasn't a pirates' hideout but a garden. An enchanted garden on a desert island.

Just below Vango, the valley looked like the palm of a hand. Mysterious stone architecture framed the lush vegetation, and this hidden paradise was surrounded by a blue haze. The heat of the sun was causing steam to rise up from the garden soil.

Vango had never seen or dreamed of such a place. He felt as if he'd been born between two stones and all he knew about was broom, dry herbs, and the thorns of prickly pear trees. Whereas here, thriving hedgerows alternated with perfectly kept squares of lawn, alongside strips of vegetable garden embroidered onto the black earth, while semi-invisible buildings were tucked away beneath the palm trees. Two low towers appeared like rocks, perched over the greenery.

And yet there was no human presence on the garden's pathways, not a single being, not a voice. There was no trace of these green-fingered pirates who knew how to make the stone burst into bloom.

Vango decided to take advantage of there being no one around by heading down to take a closer look.

Where had they locked up Pippo Troisi?

Vango immediately recognized the smell of jasmine and the sound of the water. This was where they had led him during that gap in time. Back then, he hadn't been able to see the place at all, but scent and noise can mark the memory forever.

Vango slid beneath the lemon trees and walked, crouching down, along a row of late tomatoes. The air in the garden's pathways was exceptionally fresh. There was water everywhere. It circulated through a system of hollowed-out wooden pipes, came to a stop in the stone troughs, climbed by the magic of mechanics to the top of a reed wheel, and set off again in a myriad of thin babbling channels.

Vango couldn't believe his eyes. This island of Alicudi had been deserted because it had no water source, no protected port, because nothing would grow and even the mules died of heat and boredom. And yet here he was discovering a place that was more clement, damp, and fertile than anything he could ever have imagined.

Pippo Troisi was sitting alone on a chair, tugging at the loops of a big net that completely covered him. Vango caught him unawares, out in the bright sunshine of the paved pebble terrace. Troisi was concentrating hard on the task at hand, sometimes even using his teeth.

Lying on the ground watching him, Vango felt sickened by the bad luck of this man who had dreamed of freedom in Zanzibar but who instead found himself living like a bird in a cage, trapped beneath this fishing net. The young boy started crawling between the rosemary bushes before coming out into the open, his stomach flat on the stone path.

"Signor Troisi . . ."

The farmer didn't hear him. Vango kept edging forward. Pippo Troisi almost had his back to him.

For the second time, Vango tried to save his life. Even though there wasn't a sound in the garden, Vango was still on his guard. He knew that the prisoner wouldn't be left alone for long. The pirates would be back. He needed to act quickly.

Troisi felt the net slipping between his fingers. Twice, he tried to hold on, but the movement was too strong.

"Hey!"

He ended up putting his foot down in the middle of the net to jam it. A sharp tug released the hemp string and lifted the net.

"Over here! Come this way," a voice whispered.

Pippo Troisi turned around and saw Vango at his feet.

"Don't be afraid; we'll escape together. . . ."

"What are you doing here?"

"I'm here to help you."

"No, Vango."

"Follow me, Signor Troisi. Come on."

Troisi was writhing on his chair as if he needed help.

"Go away, Vango!"

"Cheer up—I came just for you."

Vango grabbed hold of Troisi's wrist and wouldn't let go.

"Leave me alone! Go back home!" said Pippo.

His face was twisted with fear.

"Stop, Vango!"

But the boy had decided to save Pippo Troisi at any cost. He tugged with all his might.

"Never!" shouted Pippo. "Never!"

And, with his free hand, Pippo grabbed hold of the back of his chair, hesitated a second because he felt sorry for what he was about to do, and then, closing his eyes so as not to see, he hurled the chair at Vango.

"I'm sorry, little one. I did tell you. I gave you fair warning."

Pippo picked up the chair. Trembling, he sat back down and looked at Vango, who had blacked out on the terrace.

"Never . . ." he said again. "No one will ever tear me away from here."

His only fear was having to leave this place one day.

Pippo folded up the net he was busy mending. He turned it into a makeshift bed to transport Vango's body. He pulled out a cloth that was tucked into his belt, went to wet it in a fountain where papyrus reeds grew tall, and returned to lay it on the child's forehead.

"I didn't want to hit you."

He was leaning over Vango when he sensed someone behind him. Pippo Troisi turned around and said almost in tears, "Padre, oh, Padre! Forgive me, I think I've hurt him. I hit him on the head. But he was the one who started it. Please, I want to stay here. Can you tell him I want to stay here?"

Padre Zefiro was not a pirate. He was a forty-two-year-old monk.

He was nearly six and a half feet tall and carried off his monk's cowl better than any film actor. He was accompanied by four other monks, with hoods on their heads and faces burnished by the sun. They had wicker fish traps strapped to their backs that were alive with fish.

"He's come back. . . ." stated the padre, looking at Vango.

"Before you can so much as say Arkudah!" answered Pippo, who had heard this expression from Zefiro and was now using it ten times a day out of devotion to the great monk.

"He's come back. . . ." the padre repeated, his face betraying his curiosity.

"Carry him to Brother Marco, in the kitchen," he told Pippo. "Let him put some oil on his head."

Pippo Troisi was startled.

"You're . . . you're going . . ."

"What's the matter, Fratello?" asked Zefiro, who was already heading off.

"You're going to eat him?"

Zefiro stopped. A smile from Father Zefiro was rare, but when one appeared, it truly shone.

"Yes," he replied. "Before you can say Arkudah!"

In reality, Marco, the brother responsible for cooking, was something of a doctor. He nursed Vango's head with camphor oil and settled him in the warmth, close to his oven.

Zefiro was now standing in his bedroom. The monks lived in tiny cells that flanked the garden. The cells were almost completely empty, just a simple straw mattress rolled up in one corner and a horizontal slit that served as a window the full width of one of the walls. Zefiro was looking through this notch in the stone, at eye level.

He wondered what he should do with the young visitor who had come to disturb the life of the monastery.

Arkudah was Zefiro's life's work. It was what he called his invisible monastery.

For five years, thirty monks had been living there around the padre, undetected by the rest of the world. During the initial period, they had constructed the buildings and dug the gardens with their own hands and made themselves self-sufficient for food and water, and then the life of the community had taken on the rhythm of every monastery. Work, fishing, prayer, reading, gardening, meals, and sleep were allocated their hours of the day and night according to a set timetable. It was a peaceful human clock.

But Vango was a grain of sand caught in the cogs.

Nobody knew about the invisible monastery except for the pope (who had encouraged Zefiro to found it) and a dozen contacts on the Continent and across the world.

Keeping it secret was a matter of life or death for Zefiro and his brothers.

The arrival of Pippo Troisi could already have been a serious cause for concern, but, having heard what he had to say for himself, the community had decided to keep him. The portrait he painted of his wife, the fearsome Giuseppina, made the assembly of invisible monks quake with fear and laughter.

They had accorded Pippo the title of "asylum seeker from marriage," and they treated him as a survivor.

When he found out that they were going to let him stay, Pippo had jumped with joy. He felt as if he'd landed in paradise, before he could so much as say Arkudah!

But Pippo Troisi's first day nearly went disastrously wrong. He took the considerable risk of not going to mass.

He was still asleep at half past six in the morning, when

Zefiro came out of the chapel to fill a bucket of water from the cistern and empty it over the head of the poor novice.

"Are you sleeping in, Fratello Pippo?"

From the next day, Pippo, who had never set foot inside a church, was on his knees before five o'clock in the morning, with a meditative expression, hands together. Zefiro warmed to him. He had fun watching his lips move during the Latin cantos, which he pretended to know. Pippo mumbled, into his beard, the couplets of sailors' songs, which weren't strictly speaking liturgical: *"What shall we do with the drunken sailor . . ."*

Vango, the newcomer, was of more concern to the padre.

Zefiro had been observing him for three days now.

Vango was starting to feel better and was able to leave the kitchen more often. He spied on monastic life, following the monks' every gesture. He had been spotted on the chapel roof listening to evensong.

Zefiro had found out Vango's story from Pippo Troisi, including the boy's mysterious origins and the existence of his nurse. It was all fascinating. But he couldn't keep a child in a monastery. On the other hand, how could he make Vango keep the secret of Arkudah outside these walls?

Zefiro didn't hear the knocking at the door. Brother Marco, the cook, entered and walked over to him.

"Padre."

He broke off his thoughts.

"Yes?"

The conversation that followed between these two men of the church would have made their guardian angels blush.

"I've found your queen," said the cook.

"My queen . . ."

Zefiro carefully pushed the door shut.

"Really? You've got my queen?"

"I believe I've found her, Padre."

Zefiro pressed his hand against the wall. He seemed to be losing his balance.

"You believe so? Is this merely a belief?"

The cook stammered as he fiddled with his glasses, which were already half broken: "I b-b-believe so. . . ."

"Believing isn't enough!" pronounced Zefiro.

Coming from the mouth of a man who had chosen to make believing his vocation, these words represented something of a blunder. Zefiro was aware of this. He tried to calm down before his guardian angel collapsed behind him.

"You have to understand, Brother Marco . . ." he went on. They were almost whispering. "I've been searching for my queen for such a long time."

"I understand, Padre. That's why I'm telling you about it. I believe—I *think* she could be with us in just a few days, if that's what you wanted."

This time, Zefiro turned very pale. He was smiling.

"In a few days . . . my queen, my God! My queen!"

"On one condition."

"Yes?"

"You've got to let the little one go."

Zefiro stared hard at Brother Marco and his mischievous face.

"The little one?"

"Yes, young Vango. As of today."

Zefiro made a show of accepting these terms against his better judgment. In reality, he was ready to do whatever it took.

"Is this blackmail?"

"More or less."

"All right. Let him go."

"And then . . . you've got to let him come back."

Padre Zefiro was stunned.

"What? Are you insane?"

"No Vango, no queen."

"I repeat: Are you insane, Fratello?"

"No, I'm not insane. Vango is the one who knows where she is. He will bring her here."

By this stage in the conversation between the two monks, there was only one way to revive their guardian angels, who would have passed out in a cold faint from the shock, their halos askew.

The only way was to explain a few facts.

Zefiro, who had become a wise man in all matters, nonetheless kept one vice hidden, a single crazy and chaotic passion. For many years now, he had had in his service an army of young and vigorous buccaneers, which he dispatched to pillage the other islands in the archipelago.

They would come back in the evenings, trembling, laden with gold and sweet delicacies, exhausted from the many miles they had covered, and they would unload their booty in front of their master.

These pirates were bees.

Zefiro was a beekeeper.

On the first day he'd arrived on the island, he had established five hives. These roaming bees consoled him for the journeys he would no longer be able to make, since a secret had condemned him to found the invisible monastery and to stay there until his final breath.

And so for many years, alongside his life as a monk, Zefiro had been a pirate chief, seeking out his bees morning and evening on their return from an adventure. But they had all died a few months ago, destroyed by a late-summer storm. Zefiro had kept his despondency well hidden and had even managed to cheer up the cook, who wept on account of there being no more clear honey for his gingerbread.

In the aftermath of that catastrophe, Zefiro had been looking for a queen. He needed a queen bee to attract a new swarm and to build up his hives again.

From his base in the kitchen, Vango had heard Brother Marco complaining about the situation. He had told the cook that he knew of at least three or four bee colonies in the cliffs of Salina. He could easily find a queen so that the apiary on Arkudah could be reborn.

The truth was, if they'd asked him to find a kangaroo or a coconut, Vango would gladly have promised to bring one back. He would have done anything to earn the right to return. But this time, he wasn't lying. He was as familiar with the bees as he was with everything else that lived on his island. In his eyes, this kind of challenge was child's play.

The next morning, the monks lent him one of the boats they kept hidden in a deep cave that had an opening at sea level on the western cliff of the island. Vango went away for four days and came back with two queens, some matches, cakes, and beef. The monks gave him a greater welcome than if he had been a prophet.

That evening, over a stew cooked for the monastery the way Mademoiselle had taught him, Vango understood that he had won his freedom. The freedom to come and go, invisible among the invisible ones.

And from then on, he divided his time between the wild nature of his island, with all of Mademoiselle's warmth and knowledge, and the great mystery of the invisible monastery, where he would spend more and more time. He lived the life of a smuggler between two islands, supplying Zefiro with anything he lacked, posting slim letters for him in the post office at Salina, and receiving in exchange a warm welcome from the monastic community.

Vango observed the life of the monks and tried to understand it. He was interested in finding out what sustained them. And he kept an even closer eye on Zefiro.

The monk and the child didn't say much to each other. But their rugged characters were complementary. The hardest stones make the sparks fly. A deep friendship was being forged between them.

Why nobody on Arkudah had seen it coming is hard to say. But one summer's morning, when he was thirteen, Vango solemnly announced to Father Zefiro:

"I've been thinking, Padre. . . ."

"That's good news."

"I'm ready to take an important decision."

Zefiro was trying to catch a rabbit in the enclosure behind the chapel.

"An important decision?"

The padre was chuckling to himself. Vango often sounded as portentous as a judge.

Zefiro grabbed a black rabbit by the skin on its back. He looked at Vango. He was enjoying watching this boy grow up. A beautiful present had washed up on his island three autumns earlier. It seemed to Zefiro as if, by appearing in their lives, Vango had nudged the earth around a little, to make it face the sun.

"Tell me about it," said the monk.

"Not here."

"Rabbits have ears," whispered Zefiro conspiratorially. "But don't worry, this rabbit won't breathe a word to anybody."

He was holding the rabbit tightly to him.

"Tell me what you've decided."

"Not here. It's important."

"Speak, little one!"

Vango swallowed hard and announced: "I want to be a monk."

Vango hadn't anticipated the storm that was about to hit.

Zefiro let out a roar of anger. He released the rabbit and headed off to kick a pile of crates while cursing under his breath. He stumbled and fell to the ground. Then, unclenching his fists, he tried to pull himself together. He put his head in his hands, went very still, took several deep breaths, and said, "What would you know about it?"

"I'm sorry?"

"What do you know? Absolutely nothing."

"I know . . ."

"Be quiet!"

Vango looked down. The rabbits were trembling under a rock.

"I'm telling you that you know nothing!"

"I've been coming here for three years," whispered Vango.

"So what?"

The monk could feel his anger rising again.

"So what? After three years in a circus, you'd have wanted to become a clown! After three years in a rabbit hutch, you'd have wanted to become a rabbit! You know nothing, Vango! Nothing! Nothing! Nothing!"

"I know your . . ."

"But what about the world! Do you have any knowledge of the world? What have you seen of life? The islands! Two scraps of confetti floating on the sea! A nurse, a few men in hoods, lizards . . . The life of lizards, Vango, that's what you know! You're a lizard among lizards."

Vango had turned around. There were tears welling up in his eyes. He had expected the padre to welcome him with open arms.

A little bird flew close by to console him.

Zefiro went to sit on a stone. Each stayed on his own side for several long minutes before Vango approached him.

"We need to say good-bye," he heard Zefiro saying.

Another silence passed between them.

"You will leave this place, Vango, and you will leave your island too. You must go and spend a year far away from here. And in a year's time, if you want, you can come back to see me."

"But where am I going?" Vango said, sobbing.

Zefiro felt guilty.

He should have sent this boy away a long time ago.

"I'm going to give you someone's name. You'll visit him on my behalf."

"In Palermo?"

"Farther away."

"Does he live in Naples?" The boy sniffed.

"Much farther away than that, Vango."

"In another country?"

Zefiro put a hand on the boy's shoulder and hugged him.

"In another country?" Vango asked again.

"This whole planet is his country."

AIR RESISTANCE

On the shores of Lake Constance, Germany,
six years later, April 1934

In its gigantic hangar, the zeppelin was tied to the ground like a captive dragon. The mooring ropes squeaked. Spots of light lit up its flanks. It was almost midnight. Down on the ground, between the suitcases and mailbags, a radio was playing the music of Duke Ellington.

"Herr Doctor Eckener!"

These words were barked from outside.

The balloon swayed on its ropes. Its silvery bulk still gave off the salty smell of recent travels. It seemed to be dozing.

"Find him for me!"

Still barking orders, a man walked into the hangar. He was followed by three young soldiers in uniform, who froze when they saw the zeppelin.

The *Graf Zeppelin* was a balloon some two hundred and forty meters long and forty meters wide: in other words, it was as tall as a ten-story building, and it made anyone standing next to it look like a little worm. But the newcomer didn't need this difference of scale to appear ridiculous.

"Dr. Eckener! Get me Dr. Eckener!"

Drowning in a uniform that was too big for him, the man who had just walked in was the *Kreisleiter,* the Nazi chief for the region of Friedrichshafen. Two embroidered oak leaves on his collar drew attention to his rank, which was handy for anyone who might otherwise have mistaken him for a pimply teenager dressed up by his mother in order to pay a visit to an elderly aunt.

"Find him for me!"

The soldiers stirred back into action, more intimidated by the splendor of the balloon than by their boss waving his arms about. They were virtually walking on tiptoes so as not to wake the monster.

The three soldiers were barely twenty years old.

They had all grown up in the region. And they had witnessed the evolution of these balloons, invented by Count von Zeppelin at the end of the previous century. They loved and respected this crazy adventure, born on the shores of their lake and kept alive by Commander Hugo Eckener following the count's death.

They had watched out for the headlines about this most recent flying ship, the *Graf,* which traveled around the world and was a triumph in every town and city it landed in.

All three of them had visited the zeppelin on the ground, for its inauguration, when they were thirteen or fourteen, and their fingers had trembled as they touched the blue-and-gold-edged tableware made out of a porcelain so light it was almost transparent.

On pushing open the doors of the ten passenger cabins to reveal those luxurious bunks and windows that gave onto the sky, they had all dreamed of leading their fiancées in there by the hand one day.

Later on, in 1929, they had joined the hurrahs of the crowd when they saw the airship appear in the sunlight above the pine trees, on its return journey from a complete trip around the world in twenty days and a few hours.

Finally, scarcely out of shorts but already learning about weapons, they couldn't help glancing up discreetly at the sky while standing to attention in their barracks at dawn, as the zeppelin passed overhead. Two hundred shiny pairs of eyes, under the weight of their helmets, had gazed upward at this childish dream.

And now here they were back again, embarrassed at turning up fully armed in the middle of the night while the airship was having a snooze.

The chief himself didn't dare look the beast in the face. He was frantically searching for the source of such intolerable and decadent music that made people want to dance. When he had finally located the large wireless set, he rushed over and gave it a good kick. That was all it took to hush the musicians from the Cotton Club.

But a second kick turned the volume up and made the young soldiers, caught by the rhythm, sway their heads. Three or four kicks later, Duke Ellington's piano began to weaken, but the chief's boot was also in a bad way, and with the final assault, he crushed his big toe. The music stopped, to give way to his groanings.

After a few hobbled leaps in the Bavarian fashion, the diminutive chief gulped back his pain.

The music started up again. But it wasn't coming from the radio, which was in pieces.

Somebody was whistling it.

The four men craned their necks at the same time.

Up high, suspended from the ropes of a pulley system on

the back wing of the beast, was a man with a pot of paint fixed to his belt. He held a paintbrush in one hand and was meticulously painting the canvas of the zeppelin.

"Herr Doctor Hugo Eckener?"

The painter carried on working as he whistled his jazz tune.

"I wish to speak to Herr Doctor Hugo Eckener!"

"Yes?"

He turned his head.

The man suspended fifteen meters above the ground was indeed Hugo Eckener, sixty-six years old, director of the Zeppelin Company, and one of the century's greatest explorers.

"Heil Hitler!" declared the short army chief, clicking his heels.

Commander Eckener did not respond to the salute. The soldiers could scarcely believe their eyes. What was this man, who was worshipped by all of Germany, this stout old lion with his white mane of hair, doing up there disguised as a decorator?

"Didn't you hear me, Herr Doctor?"

"It seems you don't like music, Herr *Kreisleiter*."

"That's not music!" retorted the chief, who took a certain pleasure in crunching beneath his feet a piece of the defunct radio.

"You'll forgive me for not coming down. I've got this little job to be getting on with."

"Don't you have a maintenance person for that?"

Hugo Eckener, who was squeezed into his harness, smiled.

"The thing is . . . it's rather dangerous work. Some people

have died for this kind of thing. Would you mind passing me the new brush, which is just by your feet?"

The short army chief hesitated for a moment. It was an embarrassing situation. He wasn't there to serve as an apprentice. But eventually he picked up the paintbrush and clumsily sent it flying through the air toward Eckener.

"Missed!" declared the painter.

Three times the chief failed to reach his target, until on the fourth attempt Eckener deftly slackened his ropes and managed to grab hold of the brush.

"You're making progress, Herr *Kreisleiter,*" Commander Eckener said approvingly. He smiled.

The army chief realized he had just made himself look ridiculous in front of his soldiers.

"As I was saying," Eckener went on, "it's dangerous work. Which is why I'd rather do it myself, calmly, in the evening, listening to music."

"That's not music!"

"I used to share your opinion, but there's a young American who's been working here for a few days, Harold G. Dick. He's befriended my son Knut. And I'm beginning to change my mind about this kind of music."

"Only weaklings change their minds."

Hugo Eckener burst out laughing. He liked idiots. Or at least, idiots had kept him amused for a long time now.

"It's thanks to us changing our minds that we've been able to conquer the sky, you know, Herr *Kreisleiter.* Here's a little piece of advice from a wise man: you'll never go very high unless you can change your mind."

"I'll go higher than you, Herr Doctor," countered the chief.

"Yes, you'll go very high indeed . . . in your tree . . . but I was talking about the sky."

The three soldiers held their breath. The maggot was squirming in his boots.

"Do you take me for a monkey, Doctor Eckener?"

Commander Eckener stopped painting, put the paintbrush in his left hand, and raised his right.

"I swear on the memory of my master, the good Count von Zeppelin, that I wasn't thinking of a monkey."

And he wasn't lying. Eckener had too much respect for monkeys.

The short army chief tried to regain his composure. He didn't know what to say anymore. He turned to his soldiers and tried to remember what had brought him here in the first place. All of a sudden it came back to him, and he turned around to face Eckener, reinvigorated.

"Doctor Eckener, you are under arrest."

"Oh?"

His response was offhand, as if someone had just remarked on a stray hair from his short white mane.

"You have flown over Paris without authorization."

"Paris!" sighed Eckener. "Who can resist Paris? Yes, I flew over Paris."

"A certain person in Berlin is not happy. A certain person has indicated this to me. A certain person has asked me to arrest you."

"A certain person is too kind to think of me, but a certain person can't stop the clouds from passing over Notre Dame in Paris. A certain person in Berlin should know this, shouldn't he?"

His brush stopped moving.

"I had a friend to see in Paris. Unfortunately, I just missed him."

"Doctor Eckener, I am ordering you to come down!"

"Another time I would be delighted to join you over a nice bottle of wine, but I've got this little job to finish. I trust that in Berlin, a certain person will forgive my deadline — that is, if a certain person has any brain under his hat."

Eckener was taking risks. And he knew it. The certain person in question had a small mustache the size of a postage stamp, and his name was Adolf Hitler.

The commander's paintbrush was applying alumina paint to cover over a final line that was still black.

"There we go. Leave me now. This is an important job."

The *Kreisleiter* took a few steps backward.

His eyes were wide as saucers.

He had just realized what the important job the commander kept referring to was all about. For most of the conversation, under his very eyes, Hugo Eckener had been applying a layer of silver paint to cover up the gigantic swastika on the wing of the zeppelin. Not a trace of it remained.

The maggot was speechless. The soldiers had retreated with him. Since Hitler and his Nazi Party had come to power the previous year, the swastika was obligatory on the left side of all airplanes and airships.

Eckener had always fought against this symbol, which represented everything he found repellent. Six months earlier, for the Chicago World's Fair, he had performed a tour of the city in a clockwise direction so that America wouldn't see, on the left side of the zeppelin, that tattoo of shame.

Yes, making a swastika disappear was a small but rather dangerous job in Germany in the spring of 1934. None of Eckener's workers could have done it without ending up with the rope around his neck.

He put his paintbrush back in its pot.

"There we go. It looks better like that. It's more handsome."

The maggot took a pistol out of his belt.

"Come down! You're finished."

Eckener burst out laughing. An endearing laugh that suited him. It spread to his forehead, his temples, and his eyes. At the end of the day, even in these troubled times, the idiots still made him laugh.

The maggot fired into the air in the direction of the ceiling.

Eckener stopped abruptly. His face had changed beyond all recognition. Now he looked like the god of storms carved on public water fountains. He was a terrifying sight to behold.

"Never do that again."

He had spoken very softly. The thing was, Eckener tolerated idiotic behavior only in very small doses. But for some time now, all around him, the dose had become excessive, mad, monstrous. There were enough people behaving like idiots to fill whole stadiums or the Potsdamer Platz in Berlin. Even his closest friends were starting to show some of the symptoms.

"Never do that again on my premises," Eckener repeated.

How could this man, fastened by a few ropes to the tail of the zeppelin, his nose shiny with paint, speak with such authority to a representative of the Nazi Party?

"Now, kindly leave!"

The short army chief raised his chin.

"Doctor Eckener, I shall call for reinforcements," he threatened.

For the time being, the reinforcements weren't much to be frightened of. The three soldiers looked exceedingly pale, their jaws had dropped, and the youngest of them was scratching his knee with his submachine gun.

"And what will you tell your reinforcements?"

"I will tell them that you have profaned the swastika."

Eckener frowned.

"You mean that we have profaned it?"

"What?"

"You will say that we have profaned it together?"

"Together?"

"Will these three young men be able to deny that you provided me with a new paintbrush?"

Hugo Eckener watched his visitor stiffen. He continued: "Have you forgotten how, three times, you insisted on passing it to me yourself? Aren't you the one who provided me with the weapon for this crime? You have a short memory. Didn't you watch me doing my work for a good twenty minutes without intervening? Answer me, Herr *Kreisleiter*! Answer me!"

His fearsome voice rang out in the hangar.

The *Kreisleiter* of Friedrichshafen felt sick. He had a sudden desire to chew the oak leaves on his collar. At first he was speechless, then he blurted out a pulp of words, to the effect of: "I'll get you in the end."

He roared a few curt orders to his men and declared,
"Heil Hitler" two or three times while raising his right arm
in every direction. He even saluted an old railway clock that
had ended up there, before taking off his cap and tripping
over the radio he himself had kicked into that position. Then
off he clopped, clicking his heels like an ass on a bridge. His
soldiers followed him.

Eckener watched them go.

He felt a moment of pity for those boys who would be
used as a doormat for this buffoon, and then as a stepping-
stone for someone infinitely more threatening.

Silence was restored.

Slowly, Hugo Eckener let out the rope in order to lower
himself to the ground. He put down his paint pot and turned
to face his handiwork.

It was all so silly. He knew the battle was already lost,
and that soon he would have to paint an identical swastika
back in the same place. He knew he was endangering his business and his balloon—in other words his entire life—as well
as putting the men who worked at his side in danger. But he
couldn't do otherwise.

For all that he spent most of his time in the sky, his feet
remained firmly on the ground. He was frightened for his country. Slowly and tragically, it was drifting in the wrong direction.
Something had to be done. Tiny gestures. Barely noticeable. A
little resistance, some gentle friction, to break the fall.

He called this air resistance.

Hugo Eckener took off his painting smock. He climbed
across the footbridge and walked into the deserted zeppelin.

To his right the door giving onto the airship's kitchen was ajar. The toque belonging to Otto the chef was propped on a chair. Eckener turned to the right and crossed the handsome dining room, whose curtains blocked out the light from the hangar.

He opened the door giving onto the passengers' walkway. The cabins were laid out on either side. He slowed down opposite one of the cabins, then continued on his way again.

He went as far as the last door and pushed it open. It was the men's bathroom. He began to wash his hands.

He glanced up to take a look at himself in the mirror. *What an odd face,* he thought. Then he started talking to himself out loud: "Did you hear everything? As you can see, Commander Eckener hasn't changed," he said very loudly, as if he wanted to be heard in the next-door room.

"Always trying to outsmart them, you see. I won't budge. The trouble is that the world is moving. I'll end up getting into trouble. That's what my wife keeps telling me." He laughed. It was a strange monologue. He turned off the faucet and dried his hands.

"As for you, I imagine you're in trouble too."

Eckener exited and walked back up the corridor in the opposite direction, before stopping in front of the same cabin and putting his hand on the door handle.

"I know you're awake, Jonah."

He opened the door. The person Eckener had addressed as Jonah was standing in the shadows.

"I came by a while ago," explained the commander of the zeppelin, "but you were asleep on the banquette, having arrived here out of the blue! So I did a spot of painting while

I was waiting. And then I had some visitors, so you'll have to forgive me. Now, here we are at last, just the two of us, four years on. Jonah! What has happened? Come here so I can give you a hug."

Vango threw himself at Eckener and burst into tears.

9

IN THE BELLY OF THE WHALE

After a few minutes, Eckener loosened his grip and started laughing. He turned away slightly and slid his thumbs into his jacket pockets.

"I remember when you turned up for the first time, Vango. You weren't in any better state than you are today. Where have you come from?"

He studied his friend carefully. Vango looked exhausted. He had just crossed all of France, Switzerland, and Germany in order to shake off the police who were on his tail.

"The last time you turned up out of nowhere, you spent a whole year with us."

Eckener closed his eyes to recall it more vividly.

"It's five years ago now. . . . The black year, 1929, the Great Depression . . . The world was collapsing. So why was it such a memorable year for me? I developed a soft spot for you, Piccolo. I used to have fun teasing you that I didn't need you on the zeppelin. But since it was my old friend Zefiro who had sent you . . ."

Both of them smiled.

"One whole year on board with us. A strange and wonderful year. And then you left us, just like that, without a word."

"I'm sorry, Commander," said Vango.

"I'd spent so much time telling you I didn't need you, that I was surprised by how much I missed you."

"I'm . . ."

"Be quiet, Piccolo."

Vango had treasured every second of that first year far away from his island.

When, at barely fourteen, he had been thrown out by Padre Zefiro, Vango had returned to the little house in Pollara. Weighing his words, he had explained to Mademoiselle that he had to leave for a whole year but that he would be back.

She gave him a hug. She was trying to say, "Yes. That's a good idea. What a great adventure," but no sound escaped her lips.

When he disembarked at the port of Naples, a few days later, all he had was a rucksack on his shoulder and in his pocket a sealed envelope on which was written the name of Dr. Hugo Eckener in Friedrichshafen. The address was in the padre's handwriting.

That day, Vango had felt his heart being wrenched apart, split down the middle by this stretch of sea that would separate him from Mademoiselle, from his island, and from his invisible friends. It felt like an insurmountable wrench to him.

He was convinced he wouldn't be able to live, far from this little universe, even though it would still carry on without him.

On the platform of the main station, Vango was already dreaming of returning after a few days, standing on the cliff tops again, throwing his head back like a diving bird before emerging from the water, gasping for air.

He could feel the force of that first mouthful of air filling the bird's lungs, its wings outstretched. He believed that once he was back on his islands, he would spend the rest of his life there.

That said, on the train that pulled out of Naples, heading north, he was leaning out the window, already taking in the faces, the handkerchiefs waving through the smoke, the teary farewells, the children running alongside the train. He was watching the crowd: so many stories on one platform. And already, he could feel a small square of light opening up inside him.

People. He was discovering people.

He had known individuals, a few of them, back home. Mademoiselle and a handful of others he could name. Dr. Basilio, Mazzetta, Zefiro, and Pippo. But people, they were something else. These were strangers. Their lives brushing past at high speed, like telegraph poles beyond the train window.

Next to him, in the train car, was a young lady with a tiny dog.

When the station had disappeared in all the steam, and Vango had gone to sit back down, the lady asked him:

"Would you mind looking after my dog for a minute?"

Vango took the dog, which fit into the palms of his hands. The lady left. In a flash, he understood what the padre had said to him. Before anything else, he needed to see the world. He sensed it was the speed that gave these encounters their strength. Lives affecting other lives more powerfully when they jostled up against one another because they were hurtling along with such energy.

On her return, the lady gave off a flowery perfume.

"Thank you," she said, taking her dog back. "You're very kind."

That was all. She got out at the next station.

People.

Vango had carried on for many days and nights toward Rome, Venice, and Munich, only leaving the train in order to jump on board another one. Then he had taken a single-car train toward Lake Constance.

Five years on, Vango still hadn't been back to his islands.

"I loved your zeppelin so much," whispered Vango.

Hugo Eckener went over to the cabin window and sat down on the chair.

"When I got your note a month ago," said the old man, "with the drawing of Notre Dame and a date in April, telling me you were going to become a priest, I wasn't in the least surprised. I'd known for a long time that you were seeking something."

As for Vango, for a long time he'd felt that something was seeking him. . . .

They fell silent for a moment. Then Eckener asked, "Now, tell me what I can do for you."

Vango thought of the crowd in front of the cathedral, of the shouting of the police officers, of Father Jean's body on his bed, and of Vango's own escape to Germany, to the zeppelin. It had all happened in a matter of hours, a few days at most.

Not that he mentioned any of that.

"Keep me here. I don't need anything else. I'll fly with

you for a few months. I'll work. I just need a bit of time to think. Please do this for me."

Eckener sank a little deeper into his chair.

"Ah . . . so that's why . . ."

He looked troubled.

"I wouldn't have done it to help you, Vango. I'd have done it for me. . . ."

He stopped, and wiped some invisible dust off the table.

"But the zeppelin is no longer what it was. . . . I don't get to choose my men anymore. Everything is inspected on every flight. The crew is German. Exclusively German."

Commander Eckener found these last words hard to say. His zeppelin was a piece of German territory. The law of the new Nazi regime applied to it. Months of negotiations meant that he had finally been able to recruit Dick, an American from Akron in Ohio, whom the authorities already had under surveillance as if he were a spy.

Opening the narrow door of the *Graf Zeppelin* to another foreigner was out of the question.

"Have you got Italian identity papers?" asked Eckener.

"French," replied Vango. "I've had them for a few days."

Eckener made a face.

"I'd have preferred Italian. It would have made things easier."

Mussolini, the Italian leader, was already making eyes at Hitler.

"I've never had Italian papers," said Vango.

A sad smile passed across the commander's face. He remembered Vango's story, the little shipwrecked boy with no past and no origins.

"Of course—you were Jonah being spat out by the whale on the shores of Sicily. . . ."

Back then, Eckener had given him that name, in memory of the episode in the Bible where a prophet washes up in the belly of a whale before being spat back out. Eckener had sailed the high seas before falling in love with this zeppelin. He knew that the nickname Jonah was given to sailors who brought bad luck to boats. . . . Thumbing his nose at superstition, Eckener had assigned this nickname to Vango.

A thought instantly wiped away the commander's smile.

"I wish . . . I wish I could have helped you."

He stood up briskly, embarrassed by this confession.

"This is just the way it is. Good-bye."

Incredulous, Vango shook his head. He didn't recognize his former boss.

"I understand, Doctor Eckener. I'll leave tomorrow morning. I'm sorry to have bothered you. I'm just going to sleep here a little longer, if you—"

"No."

The response was curt.

"No, Vango, you can't sleep here. The crew will be arriving in a few hours. We're departing at dawn for South America. You have to leave now."

Vango stared at Hugo Eckener. The commander of the zeppelin couldn't even look him in the eye.

"Now!" repeated Eckener.

"I understand, yes, I understand. Right away . . . I'm going."

He took a step toward the exit.

"Don't you have any luggage?" inquired the commander.

"No."

Vango was exhausted. He pushed open the cabin door, and his shoulder rubbed against the length of the corridor all the way to the end.

"Good-bye, Jonah," Eckener called out after him.

"Good-bye," replied Vango reluctantly as he crossed the dining room in slow motion, half asleep.

It was here on this red carpet that he had worked as a waiter for a year, in 1929.

Above the pyramids, over the Mauritanian desert and the Brazilian jungle, in the smoke of New York, crossing the equator and the Ural Mountains, he had served the finest meals. The guests used to stand up sometimes, napkin in hand, when a herd of reindeer was racing underneath them on the Siberian steppes or when wild geese were chasing the strange silver bird of the zeppelin.

Vango knew that 1929, the year when he was fourteen, had not yet revealed all of its mysteries. It was here, in the shadow of this balloon, that he'd discovered one of the keys to his life being turned upside down. And now it was here that he had chosen to come first, on leaving Paris and the murdered body of Father Jean.

He walked down the footbridge of the *Graf Zeppelin*. There were still men guarding the entrance to the hangar. But they hadn't seen him. Vango knew how to avoid them. He headed toward the workshop.

Hugo Eckener sat down at the navigating table, where his two clenched fists rested on the leather. His anger was making him tremble. He had just refused hospitality to a nineteen-year-old boy whom he loved as if he were his own son.

He had just given in to terror.

* * *

The young, handsome Gestapo chief Rudolf Diels had hosted Hugo Eckener for lunch the previous June. Their conversation had been trivial enough to start with.

"I'm full of admiration for you, Doctor Eckener."

Eckener was eating his soup with a spoon, in silence. He wondered what this man with a scar on his cheek and impeccably slicked-back hair wanted from him. When the dessert arrived, the chief of the political police swept the crumbs off the tablecloth and placed a large file in front of the commander. The name Eckener was written in capital letters on the cover.

Leafing through hundreds of pages, Commander Eckener had remarked, "My friend, it's more than admiration you have for me: this is love!"

The file was terrifying. They knew everything. The police knew every detail about Hugo Eckener and the Zeppelin Company. Every movement, every human contact, every telephone call had been written down in this register. It was a formidable weapon for pressuring someone.

The day after that meal, the commander had been obliged to paint the swastika on his zeppelin.

The intimidation hadn't stopped there.

Two months later, on a very hot day, Eckener had been summoned by Chancellor Hitler to his house in Berchtesgaden in the mountains.

During the nights that followed, Eckener had been tormented by nightmares about that little man sitting behind his desk, the tip of his foot stroking a black dog, in that small florid chalet overhanging a valley. For the first time in his life,

as he was accompanied to the door by Göring, the air minister, who detested Eckener as much as he did his zeppelin, the
commander had felt both of his hands trembling.

And from that day on, behind his provocative behavior
and his bad temper, Hugo Eckener hid something in the folds
of his neck, a tiny bug that clung to his skin: fear.

Something in him had given way. Part of his pride had
deserted him.

All of a sudden, Hugo Eckener stood up.

He knew what to do about that misplaced bug: hold his
head up high and crush it.

A few seconds later, as he was walking across the zeppelin's
grassy esplanade, Vango heard a shout behind him.

He turned around.

Hugo Eckener was approaching. He was out of breath.

"I do remember a stowaway who hid inside the zeppelin.
These things sometimes happen on voyages. Once the balloon
has taken off, there's nothing we can do about a stowaway.
We're hardly going to throw him overboard. . . ."

Vango was waiting to hear what came next.

"That's all," puffed Eckener. "I just wanted to tell you
that. Now I'm going to get some sleep at home. My wife is
expecting me."

Eckener buttoned up his coat collar and turned his back
on Vango. The boy hadn't reacted at all. After a few paces,
Eckener turned around.

"One other thing, Jonah: I haven't seen you this evening.
I haven't seen you for four years. I can barely remember you.
Right?"

Vango agreed. Eckener headed off into the darkness. He walked tall. The lights from the hangar blended in with his white hair.

At three o'clock in the morning, when it was still dark, the hive of the zeppelin started to stir.

Cleaners were clearing the ground, picking up debris right, left, and center. The crew members appeared one by one. Pilots, officers, mechanics all arrived in their black leather coats, concentrating on the task ahead.

These flights had been a regular event for several years now, but no one ever got used to the adventure of it: they still had to pinch themselves. They got ready as if they were going on a date. They all smelled of cologne and soap. The hair beneath their caps was well oiled, and their shoes were shiny.

Coffee was being served off to one side, in one of the workshops, to avoid lighting the portable stoves close to the flammable gas that filled the zeppelin. But the men couldn't help going back into the hangar, a steaming cup clasped in both hands, to stare wide-eyed at this sleeping giant they were tasked with waking. They smiled as they looked on, full of emotion that they were part of this small group that, in less than a decade, had made the impossible happen: an ocean liner of the air, linking Europe with Brazil or any other destination, in three days and two nights, simply but in luxury.

That night, one heavyset man didn't share this sense of joy.

He was Otto Manz. He was the chef on board the airship.

He was sitting on the first step of the wooden staircase

that led up to the zeppelin. An army of porters, standing in front of him with crates and bags, awaited his orders.

"You can wait all you like! The *Graf Zeppelin* doesn't have a chef anymore."

"Doesn't have a chef?" echoed one of the men, who was balancing three heavy crates of carrots and cabbages.

"I quit."

Otto Manz declared that he was quitting before every flight, and one hour later, he would be making pastries high above the mountains for the passengers' breakfasts.

"I'm not leaving without my kitchen help."

His kitchen help was Ernst Fischbach. He had just been promoted to the post of navigator on board the airship. This had been his dream for a long time, ever since he had been employed as a ship's boy at the age of fourteen.

And so Otto found himself without his kitchen boy.

"Boss, what do you want us to do with these vegetables?"

"I'm not anybody's boss. Go and sort it out with Captain Lehmann."

They went to find the captain, who got them to store the provisions in the pantry and iceboxes located in the keel of the balloon. Lehmann was one of Eckener's top men. And during crossings, he was never without his accordion.

Lehmann was as fine a diplomat as he was a navigator. He went to sit next to Otto. He remained there in silence, despite all the frenzy in the hangar.

"She'll be disappointed," sighed the captain.

"Sorry?"

Otto had turned to face him.

"I really do believe she's going to be very disappointed," said Lehmann.

"Who?"

The captain took off his cap.

"She was so fond of your little turnips swimming in cream."

"My God, who are you talking about?"

"Haven't you heard?"

"About what, Captain?"

"Lady Drummond-Hay arrived at the Kurgarten Hotel yesterday evening."

The chef stood up and, puffing out his chest, smoothed the wrinkles in his apron.

"Lady?"

"She's on the passenger list."

"Lady!"

Otto called her Lady, as if it were her first name.

"Lady . . ."

She was an English aristocrat, a famous journalist, a correspondent for the most important American newspapers, a widow at thirty-one, an adventurer with fur coats and velvet eyes. She had been a passenger on board some of the zeppelin's most famous voyages.

"Lady, my God!" Otto exclaimed again.

He was madly in love with her. And she took advantage of this crush, even going into the kitchen to eat cookies. Otto saw all the signs of a love shared. He was already making plans for the future.

The poor man didn't know anything about the woman's life outside the balloon, about her hundreds of suitors, her friends in Hollywood, Buenos Aires, Madrid, and Montparnasse in Paris.

All he knew was that one day he had held her hand, above Tokyo, as he taught her how to beat a béarnaise sauce. And that delicate white hand in his, whisking up the scent of tarragon and chervil, was his most tender memory.

"My God, Lady!" Otto Manz exclaimed one last time before disappearing into the zeppelin.

Hugo Eckener arrived a little after five in the morning. The captain immediately welcomed him.

"Commander, we need a replacement for Ernst Fischbach, the chef's assistant."

"We'll find one."

"I fear we won't find one in the clouds, Commander."

"Who knows, Captain!"

"Do you have someone in mind?"

"Perhaps."

Lehmann didn't push the point. Eckener seemed sure of himself.

"The front right engine has been repaired," the captain continued.

"Perfect. Anything else?"

"Yes . . . I took the liberty of ensuring that a few urgent jobs were carried out at the rear."

"I'll trust your judgment. The weather?"

"The radio telegrapher has received the weather forecast from Hamburg. The wind will be in our favor, and the Rhone corridor is clear."

"Excellent. Captain, kindly join the headwaiter and wait

for the passengers in front of the hangar. Please offer my apologies. Tell them I will see them on board."

Lehmann obeyed. Standing still, Eckener took his time observing the zeppelin. Then he headed for the stairs. He wanted to check something inside. The mechanics, crew members, and officers all slowed down and tilted their heads as he went by. Distracted, he didn't respond to their salutes.

But as he walked through the door of the airship's gondola, Eckener could hear that he was being called for.

"Commander!"

It was Kubis, the headwaiter. He looked concerned.

"Customs and police are here, Commander. Lehmann is asking them to wait outside."

"Very good. Customs can check the passengers shortly. If the police officer wants a crew list, provide him with one."

"There isn't just one police officer, if I counted correctly."

"Are there two of them?" asked Eckener, unsurprised by an excessive police presence.

"No, Commander, there are thirty-five. I think we've got a problem."

10

THE GENTLEMEN FROM THE GESTAPO

Sure enough, standing at the door was every policeman in uniform they'd been able to find within a ten-kilometer radius. But as soon as he arrived, all Eckener saw were the two Gestapo raincoats. Captain Lehmann, who was talking to them, his face covered in beads of sweat, was relieved to see the commander approaching.

"Gentlemen, allow me to introduce Commander Eckener. He'll be able to answer your questions."

Eckener gave a broad smile. And in his powerful voice, pointing to the army of police officers, he said, "I hadn't seen the passenger list. We're going to feel nice and safe: a proper flying barracks! I'm only sorry we'll be arriving in Rio too late for carnival."

One of the men from the Gestapo smiled weakly.

"You're very amusing, Commander, for first thing in the morning. I tend to be witty at night. Perhaps I'll have occasion to make you laugh one of these evenings."

"With pleasure, Officer."

"Max Grund. I'm the chief of the Geheime Staatspolizei for the province of Lake Constance."

The commander noticed that Grund had given the full name of the Gestapo, as if, one year after its creation, the affectionate diminutive already froze the blood, and it was better to dilute this effect with a long and complicated name.

With excessively cold cordiality, the officer introduced his colleague, Franz Heiner, whom Eckener had never seen before.

"There are lots of new faces in the police at the moment," remarked the commander.

"You can't do anything clean with old tools," came the reply.

As a fine craftsman, Eckener thought the opposite. A tool takes a long time before it's really good. But he remained quiet.

"I don't want to make you late," said Grund. "But there is a rumor circulating that we need to put a stop to. I have been led to understand that some paintwork has been carried out here recently."

"Rumor?" echoed Eckener.

Max Grund took a deep breath. There was a persistent whiff of turpentine.

"Yes. Paintwork that calls the honor of our country into question."

Eckener smiled.

"What remains of that honor is very thin if it is endangered by a pot of paint."

"You will allow me to verify this matter with my own eyes."

Eckener didn't move. He formed a human barrier.

"Excuse me."

The man walked around him, together with policeman Heiner. They entered the hangar and strode in the direction of the zeppelin.

Commander Eckener followed them at a distance. The visitors had their eyes fixed on the back aileron of the balloon.

"It would seem that the rumor was not false, Commander."

Eckener took his time before responding.

"Kindly tell the rumor that he forgot his hat."

The commander picked up the cap that the *Kreisleiter* had dropped the previous evening in his panic to leave.

He held it out to Max Grund, who tossed it away with a flick of the hand.

"Follow me, Mr. Eckener."

"You'll forgive me, but I have a three-hundred-ton balloon due for takeoff in thirty minutes. I don't have a second to spare."

The two men from the Gestapo sniggered as they looked at each other.

"I don't think you quite understand, Commander. The years are passing. You're a man from another era. It's rather touching . . . but it's over. Follow us."

Eckener glanced at the balloon. For the first time, he really did feel as if it were all over. The adventure would stop right there. He didn't even notice Captain Lehmann coming toward them.

"Is there a problem, Commander?"

The commander didn't hear him.

"A problem?" Captain Lehnmann repeated.

Max Grund showed Lehmann the aileron covered in silver paint.

Lehmann pretended not to understand.

"Isn't there something missing?" inquired the police officer.

"No."

"Really?"

"Really."

"Be very careful, Captain."

"I can assure you that . . ."

Suddenly his face lit up. Lehmann turned toward the Gestapo officers.

"Hold on, gentlemen. I think I know what you're looking for! You're looking for . . ."

He traced the swastika in the air. He made the Nazi salute by raising his arm.

"Is that what you're looking for?"

The two men could sense their anger rising.

"I understand that you are new to your work, gentlemen," Lehmann continued. "Your mistake is crass but excusable. The . . ."

He repeated his large arm movements.

"The . . . can be found specifically . . ."

He paused for a moment. Eckener had returned to his senses and was listening to him anxiously.

"On the other side."

"I beg your pardon?"

Grund thought he must be dreaming.

"I repeat: it's really rather amusing, and entirely natural that you should be uninformed on this matter, but the ruling from the air ministry is very strict. The big crooked drawing you're looking for must be painted on the left-hand side of the aileron."

Eckener was trying to get Captain Lehmann's attention. There was no point in making things worse. Clearly, Lehmann had no idea about what his commander had undertaken the evening before with a five-inch paintbrush.

"Follow me, gentlemen," said the captain, who was taking no notice of Hugo Eckener's frantic signaling. "Follow me— you'll be amazed."

Unfortunately, I'm not sure who's going to be the most amazed out of those three, reflected Eckener with a sinking heart as he watched them heading off. They went around to the other side, where, looking up, they scrutinized the left flank of the airship.

Eckener turned away. He could hear hurried steps rushing over to him.

"Herr Doctor Eckener."

"Yes?"

Agent Max Grund was standing before him, more in disarray than ever. He didn't say a word, but summoned his colleague.

"Heil Hitler!" they chanted in unison, their arms raised in front of them.

There was no point in putting up a fight. Eckener took a step forward.

"I'm ready to follow you, gentlemen."

"We will overlook your sarcasm, Commander. Rest assured that our informer will be hanged."

Eckener was taken aback.

"Good-bye, Commander," said Grund.

"Good-bye."

They headed off through the hangar. Hugo Eckener turned toward Lehmann, utterly bewildered.

"Captain?"

The captain's embarrassed smile was the first giveaway sign. Hugo Eckener watched him closely. He was beginning to understand. Frowning, Captain Lehmann said, as if to excuse himself, "I told you this morning that I undertook some improvement jobs on the rear before your arrival."

Eckener looked down at the ground and then straight into the captain's eyes.

"Yes. You did. I'd forgotten. Thank you, Captain. You can return to the passengers now. The bus from Kurgarten should have arrived."

The captain nodded before walking off.

"Captain Lehmann!"

"Yes?"

"What time is it?"

"Twenty-five past five."

"Twenty-five?"

"Yes, Commander."

"Captain . . ."

"Yes."

"I don't see any reason to refer to what's just happened."

Lehmann frowned.

"To what's just happened? I'm sorry, you'll have to tell me. . . . What has just happened, Commander?"

Eckener felt overwhelmed. This was the humanity he loved.

Embarkation for the *Graf Zeppelin* flight looked like something straight out of the society pages of a major newspaper in Berlin, Paris, or New York. In a few seconds, you could see an extraordinary array of characters climbing the steps, each worthy of a few juicy lines in the gossip columns because they were so important, or appeared to be so important.

The felt hats were made by Christys' of London, the dresses were by Jean Patou, the suitcases came from Oshkosh in Wisconsin, and the smiles were straight out of Pathé films.

Diplomats, industrialists, writers, flamboyant characters, politicians, scientists, people of enormous fortunes, and diminutive actresses: what they all had in common was the drive to set foot in this dream and in History. That particular morning, there were seventeen of them. Each person was weighed with their luggage to check they didn't exceed the weight allowance. It was a sort of joyous cattle market that smelled of May roses and patent leather.

A well-fed German businessman with a small canvas bag stood on tiptoes in his slippers, as if that way he would weigh less on the scales. He talked a lot, saying that he lived in Paris, that he'd caught the plane from the airfield at Le Bourget, then a three-engine Lufthansa aircraft between Sarrebruck and Friedrichshafen. He was alarmed at the prospect of being too heavy and listed all the dishes he'd been offered in the course of his long journey by plane to the zeppelin: "Stuffed cabbage, cheeses rolled in bread crumbs, petits fours, vol-au-vents; I refused everything. Everything."

He was almost in tears at the mention of this diet.

The customs officers laughed. They let him embark.

Needless to say, no sooner was he on board than he fell into the arms of Otto the chef, begging that a whole leg of lamb be sourced for his breakfast. In order to get rid of him, Otto made a heap of promises, but the chef's mind was on other things: he put on his toque and headed for the dining area.

Lady Drummond-Hay was already seated at her table.

Otto walked up from behind, overcome with emotion, trying to do up the last button on his kitchen jacket. Time for a reunion.

In a small notebook, the young woman was starting to write down her account of the voyage, as requested by her newspaper in Chicago for a forthcoming edition.

"Lady?"

She swiveled a little on her chair and saw the chef.

"Thank you. I don't need anything for now. I had a coffee at the hotel."

"Lady . . ."

"No, really. You're very kind, sir. But please don't insist."

Otto was about to say something when the zeppelin started moving as it was winched toward the outside of the hangar. Grace Drummond-Hay stood up to look out the window. Hundreds of men were assisting the departure of the airship, holding its ropes.

Otto couldn't find the strength to walk to his kitchen.

She hadn't recognized him.

The passengers had left their cabins and were all flowing into the dining area. They rushed over to the windows without so much as a glance at the chef, who had turned into a pillar of salt in the middle of all the tables.

At the front of the zeppelin's gondola, Eckener unfolded the message that the telegraph boy had just received.

For D-LZ 127 Graf Zeppelin
Flying over France strictly forbidden until further orders

With both hands at the helm, one of the pilots called Eckener over. The zeppelin was now fully out of its lair.

"I'm releasing us from the winch, Commander. Takeoff in two minutes."

"Go ahead."

Eckener signaled to Lehmann.

"Captain, come with me."

They went into the map room. Two officers were working at a table.

"Gentlemen," said the commander, "the program has just changed. We no longer have the right to fly over France."

"I'll halt operations," said Ernst Lehmann calmly.

"No. Nobody has forbidden our flight, so we will fly. Draw up a new itinerary. We'll need to go via Switzerland and Italy. Look in the archives: the same flight as three years ago, when our destination was Cairo. April 1931. Once we're level with Sardinia, you'll head west to reconnect with our route for Brazil."

"We don't know about the weather in the Alps."

"Find out. And warn the ground that we're leaving in spite of everything."

Twenty-five meters above them, in the middle of a forest of girders and lying on a metal platform, Vango waited.

The zeppelin was late taking off. Vango intended to let a few hours of flying time go by before revealing himself. A large part of the crew had known him five years earlier.

All Hugo Eckener had to do was pretend to scold him and then find him a role on board. The passengers wouldn't even notice the presence of a new crew member.

Vango had remembered this hiding place near the wine cellar, just below the zeppelin's canvas ceiling. He was unlikely to get any visitors. No operation required climbing all the way up there via a labyrinth of ladders and walkways. The tiniest noise, the slightest smell reminded him of his wonderful year on board, and of young Ethel's face when he'd met her for the first time in the skies above Manhattan.

The memories gave him butterflies.

His final voyage had only lasted three weeks, but that was when it had all started. Happiness and fear. They had made each other promises, the only promises in his life that Vango hadn't kept, and which were now an open wound.

Today, those times seemed as distant to him as the memory of his island. He was a criminal hunted down in the country he had made his home for the past four years. And now he'd had no choice but to take refuge in the belly of this whale where nobody would come to pull him out. Vango felt ashamed of not having confessed to Eckener why he was on the run. By hiding the reason behind his arrival, he felt as if he were deceiving the commander and abusing his trust.

But he knew that nobody would ever have let him on board, even as a stowaway, if they'd known about the crime of which he stood accused.

Eckener was at his usual post: the starboard window of the large flight deck.

He was staring beyond the empty expanse of ground at four sets of car headlights coming toward them out of the darkness. The helmsman had just asked for a few more moments to rectify a problem with the balance. Eckener had granted the request because he took pleasure in the thought that these few late cars would also be able to witness takeoff. Commander Eckener felt extremely grateful for the enthusiasm that prompted hundreds of people to rise before dawn, simply in the hope of seeing the *Graf Zeppelin* take flight.

He sat down in his small wooden armchair, his elbow resting on the frame of the open window, and discreetly took from his pocket a crumpled piece of paper, which he glanced at once again. It was an article that had been cut out of a French newspaper. He had read it at a table at the Hotel Kurgarten, where it had been left behind by a traveler. For three days, he hadn't shown it to anyone. The article was about a sordid incident in Paris. A murder. A photograph of Vango illustrated the three columns.

Eckener had no intention of keeping his young passenger on board for long. As soon as he'd seen him, sleeping like a cherub on the banquette in the cabin, the evidence was clear: this child wasn't guilty.

But although Eckener was convinced of his innocence, he had less confidence in the courts. Vango wasn't like other boys. His whole life was a mystery. There were shadowy aspects to him, which the justice system wouldn't appreciate.

He was in danger of the gallows.

Eckener intended to drop him off at the end of the voyage, in South America, where he could start a new life. A one-way ticket to the unknown. *A strange destiny . . . he thought. With some people on this earth, we'll never know where they've come from, or where they're going to.*

The cars were only two hundred meters away now. The tooting of their horns could be heard. The commander folded the newspaper article again, stood up, and told his captain to give the signal for departure.

"I'd rather cross the mountains before ten o'clock this morning. After that, we don't know what kind of risk we'd be running. I don't want the *Graf Zeppelin* grazing the edelweiss."

"Yes, sir! The helmsman can finish regulating the ballast after takeoff. We're ready."

From the cockpit, bellpulls served to alert the mechanics of the five engines.

To the rear, among the passengers, every window was full.

Down on the ground, a crowd surrounded the airship.

The crew started emptying the water bags in order to lighten the balloon. The ropes yanked at the arms still keeping the airship on the ground. The water that was let out showered the onlookers, who gasped in surprise. Hugo Eckener assumed his position to call out, *"Chocks away!"* This was the signal to drop everything and commence takeoff.

Just then, the four cars all braked at the same time. Fifteen armed men got out. Doors slammed, and, through a megaphone, the order rang out: "Stop! Commander Eckener, remain on the ground. Orders from the minister of the interior. Don't move!"

Eckener gritted his teeth.

He didn't need a megaphone to bellow from the window:

"I have all the permission I need! Switzerland and Italy have just radioed in their consent!"

"The flight will go ahead," insisted the nasal voice, "but two places have been requisitioned for surveillance and security purposes. Open the door! I am ordering you!"

Commander Eckener let out a string of swearwords that would be impossible to repeat here, then gave a long sigh and said, "Open up for them. We'll make them sleep in the drains."

He had a ladder brought out of the hangar.

When the two agents climbed up, Eckener recognized Officer Max Grund and his associate Heiner. Once the maneuver was completed, the doors were sealed again.

"Let her go!" the commander ordered.

And the balloon rose up amid cheers. The engines started up one after the other, drowned out by the sheer volume of the zeppelin. Only the windows of the gondola were lit up at the front. The rest of the balloon formed a violet haze in the darkness.

Everything grows small, Lady Drummond-Hay wrote in beautiful handwriting in her notebook. *The dream has just begun. Lake Constance is nothing but a mirror in a bedroom where the lights have been switched off. We're leaving.*

Otto the chef was weeping against the kitchen tiles.

Looking worried, Captain Lehmann watched the police cars disappear into the distance, little luminous dots in the middle of the night.

The fat businessman was singing opera arias at the top of his lungs in the corridor, near to the kitchen, as he inhaled the aroma of bread rolls in the oven: *"Ah, dear south wind, blow once more! My lass longs for me. . . ."*

"Did you wish to speak with me, gentlemen?" Eckener asked.

"Yes, Commander. We're not just here to check on your itinerary. We have received some confidential information."

Eckener didn't move. Max Grund fixed him with a fearsome look.

"Commander Eckener, there is a stowaway on board this zeppelin."

11

A STOWAWAY

"Only one? I think I can see two of you, gentlemen!" said Commander Eckener, staring at each of them in turn. "Mr. Kubis will show you where to sleep. It's the only place we've got left. You'll have to forgive the smells, but we need to store our trash and the dirty water from the balloon in those bags, so as not to lose weight. . . . We don't throw anything away. Which is my only reason for keeping you fellows on board!"

Hugo Eckener's bad jokes fell flat. They didn't suit him. He was talking too much, and he knew it.

Who could know about Vango? How was it possible? Eckener didn't understand anything anymore. Max Grund was watching him very closely, as if reading his thoughts.

"Mr. Eckener . . ."

The officer didn't get a chance to finish his sentence. The jovial businessman passed by, singing again from Wagner's *The Flying Dutchman*.

"Papam papaaaaaaaam!"

The singer stopped.

"Aren't any of you hungry?"

He directed this question at Officer Heiner, who curtly requested that he return to the seating area.

"Ooh, are we being secretive?" The man winked. And he let out a guffaw of laughter as he pushed open the door.

"I demand complete freedom to search the zeppelin," said Grund, addressing the commander through gritted teeth. "You'll provide us with a man to act as our guide."

"Why give us permission for takeoff?" asked Hugo Eckener.

"It's more difficult to escape at an altitude of three hundred and fifty meters, Commander. And I believe we have enough time . . ."

Grund glanced at his watch.

"Seventy-two hours before landing on the Brazilian coast."

Just then, Kubis, the headwaiter, appeared.

"Show these people to their room," said Eckener.

He indicated the compartment he was thinking of.

Kubis looked surprised.

"Really?"

When Eckener gave the go-ahead, Kubis took a clothespin out of his vest and popped it on his nose.

"Follow me, gentlemen," he announced, flashing a perfect smile.

Grund and Heiner's mission was more complicated than it seemed.

The main problem was the presence of seventeen passengers and thirty-nine crew members on board. How were the officers going to spot a stowaway among the dozens of people they could run into anywhere in the balloon? But Grund was extremely smart and his memory faultless. In just a few hours, he had identified the faces of the fifty-six people on board.

He numbered them so as not to be encumbered with names.

And the balloon rose up amid cheers.

Number 1 was Eckener, and Number 56 was Lady Drummond-Hay. This obsession with numbering was something Max Grund would hold on to during the ten years that would lead him toward the peak of power and the depth of horror.

When you get rid of names, everything becomes simpler. There are no feelings involved.

Most impressive of all, Grund had managed to organize his manhunt in a harmonious fashion, without disturbing the passengers. He had politely explained to them that his mission was to study the security procedures for the great zeppelin of the future, the LZ 129, currently under construction in Friedrichshafen.

But the members of the crew were aware of his real purpose.

The Gestapo inspector treated them with no respect.

A mechanic pointed out that Grund and Heiner hadn't allocated numbers to themselves. So in secret they were known as Zero and Zero-Zero.

The officers began by searching the cabins and all the command areas to the fore of the airship, then they were taken down into the keel.

The gondola for passengers and pilots represented only a modest part of the zeppelin. You could travel for hundreds of meters along walkways in the rest of the balloon, down into the intestines of the airship. There, in that enormous space, could be found the tents pitched for the crew, the five tons of water in reserve, and the nineteen small balloons made out of cow guts containing the hydrogen that enabled the zeppelin to fly.

Max Grund was holding a plan of the airship. He was

conducting his research with the greatest care. He had immediately understood the balloon's structure and was able to
spot the possible hiding places.

The two officers were guided by Ernst Fischbach, the
apprentice helmsman and former kitchen boy. Ernst had
started work on board the *Graf* as a cabin boy. He had only
been away from his plane for one year, to learn English in
Middlesex at the home of a Mr. Semphill, an airplane pilot
and occasional passenger on the airship.

"You'll find your stowaway, if he's here."

Ernst said this with some regret. He had nothing against
stowaways. He knew that if he hadn't been accepted on the
balloon, he too would have found a way of sneaking on
board. The urge to fly was too strong and the zeppelin too
handsome.

"What have you got against him, exactly?"

"Who?" asked Heiner.

"The stowaway."

"Be quiet," said Grund.

The officers were approaching the engines, which clung
to the sides of the balloon like skiffs. Access to each engine
involved a delicate maneuver down a ladder. Then you had
to step across the void. And on this early morning above the
Swiss Alps, that void consisted of peaks and glaciers bristling
like a fakir's table. Grund had the bright idea of sending
Zero-Zero.

"Are you sure?" Agent Heiner gulped.

"Quite," snapped Grund.

Heiner opened the trapdoor and braved the wind as he
began his descent down the ladder. Grund and Ernst watched

INTERIOR VIEW OF THE *GRAF ZEPPELIN*

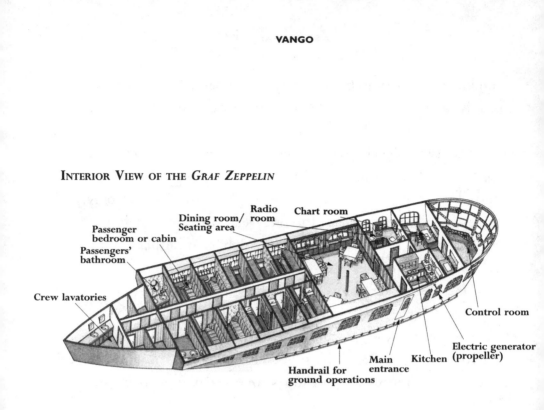

Max Grund was holding a plan of the airship.

him. Barely had he reached the engine than he glanced beneath him and hurriedly climbed back up again.

"There's somebody in there!" he shouted.

Max Grund turned triumphantly to the young Ernst.

"We haven't wasted any time!"

Now that they were this close to it, the engine was extremely noisy.

"I can't really hear what you're saying!" shouted Ernst.

"He's just found somebody!"

"Yes, of course."

"I'm telling you that somebody is hidden in that engine!"

"And my answer is: of course!"

"I'm sorry?"

"It's lucky there *is* someone—you wouldn't want the engines turning all by themselves!"

Max Grund's expression changed.

"There are two mechanics who alternate day and night shifts in the gondola for each of the five engines," Ernst explained. "So we have ten on board for that job. Which makes an awful lot of stowaways. Your bosses will be very happy!"

"Search the engine and tell the man to show himself!" Zero called out furiously to Zero-Zero.

Heiner climbed back down and entered the hull, and a few seconds later, they saw the smiling face of Number 47 appear: Eugen Bentele, a former worker at Maybach's, and an onboard mechanic since 1931. They didn't find anything else either in that engine or in the four remaining engines. But, because of all the noise and as a thank-you for his efforts, the sound of small portable engines continued throbbing in Officer Heiner's ears for several hours afterward.

* * *

The atmosphere in the seating area was calm and muffled. Some people were reading. Many were peering out the windows. Others were playing cards. The fat singer was snoring in an armchair. The room was agreeably warm. The women had thrown on traveling scarves, nothing more. A Frenchman, who was half deaf, complained about the way his fellow card-players kept standing up all the time to admire the view.

"Stupid tourists," he grumbled.

The view was extraordinary. A frosted sun had risen to the left of the balloon, like an orange sorbet. The snowy mountains gave off a pinky haze. The zeppelin was playing a gentle game of leapfrog over the peaks and passes. In the distance, Mont Blanc watched over its immaculate flock of sheep.

"My God," said an old man with a goatee, leaning out the window. "I can hardly believe what I'm seeing."

Behind him, the opera-singing businessman opened his eyes and yawned. He stood up and looked out the window too, but his gaze was toward the rear of the balloon, to the country the zeppelin had just left behind. When the old man caught his eye, moments later, it looked to him as though the jovial singer had been crying.

"Do you . . . ? Do you need anything?"

The well-fed businessman was startled.

"Me?"

"There are tears in your eyes."

The singer burst out laughing.

"I slept like a sea lion! That's all! I just need time to wake

132

up properly. And while we're on the subject of sea lions," he went on, rubbing his eyes, "did you know that in the Berlin Zoo . . ."

The singing businessman insisted on telling a ridiculous story about a penguin and a sea lion, a story he narrated in a very loud voice, so that even the deaf bridge player would be able to get the joke. But it was met with weary sighs.

By midday, the airship was already flying over the city of Florence.

Eckener walked into the passenger cabin.

Kubis was setting the tables for lunch. Down below, the Tuscan sun was making the rooftops glisten. The headwaiter had opened the windows and put a gentle waltz to play on the gramophone. Nearly all the passengers were in their bedrooms.

Since leaving the mountains, the zeppelin was flying at its cruising altitude: three hundred meters was low enough to hear the children shouting in the squares and the peals of bells, and to see the Florentines coming out into their courtyards to watch the ship passing overhead. The music from the gramophone accompanied this spectacle.

Eckener stood in the doorway to the cabin. He was struck by the contrast between a perfect moment and the anguish he'd been feeling since this morning. He knew that they would find Vango. He had no means of warning the stowaway about what was in store for him.

"Kubis."

"Yes, Commander?"

"Tell those two men from the police that they can take lunch with the passengers."

The headwaiter nodded.

Eckener wanted to buy some time. He was the one who had given Vango the idea of boarding the zeppelin as a stowaway in the first place. The idea risked proving fatal for the young man. Once he was discovered, he would be handed over to the French police, who would immediately recognize him.

Who could have tipped off the German authorities? It remained a complete mystery.

The devil himself seemed to be after this child.

Two hours later, the guests were sitting around the tables and finishing off their meals. They had been served duck with white wine from the Jura. Max Grund was sitting silently at one table. He had forbidden his assistant to join in the meal, so that surveillance on the comings and goings in the keel could continue.

Eckener had been hoping to get to Vango at lunchtime, but he had to give up on that idea when he saw Grund sitting alone. The commander had therefore sat down in a corner with a cup of coffee and was answering the passengers' questions in a friendly fashion.

He was telling them how, for example, in 1915 during the war, a military zeppelin had been struck down at Ghent, in Belgium, above an orphanage run by nuns. A soldier named Alfred Mueller had fallen through the roof and landed in the bed of a young nun.

"Heavens above!" exclaimed Lady Drummond-Hay.

"The nun had just gotten out of bed. And soldier Mueller swore the sheets were still warm."

Only Max Grund failed to join in the laughter.

"And that's why we don't have parachutes on board," the commander concluded. "I believe in providence."

"Ooh, and it encourages all sorts of liaisons," added the opera singer, drooling.

Lady Drummond-Hay rolled her eyes. She was appalled by how vulgar this man was. From the first hours of the flight, all the passengers had been avoiding his company.

Only the old gentleman with a goatee, who was sure he'd seen the opera-singing businessman crying, was keeping a close eye on him as he tried to see through his clownlike mask.

Kubis was getting ready to serve a second round of coffee when a shout rang out from the front of the airship.

Grund stood up.

A second later, the cabin door was flung open.

It was Agent Zero-Zero. His clothes were ripped, and his right ear was bleeding. He seemed unaware of his sorry appearance and was trying to behave in as relaxed and natural a manner as possible. He was smiling stupidly with one hand in a pocket while twirling the fingers of his free hand, as a sign for the passengers not to worry about him.

He limped over to his superior and whispered something nobody else could hear. Max Grund pushed him gently toward the door, and they exited together. Eckener apologized to the guests, then followed the agents into the corridor.

"What is going on?" demanded the commander.

"We've got him. Agent Heiner has found him."

"I spotted somebody climbing a ladder in the dark. I called out several times, but he didn't answer. He was trying to escape through a trapdoor up there."

"There's an exit up there?" asked Max Grund.

"Yes," said Eckener somberly. "That's the route if someone needs to go outside to repair the exterior canvas of the zeppelin."

"This exit is not on my plan."

"I don't give a fig about your plan! I command an airship. Not your piece of paper."

Eckener turned to face Heiner.

"Where is he now?"

"I knocked him out. He's on a landing near the wine cellar."

"Did he put up any resistance?"

"I grabbed him by the ankles just as he was about to go outside. He said he would rather die. We fought."

Poor little one, thought the commander. But out loud he said, "I want to see him."

"You will see him when I decide," Grund barked.

"In that case, I will have you disembark immediately."

"I am the representative of the Reich's police."

"And we are in Italy. The Reich doesn't extend this far. For the time being."

Max Grund was wary of the mad old commander who was only too capable of acting on his words. He paused for a moment, before remarking, "You seem to be very concerned about this man. I trust you've had nothing to do with him being here in the balloon, Commander. Go ahead, Heiner. We'll follow you."

A minute later, they reached the platform via a narrow passage. In the gloom, they could clearly see the body lying on the floor, facedown. Eckener was the last to reach the top of the ladder.

"Do you know him?" Grund grilled the commander.

Yes, even without any light, Commander Eckener recognized the figure.

"Do you know this man?" Grund barked again.

"Yes," admitted Eckener. "I know him."

"Who is he?"

The commander wiped his forehead with a handkerchief.

"That is my chef, Otto Manz. You have just knocked out my chef."

Max Grund turned the body over.

It was indeed Number 39, the zeppelin's head chef.

Commander Eckener grabbed Franz Heiner by the collar.

"Get out of my sight! Go and find Dr. Andersen, and four men to carry him!"

Zero-Zero obeyed without even asking permission from his boss.

"As for you," said the commander, turning toward Grund, "from now on, you'll do everything I tell you. You are in my zeppelin!"

"The *Graf Zeppelin* belongs to the Führer of the Third Reich," Max Grund countered chillingly. "You own nothing. I can crush you like an old dog run over in the road."

Eckener was shocked by this violence. From now on, civilized men were all on a stay of execution, like animals on a busy roadside.

"You . . ."

The commander didn't know what to say.

"You . . ."

He was stunned. He didn't recognize this language. He saw Max Grund laughing for the first time, coming up to him and patting him on the cheek.

"There you go. I do believe you've understood."

The police officer turned his back and headed toward the passengers' gondola.

Slowly, Otto Manz was regaining consciousness.

Eckener sniffed and leaned over him.

"You'll be all right, Otto. We're going to get you down into the officers' ward room. But what were you doing up here?"

"Lady . . ."

Eckener lent his ear.

"I wanted to die. To climb up there and throw myself into the sky."

"It's over now, my friend," the commander reassured him.

"Lady," Otto repeated. "She didn't recognize me."

Eckener smiled and rubbed his cheek.

"So that's why . . ."

"Lady . . ."

"Are you in pain?"

Otto didn't reply, so the commander kept going: "You've been working too hard. I had an idea for a boy who could have helped you in the kitchen. But I don't think it's going to work out after all."

There was a small whimper and then Otto said, "She didn't recognize me."

The commander sighed.

"Women—what can I say, old friend? Women."

There followed an unexpected moment of peace. Two men, both wounded in different ways, on the floor, chatting away like a couple of friends camping under the stars and exchanging everyday banter. Sometimes, the simple things in life make us feel better.

"Ah, women . . ."

Eckener was lying next to his chef, his hands under his head.

"I got to know my wife on solid ground," he said. "I prefer it that way. Up in the air, nothing is quite real. It's all just stories: our balloon, Africa, Amazonia, the winds that carry the birds over the Black Forest. Do you believe in any of them?"

Otto was listening with his eyes shut.

"They're just fine stories, my friend. We say we're flying, that we travel the world. We say that. People like it. One day, everything will stop. History will be over. We'll open our eyes. And the campfire will be a distant memory. Get married down below, Otto. Find a real woman, with earth all the way up to her knees. Find someone who's right for you."

Otto smiled in the dark.

"Find someone who's right for you," repeated Hugo Eckener. "Someone who stays on after the stories are over and who doesn't fly off when you breathe on her. Are you listening, my friend? Will you think about what I've said?"

"I'll think about it, Commander."

Otto tried to roll onto his side to talk to the boss.

"Commander . . ." he said. "I wanted to tell you . . . I heard the way the police officer was talking to you. You mustn't allow yourself to be treated like that."

Eckener looked up. He had sensed the presence of someone, to the side of them. Scanning the gloom, he allowed a little time to go by, but already they could hear the men climbing up.

"And as for you," he whispered, "don't budge. Not a single move until I tell you."

He sounded authoritative but gentle.

"Are you talking to me, Commander?" asked Otto.

"No, I'm . . . I'm talking . . . I'm talking to myself."

"What do you mean?"

"It has to do with that police officer you overheard. . . . I'm talking to . . . my pride, my sense of personal pride. . . . I'm telling it not to budge. The time will come."

In the shadows, Vango knew the message was for him.

12

OLD HEROES

Everlund, Scotland, at the same time

It was raining. Three horses were galloping through the birch trees. A man was riding the first horse and leading the two others by a rope.

They formed a tightly packed group. At each bend, it looked as if their hooves might get caught up or the leash tangled in the branches.

But the rider led his team ably through the forest. Silently, the horses obeyed his orders. They enjoyed the sensation of the papery bark rubbing against their flanks. They barely noticed the rain, unlike the young man, who had soaking-wet hair and needed to blink every now and then to stop the rain-drops from blinding him.

They galloped across a stream, over fallen trees. After the birch wood came a great expanse of red that accentuated the gray sky. The horses picked up the pace through the heather to reach the top of the hill, from where all three of them sped in a single movement when they saw the rooftops stream-ing with water in the distance: a misty black castle, like an engraving that had been left out in the rain.

The rider made his charges pause for a moment. They'd set off again soon enough. But he had noticed a white smudge in front of one of the towers. Something had changed since he'd left the castle in the early morning to collect two horses from the other side of Loch Ness.

A small white smudge on a moor in a season when white didn't exist.

The horses were champing at the bit. He relaxed the bridle on his mare, and the team set off again at its triple gallop.

On spotting the rider approaching between the low stone walls, two grooms hurried down the steps. But he didn't make for them, directing the horses instead toward the tower and that patch of white.

Still at a gallop, he released the two other horses and continued alone.

He rode up to what looked like a white shroud. And, coaxing his mare to get as close as possible, he tugged at the sheet, which slid off to reveal a small, gleaming Railton automobile.

"Ethel!" he called out, heading for the main steps.

She was back.

"Ethel!"

He jumped off his horse and dodged the small gaggle of house servants rushing toward him. The castle door opened as if by magic. Behind him on the stone floor of the entrance hall, he left a trail of earth and muddy grass.

"Would Sir like to give me his coat?" the butler inquired in vain.

"Where is she?" the young rider called out, climbing the stairs.

"In the Master and Mistress's bedroom," replied the man, already bending down to pick up the clumps of earth as if they were precious objects.

*   *   *

The rider rushed down a final corridor and pushed open the door.

She was there, with her back to him, buttoning up a large pair of men's trousers. She was wearing a yellow striped shirt. Her hair was wet.

"Ethel?"

She saw him in the mirror, ran over to him, and threw her arms around his neck.

"Paul."

He stood there, arms by his sides, his face giving nothing away.

"I got here two hours ago," said Ethel, burying her head in his neck. "I was waiting for you."

Paul was almost leaning over backward now; he was distant, his chin held high, as if a child with jam smeared all over her had thrown herself into his arms.

"I was waiting for you," she said again.

"*You* were waiting for *me?*"

"Yes. And it felt so long."

"*You* were waiting for *me?*" echoed Paul, who thought he must be imagining this.

She winced with embarrassment, but he couldn't see.

Ethel had made it to the castle before the rain, but she knew she wouldn't escape the downpour of Paul's anger.

"*You* were waiting for *me?* You say you were waiting for me when you were the one who left without any warning, seventeen days ago?"

He removed the hands that had been thrown around his neck and pushed them away.

"I sometimes wonder if you realize what you're doing, Ethel. Seventeen days!"

She pretended to be surprised by this number and made a vague show of doing a recount on her fingers.

"And so for seventeen days, I've stared out of the window at the horizon, scanning the woods, being consoled by Scott, Mary, and the staff from the kitchens. Dining alone downstairs without knowing whether you'd ever come back."

"I'm back; you know I always come back."

He stamped his heel on the parquet floor and turned away from her.

She took a step toward him. She loved Paul. She blamed herself when he suffered.

"Paul . . ."

"Yesterday evening, Thomas Cameron and his father came over. You invited them a month ago, I believe. You'd promised them a trip in the car."

Another embarrassed face from Ethel. Yes, that dimly rang a bell.

"They were dropped off at the end of the driveway," said Paul. "I didn't know what to say when I saw them arriving."

"The Camerons? I'd said 'perhaps,'" muttered Ethel.

"Everything is 'perhaps' with you, Ethel. You might as well be named Perhaps."

"Sorry, Paul."

"I lent them horses to ride back home. I don't understand why you weren't here."

"I don't care what the Camerons think," she said.

"Well, I felt embarrassed. The truth was, I didn't know

if you were dancing in the cellars of Edinburgh, London, or somewhere else, or lying half dead in a ditch behind the hill."

"This time, I wasn't dancing."

"Oh, really?"

Her wet hair was going curly around her eyes.

"I was in Paris."

"I know."

"How?" blurted Ethel.

"Because a Frenchman called for you last night. And there was a telegram from him this morning."

He was watching her closely now.

"Do you know his name?" Ethel asked sharply.

Paul didn't answer.

"Where's the telegram?"

"In my pocket."

"And you opened it?"

Silence.

"I'd decided that I would open it this evening if you hadn't returned."

"Give it to me."

Slowly, he held it out.

Her trembling hand took the telegram, and she went over to the window. She turned her back to Paul, but he could see from the way her shoulders were moving that she was breathing heavily.

Vango, Vango, Vango.

She kept saying his name over and over again to herself in the hope that it would be printed in blue at the bottom of the folded piece of paper between her fingers. Did he remember her?

She opened the telegram and scanned it, and Paul saw her shoulders fall in one movement.

"Is he handsome, at least?" he asked.

She turned around and gave a disarming, disillusioned smile. At last, he let her hold his hands.

"He's an old gentleman with a face like a Scottish terrier," she replied. "He's named Superintendent Boulard. He says he'll be here tomorrow."

Paul looked at her. Nothing surprised him anymore. He stared at the bed and then the whole bedroom.

The windows were streaming with rain.

They let a moment or two go by.

Ethel's dirty clothes were hanging off a leather armchair. Three or four ancestral portraits, with peepholes in their eyes, were secretly spying on them.

"It never changes in here."

"No," said Paul. "Mary puts out fresh flowers every day."

"She even changes the sheets."

"She says, 'I've tidied the Master and Mistress's bedroom.' I don't know what she finds to tidy!"

They both laughed at the same time.

"Yes," said Ethel.

"Even though the Master and Mistress haven't been here for ten years. Nobody comes into this bedroom."

Then he stared at Ethel and added, "Apart from you, who's always trying on Father's clothes."

Together, they stared at the mirror.

And then they lost any desire to laugh. They could see themselves at four and twelve years old, coming into their parents' bedroom at daybreak, climbing aboard that big bed like highway bandits. With one eye open a crack, their father would call out to an imaginary coachman to pick up the pace, and then he'd grab his sword to defend his wife, who was hiding under a pillow. The little bandits would roll onto the carpet.

When Mary, the housekeeper, came in to open the cur-tains, she would witness this crazy family writhing about on the bed and on the floor, looking exhausted, the little girl often planting herself underneath the chest of drawers, wear-ing her father's enormous boots.

"They're mad. My God, they're mad," Mary would often say.

But in her bed at night, she prayed for them to stay like that forever.

Ethel and Paul closed their parents' bedroom door softly behind them. Dinner was ready downstairs. There was a fire in each room. The two of them sat down, side by side, not far from the fireplace, at the head of a vast table that ended somewhere in the mists of Scotland.

There were three people to serve them and two butlers at the doors.

The candlelight from the chandeliers blended with the light from the fire.

"I know who it was you wanted to see in Paris," said Paul.

She looked down.

In the food on his plate, her brother had drawn a *V* with a knife.

* * *

Above the Mediterranean, the same evening

At about ten o'clock, on board the zeppelin, somebody put an armful of rope next to Vango in the darkness. The stowaway was getting ready to jump when he heard Captain Eckener, out of breath, whispering: "They're looking for you. When I give the signal, you'll go out onto the roof of the zeppelin. Lower yourself to the ground with the rope. We'll fly very low. Good luck, Jonah."

What signal? What ground? Vango was about to ask. But just then a voice nearby on the ladder called out, "Commander? Are you looking for something?"

A beam of light was trained on the commander's face. It was an electric lightbulb fixed to a square battery as big as a tin of biscuits. Yet again, the voice belonged to Max Grund.

"You take your evening strolls in very out-of-the-way places. . . ."

Since the incident with Otto the chef, the two men from the Gestapo had called off their search. They planned to start again the following morning by requisitioning ten crew members. Within a few hours, they'd be sure to find their stowaway.

"Can I help you?" asked Grund.

Hugo Eckener was using his hand to shield himself from the light.

"I don't think there's anything you can do for me."

"Perhaps you have a problem?"

"Yes."

"Everybody has dirty little secrets, Commander. Even heroes."

"I am not a hero," said Eckener.

"Well, you certainly won't stay one for long in the eyes of the people. I get the impression that . . ."

Ever since takeoff, Grund had sensed that Captain Eckener was bothered by this business with the stowaway. The policeman had promised himself to make two arrests instead of one, by unmasking Eckener at the same time as his main target.

"Come on, then. Show me what you've got to hide, Commander."

"I'm no hero," Eckener said again.

His voice was trembling.

There was the sound of broken glass under his feet.

Max Grund lowered the light. There was a broken bottle. Wine was leaking onto the floor and soaking Eckener's shoes as he held another bottle by the neck. He seemed to be having some difficulty standing upright. The stench of alcohol was overpowering.

Grund looked disgusted.

"The old heroes are the best. . . ."

"I'm not—"

"So that's your dirty little secret," Max Grund said, cutting him short. "Fortunately, there's a new Germany coming whose idols are not old drunkards who hide away to hit the booze!"

He shone his light over the wine store. Vango was just behind, invisible. Grund spat on the floor and turned around.

He went back down the ladder, annoyed that he hadn't captured his prey but satisfied with his discovery. Eckener's file was growing heavier by the day.

"I am not a hero," repeated the commander, staggering along behind him.

Hugo Eckener had just paid the price of Vango's freedom with his own honor.

Two hours later, the stowaway was still there, waiting for the mysterious signal. He'd wound the rope around himself. The zeppelin was silent.

Vango hadn't left his hiding place. Not even the engines were making a sound. The hydrogen balloons were gently pushing at the airship's canvas, making the seams creak and groan. It must have been midnight.

Down below, after spending quite some time alone, Eckener had returned to the seating area, where a few passengers were still up despite the late hour. Captain Lehmann was standing next to him.

"Commander, we've lost a considerable amount of time by not flying over France. So I don't understand this new detour."

"I've told you, Captain. We're making this detour to thank Dr. Andersen for saving our chef's life."

"I'm sorry," said Andersen. "I wouldn't want to . . ."

Dr. Andersen was the old gentleman with the goatee whose eyes didn't miss a trick.

"You've always dreamed of seeing Stromboli, so now you're going to set eyes on the volcano for yourself!"

"I . . ."

"Doctor, haven't you always dreamed of seeing Stromboli?"

"Of course, Commander, but . . ."

"You heard that, Captain—he's always dreamed of it."

As a matter of fact, Dr. Andersen had dreamed of and was curious about everything imaginable: one life just wasn't enough to satisfy all his interests. If someone had suggested setting off that very night to find out whether the North and South Poles were in fact flat, he would have risen to the challenge.

Captain Lehmann simply didn't understand his boss anymore.

At ten o'clock that evening, just as the airship should have steered full west, level with Sardinia, Hugo Eckener had decided to hold his southward course in order to get close to the volcano of Stromboli. This kind of whim was so uncharacteristic of Eckener that Lehmann wondered what was going on. He had found the commander, just before, washing the soles of his shoes. And there was still a concerning whiff of wine about his person, even after his trip to the crew's bathroom.

"We're going to arrive in Brazil eight hours late!" the captain had implored.

"Lehmann, I'm just asking you to obey."

The zeppelin had been holding this new course for some time when one of the pilots walked into the saloon.

"Stromboli, Commander."

The passengers who were still awake were authorized to go up onto the bridge to witness this phenomenon.

They called it the lighthouse of the Mediterranean. For millennia, it had lit up once or twice an hour. The reddish glow of Stromboli, more than a thousand meters high, could be seen from far away at nighttime.

Four years earlier, a gigantic eruption had proved fatal, but Stromboli had now resumed its innocent rhythm. It was a volcano island in the middle of the sea, with a few brave fishermen's houses on its slopes.

"It's magnificent," said Dr. Andersen when the orange glow dissipated.

"If you'd like," answered Eckener.

"I'm sorry?"

"If you'd like, then that's what we'll do."

"Do what, Commander?"

"The doctor wishes to get closer to the volcano," Eckener told the pilot.

Andersen appeared to be choking.

Captain Lehmann came over.

"Commander, it's time to steer to the starboard side."

"Not yet," said Eckener.

"We shouldn't get too close to the volcano, with the amount of explosive gas we've got on board."

"I know better than you what we've got on board. Go to bed, Captain."

Twenty minutes later, Eckener gave the order for the engines to cut out.

He had the balloon's horn sound three times.

Vango sprang to his feet.

The signal.

The passengers came out of their cabins in dressing gowns. The crew members emerged from their dormitories. They all ran into one another in the corridors and wondered what was going on.

Commander Eckener's good mood quickly put them at ease. Transformed into a circus ringmaster, he clapped his hands and called out, "Everyone over to the port-side windows. Roll up! The show is about to begin!"

Lady Drummond-Hay hadn't been able to find her silk slippers. So she was barefoot, curled up in an armchair in front of the bay window.

"Port side! The show is about to begin!"

Everybody was peering into the darkness, which was unrelieved by any sign of a glimmer. The businessman was humming circus music.

Next to him, Dr. Andersen was feeling extremely embarrassed about being the cause of all this upheaval.

"But I didn't ask for any of this," he kept saying, wide-eyed behind his spectacles.

Otto the chef, with bruises on his face, was walking around with a basket of warm brioches, which he was offering to the passengers. If he'd been dying in the trenches of 1916, Otto would still have made pastries and strudels.

When he came close to Lady Drummond-Hay, he wanted to avoid catching her eye. So he looked down as he held out the basket. His eyes fell on her two dainty bare feet, and when he sensed his heart racing, he realized he wasn't over her yet.

"You're going to enjoy this," said Eckener, passing Max Grund, who hadn't removed his black raincoat since the airship had taken off.

Grund didn't respond. He was in a bad mood. He'd slept very little because the stench in his room was so appalling.

Captain Lehmann was feeling moderately reassured. Eckener had finally stopped the balloon at a reasonable distance from the volcano. There was no immediate danger.

Now, with the engines and lights switched off, the zeppelin was perfectly silent. Everyone was waiting for the big event. A few minutes went by in total darkness, only partially spoiled by the fat singer's bad jokes.

When the volcano finally lit up again, and a huge "Oooooh!" went up from everyone in the balloon, it might also have been possible to discern, standing on top of the zeppelin, with the starry sky above him, the figure of Vango emblazoned in red.

Glowing swallows flew like sparks around him.

The air was mild.

Vango had just realized where he was.

He fixed the end of the rope to a snap hook on the dorsal spine of the airship and proceeded to lower himself down the length of the balloon canvas by letting out the rope.

Down below, in the seating area, the chief helmsman came to see Eckener.

"The balloon is losing height. There's ground below us. We need to start up the engines, Commander."

"Let's take our time—there's no hurry."

"We're less than a hundred meters from the ground."

"Let us descend to twenty-five meters," ordered Eckener. "At twenty-five meters, you can fire up the engines again."

"That's too tight a margin," Lehmann pointed out.

"You're the one who's being uptight tonight, Captain."

As he said this, Eckener tottered a bit.

The captain made as if to help him, but Eckener righted himself.

"Sorry. Just a bit of fatigue. Forgive me, Captain. I was rude to you."

In reality, he had just seen Vango's shadow passing vertically in front of the window.

Vango had commenced his descent on the right-hand side. Nobody else had noticed him.

A minute later, the sounder announced that they were at twenty-six meters. The throbbing of the engines kicked in again. The seating-area lights were switched back on. Champagne was poured. The horn was blasted. The balloon was heading toward Gibraltar, on its way to South America.

Vango rolled onto solid ground, his body tucked in a ball. A few kilometers away, across the sea to the southwest, a woman had come out of her house with a lantern. She was wrapped in a cape. She thought she'd heard a ship's horn. Later, she could just make out a light shining among the stars above the horizon.

At the end of the path, Mazzetta watched Mademoiselle going back inside the house. The nurse had been living alone for at least five years, ever since the little one had left.

An east wind pushed the zeppelin along at top speed. The next day, at teatime, it crossed the equator. The day after that, while the passengers were sipping their morning hot chocolate, the

Brazilian coast was in view. They passed Pernambuco not a minute late and continued as far as Rio de Janeiro. The passengers were driven to their hotel, the Copacabana Palace, set back from the city center, on the beach. Barely had he gotten through the revolving door than Max Grund rushed over to a telephone. He had reception call Berlin.

"Hello . . ."

It was a bad line, but he could hear the bellowing on the other end clearly enough when he had to admit that no, he hadn't found anybody on board the zeppelin. Grund swore that he simply couldn't understand it. He knew that the person they were looking for was a priority for the regime and that his escape had been denounced by somebody very reliable and very close to the authorities. The mission was fail-proof.

"Fail-proof!" the voice on the other end shouted.

Max Grund was swimming in the tropical heat. The telephone handset was melting in his fingers. A large fan was turning, to no avail, on the ceiling.

Close by, in the men's lavatories, the fat opera singer was standing in front of the mirror with a serious expression on his face.

He ran his hand through his hair and slid off the wig that had been hiding his bare scalp. He pushed his fingers into his mouth and pulled out the piece of rubber that had been padding his gums and cheeks, thereby transforming his face. Then he undid his suspenders and opened his shirt to remove the large rubber pouch that had provided him with his paunch.

He buttoned up his shirt again and stuck his head under the faucet.

The face that appeared in the mirror was that of the actor Walter Frederick, star of the Deutsches Theater in Berlin and a fervent opponent of the Nazi regime. After living under a death threat for the past eighteen months, he'd had no choice but to leave Germany hastily in order to reach California via Brazil.

He thought his life as an actor was at an end. Little did he know that a few years later, he would triumph in Hollywood and that his and Vango's paths would cross again.

He went out into the lobby and performed, as a final number, a few tap-dancing steps behind Max Grund, who had just hung up furiously.

The stowaway Grund had just failed to capture was Frederick.

PART TWO

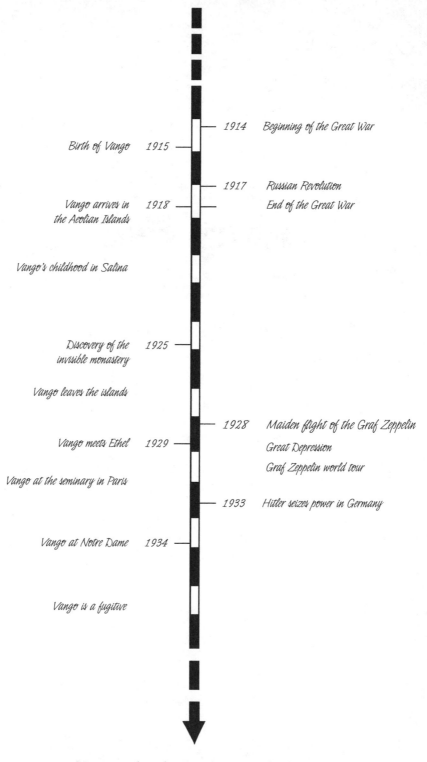

1914   Beginning of the Great War

Birth of Vango   1915

1917   Russian Revolution

Vango arrives in   1918   End of the Great War
the Aeolian Islands

Vango's childhood in Salina

Discovery of the   1925
invisible monastery

Vango leaves the islands

1928   Maiden flight of the Graf Zeppelin

Vango meets Ethel   1929   Great Depression

Graf Zeppelin world tour

Vango at the seminary in Paris

1933   Hitler seizes power in Germany

Vango at Notre Dame   1934

Vango is a fugitive

He remembered Vango's story, the little
shipwrecked boy with no past and no origins.

13

THE YOUNG LADY AND THE SUPERINTENDENT

Everland, Scotland, May 1, 1934

The superintendent arrived at the castle at midday.

He had just spent three days traveling. He had already caught two trains and one boat when his suitcase got stolen somewhere between Victoria and King's Cross Stations, in London. He was hopping mad and cursed the English first, then Napoleon for having lost the battle of Waterloo. Passersby stared at him as he kicked the pavement, his face turning as red as a poisonous mushroom.

There was nothing for him to do but catch the Flying Scotsman, the new train that linked London to Edinburgh in seven or eight hours. Once safely on board, the superintendent enjoyed the comforts of one of the world's great railways. He spent half the journey eating lunch, and he even found a barber's booth where he could freshen up ahead of his meeting the next day. On arrival, he spent what was left of the night near to Edinburgh's Waverley Station, in a hotel that was so jam-packed he had to share a room with a redheaded giant who suffered from insomnia. By the time his neighbor finally dropped off to sleep at five o'clock in the morning, Boulard had already left.

For the last leg of his journey, Boulard got a carpenter with a horse and cart to drop him off at the end of a long driveway. The superintendent stared at the castle for some time, at a loss for words.

"Are you sure?"

He repeated the address several times for the benefit of his driver, who nodded to the effect that this was indeed the right place.

"Everland Castle," the carpenter confirmed.

Boulard thanked him in his impenetrable French accent, before watching the cart drive off.

"Well, my little pussycat . . ."

He smoothed his hair under his hat.

"Well, my little pussycat, you don't exactly live in a basket . . ." he muttered, recalling the fragile young woman he'd met briefly in Paris, upstairs at the Smoking Wild Boar.

Boulard had been expecting a pleasant little house in the hills. But this was a fortress that would have made Mordachus, King of Scotland, quake in his boots.

The superintendent didn't feel dressed for the part of charging the castle. He could have done with a chain-mail coat, a helmet, and two horsemen, but he didn't even have a spare pair of socks.

He hid behind a tree, where he straightened out his clothes. Luckily, he still had his umbrella. His umbrella was key to his elegant appearance, or so he believed. He was thinking of his elderly mother, who had packed his case for him back in Paris: *I've put in your flannel trousers, in case you need to dress up of an evening. . . .*

His thief back in London was probably passing himself off as a prince, drinking to the superintendent's good health while sporting his dapper evening suit. Above all, Boulard was annoyed about his notebook getting stolen, because it contained what little information there was of the Parisian investigation as written up by his faithful Avignon.

"Onward, Boulard!"

He marched toward the castle. He was using his umbrella as a walking stick. The double doors of the main entrance swung open when he was still a hundred meters away.

Knight Boulard was expected.

A man showed him inside, greeting him in perfect French: *"Soyez le bienvenu, Monsieur le Commissaire!"*

He helped Boulard take off his coat before reaching for the superintendent's umbrella. Caught by surprise, Boulard tightened his grip on the handle.

The umbrella. He mustn't let go of his umbrella. The man was tugging at it, but Boulard clung on with both hands.

They stared at each other and began walking in a slow circle around the umbrella, which was firmly planted on the stone floor. It was a strange samurai duel between a Scottish butler and a French police officer.

"Sir, allow me to take your umbrella," the butler finally insisted.

"I'd rather keep it," retorted Boulard, as if fearing a small outbreak of rain in the drawing room.

Being a good sport, the butler gave in to the visitor's wishes. Boulard felt thoroughly relieved. After the robbery, this was all he had left. His mother thought he looked much more stylish with his umbrella. Without it, he would have felt naked inside this citadel.

The guest was bidden to sit by a fire in what was referred to as the small hunting room, but which was in fact large enough to park two or three planes from the French airmail service. A glass was poured for him. And he didn't say no to a second. Boulard's feet were warming up nicely by the flames. He had discreetly removed his shoes in the hope that his socks would dry out.

Ordinarily, the superintendent hated waiting. He only had to be left on his own for a single minute before his blood pressure started rising in much the same way as in a dentist's waiting room. But on this occasion, he felt relaxed in the corner by the fire, in the middle of all these carpets and paintings. He was almost snoring.

He realized that he had never waited for a young lady in a castle before. It was a giddy sensation. At sixty-nine years of age, he suddenly felt that it was high time he experienced the life of a Prince Charming.

Boulard was starting to worry about his mental faculties when he saw the door being pushed ajar and a young doe with white spots walk through the gap.

Yes, a doe.

A doe.

He stared at his glass and the animal in turn, then at his glass, then at the animal.

Boulard, old boy, you're worn out, he told himself.

He threw the contents of his glass onto the fire, producing a high flame that made the young doe shy away.

A doe.

Boulard stood up abruptly.

The animal was approaching him.

"Shoo, shoo, shoo!" tutted the superintendent, waving his fingers to make it go away.

The doe liked this game. She pranced around the room a bit before heading back toward her new friend.

"Shoo, shoo, shoo!" Boulard tried again, realizing that he had left his umbrella and shoes by the armchair.

The doe was delighted. She was dancing about on the spot.

"Shoo, shoo!"

This time, she jumped on top of a large table, took a sharp turn along a leather banquette, and threw herself at the superintendent.

When Ethel walked into the small hunting room, she could tell that something was up.

The superintendent was standing in his socks on the chest of drawers, holding on to a chandelier. The doe was staring at him, batting her long amorous eyelashes.

"Could I ask you for my umbrella, please, Mademoiselle?"

Ethel clicked her fingers and the doe, looking moody, sloped off toward the door.

"I'm sorry. You've met Lily," said Ethel, holding out the umbrella and shoes.

Boulard stayed on top of the chest of drawers long enough to tie up his shoelaces, while checking that Ethel closed the door firmly behind Lily.

"Does she . . . does she live with you?"

"No. She comes from the woods, but she sneaks into the house whenever a door or window is left open."

The superintendent was astounded. In Paris, not even the pigeons got close to his windows.

"I bottle-fed Lily for the first year of her life," Ethel explained in her faint accent. "She's become very . . . clingy."

It always took Ethel a while to get used to speaking French again.

Boulard had to admit he'd never bottle-fed a pigeon. Which might explain why they never ventured into his apartment.

Once the superintendent had set foot on the parquet floor again and was reunited with his umbrella, it was only a matter of seconds before he was back in the character of Auguste Boulard, the impressive police superintendent from Paris, who had solved some of the century's greatest crimes.

"I don't imagine you're paying me a visit just because of your love for animals," said Ethel.

"Indeed not, Mademoiselle. Indeed not."

It had only taken two days—the two days following the events at Notre Dame—for Boulard to realize that he wouldn't find out anything about Vango Romano in Paris. He had never been confronted with a situation like this before: a boy who had lived for four years in a seminary, alongside dozens of others who all viewed him favorably, and even admired him; a boy who had fit well into a close-knit community but about whom people could say nothing at all. Nothing.

Boulard sometimes investigated street crimes, and now and then, a witness might not be able to state his own name, answering, "They call me Mosquito around here—I don't know my name." But Vango wasn't a street urchin: he had been a boarder in a Carmelite seminary for four years.

From the other students, Boulard had tried to track down any piece of information that could have rooted Vango Romano somewhere on this earth: his place of birth, the surname of a family member, his parents' address. The superintendent had inquired about the boy's hobbies, where he spent his holidays, what visitors he had, what mail he received . . .

Nothing. Nothing at all.

Nothing. Nothing. Nothing.

"You're making fun of me, Canon!"

Boulard had ended up in the office of Canon Bastide, whose responses to the same questions involved his eyes bulging as he tied knots in his cassock.

"Nothing," the canon replied over and over again, fueling Boulard's outrage.

"You're making fun of me! You can't seriously be telling me that you don't know his date of birth!"

This time, Bastide's face lit up.

"Oh, yes . . . his date of birth, I should be able to help you out there."

Lieutenant Avignon, who was standing behind Boulard, looked interested and got out his notebook.

"Around 1915," said Bastide. "Or perhaps 1916."

Boulard gritted his teeth.

"Or 1914," ventured Canon Bastide somewhat abashedly.

Augustin Avignon had noted down the three years in his notebook.

"That's about as accurate as the year in which Abraham was born," thundered the superintendent.

"As a matter of fact," admitted the canon, "I believe that Vango tried to pass himself off as a little bit older than he really was, in order to make it to the priesthood sooner. He was just a kid. He requested a special dispensation from Rome. I don't know how he got one. He spoke Italian, had connections."

Had connections! The whole problem was that Vango didn't appear to be connected to anyone.

The canon did, however, say a word or two about the paranoia from which Vango suffered.

"Paranoia?"

"Yes," confirmed the canon. "He was a vulnerable boy. Unfortunately, the accusation is only too clear. It's written on the victim's desk."

Boulard had enough schoolboy Latin to understand what *Fugere Vango* meant, but he didn't trust the evidence. He could tell that Bastide didn't like Vango. He changed the subject.

"Do you have the file for that special dispensation?"

"Nothing," muttered the canon, for the fiftieth time.

Boulard collapsed into an armchair. He glanced behind him at Avignon.

"Well, do you have anything else to ask this good father?"

"Nothing," the lieutenant replied.

"Right!" groaned Boulard, checking his pocket watch.

The superintendent stood up and headed for the door. His thoughts had now turned to a bistro behind Saint-Sulpice. A bistro that served up veal cheeks to die for.

Boulard was hungry.

Just as he was about to turn the handle, he heard the canon remark, "When all's said and done, there's only one person who could help you. He knew everything, I think. He vouched for the boy from the outset."

Avignon got out his notebook again.

"He was the person," revealed Bastide, "who introduced Vango to me. He got him in here."

"And he is?"

"He *was* Father Jean. And Vango killed him on Friday night."

"The day you find a witness who's alive, Father, do let me know."

Boulard slammed the door. The wall quivered, making the crucifix perform a half turn.

Now that he was standing opposite Ethel, the superintendent adopted a different tack.

"Yes, of course we're making progress with the investigation. We're not far from getting to the bottom of this business. The noose is tightening. It's in the bag. The secret won't go with him to the grave. . . ."

Boulard was playing for time with this string of clichés, while working out the best way to interrogate Ethel.

He never prepared his line of questioning.

His mentor, Jacques Aristophane, chief commissioner of the Paris Police when Boulard had started out in 1891, had always told him that to arrive with questions meant already providing the answer.

Aristophane used to explain his method with quick-fire examples, sometimes referring to nursery rhyme characters. "You see, Boulard my boy, if you ask the milkman whether he saw Mother Michelle's cat last night, you're already letting him know that Mother Michelle has a cat, that there's a problem with that cat, and that the problem happened last night. But, Boulard my boy, if you just say 'Hello,' you have a chance of hearing something."

Boulard, who was very young at the time, would listen religiously to his mentor and from then on viewed his childhood nursery rhymes in an entirely new light.

"Because, you see, the milkman will tell you, 'Now, look here, today's got off to a bad start. Someone has spilled all my milk. It's bound to be the neighbor's son, because he's always playing with his ball in the courtyard.' Well, he'd never have told you that, Boulard my boy. He'd have answered you with, 'No, I didn't see any cat.' And that would have been an end to the matter. He'd never have made any link with the overturned milk, because he was so primed to blame the neighbor."

Jacques Aristophane had taught Auguste Boulard everything he knew.

The chief commissioner died from a pistol shot in 1902 while attempting to intervene in a gangster street fight at the end of Rue Planchat, by the gates to Paris. The young Boulard, leaning over him, had harvested his dying words: "The shot has gone under my rib, Boulard, my boy, so it must have been the shortest one who fired."

Even his final sigh was a police investigation.

As Boulard recalled those early days, he was also mindful of the fact that young Ethel was smart and wouldn't easily volunteer any information.

"So, as I was saying, we're very close to solving it. . . ."

He stopped to look at her and added:

"In any case . . . the guilty party, Vango Romano, is under lock and key."

It came to him just like that, the way you flick a ball over the tennis net. It was worth a try.

The results weren't long in coming. Ethel clenched her fists and hid them under her short hunting jacket, as if she were cold. Boulard noticed this, but a normal observer would only have seen the girl's apparent indifference. Just in time, she caught the ball: "You're very efficient. Bravo, Superintendent! But I'm not sure why you've come all the way here to tell me that."

"Because I've been told that only you can give me the information I need."

"Who?"

"You."

"No, I mean who told you that?"

"Vango."

TWO YOLKS IN ONE EGG

This time he had her. The Aristophane method was working.

Ethel sat down in an armchair beside the fire. They fell silent for a while. Ethel knew there was no point in denying it. If Vango had given her name, she couldn't contradict him.

Deep down, she was also enjoying imagining the shape that her name formed on Vango's lips.

Ethel.

Ask Ethel.

That's what he must have said.

Boulard, who was pretending to be very offhand about it all, was miming playing the double bass with his umbrella.

"Can I see him?" Ethel finally ventured.

"Who?"

"Him."

Boulard shrugged, making an apologetic face as if to say, *It all depends on what you're about to tell me.*

Ethel's foot gently nudged a log, about to escape the flames, back into the fireplace.

"I knew him a little for a few days. We were very young."

Now it was the superintendent's turn to sit down. She amused him. At barely seventeen years old, she sounded like a respectable old lady referring to a love affair in her youth.

"I was traveling with my brother, Paul. Vango was there. We became friends."

"Was it a long time ago?"

"Oh . . ."

She flung her hand over one shoulder as if talking about a bygone era, about a period in time that the old superintendent could never have known.

"Your parents allow you to travel like that?"

Ethel smiled.

"Our parents leave us a little too much to our own devices, Superintendent. Our parents aren't very . . ."

"Clingy?" guessed Boulard.

"Yes. It's a real word, isn't it? *Clingy?*"

Boulard shrugged again.

"Our parents," she repeated, "aren't what you might call 'clingy' at all."

Her eyes were moist, but she tried to smile and continue talking.

"So, as I was saying, I was traveling with my brother, and Vango was there—that's all."

"What do you know? What did Vango tell you about himself?"

"Very little. He told me very little."

At least she had avoided the dreaded refrain of "nothing," which everybody used when talking about Vango.

"Well?" asked Boulard.

"I know he grew up on an island. Or a few islands."

"Where?"

"I'm not sure. He used to say 'on my islands.' Because he spoke such good Russian, I imagined them as islands in frozen seas or on the Amour River."

Or was it Amur? She knew it sounded like the River of Love, anyway.

"I . . . I mean—"

"He spoke Russian?" Boulard interrupted her, frowning.

In Paris, a German seminarian had claimed to be very close to Vango because he spoke German just like he did. And Canon Bastide said that he knew Italian. Were they all talking about the same boy?

"Yes, he spoke Russian. He spoke with . . ."

Ethel's expression became agitated for a moment. She appeared to be troubled by something.

"With?" quizzed Boulard, who wasn't going to let the matter drop.

"With a Russian who was traveling with us."

Ethel was silent for a moment.

The Russian.

His face had just flashed into her mind. She had been searching for the owner of that face for several days now, and it belonged to the man who had taken out his weapon on the square in front of Notre Dame. The man with the waxen face, the man she'd already seen somewhere before, and she had suddenly remembered where: their paths had crossed in 1929, during that long voyage with Vango. But she didn't want to mention any of this.

Boulard stood up sharply.

"Why on earth did he speak Russian? I mean, is he Russian?"

"No," she said, "I think one of his parents must have been British or American."

"Why?"

"Because he spoke my language perfectly."

Boulard couldn't make head or tail of any of this. He rubbed his ear, which was something he always did on a bad day. During the last week, he had developed a sketchy sense of Vango, as a rather bland and mild character, but now, all of a sudden, it felt like he was hunting down a globe-trotting chameleon who was sticking out his multicolored tongue at him.

"By heck, I'll get him in the end!"

Ethel's eyes widened. Too late, the superintendent realized what he'd just said.

The girl's eyes were as green and shiny as polished bronze.

"You haven't got him yet!" she gasped. "You just wanted to make me talk."

Boulard bit his lip.

"I must tell you, Mademoiselle . . ."

She stood up.

"No. You're not going to tell me anything. You are welcome here, Superintendent. Do at least stay until tomorrow."

She kept on talking, with no letup.

"Mary will show you to your bedroom. Lunch has been laid out for you in there. Along with some clothes, because you appear to be rather short of them. Do take a walk this afternoon. I can show you the view from the hill. We shall dine late tonight. My brother, Paul, will be joining us, but he won't be back until nine o'clock. It will be a fun evening: the three of us have plenty to tell one another."

She sounded sad and severe now as her voice betrayed a hint of emotion: "But as for the subjects we've touched on, Vango and everything else, I don't want to hear another word. Do you understand? Not a single word or I'll throw you out, even if it's in the middle of the night, and even if Lily and all the other wild animals are out there roaming the Highlands. Until later, Superintendent. And not another word."

Ethel nodded and walked away with her head held high.

Boulard's day was certainly memorable.

He settled into a bedroom the size of a concourse in the railway station of a large provincial city. For Mary, the housekeeper, it was love at first sight, and in the kitchen she was constantly referring to their guest as "the handsome Frenchman." Nobody else recognized this description of the short superintendent.

Boulard went for a stroll over the hills, dressed in a pair of Scottish laird's trousers whose hems had been hastily taken up by Mary while he was having a bath.

That evening, the dinner was as much fun as predicted. Paul simply couldn't understand what this man was doing at his table, but he welcomed him like an old friend. At midnight, Mary led the superintendent back to his bedroom by candlelight.

"Tell me, dear child," said Boulard before attempting to leave Mary in the corridor by closing his door, "the parents of these young people, where are they at the moment? Are they far?"

"Oh, no! They're never far, Mr. Poolard. That would be out of the question! The four of them love each other too much. . . ."

She drew him over to the landing window and pointed out some flickering lights less than a hundred meters away.

"Just there, look, the little graveyard is under the tree."

The superintendent nearly keeled over.

"Ah, right, yes . . . you've put my mind at rest. And how long have they been there?"

"Ten years. Ten years in four days' time."

The next morning, Ethel offered to drive Boulard to Inverness station. Mary had crammed a bag full of souvenirs for the handsome Frenchman. He made his excuses for not taking the stag's head she wanted to give him.

She must think he lived at Versailles. He was trying to picture his mother's face when, on opening the front door of their three-room apartment in Rue Jacob, she discovered those antlers.

"Good God, Auguste!"

He already had to hide his collection of toy soldiers under his mattress because, according to Madame Boulard, they were a dust trap.

"The superintendent is rather overladen," Ethel explained to Mary. "We'll send it to him."

The two of them slid into the twelve-cylinder Railton. The racing car wasn't built for two people, but Ethel was very slim. And Boulard pulled his stomach in.

The young woman and the superintendent made a funny sight, squeezed in like two yolks in one egg, with a suitcase into the bargain.

The automobile drove away from the castle. It took a left bend, and then its engine roared as it vanished on the horizon.

Mary went back inside, forlorn and still holding the stag's head.

*   *   *

The superintendent felt out of his depth, glued to this young woman at eighty miles an hour on a bad road.

"She made it to a hundred and sixty an hour on the circuit at Brooklands!" shouted Ethel.

"I'll take your word for it."

"Sorry?"

"I'm saying you don't need to give me a demonstration!"

"Sorry?"

"NOT SO FAST!" roared the superintendent.

And Ethel broke into a dazzling smile, unlike anything he'd seen from her.

On a bend, she wanted to stop to show him the view. The pneumatics sank squeakily back down to the ground.

His legs still trembling, Boulard took a few steps through the long grass behind Ethel.

They could see Loch Ness in the distance.

"It's a fine sight," said Boulard.

Ethel sat down on a rock and was very quiet.

The superintendent stayed standing. The countryside reminded him of his birthplace, Aubrac: the high plateau where he had grown up between the Aveyron, the Lozère, and the Cantal, with five months a year of snow underfoot.

"How many kingdoms know us not," Ethel murmured.

Boulard frowned.

Her eyes were closed.

The sky was turning black toward the west.

"It's a phrase that was written on a scrap of material he always had on him," Ethel explained. "'*Combien de royaumes nous ignorent.*'"

Coming to her senses again, she added in a different tone

of voice, "I'm telling you that because it won't be of any use to you."

"Thank you," came Boulard's sarcastic reply.

It was the kind of clue that served no purpose except to look good in detective novels.

"It's a quote from Blaise Pascal's *Thoughts*," remarked Boulard, who never read detective novels.

"Does the name 'the Cat' mean anything to you?"

Ethel fell silent.

"It's the only clue I've been able to find," the superintendent conceded. "The only one. Somebody came to ask for Vango Romano at the seminary the day after he'd fled. A fourteen-year-old girl. She told the caretaker to let Vango know the Cat was waiting for him. But when we turned up with two of my men, the girl was no longer there. . . ."

Ethel stared at the police officer.

"Well, does that name mean anything to you?"

"It's time to go, Superintendent. But if you keep pestering me, I'll have to leave you here."

She ran toward the car.

She didn't much like the idea of another girl looking for Vango.

Twenty minutes later, they arrived at the station. The train was already there, ready to leave, and the platform was empty apart from the superintendent and the young lady.

"I've never heard that name before," Ethel conceded reluctantly, shaking Boulard's hand. "But let me know if you find her."

He already had both feet on the train outboard.

"You mean the Cat?"

She nodded. A young man in a cap came out of the station and rushed onto the train just as it was pulling out. Two blows of the whistle cut through the chill of the May morning.

When the train had gone, Ethel, alone on the station platform, was musing about how she would have loved to spend all night talking about Vango, sharing everything she knew, which is to say nothing apart from what she had experienced onboard the zeppelin.

Vango. The way he opened and closed his eyes, the way he walked, the way he told stories, the way he pronounced certain words, like *Brazil,* the way he peeled potatoes by giving them eight perfect sides, the way he gazed at the waves down below, the way he recited short poems in unrecognizable dialects, the way he prepared French toast above the Pacific Ocean at two o'clock in the morning that was so good it made your teeth feel like they were sinking into a dream.

She couldn't have recounted anything other than those little memories because, during the precious few weeks she and Vango had spent together, she had lived only in the present. On the day when she had suddenly thought about the past and especially about the future, it was already too late.

As the superintendent watched the girl on the platform shrinking, he felt curiously satisfied by his visit. He had gotten what he wanted, the trail that he'd been missing up until that point.

He settled comfortably into his seat.

That same morning, at breakfast, when Mary had brought him his tea, he had been able to ask what he needed to know, between two compliments about the blueberry muffins.

The voyage that had made such a mark on Ethel and Paul had taken place between the tenth of August and the ninth of September 1929.

"Yes, Mr. Poolard, the pair of them set off, those poor children. I can remember it only too well. Ethel was in such a bad way. So fragile since the death of her parents. She came back a completely different person."

"Better?"

"Cured, Mr. Poolard! Cured!"

Mary wiped her nose. The superintendent was listening.

"It happened on board the zeppelin, five years ago. The grand world tour of 1929, you understand! They were even in the newspaper. Those poor little bairns . . ."

"Poor little ones," Boulard echoed joyously.

That same zeppelin had flown over Notre Dame in Paris the day after the murder, as Vango was running away.

It might not seem much. But for someone like Boulard, that kind of coincidence looked like the beginning of a solution.

3

A CRAZY LITTLE HORSE

The Ritz, Place Vendôme, Paris,
three days later

Boris Petrovitch Antonov had shaved off his mustache.

He was furious about this, but the orders had come from so high up that personal vanity was out of the question.

Now he looked like a white-haired baby.

"Is that all you've got?"

Boris was leafing through a small notebook across the table from a student who was crumpling a cap between his ink-stained fingers. They were sitting in a bar at the hotel. Three old ladies were sipping tea. They gave off a scent of white lilies and bergamot.

"Where's the rest?"

"In the Thames."

Boris smacked his hand against his forehead.

"You threw the rest of the suitcase into the river?"

"Those were my orders."

They were clearly Russian, but they were speaking in French to avoid drawing attention to themselves. A pianist was playing slow melodies in the adjacent room. The sound of footsteps rang out in the lobby.

His complexion looking paler and more waxen than ever, Boris paused over a page in the notebook on which a portrait had been reproduced.

"It's a striking resemblance, isn't it?" said the student, who had finally put his cap down on the table.

Boris glared at him. It was a portrait of Boris Petrovitch Antonov himself, drawn by Ethel and copied into the notebook by Augustin Avignon.

This portrait of the mysterious marksman at Notre Dame was in the hands of the police.

Boris turned the page roughly, exasperated at seeing the sketched version of the mustache he'd had to sacrifice because of this kid, so as not to be recognized.

"Did you at least see the girl?"

"Only from a distance. It was impossible to get close to the castle. The place is buzzing with servants. When she goes out, it's in her car or on horseback. You can't see her for the cloud of dust. But she took the superintendent to the station at Inverness the next day. I followed him as far as Paris."

"Who?"

"Boulard."

"Where does he live?"

"Behind Saint-Germain-des-Prés."

"Alone?"

"With his mother."

Boris grabbed a passing waiter and ordered two more coffees. Next to them, a little girl was eating an enormous bowl of ice cream, one scoop taller than she was.

"So the bottom line is, you haven't found anything?"

"I haven't found anything because they haven't got anything," the student explained.

"You haven't found anything," Boris repeated.

"I'm telling you . . ."

"Be quiet. You took the suitcase too early. You should have stolen it on his return from staying with the girl, when he was passing through London again. She might have said things to him. They would have been in the notebook."

"I took the suitcase when I could, Boris Antonov."

Livid, Boris banged his fist on the table. First his mustache had been sacrificed, and now his career and his life hung in the balance.

"We already knew about the portrait. As for the rest, there's nothing," he declared, summarizing the situation. "Is that correct?"

"Yes."

"I'm disappointed in you, Andrei."

"I fulfilled my mission."

"Did you at least pay a visit to the monks?"

"Yes. They buried Father Jean this morning. There were a lot of people. I went into his room last night. They've cleaned everything up. There's nothing left."

The little girl knocked over her glass of water and nearly drowned the notebook. Andrei rescued his cap, but Boris felt his trousers soaking up the water. The pair of them stared at the girl. Blond and pretty, she apologized with a big smile before continuing the ascent of her ice cream via the north face.

Boris gritted his teeth. How could people leave a child of twelve or thirteen all alone in the lobby of a hotel? He spat into his handkerchief, disgusted by French society.

"So you haven't got anything," said Boris Antonov, returning to the subject.

"I did what you asked me to. You found an address at the priest's. Perhaps that will lead to something."

"It's far away. Somewhere in the middle of the ocean. We've sent some of our men to go and check it out."

"Oh, and don't forget, there's also this name in the notebook."

Andrei took the notebook from Boris and showed him a page.

"Yes," said Boris, "I saw that. The Cat."

He sniggered.

"A big thank-you for finding that. The Cat! Bravo! Now there's a suspect, if ever there was one!"

Boris stood up, clapping softly, then he shook Andrei's hand. His fingers were icy.

"Are you leaving?" the student asked anxiously.

"Yes. I'm on a special mission."

Boris whispered something in his ear: "I'm going to the zoo at Vincennes, to ask the lions if they can tell me where to find the Cat."

Andrei smiled tensely.

"Do you think it's funny?" Boris barked.

Andrei froze. The big man grabbed him by the ear.

"Where will I find you if I need you?"

The student kneaded his cap in his hands without giving an answer.

"Where?" Boris pressed him, ready to rip off his ear.

"Boris Petrovitch Antonov, I've been meaning to say . . ."

"Yes?"

"I think I'm going to have to stop . . ."

"To stop?"

"Working for you."

The man looked pityingly at him.

185

"No? Really?"

"I've been mulling it over. And I really do feel I should stop."

"Is that so?"

Boris Antonov had let go of his ear and was using the tablecloth to wipe his wire-framed glasses clean. His near-sighted eyes were taking a hard look at Andrei.

"I don't think that's a very good idea. You're young, Andrei."

"Exactly. I need to consider what I'm doing with my life. I'm a violinist."

Boris couldn't help smiling. *Consider: the boy still thought he had a choice!* He put a few coins down on the table.

"I'm leaving. Have a drink on me. And don't disappear, little one. I'm counting on you. And so is your family."

"I'm telling you, I want to stop everything."

Boris Antonov laughed and placed his index and middle finger on the boy's forehead, so that his hand made the shape of a pistol.

"Stop what? Living? There are some things we don't stop doing, Andrei."

He pinched the young musician's cheek and headed off with another guffaw.

The student stayed sitting there for a long time, both hands gripping his cap to stop himself from falling over.

He was thinking of his family in Moscow.

He had come to Paris to study music. He had been sur-prised by the ease with which he'd been authorized to leave his country. But it had all become very clear once he'd been contacted by Boris Antonov. At the beginning, they'd talked to him about his family, who wasn't well thought of in Moscow. Then, they'd started asking him to do things. As long as he obeyed, his family need fear nothing.

How was it all going to end? How?

"Do you want to finish this off for me?"

He was startled.

The little girl next to him had pushed her ice cream his way.

"It's too big for me," she said. "I can't eat it all."

He looked at her. She wasn't so young after all. Fourteen, at least.

"No, thanks, I've got to go."

He stood up and left.

To pay for her ice cream, the girl piled up her coins on the table, a pile as tall as the column in the Place Vendôme, and then she left as well.

The doorman nodded at her. "Good evening, Mademoiselle Atlas."

The head receptionist greeted her as she walked past.

The baggage handler turned the revolving door for her. "See you soon, Mademoiselle Atlas."

Outside, the valet repeated the same words.

She didn't respond to any of them.

Ever since she was a little girl, they had all insisted on calling her Mademoiselle Atlas, which she found ridiculous.

She wandered off into the square.

Her real name was the Cat.

*　　*　　*

The Cat had met Vango eighteen months earlier, on December 25, 1932, at three o'clock in the morning, between the second and third levels of the Eiffel Tower.

The place, the date, and the timing weren't the most propitious: the final meters of the Eiffel Tower, on Christmas Day, at three o'clock in the morning. But up there, where there's only one route, there's a far higher chance of meeting other climbers than lower down, where the tower's four legs multiply the options.

"Hi."

"Hello," answered Vango. "Are you all right?"

"Yeah."

Vango wasn't the sort to engage in small talk during his nocturnal escapades, and on the rare occasions when he'd encountered people on the roof of the Opera, in the clock at the Gare de Lyon or, years later, in the cables of the Brooklyn Bridge, he had hidden before anyone could see him.

That night, the first thing that struck him was the Cat's age. She looked like a little girl on a seesaw in a children's playground. Except that she was sitting two hundred and twenty-five meters up, astride a metal arch.

Despite the cold, the Cat wasn't wearing gloves.

It took a lot to get her to admit to being thirteen.

"Do you come here often?" asked Vango.

"Reasonably," she replied, her gaze cool.

Which meant this was the first time.

"Would you like to continue together?"

"I'm just having a bit of a rest, thanks."

Breathing heavily in the freezing air, she exhaled little round clouds of white steam.

"Right."

Vango made a show of continuing his ascent. At this height, the paintwork had flaked beneath the frost. He had to check every handhold so as not to slip. He turned around again.

"Are you sure you're all right?"

Vango hated insisting like this, but the girl didn't seem comfortable. She didn't answer. He lowered himself and took another look at her. She was wearing a silk scarf that was too long for her, so she'd wound it five or six times around her slender neck. The steel crossbars that framed them both weren't well lit.

"Your left foot's hurting you," he pointed out.

"No."

And then she asked instinctively, "How did you know?"

"Can I take a look?"

He took her foot, and she let out a yelp.

"You've sprained your ankle."

"And?"

"Can I help you move from here?"

She stared at the lights in the distance and shrugged, like a polite child being offered a sweet.

"Yes, please."

Carefully, he took her on his back. They could hear an owl, very close by. From the way she held on to his shoulders, he could tell that this girl was just like him, that she had known how to climb before she could walk.

"I'm guessing you don't want to take the steps," he said.

"No."

They both knew that on the stairs there was a guard with a scary black dog whose teeth glowed in the dark.

"All right."

He started climbing.

"Where are you going?"

"Didn't you want to go higher up?"

"Yes . . ."

She was warming to him.

"So let's go, then."

"Fine. Whatever you say."

They stayed at the top of the tower until sunrise.

Vango got out some bread, which they shared. Seagulls came to screech around them. They played with Vango.

"Do you know them?" the Cat asked, fascinated.

Vango was watching them closely. Looking up from down below, a ring of feathers circling in the red of the rising sun would have been visible at the top of the tower.

Vango pointed at an owl hovering just above them.

"That one, yes, I've seen her before, where I come from, a long way away from here."

The young girl tried not to show her surprise.

They could make out the forests beyond the city's outskirts, and the Cat even claimed to be able to see the sea.

"Perhaps," said Vango.

"Over there, look."

Clouds were stretched across the horizon.

Her eyesight was good. You would expect no less of a cat.

Neither of them shared their life story.

* * *

He dropped her off in front of her house in the morning.

"Why are you called the Cat?"

"Because if I'm not at liberty to prowl, I suffocate."

Vango smiled.

"Don't laugh. I really do suffocate."

"I'm laughing because it's given you a taste for luxury. Your home looks pretty big to me."

They were standing in front of a beautiful house at the bottom end of the Champs-Élysées.

"The rooms aren't bad. But I live up there."

She looked up. A hammock could be glimpsed hanging between two lightning conductors on the roof.

"I'm claustrophobic."

"Pleased to meet you! I'm paranoid."

They smiled and shook hands, and she hobbled off.

From that day on, they spent many nights on the Paris skyline. She taught him how to slide down the roof of the Théâtre du Châtelet and how to venture into the flies above the dancers during a performance.

He showed her the Saint-Jacques Tower, close by. An obsessive security guard spent all night long patrolling it. This was a game for them. They had to climb seventy-seven meters in under ninety seconds, which was the time it took the caretaker to walk all the way around. Once they were up there, they could see the winding Seine with its islands; they could see the ship of Notre Dame standing out in a sea of gray rooftops.

They became friends without knowing anything about

each other. Sometimes they would accompany each other back home. But both of them only knew the front door of where the other lived. And this door would close again without them being able to glimpse, through the gap, any hint of the rest of their lives.

One day in April, Vango didn't show up. After a few hours of waiting, the Cat stood at the main entrance to the building where she knew he lived. From the caretaker's expression when she asked, "Could you let Monsieur Vango know that the Cat is waiting for him," she immediately realized that something was wrong. She narrowly missed the police.

During the hours and days that followed, she tried to figure it out.

From positioning herself nearby, listening at the entrances to cafés where those conducting the investigation were sitting, she was able to piece together the story.

Her first surprise was to discover that Vango was training to become a priest. She didn't know any priests personally, she barely knew what that life involved, but she certainly couldn't imagine a priest hanging upside down off the Eiffel Tower or sleeping in the park trees, as the two of them had often done.

She was almost less shocked to learn that he was accused of having killed a man. Perhaps he had his reasons. And anyway it was none of her business. Now she understood why he hadn't come, and that was all she wanted to know.

And so she thought that she would be able to pick up her everyday life again.

But one night, lying in her hammock, she felt something in her ribs.

It wasn't a pain exactly, but it climbed up as far as her chest and shoulders. She turned over on to one side, then the other. She sighed. She took a few steps in the darkness, on the roof.

She watched the flame in a streetlamp flickering.

After a while she crossed her arms, clutched her shoulders, and sighed again. Perhaps this was what books referred to as loneliness.

It was something she had never experienced before.

The Cat had grown up alone.

She had three much older brothers. The last one had left home the day after she was born. They were all over thirty-five now, which to the Cat was the age of her ancestors in the family's oil paintings.

She was the offspring of her father's second marriage. Her parents were very busy. They lived in three cities at the same time, never emptied their suitcases, and even kept their fur coats on when they popped home to give her a kiss.

She had been through twenty-two governesses, who'd had the bad idea of calling her Mademoiselle Atlas and of wanting to make her stay inside the walls of the house. The last one had fallen from a tree, trying to catch her.

The Cat had ended up taking up the post herself. She had become her own governess. The twenty-third.

But never, in all her fourteen years, had she experienced loneliness. Not even when the seventh governess had locked her in a cupboard all night long to stop her from sleeping on the roof, nor even when she'd spent a year in a sanatorium in the mountains because she was sick, had she ever really felt alone.

And now this idiot Vango had knocked her armor right off, with a din that sounded like the clattering of saucepans.

The Cat decided that she had to find him in order to settle the score.

And so she moved into the small bell tower at the Carmelite seminary and waited for him. She didn't want to stray too far from the site of the drama. She was convinced that this was the only spot where she'd be able to find something out.

Nothing happened for three days.

The memory of the murder had, little by little, become diluted.

On the fourth night, someone started playing the foxtrot on the organ below her. She didn't know that it was Raimundo Weber, the Capuchin caretaker, who was resuming his nocturnal concerts after a brief period of mourning. Life went on.

The following day, the police came to empty the victim's bedroom. A large van drove off with a desk, a chair, a few boxes of books and notebooks. Five boys from the seminary sluiced down the floor and the walls, before opening the window so that the memory of Father Jean would evaporate.

By the fifth night, the Cat was beginning to think she was too late.

It was a very mild night, partly because a May breeze filled the city with the scent of cherry trees, and perhaps also because Weber was playing more peaceful music than usual on his organ. It didn't consist of more than four notes, but he was playing them in a magical order that changed with each new musical phrase.

The Cat strained an ear.

Someone was ringing, by the grille at the entrance to the seminary.

Weber was too heavily under the music's spell to hear anything.

Judging from the appearance of the person waiting behind the grille, the Cat realized this was an unusual visit. She had only seen priests, nuns, a bishop, seminarians, and policemen entering on the other days. But this person was wearing a street urchin's cap. He was carrying a black case as well as a leather briefcase, like the students in the Latin Quarter.

The Cat was watching him. He might give up if nobody answered his ringing, which would be very frustrating for her.

So she slithered down to the bottom of the roof and looked in through a window that gave onto the chapel. Weber only seemed to be half conscious. His small body was motionless, hunched over the instrument, but his great big hands were spread wide like bats dancing over the keyboard. He had moved on from the four opening notes now. From the deepest to the most high pitched, he didn't want to leave a single note unplayed.

The Cat flung her blanket like a fishing net. She glided a bit under the dome before landing on the organ pipes, which started wailing like a sick elephant. In a flash, Weber emerged from his musical ecstasy. He could hear someone calling out. He jumped up off his stool and exited the chapel, muttering, "I'm coming, I'm coming. . . ."

The hem of his dressing gown trailed over the courtyard cobbles.

He peered through the grille and saw a young man on the other side.

"Are you lost, my boy?"

"Good evening. I'm a boarder at the school across the way, on Rue Madame. I'm locked out. Could you find me somewhere to sleep?"

"To sleep . . ." repeated the Capuchin monk, biting his lip.

Weber patted the keys in his pocket; he seemed to be bothered about something.

"Normally, I would have opened up for you. . . ."

He glanced around and whispered, "But I've been asked to be extra careful. There have been some things happening. . . ."

"I'll leave very early," the boy promised in a Russian accent.

"I believe you, my son, but I have my orders."

The boy nodded.

"Under normal circumstances . . ." Weber went on.

"I understand. I'm sorry to have troubled you."

The boy headed off down the sidewalk.

"Hey!"

Raimundo Weber called him back. The boy returned to the grille.

"What have you got in that case?"

"What case?"

"There, in your left hand."

"Nothing. A violin."

Weber inserted the key into the lock. He opened the door.

"A violin?"

The caretaker shook the boy's hand.

"Do you play?" He was eager to know.

"Yes."

"Zing zang zang zaaaaaang."

Weber was singing and miming on the sidewalk.

"Ziiiing . . ."

He was looking questioningly at the boy.

"Zaaaaang zooing . . . Do you recognize that?"

"Shostakovich," the boy declared.

Weber almost leaped into his arms.

"Are you Russian?"

"Yes."

"Come with me."

The Cat saw him ushering the boy inside and leading him over to the chapel. Weber climbed back up to his organ. He started playing a new piece of music.

"Take out your violin!"

They played together for an hour.

It sounded like a village feast day in Stromoski, Siberia. Even the kneelers wanted to dance. At the end of that hour, an exhausted Weber slid down between the organ pedals, dead to the world.

The Cat didn't take her eyes off the young man.

He put the violin back in its case, checked that Weber was sleeping soundly, stole his keys, and left the chapel. He went over to the small house in the second courtyard, opened the door with the biggest key, and went upstairs.

The Cat followed him via the roof.

The boy soon reappeared and walked back over to the grille. He went out into the street.

The Cat trailed him to where he was staying, in student accommodation, and the next day, to the burial of Father Jean in Montmartre Cemetery, and finally all the way to the Ritz Hotel at the end of the afternoon.

There, she discovered that he worked for a man named Boris Petrovitch Antonov and that he was also looking for Vango.

By the time she was back home, safely on her roof, the Cat was feeling very pleased with herself. She had a lead, that lead was named Andrei, and he was a violin student. The Cat knew the sound of his voice, his address, and the name of the person he worked for.

That evening, though she wasn't yet ready to admit it to herself, this lead, with his violin and his tousled hair, with his sad eyes and his handsome face from a cold climate, made her heart beat as fast as the hoofbeats of a crazy little horse in the Siberian taiga.

MADEMOISELLE

Aeolian Islands, May 1, 1934

Vango had been dropped off by the *Graf Zeppelin* on the islet of Basiluzzo. He had instantly recognized that rock perched in the sea between the volcano and the island of Panarea.

At dawn, he'd called out to the fishermen who came to comb the rocks just above sea level, to dislodge fish and octopuses. They didn't ask what he was doing there. They just let him slip in between the baskets of fish. One of them, at the bow of the boat, was singing.

Listening to them speak, and feeling the swaying of the boat, Vango understood that he was back.

The fishermen came from Lipari. They took him to their large island.

From there, he caught a regular boat for Salina. There were no seats left. Vango squeezed in behind a man sleeping on his suitcase. He watched the twin peaks of his island slowly getting closer. He was at the stern of the boat, the only traveler without any luggage, while the other passengers were transporting enormous packages of supplies and hardware. Some of them wouldn't be leaving their islands before the autumn. They would have to hold out until then.

The boat sailed around the pumice stone quarries of Lipari. The current was against them. The journey felt terribly long to Vango—even though his island was right there, behind that big square sail, which wasn't coping well with the wind.

Vango was huddled with his arms across his knees. Around one ankle, he'd knotted the blue handkerchief that never left him. He had time to rehearse his big reunion with Mademoiselle several times over in his head.

He knew she wouldn't reproach him for anything, that she would stand back a little to see how tall he'd grown, that she would run a hand through his hair, apologize for her dress, put his plate and glass on the table, say it just so happened there was still a warm vegetable gratin in the oven, and some sweet biscuits, and then she would add a tender word or two of endearment in one of the languages she loved, before immediately giving herself a telling-off because he wasn't a child anymore.

She would do everything to ensure he didn't have time to ask her forgiveness for not coming back, for only having written four letters in five years, four letters that gave no address and that simply said:

Always thinking of you, Mademoiselle.
I'm well, and sending you a kiss.

Four letters as empty as letters written by soldiers in a war. Health good, morale good.

Vango advanced in life by erasing all trace of himself. He didn't call this paranoia but survival. He was like a man on the run, dragging branches behind him so as not to leave any tracks.

He believed he was protecting Mademoiselle by not telling her anything.

Thanks to his silence, they wouldn't be able to get to her.

They had been spying on him for five years.

Those who wanted him dead.

Those whom Father Jean had referred to as "your illness," but who had managed to take Father Jean's life in the end.

But at Notre Dame everything had changed. Thousands of people had seen bullets exploding all around him.

And Vango had felt the urge to call out, "See! See! Am I really mad? They're real! They're here!"

For a moment, when he was up at the top, he had even stretched out his arms, ready to receive the shot in his heart so that there would be a mark on his body, the kind of evidence that a surgeon could remove with his tweezers and place on the table. But instead, the impossible had happened. He had seen a sparrow flying toward him in slow motion, batting its wings feebly, almost to the point of stopping, in a way that no sparrow can do.

A gunshot rang out, and the sparrow had stopped, pierced through, before plummeting the full height of the cathedral.

The bullet had been knocked off course, so that it only brushed against Vango's side rather than piercing his heart.

In Salina, Vango disembarked at the port of Malfa.

It was growing dark. People were waiting for the boat.

They were out on an evening stroll, turning up to see the crew, to help them unload the packages, to watch those passengers who remained on board headed for another island, or to dream about seeing new faces. Vango could tell that nobody recognized him. There were couples sitting, legs dangling just above the water. An old man was counting the fish in his basket again.

As Vango took a few steps on the quayside, he sensed how much he had changed. He was no longer the same person. The boy who had spent his childhood running away from the inhabitants of his island was now interested in looking at them.

"Can you help me out, young man?"

A man had put his hand on Vango's shoulder.

"I've got to carry the mail up. One bag each."

Vango took the bag and slung it on his back.

He recognized this man, Bongiorno, who handled the mail and the boat tickets, who sold vegetables and shoes, and who repaired broken windows. A man who had replaced five or six of those who had left to try their luck on the other side of the world.

"Normally," said Bongiorno, "that fellow comes with his donkey, but he isn't here this evening. We've just got to get it up as far as the square. I'll pay you something."

"Don't worry," said Vango. "I'm going that way anyway."

He was watching some children diving off a rock. They disappeared into the inky black water. A man and a woman were running down the winding path toward the boat. They were calling out, begging for it to wait. Someone struck the ship's bell, just for the fun of making them run even faster. The young girls sitting on crates burst out laughing. A boy dived off the prow. Vango wondered why he'd never swum with the children from his island.

He saw a woman who looked like a vagabond, crouching under a roof of planks that hung off the seawall of the port.

"Who's she?"

"You're not from here!" said Bongiorno.

"No."

"But you've got a faint accent from these islands."

"I came here a long time ago."

Bongiorno was walking in front of Vango.

"That woman is mad. She's been waiting for her husband for . . . I don't know how long . . . many years. She stays there so she'll be able to see him when he arrives."

"Where did he go?"

"If you ask me, I think he's dead. I feel sorry for her."

He threw her a coin and shouted, "You need to eat, Donna Giuseppina!"

Vango slowed down as they walked past. He had just recognized Pippo Troisi's wife.

"She's always there," Bongiorno said. "She stays to weep."

Vango couldn't take his eyes off her.

"What about you? Where are you going?"

"Me?" asked Vango, a bit lost.

"Yes. Where are you going on to, afterward?"

"I'm going up there, to the Madonna of Terzito, on a pilgrimage."

Vango was referring to the tiny forgotten sanctuary on the pass, between the mountains. He couldn't think of anything better to satisfy Bongiorno's curiosity.

And it worked: the postmaster didn't ask any more questions on the way to the square in Malfa.

When they got there, Vango left Bongiorno with his bags,

203

explaining that he wanted to complete his climb before it was fully dark.

"Take these coins," the man offered. And when the boy refused, he added, "Light some candles to the Madonna for me. You won't be alone; there were two foreigners this morning who were headed that way."

Vango took the coins. He left the village on the west side. He was almost running. In less than an hour, he was above the crater of Pollara. A light was shining in the village, hundreds of meters below him.

At that moment, in the house at Pollara, Mademoiselle was sitting in a small armchair made by Vango at age twelve from driftwood—the kind of wood that rolls in the sea for a long time and ends up polished and bleached by the pebbles. The chair was a nest made of pieces of wood tied together. It was very comfortable to sit in. Mademoiselle spent her evenings in it, reading or sewing, and sometimes she would wake up in the morning with a book on her knees.

That evening, her book had fallen to the floor, but Mademoiselle wasn't sleeping. She was simply staring at two men who were destroying the interior of her home.

They had entered without saying a word, just a thin polite smile for Mademoiselle.

There were so few objects inside these walls that the intruders were almost disappointed. Mademoiselle was petrified. She couldn't move at all. They paced about a bit, then started by ripping out the pages of the books in the small bookcase. They found a pile of papers in a folder made of blotting paper and emptied them into a travel bag. They also threw in a stitched notebook in which Mademoiselle used to copy out her accounts and some poems in no particular order.

Then they broke a few plates. And, as if that wasn't enough, they started smashing the blue china tiles that covered the walls. These didn't fall off but splintered into a thousand slivers. The whole room was like the inside of a kaleidoscope that would make anyone's head spin.

They did all this without saying a word, as if carrying out an intricate job that required complete concentration. To free up their hands, they had put their weapons down on the table: two Tokarev TT33 automatic pistols and a double express pump-action shotgun that must have weighed six or seven kilos.

When they'd entered the home, Mademoiselle hadn't looked particularly surprised.

She'd told them in Russian that she'd been expecting them for fifteen years.

Vango rushed down the path. All he could feel now was the euphoria of the moment. He was returning to the place he loved, the house that was his homeland, the woman who was his family—a race on a May night after five years of exile. He forgot about everything else.

He took a shortcut to the left. This time, he could clearly see the white roof of the house and then, as he got closer, the lamp alight in the window. She was there.

Vango didn't want to give Mademoiselle too much of a shock. So he thought he would knock, to indicate his presence on the other side of the door. But first he made a small detour via the olive tree. Its leaves rustled as he approached, and he put his hand on the bark, pressing his forehead against the tree.

Inside the house, through the tiny windows, it was possible to make out some signs of movement. She wasn't asleep.

Mademoiselle.

He owed her so much. Mademoiselle was a world in her own right. She seemed to know all of life's secrets, but she let you into them one by one, almost without your noticing. Like this olive tree that shed its leaves throughout the year, without ever seeming to be missing a single one.

Whenever Vango had been feeling sad for too long, she would say things like, "That's enough of the day wasted on one set of troubles." She invented her own wisdom.

Before leaving the cover of the tree, he paused for a few seconds.

An enormous shadow was advancing toward him from behind. It was as if Vango was deliberately giving it time to get close. But he hadn't seen anything and simply wanted to make a sweet moment last a little longer, as he leaned against his tree.

I'm coming, Mademoiselle . . . he thought.

As Vango took a step toward the house, he felt a hand grab hold of his jawbone while he was tackled by the waist and lifted off the ground. It had been the first time in years that Vango had really relaxed, the first moment he had let his guard drop.

But one second was all it took.

Mademoiselle saw the two men rush for their weapons. Like them, she had heard a noise outside. They must have had a third companion keeping watch. One of the men went outside. He returned promptly and nodded reassuringly at the other man. They resumed their infernal task. Mademoiselle had closed her eyes.

Vango was dragged off into the night. The person holding him was prodigiously strong. Vango didn't put up a fight.

At one point, he could feel himself being put down on the ground. He was in a sort of hole with a hard lava floor. At the back of a small fireplace, flames lit up the room. Vango stood up. There was a gun pointed straight at him.

"Don't move."

The man spoke Sicilian.

"You've got no chance against them."

Vango recognized Mazzetta.

"They've got more munitions than all the carabinieri from the islands to Milazzo."

Mazzetta was right. The tilting-block rifle that had been put on Mademoiselle's table was loaded with 600-caliber nitro, renowned for the past quarter of a century as the ideal weapon for elephant hunting. And one of the men, the taller one, had, in addition to two Tokarev TTs, a handsome English submachine gun hanging beneath his shirt like a christening charm.

Vango got up.

"Sit down," Mazzetta ordered. "I'll kneecap you if you try to leave. I don't want them to get you."

When he saw the men entering, Mazzetta had intended to take the house by siege. But then he had spotted the arsenal by the window. He knew the power of weapons. He wasn't frightened for his own life, which he had given up a long time ago. He was frightened for Mademoiselle. He wanted to stay alive so that he could keep an eye on her.

"Let me go over there."

"No. They'll leave in the end. They won't do anything to her. I'm sure you're the one they're looking for."

A stamping sound could be heard just in front of Mazzetta's hole. Someone was crushing the dry grass. Vango held his breath.

"Who is it?" he whispered.

Mazzetta put a finger to his lips.

Someone was breathing heavily only two meters away, if that.

"Who is it?" Vango wanted to know.

Mazzetta's bearlike face nodded gently.

"It's my donkey," he breathed eventually. "He's warning us they're leaving."

Tesoro the donkey, still wearing his enormous studded leather collar, poked his head around the door. Mazzetta stroked him between the eyes.

They waited several long minutes before Mazzetta went outside. Vango didn't move.

Eventually, Mazzetta returned and sat down next to Vango.

"They've gone."

"What about Mademoiselle?"

"They'll stay around these parts for a long time. You must leave."

"Mademoiselle?"

"She's in front of the house. She's not hurt."

"I want to talk to her."

"They're watching. If you talk to her, she's dead."

Vango wiped his hand across his face.

"My God," he uttered.

"Go."

Mazzetta had put down his hunting gun. For the first time, Vango was actually talking to him.

"What about Mademoiselle? Are you going to look after her?"

"She doesn't want my help. But I know someone who'll be there for her."

"Do whatever she needs. Please."

Vango made his way out of the hole and crawled through the undergrowth.

Once he was far enough away, he ran toward the sea and climbed down the cliff. He chanced on a boat and pushed it off from the pebble beach, making straight for the open sea.

At two o'clock in the morning, Dr. Basilio heard someone knocking at his door.

He recognized the familiar sound of a man crying outside his house. For him, these male cries were always a few hours ahead of those belonging to the wife who was about to give birth, and the child who was about to see the light of day.

"The men must be able to let it all out too, at some point. It's their right."

Half asleep, the doctor chewed his words, put on a pair of trousers, grabbed his bag, and opened the door.

It wasn't what he'd been expecting.

Before him stood Mazzetta, breathless.

"Is it . . . ?"

From the look in Mazzetta's eyes, the doctor could tell that something serious had happened.

"Mademoiselle?"

He followed the lone character, running through the night.

Arkudah, the next day

Zefiro had never been gifted when it came to reunions. His real talents lay in saying farewell, offering colorful benedictions, and hugging a person hard before a journey. But when he was reunited with someone, he didn't know whether to open his arms, lower his head, or hold out his hand. So most of the time he did all three at once, resulting in some unfortunate collisions.

Zefiro never knew what to talk about first or how to broach the long absence that had separated them since their last farewells. Their time apart was like a curtain of ice for him.

Finding himself face-to-face with Vango once more, he ventured that the young man's hair looked a bit shorter than before, stammered something about the weather they were having, and offered him a glass of water.

Next came an unorthodox welcoming phrase: "I've got some new rabbits."

Vango was standing there in front of him, at the door to the invisible monastery, exhausted, his clothes in tatters. His eyes were red, and he was famished.

But he hadn't forgotten Zefiro. And so he followed him.

As they were walking toward the rabbit hutches, the ice began to melt. When Vango held out a trembling gray rabbit,

Zefiro moved the furry animal to one side and took hold of the boy instead, crushing his head against his shoulder. Five years had gone by.

"You were such a long time."

Vango wanted to look up, but Zefiro refused to stop hugging him because he didn't want the young one to see his tears.

"You were the one who told me to leave," Vango said with a sigh.

"One year! I gave you one year to come back. . . ."

Vango looked at him.

"I had a few problems, Padre."

Moscow, the Kremlin Palace, the same evening, May 2, 1934

Setanka was only eight and a half years old. But when she went to see a film, at night, in the former Winter Garden transformed into a cinema, she was followed by a convoy of armored cars and dozens of guards.

She trotted along in front.

This evening, her father, who was walking just behind her, was listening to a man giving his report.

"We found the house and the woman who brought him up. But no trace of the boy. It seems he hasn't lived there for a long time."

"Find him."

She strained her ears. They were talking about the Bird.

For a long time, Setanka had thought her father was a gardener. In the country houses in Sochi, the Crimea, or just outside Moscow, he liked to touch the flowers and the trees. She could see his handsome mustache quivering at the scent of roses.

A year after the death of her mother, when she was enrolled at a school known as the Twenty-Fifth Model School, standing in the corridor that looked out on to Gorky Street, she had been surprised to see portraits of her father hanging on all the walls. It was then that she realized her father wasn't a gardener.

He was the absolute master of a vast country that extended as far as Mongolia and the Pacific.

His name was Joseph Stalin.

"Find him," she heard him saying again. "And leave me in peace."

When she turned around, she saw him shooing away the man he was talking to with the back of his fingers, the way you swat a fly on a plate of meat.

He took his daughter's hand.

"Well? Is my little boss happy to be going to the cinema?"

But Setanka didn't feel like answering. She was gazing at a star above the roof of the Winter Garden. She was thinking of the Bird, who was flying through other skies and who could, at any moment, be struck down in full flight.

GOING ON A DATE

Friedrichshafen, Germany,
one year later, May 1935

Waiters know all about diners in restaurants who make a reservation for two but arrive alone. They've dressed up for a romantic dinner. They check their watch and do their hair again by glancing at their reflection in their glass or their spoon. Nobody comes.

The waiter suggests removing the second plate, but they refuse. "No. My guest won't be long now. She'll be here in a minute. She's often late!" One hour later, the restaurant offers an aperitif on the house as a consolation prize. The other diners look on pityingly.

That evening, at the Kurgarten Hotel, the table by the lakeside was set for two. The restaurant was full. Hugo Eckener had been waiting for three quarters of an hour, but he didn't look unduly concerned.

The headwaiter, who had recognized him, kept passing by to see if he could be of any assistance.

Three paces away, trees were overhanging the water's edge. Eckener could see the lights of a village on the other side of the lake. The neighboring tables were filled with couples whose legs were intertwined under the tablecloth.

"A newspaper, Herr Doctor?"

A waiter held out a pile of the day's newspapers.

Eckener brushed them away.

"Never."

Whenever Hugo Eckener opened a newspaper, he instantly had to close it again as if it were a basket of snakes. In Germany, the press didn't talk about anything freely anymore, and if by chance some real news managed to get published, it gave you goose bumps.

Ten months earlier, in July 1934, Eckener had escaped a dreadful night during which Hitler had ordered the killings of dozens of people who irked him: the Night of the Long Knives.

Protection from a minister had narrowly saved Hugo Eckener. Reading the papers the next day, he hadn't found a single one that denounced the massacre.

Such crimes were becoming increasingly commonplace. Why exhaust yourself trying to convince people when you could just annihilate them? The years of financial crisis had left so many people unemployed that they were ready to believe every promise uttered by Hitler and to pounce on all those he accused as guilty parties.

Eckener spotted a boat crossing the lake in the darkness.

The waiter brought him a glass of wine on a tray.

"I said I don't want anything for the time being," huffed Eckener.

"It's on the house."

Eckener stared at the glass that had been put in front of him. He was thinking about his wife. He had told her that he was having dinner with an old university friend named Moritz, who had become a psychologist in Munich.

"Apparently, he's lost all his hair!" the commander had joked to Mrs. Eckener, to make it sound more plausible.

The waiter tiptoed away.

"I'm glad you didn't wait for me to have a drink."

Eckener stood up. The young lady was standing in front of him. Eckener thought she looked ravishing. All the customers in the restaurant fell quiet as they watched this strange couple. They shook hands.

"My, how you've grown up, Ethel!" said Hugo Eckener.

It wasn't the most romantic welcome for a guest at this sort of restaurant, but then he had known her when she was only twelve. Now she was almost eighteen. She was hardly the same person.

"I'm sorry, Doctor Eckener. I kept you waiting."

"It was my pleasure."

"Two escorts on horseback have been following me since yesterday. I wanted to lead them on a merry dance through the woods. My car goes much faster than their horses. I can relax now."

"Do you think you've shaken them off?"

Ethel nodded.

Agents who weren't as secret as all that had been trailing her since her arrival in Germany. She'd ended up taking a path through the forest at eighty-five miles per hour. Her little Napier-Railton flew through the pine trees. It was impossible to follow her.

An accordionist started up a few tables away from them.

"Can you see that boat over there?" asked Eckener, helping the young lady into her seat.

"Yes."

She could smell the slightly musty scent of Lake Constance as well as that of the peonies on the table, between the candles. She remembered a boat trip she'd made years earlier on this lake with her brother, before going on board the zeppelin. It had been here, in front of this hotel. Right here. At the time, she had been a little girl in whom the light had gone out four years previously: she was in pieces following the deaths of her parents. She had stopped talking. Not a word in four years.

That balloon trip had changed everything.

She kept looking at the rowers, who must be able to see this restaurant, lit up on the shore.

"Why do you ask? Would you like to take me for a spin, Commander Eckener?"

"Your escorts are in that boat."

Ethel stared at Eckener, aghast.

"You'll never be able to shake them off," he added. "Mine have been following me for a year."

"Where are yours?"

"One is sitting inside, at the bar. The other is busy murdering that accordion tune you're listening to."

Ethel turned toward the musician, who had his eyes fixed on them.

"Which is why I asked you to meet me here, my dear Ethel. I always choose the most exposed place so they don't think I've got anything to hide."

He took a good look at her and added, "Especially when I'm spending the evening with a young lady who is the classic English spy of everyone's dreams."

"Scottish."

"Yes. Scottish. I do beg your pardon. How is your brother? Still a pilot?"

"Yes. He's got a plane now."

"And you?"

"He won't lend it to me," said Ethel.

She spoke the words as petulantly as if she were seven years old.

"And you let him get away with it?"

They ordered dinner. Their time together passed very enjoyably. They talked about engineering, clouds, the difference between Scottish and German cabbages, and above all about their memories of that voyage they'd made together around the world in the zeppelin.

Ethel could paint the portraits of several passengers. Eckener was struck by how accurately she could recall them. Each moment was engraved on her memory. She could describe the leather braces of one traveler or the entire hangar where they had stopped off at Kasumigaura, in Japan.

Ethel ate enough for four. She looked stunning in a dress her mother must have worn to dance the Charleston in America after the war, flicking her heels behind her to the rhythm, first one then the other, until they touched her hands.

Ethel listened to Eckener telling her about an expedition he'd attempted to the North Pole. The *Graf Zeppelin* had been able to land on the Arctic Ocean, near Hooker Island. Ethel shivered and then laughingly begged for some tropical destinations instead.

So he spoke to her about the pyramids and about Jerusalem. Ethel had taken off her shoes.

The people around them were whispering. Perhaps they thought she was old-fashioned, with her 1920s dress. They whispered that she was laughing too much. But neither the women nor the men could take their eyes off her.

Everybody was craning their neck. And Hugo Eckener was enjoying himself greatly.

But the only thing on his mind was a name neither of them had mentioned yet. Which proved they were both thinking about him.

"I was wondering about something," said Ethel.

Hugo Eckener put down his glass. The time had come.

"Do you remember," she asked, "that boy . . . Vango?"

Eckener smiled. She had screwed up her eyes as she uttered his name, as if she wasn't quite sure whether or not she'd gotten it right, even though she'd just shown herself capable of recalling exactly what color socks the lowest-ranking engineer on board the zeppelin was wearing.

It didn't ring true, and this was the third time in a few months that Eckener had experienced such a scene.

First of all, there had been that Frenchman, claiming to be a canned-goods businessman, who had come to pay him a visit. One Auguste Boulard.

After talking about canned meat and spinach while heartily recommending them for the provisioning of the *Graf Zeppelin,* after refereeing the match between dried beans and canned beans, after a poignant depiction of the agony of the fresh bean (flaccid, sad, and bound to turn yellow after three days of travel), he had finally popped the question: "Do you remember that boy . . . Vango? Do you have any news of him?"

Then there had been the passenger on a crossing to

Lakehurst, near New York. A Russian whom he already knew and who had asked him, "Do you remember that boy . . . ?"

To each of them, Hugo Eckener had replied that he remembered him very well, yes, absolutely, a delightful boy, but he hadn't had any news of him for five years now.

"My dear Ethel, might it by any chance be on account of your last question that I have the privilege of dining with you this evening?"

Embarrassed, she fiddled with her glass.

"You do know that you're not the only one looking for him?" Eckener pointed out.

"You must have had a visit from a short, rather round gentleman with an umbrella," said Ethel.

"Yes," Eckener agreed, "with an umbrella."

"And perhaps a Soviet gentleman with glasses, a mustache, and a complexion like a melted candle?"

"Perhaps," Eckener acknowledged, "but without the mustache."

"The Russian who traveled with us in 1929 in the zeppelin?"

"That's the one, yes. Quite so. But without the mustache."

It was because of his visitors that the commander had decided not to say anything to his young dining companion. They frightened him. Eckener had known Ethel's father, a long time ago, in Ohio. In memory of his friend, he had invited the little orphan girl and her brother to embark on a tour of the world in the zeppelin, in August 1929. He had felt in some way responsible for her.

"Thou shalt not covet the prey of the scorpion."

"Is that in the Bible?"

"It would do well to be!"

Eckener wasn't very familiar with the Bible. He distrusted religion and had refused to get married in church.

"*Thou shalt not covet the prey of the scorpion,*" he repeated, even more darkly.

"What does that mean?" Ethel wanted to know.

"It means that in looking for Vango, you will first encounter those who are after him."

"I'm not afraid."

"They're dangerous."

"I'm not afraid."

Eckener ran his hand through his beard.

"Where is he?" Ethel asked softly.

"I don't know."

"I'm sure he's been here."

"He visited the shores of this lake, yes. Five or six years ago. But you know that already because you were there."

Ethel raised her voice.

"You shouldn't be giving me the same answer as you did to the others, Herr Doctor. They want to destroy him, but I . . ."

She couldn't finish her sentence. Why was she looking for Vango?

"You know that he was ordained a priest in Paris," said Eckener calmly.

"No!"

She brought her fist down on the table. Vango was not a priest. He had missed becoming one, admittedly only by three or four minutes. Eckener sensed that nothing was going to stop Ethel. He tilted his chair back.

Why not reveal the existence of Zefiro's invisible monastery to her after all? Vango was bound to be there, after the zeppelin had dropped him off near the volcano of Stromboli.

Only a handful of men on the planet knew the secret of this monastery. And Eckener was one of them. They would all have died rather than reveal it. But Ethel's determination seemed stronger than anything.

Yes, he thought, *I'll tell her where he is. She'll be in less danger if she's ahead of them all. And she might be able to help him.*

He glanced around him. The neighboring tables were empty, their candles blown out.

Ethel was waiting. Eckener folded his napkin with great care. He was weighing his responsibilities here. The danger for his friend Zefiro. And the fact that he also wanted to protect this girl.

"You see, Ethel . . ."

Someone was walking toward Hugo Eckener.

"Sir," he said, leaning over the commander.

It was a waiter.

"Later," growled Eckener.

"But sir . . ."

"I said later."

"It's Frau Eckener for you," the waiter dared to add.

"Well, I'll be damned! My wife! Where's the telephone?"

"She's not on the telephone, Commander."

"Where is she?'

"Right . . . right behind you."

THE THREE SWIMMERS

Johanna Eckener had hung back in the shadows and was watching Hugo with an amused expression on her face.

"I'm sorry," she said. "Forgive me, young lady. I have a very urgent message for my husband."

Eckener was completely paralyzed.

"Good evening, Hugo."

He couldn't even open his mouth.

"Tell me, is this your university friend Moritz, the one you'd lost touch with, a psychologist . . . and bald?"

Ethel was wide-eyed.

Hugo Eckener, who was unaccustomed to this kind of scene, was on the verge of agreeing that yes, Moritz had indeed changed a great deal. To tell the truth, he hadn't recognized him at first either . . . but he returned to his senses just in time: "Johanna . . ."

She was deliberately not saying anything, to make him flounder.

"Johanna, I don't know why . . ."

The reality was, he knew perfectly well why he had lied.

Because he hadn't been out for a romantic dinner with his wife in a restaurant for seven or eight years, because he knew this was something that she dreamed of doing, because he spent his life between his balloon and his crew, and because he hadn't wanted to tell her that he was going to dine with a young lady who'd only had to write him three lines for him to rush to reserve the best candlelit table in the finest restaurant.

"I promise you that . . ."

Johanna smiled wanly. She knew how obsessively loyal he was and didn't believe him capable of anything more than this dinner. But this dinner was crime enough.

She had always believed that she'd grown more mature over time, but she had to admit she was jealous. Not of Ethel, but of this moment, of the stars, of the peonies between them, of the white melted wax on the tablecloth.

"I'm sorry, I know this is nothing to do with you," she said to Ethel, her voice breaking a bit. "This is between me and my husband. And I hope you'll forgive me for making you witness it."

"No, it's my fault," said Ethel, standing up. "I didn't know that . . ."

"Please don't get up. It will only take a moment."

Johanna turned to Eckener and spoke in a hushed voice.

"Hugo, I just came to tell you that someone appeared at the house. He needs to see you urgently and discreetly."

"Who is it?"

"I don't know."

She hesitated, glancing at Ethel.

"You can talk in front of her."

"He mentioned Violette. . . ."

The word struck Eckener like an electric charge.

"Where is he?"

"I told him to wait in front of the beach hut opposite the island."

"And what am I supposed to do about this crew?"

He indicated the three or four shadows waiting on a bench, ready to start tailing them again at the slightest sign of movement. They blended in about as well as ducks in a tearoom.

"I'll take care of them," said Ethel.

"Me too," agreed Johanna.

Eckener looked skeptical.

"Get your car," Johanna ordered. "Young lady, are you coming with me?"

"Gladly."

And Johanna took Ethel's arm.

Eckener wondered what they were scheming. But knowing their characters, he decided it was better simply to trust them.

The three of them made a show of leaving the restaurant together, waving at the headwaiter on their way out. Eckener requested that the bill for the dinner be sent to him the next day.

There were still a few cars in the courtyard. Eckener got into his vehicle, and his wife slid next to Ethel in the little Railton that was parked by the wall. They exchanged a few words. Two other cars were already revving up and getting ready to follow.

"You go in front!" Ethel called out to Eckener above the din of backfiring.

The commander waved from his black sedan.

To exit the courtyard, they had to negotiate a narrow

passage between two enormous flowering rhododendron bushes that only one car could get through at a time.

So Eckener went first. Ethel and Frau Eckener followed.

"Wait. . . ."

In the middle of the narrow passage, Johanna Eckener made Ethel stop the car.

"Oh! Will you take a look at that!"

She got out and went to pick one of the biggest purple flowers on the bush. Ethel switched off the engine and joined her. They started talking about gardening, fertilizers, and cuttings. Behind them, engines were revving, but the cars were unable to move.

Horns tooted and there were loud words.

"It's so pretty," said Ethel, stroking the petals as if she'd never seen anything like them before.

The lights from Dr. Eckener's car were already far away.

Doors banged furiously behind the two women.

"Did you know that the rhododendron layers perfectly?" Johanna inquired of Ethel.

"No!"

The Scottish heiress looked completely taken aback, as if someone had just announced that the sun had disappeared for good.

"Yes!"

A man came up behind them.

"And what about mallow plant?" Ethel was impatient to know.

"Ah! Mallows! Don't even mention them to me. Mine aren't doing very well this spring. . . ."

"Are you going to get your car out of here?" bellowed a man who was spitting with anger.

"No, for me," said Johanna, "mallows are a real problem."

"Clear this passage!"

"And that's despite the fact that I put manure on them to help get them going again. . . ."

She was still talking about her flowers, but the man was looking at her feet.

"Let us through!" another man roared as he rushed toward them.

"I beg your pardon?"

The women appeared to have only just noticed the two men.

"Are you in a bit of a rush?" simpered Ethel.

She looked thoughtful and pointed at one of the men.

"Oh, my goodness, aren't you the same man I saw dragging your heels by the shores of the lake all evening?"

She spoke German with a singsong accent.

"Remove your car," said the man, "or I will crush it."

"Your romantic moonlit walk with your little friends was so touching. I wanted to throw you rose petals."

"Come on," said Johanna Eckener, tugging Ethel's arm. "The gentleman is right. Our car is in the way."

Ethel allowed herself to be led away. Their mission was accomplished. Sometimes it's good to know when to stop.

Hugo Eckener parked his car on the side of the road, by the lake. It was almost completely dark now. The beach was deserted. He couldn't find anyone in front of the hut. It was a white chalet, Atlantic beach–style, on low stilts. He waited for several minutes on the steps. He lit a cigar. A breeze rose up.

Eventually, Eckener strolled toward the lapping shore of the lake. He stopped.

He had just noticed something.

The commander removed his pants, his jacket, and the rest of his clothes. He was down to a long white pair of boxer shorts. He waded into the lake.

A man was waiting for him in the lake, with the water up to his shoulders.

"Are you alone?" asked Eckener. He still had his cigar in his mouth.

"No," the other man replied, "I'm with the invisible man."

Eckener had no trouble recognizing Esquirol, the renowned Paris doctor.

The commander was a quarter of a century older than the medic, but their affection for each other was like that of boarding school friends or soldiers in a regiment. They regretted seeing each other so rarely and only on grave occasions.

Suddenly, Eckener felt the cigar being ripped out of his hand.

"Dammit!"

The glowing red ember flew above them before being extinguished in the water four or five meters away.

"Who's there?"

Caught by surprise, Eckener had nearly lost his footing. Esquirol hadn't made a single move during all of this.

"I warned you I'm with the invisible man!"

No sooner had the doctor said this than a quiet chuckle was audible in the gloom, and Hugo Eckener felt a hand on his shoulder.

"Hello, Doctor Eckener."

It was Joseph Jacques Puppet, a small man impossible to detect in the darkness. Against his black skin he wore a one-piece knitted swimming costume of the same color, which was the latest male fashion from the beaches of Monte Carlo.

He had been born in Grand-Bassam, Ivory Coast, in West Africa. He had nearly died at Verdun during the war, and then in the boxing rings at the Velodrome and Holborn Stadium, where he was a featherweight by the name of J. J. Puppet. He had stopped boxing just before the venues had been demolished, and now he was Joseph, the barber of Monaco, whose scissors were sought after from one end of the Côte d'Azur to the other.

Eckener was delighted to see his friends again but guessed that the situation had to be an alarming one. They had come to a dangerous country, despite instructions to meet as little as possible and never with witnesses. So this had to be a serious business.

They swam out into the lake.

"Tell me what's going on," said Eckener.

"We need Zefiro," replied Esquirol, scanning the gloom around them.

"Why?"

"Because of Viktor."

"Viktor?"

"The Paris police think they've found Voloy Viktor. They want Zefiro, so that he can be identified."

Eckener was floating on his back.

He felt relieved. For a moment, he'd thought they were going to talk to him about Vango again.

"How did they find Viktor?" he asked after a pause.

"By chance, at passport control on the Spanish border."

"Impossible," gulped Eckener.

How could anyone believe that one of the most dangerous and elusive men in Europe would allow himself to be caught like that?

"They're almost certain it's him. But if someone can't formally identify him, they'll have to let him go. There's plenty of pressure being put on them from on high."

"And you want to risk Zefiro's life for this kind of game?"

"Yes."

"He's already taken enough risks. Leave him in peace."

"We need him one last time. It'll all be over after that, but he's the only one who can identify Viktor. We've got to ask him. Tell us where he is."

None of them moved; they were floating on their backs in silence.

"Look, it's 1935," said Joseph Puppet, who had spoken very little up until this point. "The war has only been over for seventeen years, and it could break out again from one day to the next. You know what's happening in the world at the moment, Dr. Eckener. You're well positioned to be aware of all this."

"I won't reveal where Zefiro's monastery is."

They fell quiet. A car drove past on the road. They waited for the sound of the engine to fade into the distance, and then Eckener reiterated, "I won't tell you anything."

"Always the same, Eckener," murmured Esquirol.

"Meaning?"

"Stop it, Esquirol!" Joseph intervened.

"Meaning," Esquirol went on, "that you've never done anything to change things."

"I don't know what you're talking about," gulped Eckener with a lump in his throat.

All three of them knew exactly what Esquirol was talking about.

Before Hitler had come to power, plenty of voices to the political left and center in Germany had asked Hugo Eckener to run for office. He had refused so as not to offend old Marshal Hindenburg, who would have been his opponent.

The marshal was elected. But he couldn't halt the Nazi rise to power.

Hindenburg had died the previous August, and Hitler had pounced on his seat.

This episode was perhaps Hugo Eckener's greatest regret.

In the dark, he could hear the voice of his friend Esquirol: "Now I understand why your zeppelins bear the Nazi insignia. . . ."

Eckener sliced through the water to throw himself on the doctor, but Joseph got in the way. Despite his small stature, one wouldn't want to cross the boxer-barber of Monaco.

"Stop it!"

All three of them looked at one another.

In the small hours, returning to his house, soaking wet, Hugo Eckener found that his wife was still up.

"Did you go for a swim, Hugo?" she inquired, taking a towel to rub him down.

For some time, her husband had been behaving like a teenager going through an identity crisis. . . .

"Where's Ethel?" he asked, purple lipped.

"I offered her a bedroom, but she's back on the road. I've taken rather a shine to her."

"Yes," agreed Eckener. "Me too."

He closed his eyes but didn't sleep a wink.

Eckener already regretted what he'd done. He spent the rest of the night thinking about Zefiro and Vango. It was a curious destiny that had reunited these two hunted lives on one island.

Eckener had just provided his friends with the exact location of the island of Arkudah.

THE BEEHIVE TRAITOR

Arkudah, two weeks later, June 1935

Small damp clouds caressed his face.

Vango was hanging from the top peak of the island in a giant cotton net. He had climbed up there that morning before the mist had cleared and was gazing at Mademoiselle's house in the distance, a tiny white dot among others on the island of Salina.

As far as he could tell, his nurse's life was almost back to normal again following the incident with the two armed intruders one year earlier. The good doctor Basilio had restored the blue tiles on the walls, while Mazzetta stood guard with his donkey, a few strides away.

On the first day of each month, since returning to the monastic life, Vango had borrowed a boat without mentioning it to anyone, tied it up at the foot of the cliffs of Pollara, and gone to stalk around Mademoiselle's house. Always waiting in ambush, Mazzetta would suddenly rise up and nearly knock him out.

"It's me!" Vango would whisper.

Mazzetta would groan and lower his arm.

"It's you?"

When he finally recognized Vango, Mazzetta would lead him into his cave without making a sound, so as not to attract Mademoiselle's attention.

She had taken a long time getting her strength back after her house had been ransacked. She was convinced that her aggressors were after Vango. But she chose to explain to the doctor that they must have been hoping to steal her savings in the belief that this woman who lived all alone, and who came from a foreign country, had a pile of gold stashed away in her underwear drawer.

After loitering in the area for a few days, the visitors had set off again. Mazzetta had discreetly escorted them as far as the port of Lipari, to make sure they actually left the Aeolian Islands.

"Let me speak with Mademoiselle, now that they've gone," Vango would beg Mazzetta.

But the older man always managed to discourage him.

Don't say anything to her, remain hidden, don't pay her a visit. This was the only way to protect her. If the two men came back, they would stop at nothing to make her talk. Vango had to resist the temptation to rush over to the white house and throw himself into the arms of his nurse.

And so, perched in his net every morning, with his head in those clouds of mist, he would stare emotionally across the sea at the island of Salina. Then he would clamber down, loop by loop, until he reached the ground, where his work awaited him.

Vango began by untying the ropes that held the masts in place. These five gigantic nets were hoisted every night above the monks' island. Zefiro had devised this system. And it was the secret to his enchanted gardens.

One day, when Vango had first discovered the island, while staring at the abundant and healthy lemon trees, he had quizzed Zefiro: "Where does the water come from for all that, Padre?"

Zefiro had pointed one finger at the sky, and at first Vango had thought there must be a metaphysical explanation. But he had quickly realized that the monk was simply pointing to the clouds.

There was no water source on the island.

Water from the clouds, captured each night on the summit, slowly soaked through the cotton nets and flowed as far as the little channels that supplied the underground cisterns.

Two thousand liters, per net, per day. The winter and autumn rains were carefully collected to supplement these enormous reserves of pure water.

There was enough to slake the thirst of a herd of a hundred cows in this desert.

When he left the chapel in the mornings, Vango's first task was to lower the nets from the top of the island in much the same way as the sails of a boat are collapsed.

In twelve months, Vango had got under the skin of what it meant to be an invisible monk. Everyone admired the speed with which he had re-adapted.

He studied and prayed just as they did. He was able to conform to the strict order of this existence, following each stage of their day.

In chapel, his voice blended in perfectly when the monks were singing.

And he was always ready to work hard.

"For it is thus that they are truly monks, if they can live from the labor of their hands," Brother Marco used to say, citing the rule.

Vango did everything to enter into the monastic rhythm.

Since the early Middle Ages, the centuries had polished and perfected the equilibrium of these monasteries so that it was like a beautiful pebble that had spent thousands of years in the waves.

Vango would have given anything to enjoy the kind of peace that people thought he experienced.

But he knew that his life was an illusion. Despite all his best efforts, he was in a cyclone. The mysteries of his past troubled him from morning to night, and from night to morning. Where did he come from? Who was after him?

He didn't sleep, but spent his nights kneeling on the stone floor of his bedroom. He was trying to understand. His prayer was a silent cry.

And yet for ten years he had dreamed of this existence. At the seminary in Paris, despite the walls surrounding him, he had questioned himself every day to make sure his choice wasn't merely a childish whim. Despite Zefiro's reticence, he was sure this was the right path for him.

He wanted a life without limits. And for him, that meant a life here.

He had reached this decision so simply, one rainy day when he was twelve years old. It was as if someone had entrusted him with something, saying, "Look after this for me; I'll be back."

But now he found himself alone, still holding this "something" in his hands, and life was going on all around him, full of mystery and pain. He couldn't let go of what he'd been entrusted with, still less bury it; he couldn't leave it or hand it over to the first person who came along. Because in his eyes it mattered.

And then there was Ethel, another horizon that never left him.

Some evenings, lost in the midst of these desires and fears, he would dive from the cliff tops, behind the monastery. Vango was no longer afraid of the sea. He launched himself off like a bird. He emerged from the water, his skin glowing white in the moonlight.

Vango headed back down toward the monastery. As he approached the gardens, there was a freshness hovering in the air, even though the hottest months of the year would soon be upon them. He entered the kitchen garden overhanging the cloister, on the south side. The water was flowing through channels of baked earth alongside a low wall a meter high. He could smell the melons on the ground, splitting in the sun. White bindweed wove knots through the low chestnut-wood fencing. It looked for all the world as if Adam and Eve might appear at any moment in this Garden of Eden, but that morning, the first man was wrapped in a black apron and was busy sifting through the lettuces.

His name was Pippo Troisi.

"Ah, Vango, it's war! Can you take these into the kitchen

for me? The padre's rabbits attacked my lettuce in the night. It's all-out war, Vango. They're burrowing! My chickens would never do anything like this. Zefiro should throw his rabbits into the sea. . . ."

As could be heard, Pippo Troisi had not made a vow of silence. The quieter the monks were around him, the more he babbled. His one-man shows amused the community. Not counting the rabbits, he had forty pairs of ears bent in his direction, which was enough to fulfill the dreams of any chatterbox.

Vango noticed the hunting gun by Pippo's side.

"And anyway, you don't go putting rabbits on an island. It's a question of principle. When will Zefiro understand this? I'm telling you, if they get anywhere near my lettuce again, there's going to be some lead shot in everyone's stew — before you can so much as say Arkudah!"

Vango bent down to pick up the crate of lettuce.

"And another thing," Pippo went on. "The padre's not thinking straight. . . . He's got a visitor this morning. A visitor! If we start letting just anyone come here, there won't be anything invisible left about this monastery. It starts with one visitor, and before you can so much as say Arkudah, you'll end up with boatloads of pilgrims. I'm telling you, it's just like the rabbits: we're not dealing with the invisible here, but an invasion!"

He paused for the warning to sink in, but Vango was already on his way. He could hear Pippo still yammering on about his lettuce.

"Invisible, invisible . . . I ask you . . ."

What was so comical was that Vango knew Pippo Troisi was the only real invader of the island.

* * *

Vango just had to pass by the orchard, to add some fruit to his crate. Then he would make his way to the refectory to start work with Brother Marco, the cook.

He spent two days a week in the kitchens, and all the monks looked forward to those days as if it were Easter time. Vango's culinary talents and know-how, passed down from Mademoiselle, had been polished during his year of travel in the zeppelin, followed by his time at the seminary.

In Paris, he had even prepared a Shrove Tuesday dinner for three bishops. He had become a proper chef.

On the days when he was working in the kitchen, the monks tended to stray oddly in the morning, so that they could carry out their holy readings close by, inhaling all the aromas. During the midday prayers, their nostrils could be seen quivering like butterfly wings. And at a quarter past midday, Zefiro would bless the food in record time, they would all sit down together, their napkins tucked into their robes, their cheeks already turning rosy, and, according to the season, they would sink their teeth meditatively into a morel mushroom clafoutis or stuffed apples.

When it came to doing the washing up, there was no lack of volunteers to scrape out the bottom of the saucepans.

For the forty days of Lent, a period of fasting and privation, Vango didn't set foot in the kitchen.

Brother Marco was far from being jealous. He admired Vango's handiwork. He would sit in a chair not far from Vango, his glasses pushed up on his forehead, staring at him just as, two centuries earlier, the greatest musicians in Vienna had sat behind the young Mozart in order to watch his hands on the piano keyboard.

Vango arrived at the orchard. The trees were young but collapsing under the weight of their fruit. The monks couldn't keep up with them. All the coulises, compotes, fruit pastries, marmalades and jams, tarts, candies, and liqueurs they concocted weren't enough to use up the fruit harvest.

Twice, Vango had secretly left a laden basket by Mademoiselle's front door. The next day, with his nose in the wind, he had tried to sniff out, across that stretch of sea separating him and her, the scent of the cordials she used to brew slowly with thyme.

Vango began picking the cherries. They kept slipping through the gaps in the crate, so he went hunting for some large leaves to cover the bottom. But as he was making his way over to the clump of fig trees, he heard voices.

Zefiro was by his hives, behind the tree. Vango could glimpse him between the branches. He was talking. His voice was muffled by his beekeeper's hat, which was like a helmet with wire mesh. There was another man with him, clad in the same fashion, but because he was shorter, the wire mesh came down to his chest.

"The law needs you one last time. Once he's safely locked up, you'll be left in peace."

Vango dropped down into the grass. It seemed improbable, but he recognized the voice, which was speaking in French.

"Be reasonable," the short man advised the monk.

"You know I have no choice but to obey," said Zefiro. "You've trapped me with your barbarian methods. . . ."

"Don't be angry, Padre."

"Last time, in Paris, you weren't up to the job of catching him."

Superintendent Boulard didn't answer the accusation leveled at him. He was sweating beneath his mask. His travel suit was too heavy for this climate.

"Ask someone else," said Zefiro.

"Nobody knows him like you do. I promise your life won't be in danger."

Zefiro lost his temper.

"I'm risking a lot more than my own life," he retorted. "I don't care about my own life."

Boulard knew the monk wasn't lying.

"Well?" asked the superintendent. "Are we agreed?"

Zefiro removed his helmet, and the bees started dancing around their master's face. Boulard took a step backward.

"You're a bully, Superintendent," said Zefiro.

"Is that a yes?"

This time Vango heard a clear and resolute reply.

"Yes."

"Right, then, you've got all the instructions," said Boulard, heading off. "I'm leaving now. I'll see you back there. Remember: before the end of the month. Good luck, Padre."

Zefiro was alone again.

He crouched down and watched his worker bees sniffing the air at the door to their hives before setting off, each in its own direction. Others were coming back in, slightly tipsy, like workers at dawn just finishing their day while others were about to begin.

Zefiro could have spent hours in that spot, mulling things

over, but when he looked up, he saw the barrel of a gun being pointed directly at him.

"What are you doing, Vango?"

"Don't move. I won't show you any mercy."

"Put that weapon down."

"What do you know about me? Tell me everything you know."

"What on earth are you talking about?"

When he'd heard Zefiro say yes, Vango had run toward the kitchen gardens. Pippo Troisi had his back to him. He was bent double, his nose virtually in the soil. He was pulling out the weeds around the artichokes and still grumbling: "Invisible, invisible . . . What about my backside, then, is that invisible?"

In fact, Troisi was all you could see, in the midst of that lettuce and cabbage.

Undetected, Vango had picked up Troisi's gun and made his way back to the orchard.

He had checked the cartridges before aiming at Zefiro.

"Tell me what you know, and then I'll disappear."

"I don't know anything about you," the padre said. "I'd like to be able to help you, but I don't know anything. You've never told me anything."

"You're lying. Boulard said that you knew about my life better than anyone."

Zefiro stood up. Vango loaded his gun.

"Don't move," he ordered.

"Were you here when I was talking to the superintendent?"

Zefiro made his way toward the boy, who stood his ground.

"You're mistaken, Vango. You haven't understood properly."

"I'm warning you: I will shoot."

"If you really did hear what I was saying, you would know that I don't care about my own life."

"Don't move, I'm telling you!"

"But I do care about your life, Vango. So put that weapon down. You don't know what happens to the life of a man who has killed another man."

"Oh, yes, I do. I know only too well."

They stared at each other.

"Put that weapon down."

"I'm defending my life," said Vango, who was loading the second shot into the hunting gun.

The worried buzzing of the bees could be heard.

"Don't get any nearer," Vango warned again.

His finger was trembling on the trigger.

It took less than a second for the weapon to change hands.

Zefiro grabbed hold of the gun, wrenching it away in one clean movement and turning it to face the other way. At the same time, his leg flattened Vango, who found himself lying in the dust.

20

PARADISE STREET

Zefiro removed the cartridges from the gun, slid them into the pocket of his brown cassock, and threw the weapon down onto the grass.

Vango was lying on the ground in front of him. He tried to raise his head, leaning on his elbows. The sun was falling directly on him, and there was no shade.

The monk wasn't looking in the boy's direction. He picked a fig from behind him, sat down at the foot of the tree, and, digging his thumbs into the red-fleshed fruit, began talking.

"Listen to me, Vango. I'm going to tell you a story. You'll understand everything if you hear me through to the end.

"When I was thirty years old, I signed up as a war chaplain in the French army. It came about by chance. I was already a monk, in the west of France, in 1914, when war was declared. Two years earlier, I had been entrusted with the garden of an abbey, at the end of an island, in the middle of the ocean. I had been dismissed by two Italian monasteries before ending up there. I'd been given my own space in that community of fifty nuns. The only man alongside all those sisters. I was happy in my garden. I was an untamable monk, but I was a monk, and I didn't want any other life than the one I had chosen. I often worked with the peasants from the marshes. I was a friend of the millers, the salt-marsh workers, and all the sailors in the port. I had the finest garden in the Atlantic.

"At the beginning of September 1914, all the young people from the island left to fight. Germany had invaded Belgium. France was going to war. I was the same age as them, and I wanted to join up too.

"The superior at the abbey was named Mother Elisabeth. She gave me her consent. She thought it would make me wiser. I took the train to Challans. I went to see the bishop in Paris, warning him that I was Italian. He replied that this wasn't a sin. He needed men, so he took me.

"We were expecting a quick war, and I thought I'd be back in Rome the following summer to relax for a few days, climbing in the hills, walking through the orange trees of the Villa Bonaparte, where I had friends. After that, I hoped to rejoin my monastery at La Blanche, facing the ocean, surrounded by green oak trees, prayers, and potato fields.

"But, two years later, the war had sunk itself into the trenches of Verdun, in Lorraine. And I was blessing more corpses than fighters. We lived underground, together with shells that rained down into the mud, rampant epidemics, and men with beards who had aged by a hundred years and who cried like children. I had become chaplain to the rats.

"When I said mass in my trench, I didn't know if the arm of one of the faithful would be ripped off by a grenade before it had made the sign of the cross. That's war for you, Vango.

"On August fifteenth, my trench was filled to overflowing with bombs. Filled to overflowing, do you hear me, Vango?

My battalion disappeared. But I was spared. I left with a young doctor I liked very much. He was named Esquirol. On his shoulders he carried a black soldier, Joseph, an infantryman whose stomach had been ripped open by a burst of shell fire. That's war for you, Vango.

"There's a small wood near the village of Falbas, with a clearing in the middle and a large five-hundred-year-old oak tree. The three of us stopped there. An airplane was caught in the tree's branches, like a child's toy. It was a German plane. The canvas on the wings wasn't even torn. I climbed up to see if the pilot was alive. He wasn't there, but the engine was still warm.

"The doctor lowered Joseph the infantryman and put him down on the grass. It was a fine day. The explosions seemed far off. Esquirol took out the implements he needed to stitch the soldier back up.

"Half an hour later, Joseph was saved. We lay down twenty paces from him to sleep.

"A man woke us up. A German officer in an aviator's uniform: the pilot of the plane in the large tree. He was aiming his pistol at each of us in turn. He hadn't seen Joseph.

"The German was wounded. His thigh was open just above his knee.

"'You, you're a doctor,' he told Esquirol in French. 'Treat me.'

"'Throw down your weapon.'

"'No.'

"Esquirol wiped his instruments. He operated on the pilot's leg with the pistol butt pressed against his forehead.

That's war for you, Vango. But thanks to Esquirol, the soldier could soon stand.

"That evening, infantryman Joseph, coming up from behind, was able to disarm the German with his bare hands. Joseph had fists as tough as shell heads, and he went on to use them after the war. Under the name Joseph Puppet, he boxed against the greatest.

"And that is how the four of us—a German, an African from the Ivory Coast, an Italian in a combat cassock, and a French doctor—came to find ourselves lying under the oak tree, stunned, exhausted, half crippled, not understanding what had brought us there or what we were going to do next.

"Night came, and one of us dared to open his mouth. It was the German officer. He was called Mann. Werner Mann. He spoke perfect French.

"'I'm trying to remember the name of a street in Paris just beyond the Porte Saint-Denis—do you know the one I'm thinking of?' Mann asked.

"Nobody answered.

"'A street with a little café called Chez Jojo,'" he continued.

"It felt as if the question had come from another planet. A planet with shiny brass counters that smelled of ground coffee, a planet where someone named Jojo could chat with his customers while drying the glasses about the nice weather they were having.

"'Chez Jojo, Rue de Paradis,' said Esquirol.

"'Yes, that's it.'

"We couldn't hear the sounds of the fighting anymore. Mann and Esquirol fell quiet for a long time. But since none of the four of us were able to sleep, Werner Mann picked up again: 'In that street, there's a girl who sells flowers. When I went to study in Paris, I had a room on Rue Bleue, the next street along, and I was very fond of that girl. Does anyone here know her?'

"That's people for you. If you're a native of New York and you're far away from home, on a journey, people will ask you if you know someone named Mike who's blond and also lives in New York. And they'll want to know if you've got any news of him.

"Esquirol looked like he wanted to say something again. I think he was wondering if it was legal to talk to a German about a girl who sold flowers next to Chez Jojo. Men had been shot for less. They called it 'fraternizing with the enemy.' It was a crime. And so he tried to keep quiet, but after half an hour, Esquirol couldn't resist revealing, in one breath, 'The girl, she's named Violette.'

"It was thanks to those words, thanks to Violette, that it all started. In a flash, the absurdity of war was clear to all four of us. If combatants could find themselves on the edge of a battlefield that was dug over like a cemetery, sharing a memory as fragile and fleeting as the face of a girl, then anything was possible.

"War was not inevitable. We talked throughout the night. And in the morning, Project Violette was born. Each of us rejoined our ranks. Mann on the German side and us on the French side. We finished the war as soldiers, without our paths crossing. And when the peace was signed, on November eleventh, 1918, I went back to my monastery at La Blanche on the island of Noirmoutier.

"I was so weakened, Vango, so shocked by my years

serving on the front, that at night, the crashing of the waves behind the abbey terrorized me like the sound of canon fire. I took my time getting my strength back. The nuns baked me walnut tarts with salted butter.

"On Christmas Eve 1918, still feeling a bit shaky, I asked for permission to go to Paris for three days. Mother Elisabeth gave me leave. Which is how I found myself, on Christmas night, walking through the snow on Rue de Paradis. I got to Chez Jojo's a little before the agreed time.

"Two years earlier, in our clearing in Verdun, we'd arranged to meet there. On the first Christmas after the end of the war, whenever that might be, in the café that had started it all. Chez Jojo, Rue de Paradis.

"Joseph Puppet arrived after me, dressed like a prince with a silk waistcoat under his jacket. I whistled to him. He stared at my medieval attire. He laughed out loud and told me that if I was looking for a tailor, he could recommend Michel, near the clothes market at Temple. We fell into each other's arms.

"A man sitting nearby waved a newspaper.

"'Is that you?'"

"He pointed to a photo at the bottom of the front page. It was indeed Joseph, J. J. Puppet, victorious the previous evening after knocking out Kid Jackson, the champion boxer from Liverpool, in the seventh round. Joseph laughed as he signed the photo. Then Esquirol appeared. He hugged us. I hardly recognized him in his gray hat and his wool coat with its upturned collar. Each of us spoke about his experience of the last months of the war.

"Esquirol kept checking his watch. Mann hadn't showed

up. Joseph tried joking: 'I bet he's one street along, in the arms of young Violette. He wanted to see her first before joining us.'

"But we all knew what his absence really meant. He didn't come. A man arrived in his place. He was in his midforties and had been Mann's flying instructor. Mann's plane had gone up in flames on the last day of the war. Despite putting up a fight, he had died from his burns the next day. We were shattered. Our friend was dead.

"Project Violette had kept me going for the rest of the war. Nothing made any sense if there wasn't a German in our group.

"'Werner asked me to replace him,' the man added. 'If you'll have me, then I am on your side. My name is Hugo Eckener.'

"We were slightly suspicious at first. I stared at Eckener, who hadn't taken off his snow-flecked hat. Esquirol was the first to shake his hand, saying: '*Willkommen* . . . welcome . . .'

"We stayed at Chez Jojo's until late. Afterward, setting off alone down the street, I was thinking about Mann. I wanted to pass by Violette's shop. The shutters were down. I asked the caretaker what had become of the flower girl. He replied that she had died of tuberculosis the previous autumn. So Joseph had been right all along. Mann was in Violette's arms, somewhere. . . ."

Vango had been listening all this time. He had slowly crawled under the fig tree to stay in the shade.

He couldn't see what any of this had to do with a French superintendent turning up on the island of Arkudah more than fifteen years after the events described. But he felt shattered by what he had heard. He suddenly had a better understanding of what war meant. Before, war to him had been about flowers on monuments, medals, mothers who had lost their only son, drums beating out their rhythm once a year, men who were missing an arm or a leg.

War . . . Zefiro's memories turned that word into flesh and blood.

"We met up again two years later. Things got off to a very bad start for Project Violette. It was an idea dreamed up by choirboys, a simplistic and naive plan that could be summed up in just two words: *never again*. Fight the war before it began. Attack its roots before it grew out of the earth. All that remained was to put this into action.

"But something was happening. The dragon's head was growing back exactly where it had been chopped off. Arms dealers and others were rubbing their hands with glee. From early 1919, they were there, just ahead of us, the future wars. The treaty that would be signed at Versailles was an invitation to further battles. The punishment against Germany was so violent that it would inevitably lead to hatred and revenge.

"Hugo Eckener made us weigh all this. On the maps where he showed us the new borders that had been drawn up, everything looked like a minefield. We didn't even have time to react. What could four ordinary men do, faced with this war machinery?

"Project Violette was going to perish before it had sprung to life. We wrote letters and opinion pieces in the newspapers, and met with MPs who smiled and took us for dangerous pacifists.

"I remember Puppet wanting to make a speech at the end of a boxing match he'd won, but the cries of the crowd drowned out his voice. From the front row, Esquirol told him to abandon his plans. And so the public carried off their champion triumphantly, without him being able to say a word. That day, looking at the newspaper photos, everyone thought he was weeping with joy."

Zefiro paused for a moment. Who doesn't recall the day when they gave up on their greatest dream? His next words sounded like a funeral dirge.

"Christmas 1919, over a hot chocolate at Chez Jojo's, Project Violette was buried by three voices against one. A freezing wind was blowing across Paris. Over on the upholstered bench, Hugo Eckener in his fur hat looked like a washed-up polar bear. I held out for several minutes, saying that I still believed in it, that I had a plan.

"That day, we hardly dared look one another in the eye. Esquirol had recently opened a swish doctor's office in Paris. Eckener had settled by the shores of Lake Constance. J. J. Puppet had just broken Joe Beckett's nose magnificently. And I had become the wise monk the hierarchy had wanted to make of me, with the result that my name was being mentioned at Saint Peter's in Rome.

"Most of us had our eyes in our hot chocolates. Joseph was looking at the clock. We said our good-byes. I was thinking about what Mann's judgment on the four of us would have been. We walked for a while together down Rue de Paradis. And when we passed the hardware store that had replaced pretty Violette's flower shop, I saw Esquirol cross over to the other side, because he felt so ashamed.

"Perhaps it was that image that stopped me from giving up on our idea. I worked alone. I followed a lead I had, and eleven months later, I became confessor to Voloy Viktor, an arms trafficker working for the worst warmongers. Europe and the whole world made a show of pretending to be after him, but all the while they were signing contracts with him.

"He switched identity every three months, transforming his face and his nationality. He had been an English lord, a Spanish merchant, a circus ringmaster, and even, according to some people, the star singer in an Istanbul cabaret. There were plenty of people who claimed he didn't really exist.

"Viktor only had one fear: burning in hell after his death. And so he sought out a confessor to reassure him. I volunteered my services with a view to getting close to him. He would arrange meetings in deserted churches, a different one every time: a bell tower in the Italian mountains, a chapel in the Alpilles. He always came alone. Back then, Voloy Viktor was only twenty-five or thirty years old. He was mostly unrecognizable. He spoke with the voice of a child trying to be good. He would complain about a big boss, whom he called the Old Man. He said the Old Man was too hard on him, that he felt frightened. He would rant and rave.

"He only revealed his tiniest sins to me: a fly he'd drowned in his honey at breakfast, a swearword that had escaped his lips. 'Oh, Father, I am so wicked,' he would say, beating his chest. He would start crying, clinging to the confession grille. I tried to pass myself off as indulgent in my handling of him, but the violence was mounting inside me.

"I was hatching my plan. In November 1929, I wrote to Esquirol. I asked him to warn Superintendent Boulard, at the Quai des Orfèvres, that Voloy Viktor would be at Sainte-Marguerite church, in the suburb of Saint-Antoine, five days later at three o'clock in the afternoon. They couldn't miss him.

"A hundred men were conscripted. The streets were marked out all the way to Bastille. There were even marksmen on the rooftops.

"At a quarter past three, I gave absolution to Voloy Viktor and he went outside. There was a policeman behind each pillar. The church was surrounded. But they missed him. Yes, Vango, they let him get away. And from that day, Voloy Viktor put a price on my head. The traffickers wanted me dead. They were prepared to pay anything for it.

"I would never get away from them. I made it as far as Rome by foot, crossing the mountains, and requested an audience with the pope. The next day, in the newspapers of France and Italy, the death of Padre Zefiro, priest, monk, gardener, and beekeeper, was announced against a black background. He had died in his thirty-seventh year. The funeral would be an intimate affair. No flowers or wreaths.

"The day of the burial, while Puppet, Esquirol, and Eckener, along with a few monks, were bearing a coffin that was too light, I landed on this tiny island of Alicudi, which I rebaptized by its Arabic name: Arkudah.

"I founded the monastery in order to continue living while being dead for the rest of the world. Not even Joseph and

Esquirol knew where the monastery was. Eckener was the only one I told. So it must have been him who sent Boulard to me."

"And what about the others?"

"Who?"

"Brother John, Brother Marco, Pierre—all the other monks in the monastery," Vango said. "Where have they come from?"

"Those here with us are religious men who all have good reasons for being on this island. They come from all over."

And so Zefiro started telling their stories. The story of the men with whom Vango lived was the story of their century.

Some monks had escaped the fascist regime of Mussolini, others that of Hitler, or Stalin in Moscow. There were enemies of the Mafia, those who had infiltrated them, those who had repented. There were even two orthodox monks who had confronted the wolves of Siberia after escaping a gulag. They had arrived close to a hermitage in a forest in Finland and told their story. After being listened to (and their case being referred from Constantinople to Rome), they had been directed toward Zefiro's little paradise, where they were able to practice their religion while joining in the life of all the monks.

Some had escaped the penal colonies of Lipari, the neighboring island, where opponents of the fascist regime were kept in captivity.

Another monk, John Mulligan, was an Irish priest who had baptized the son of Al Capone, king of the Chicago Mafia. Mulligan had accidentally seen something he shouldn't have in Al Capone's office: two corpses wrapped in red-and-white-checked restaurant tablecloths. He'd had to vanish.

"None of my brothers still exist outside of this island," Zefiro summed up. "They've all been reported dead or missing. Which is why we call it the invisible monastery. This is a hideout for ghosts."

The padre was overcome with emotion. He was gently rocking his head.

"Yes, ghosts."

He looked at Vango.

And what about this boy? Who was he, really? What was he fleeing?

The sun was high in the sky now. The fig tree gave off a sugary scent above them.

"And Boulard, this morning?" Vango finally asked.

"Boulard came to tell me that he's got Voloy Viktor, who was arrested at the Spanish border. I have to go to Paris to identify him. It's impossible to recognize that man from any photograph. He's a chameleon. But I could recognize him from the slightest movement. We used to be twenty centimeters apart when he visited me in the churches."

"You're going to Paris?"

"Yes. I'm positive it won't be him."

Vango turned to face Zefiro.

"It's a trap to make me come out of my hiding place," the padre explained. "Viktor wants to make sure I'm still alive. He wants my skin."

"So why go?"

"Because if I don't, Boulard swore that he and his men would come to get me and arrest me for nondenunciation of a crime, consorting with criminals, and being party to arms trafficking as the friend and confessor of Viktor from 1919

255

to 1920. If the police come here, all my brothers will fall with me."

They both went quiet, and so did the bees.

"What about you, Vango? How do you know Superintendent Boulard? What do you have to fear from him?"

Vango wished he had a life story to tell Zefiro. A heroic life in which everything made sense and even the shadier parts of which could be clarified in a sentence.

But if he'd been able to speak, Vango's words would have sunk like flares down a bottomless well.

Zefiro held out his hand to help the young man stand up again.

"Good-bye, Vango. I'm leaving. I'll be back soon."

"I'm coming with you."

21

ROMEO AND JULIET

"You do love me a bit, don't you?"

Thomas Cameron was sitting next to Ethel in a red velvet box in the dress circle. The theater was full and buzzing. It was hot. Down below, in the stalls, female members of the audience were fluttering their fans.

A sweltering summer had taken hold of Paris. The men in the auditorium were pushing up their sleeves and unfastening their waistcoats. The ladies left their shoulders exposed. It felt more like a scene under the weeping willows on the banks of the River Marne than an evening in a majestic theater.

Ethel was leaning over the edge of their box so as not to miss a single word of the performance.

In the next box, a group of foreigners was proving rather noisy. And beyond them, in a box carefully chosen so that they could watch the young couple without disturbing them, Lord and Lady Cameron were grabbing the opera glasses.

"Look, he's talking to her! She's accepted the flowers!" cooed Lady Cameron, blushing with excitement.

Ethel appeared to be the only person interested in what was happening onstage.

It was the second act of *Romeo and Juliet*. Romeo had just entered the garden of his family's enemy: Juliet's garden. All that was visible in the darkness were handsome Romeo's eyes. The cicadas were chirruping in cages hung up in the wings. And, for once, Juliet wasn't being played by an aging thirty-something actress. She had black hair that cascaded down as far as the jasmine beneath the window.

"Don't you love me a bit?" Thomas whispered into Ethel's ear, gently changing the word order to try his luck again.

Ethel put a finger to her lips to make him hush. But poor Tom was talking very quietly already, in a voice that wavered.

He repeated his question one more time, almost inaudibly.

"Yes, Tom," she whispered so as to be left in peace.

She was watching Romeo climbing toward Juliet's window.

What else could she say to someone she had always known, who had grown up not far from her in Scotland, on a neighboring property? She loved Tom Cameron the way she loved the landscape of her childhood. She loved him as she did the white sky in the Highlands, the memory of the games she used to play with Paul, the shape of a boat on Loch Ness, or the smell of stuffed pork belly cooked by Mary. No more, no less.

But she knew that, for several years now, Tom had been expecting much more from her.

For Ethel, it was exactly as if one of the twisted beech trees behind the castle had knocked at her door one morning to ask for her hand in marriage. What could she say? Yes, she loved those little trees beneath which she used to build her dens. She loved them dearly . . . but would she have wanted to marry them?

On stage, Juliet could be heard sighing to Romeo:

What man art thou that, thus bescreen'd in night,
So stumblest on my counsel?

Even though Ethel could recite the play by heart, she felt as if she were hearing it for the first time.

In the neighboring box, the foreigners were talking in Russian. One man was watching the play, hypnotized. The others seemed to be discussing matters more serious than the love affairs of a young Italian girl from Verona.

Their eyes glued to their opera glasses, the Cameron parents couldn't have cared less about Juliet either. They were trying to gauge the reaction on Ethel's face.

"Got her!" yelped the father. "He's got her!"

You'd have thought he was commentating on a clay pigeon shooting session.

Yes. Ethel was deeply moved. She was stroking the roses Thomas had given her. But if she had tears in her eyes, it was because, on stage, Juliet had said to Romeo:

If they do see thee, they will murder thee.

Ethel was fond of impossible loves.

Ronald and Beth Cameron had always believed that Ethel would marry their Thomas. It would make an ideal alliance between the families, two estates, two sides of Loch Ness. The death of Ethel and Paul's parents had been interpreted as a sign of fate by the Camerons. They had shown a great deal of compassion toward the two orphans. And there's nothing like compassion to make certain people feel they have some kind of ownership over others. . . .

Not only that, but it wasn't all for the worse. The Camerons had always been oddly afraid of Ethel's mother and father. They found them rather wild. They agreed in private that they were aloof, over the top, and even, "Yes, Ronald, let's be honest about it: pretentious."

At their funeral, Lady Cameron had whispered into her husband's ear something along the lines of "It was always bound to happen," as if those who had departed this life had been foolhardy enough to live life to the full.

Their untimely deaths had not, therefore, changed anything about the Camerons' project to marry off Tom and Ethel. On the contrary. As a twelve-year-old heiress, Ethel was suddenly very rich, which was far from being a nuisance in the eyes of the Camerons.

In her box now, Tom's mother was thinking about all the little Camerons this lovely young couple was going to provide her with. When she closed her eyes, she could imagine nine or ten of them. They were all the spitting image of their father. Even the girls.

As for Sir Ronald, he was busy congratulating himself on his decision to invite Ethel to Paris for the month of July. The Camerons often spent the summer in a different city: Vienna, Madrid, or Boston. This year, they had rented an apartment opposite the Eiffel Tower and were living in an idyllic postcard between the big department stores, the Opera, and the Longchamp Racecourse.

* * *

For Ethel, the invitation fit perfectly. She would be in Paris, chaperoned by the Camerons and so would be able to continue her search for Vango while being able to reassure her brother, Paul, at the same time.

Paul, for his part, had been very surprised by his sister's enthusiasm as she was leaving Scotland, given that she had been starting to distance herself from Tom Cameron and openly despised his parents.

Ethel hadn't traveled with her hosts. She had explained that she would rather have her own car, but in reality she wanted to make a little trip to Germany in order to question Hugo Eckener.

In the course of their dinner on Lake Constance, Eckener hadn't volunteered anything, not a single piece of information as to Vango's whereabouts, even if Ethel had fleetingly detected that he knew something. She had arrived in Paris two days later.

Theater, museums, and horse races—this was the style in which Ethel was concluding her third week in Paris. She dragged Thomas to dances at which he didn't see her all night long. For the Bastille Day celebrations on July 14, she had crossed the whole of Paris without ever being out of earshot of accordion music. There was dancing on every street. At dawn she scooped up Thomas, asleep on a bench.

She was starting to be noticed and talked about in the newspapers. A society columnist had taken to signing off his daily write-ups that summer with lines such as "And the mysterious young lady was in the auditorium again" or "It didn't matter that the orchestra was out of tune; *she* was there."

Lord Cameron, who read the French press, had vaguely advised his son to challenge the journalist to a duel. But son and mother were less keen.

Ethel hadn't been informed about her reputation preceding her in the press, and Thomas nearly coming to blows to protect it. She had enough on her plate already.

Before setting out from the Highlands, she had warned the Cameron family that she would have to absent herself from time to time in order to visit an aunt who lived in the center of Paris, on the Île de la Cité. At first, the Cameron parents had been annoyed by this news, but they positively encouraged Ethel when they discovered that the aunt was very rich, very old, and childless.

And so Ethel had caught the bus and arrived at the Quai des Orfèvres, a stone's throw from Notre Dame. Her elderly aunt was named Auguste Boulard. Ethel wanted to ask him about the latest news on Vango.

But when she got there, the only person she could see was Lieutenant Avignon. Boulard was away.

"Will he be here tomorrow?"

"No, Mademoiselle."

Avignon had recognized Ethel. He offered her a seat in Boulard's office, but she immediately stood up again. She walked around the room, browsing the files and papers and checking the photos on the walls.

"Where is he?"

"I'm not at liberty to tell you."

"When did he leave?"

"Yesterday."

"And where did he go?"

"As I said, I'm not . . ."

Avignon, who was feeling intimidated, put his hand down to close a file she had just been leafing through.

"Please, Mademoiselle . . ."

"Monsieur?"

By accident, his little finger had landed on Ethel's. She didn't move. He started to blush dreadfully. She removed her hand once he'd nearly fainted from embarrassment.

"Well, from what I can tell, Monsieur Boulard is always on holiday. I believe I saw him this winter in a striped swimming costume on Lake Constance."

"It's for w-work," Avignon stammered, his eyes bulging at the prospect of his boss in a bathing suit.

"And where did you say he is now?"

"As I've explained, I'm not at liberty to tell you."

"Oh, no, you definitely did tell me."

Avignon was startled. What had he said?

"Only joking," Ethel murmured, removing the thumbtacks that held a picture in place on a corkboard. "Did you copy that?"

"Yes."

"Not bad."

It was based on Ethel's portrait of the assassin, which she had handed over fifteen months earlier in the upstairs dining room at the Smoking Wild Boar.

"Will I be able to see the superintendent soon?"

"In two weeks."

Ethel dropped the portrait.

"Two weeks! But what if it's urgent?"

"The same answer. Come back in two or three weeks, Mademoiselle."

Boulard had set off in search of the only witness capable of identifying Voloy Viktor with any certainty. This was his top priority as far as he was concerned. He had gone alone and hadn't wanted to reveal his destination to anybody. Not even his faithful Avignon.

Ethel scooped up the picture of the killer's face off the floor. It was in three pieces. She glanced questioningly at Avignon.

"Yes," the lieutenant explained, "I draw the mustache and the hair on separate pieces of paper. These are the first things a wanted man can change about himself. He'll cut his hair or his mustache."

Feeling rather proud, he took out a box containing different hairstyles and sideburns that could be put together in any combination on the portraits.

"So you see, it's really very easy. I always do it this way."

Ethel put the pieces of paper down on the desk and played with them for a few seconds, adding and then removing the Russian's little mustache.

"You're terribly clever, Lieutenant."

He blushed again. Ethel headed for the door.

"Do you have a message for the superintendent?" asked Avignon, following her out.

"No. I'll be back. Thank you."

She shook his hand firmly.

When Avignon returned to his office, he smiled on discovering that she had added two chunky braids and a thin beard to the assassin's portrait.

The lieutenant remained in a dreamy frame of mind for

quite some time. That girl seemed to have stepped out of a novel. Even her perfume had a make-believe quality.

Once she'd sat down in the bus, which was heading along the Quai des Grands-Augustins, Ethel took out of her bag a small and very slim brown file that she'd found on one of the shelves in Boulard's office. A file on which two words were visible: THE CAT.

And below that were two more words, underlined in red ink: "Investigation abandoned."

It was the only file that had looked interesting to her. And it just happened to be the file of a girl with a close interest in Vango. Ethel opened it. It was empty.

In the theater, it was now Act Three. Ethel was listening to Juliet's father swearing that his daughter would be forced to marry the man he had chosen for her. Juliet was resisting. Her heart belonged to Romeo.

Slippery as an eel, Ethel was avoiding Tom's hand. She was watching Juliet standing up to her father.

Cameron senior kept sending satisfied signs to his son. Thomas Cameron was trying to put on a brave face, but he was clinging to his seat so as not to throw himself into the orchestra pit. She didn't love him. How would he survive? How could he ever tell his parents?

On stage, Juliet's father was booming:

But fettle your fine joints 'gainst Thursday next,
To go with Paris to Saint Peter's Church,
Or I will drag thee on a hurdle thither.

In the box next to Ethel and Tom's, silence had been restored. The blond man was still watching the performance attentively.

His name was Sergey Prokofiev. And during the summer of 1935, he was working on a ballet score inspired by *Romeo and Juliet*. He had heard about this production in Paris and had been granted permission to come and see it.

But he was under escort and would be heading back to the Soviet Union the next day.

The curtain fell. The houselights came up. It was intermission.

Three quarters of the auditorium leaped to its feet, as if this were the moment everyone had been waiting for. Plenty of spectators only go to the theater for the intermission.

"Are you coming for a drink, Ethel?"

"No, thank you. I'll stay here."

Thomas stood up, trembling at the prospect of what he had to reveal to his father.

Ethel glanced over at the blond man. He hadn't moved. He was staring at the curtain as if he could still see shadows moving on it. Someone leaned over and whispered in his ear. Ethel could only see the back of this second man. When he turned around, she felt her heart pounding very fast.

It was the marksman from Notre Dame.

He had shaved off his mustache, but his portrait, which she'd seen only a few days earlier in the office at the Quai des Orfèvres, was so clear in Ethel's mind that there could be no doubt about it.

Boris Petrovitch Antonov might not have seen Ethel.

He was there to accompany Comrade Prokofiev, the

composer. There were also two representatives from the embassy as well as Comrade Vladimir Potemkin, the ambassador himself, plus four security guards. It was a major responsibility.

And so he might not have seen Ethel, but for the fact that the composer's eyes met those of the young woman at precisely the moment Boris was staring at the composer. It was like a ricochet effect. Ethel's look of astonishment piqued the composer's curiosity. And seeing that curiosity in Prokofiev's eyes made Boris turn his head to discover Ethel, a few meters away, sitting in an almost deserted theater, with Tom's bunch of flowers still in her hands.

They stared at each other.

For a moment, Ethel thought he was going to run away. She was ready to give chase and was already cursing the fact that her choice of dress would make her hobble. It was a black dress in which Ethel had disguised herself in her bedroom, during those years of mourning when she was just a little girl, with the dress trailing behind her to form a long, tragic train.

Ethel was already unbuttoning a short tight coat that came to her hips and restricted her movements. She wasn't going to let this man get away a second time. Suddenly she froze.

Their roles had just switched.

No, the man wasn't going to get away. Boris Petrovitch Antonov was staring at her intensely. He had gauged Ethel's determination. He knew she would always be behind him, getting in the way of his work. And so he had just decided to eliminate her.

"Will you excuse me for a moment, Comrade Prokofiev?" he inquired with a polite smile.

Addressing the composer in what was now a completely empty auditorium, he exited the box.

"Well?"

Two floors lower down, in the theater foyer, surrounded by the throng of spectators, Thomas was looking very pale in front of his parents. Lord Ronald Cameron had a bottle of champagne in one hand and was filling the glasses.

"What are we drinking to, Junior?"

Tom hated it when his father called him Junior.

Lady Cameron was blushing and in a state of suspense at the news her son was about to announce.

"Well?" she urged him again.

"Well, I spoke to her. . . ."

"And?" his father went on, his face contorted with excitement.

"And she said . . ."

Suddenly, the lights went out. All around them, people shrieked in fright.

A second earlier, Boris had appeared in Ethel's box. She was standing in front of him. He was holding a knife between his fingers, the blade hidden in his jacket sleeve.

"You really do get everywhere, Mademoiselle. But not for much longer."

He lunged in her direction, and right at that moment, the lights went out. Refusing to deviate from his plan, he plunged the knife with the precision of a street fighter. When the lights came back on ten seconds later, Boris Antonov let out a roar of anger that was drowned out by the racket going on elsewhere. He had sliced through the red velvet of the chair. Ethel had vanished.

Over in the theater bar, the moment when the lights came back on was met with a sigh of relief. Champagne flutes and glasses started clinking again.

The Camerons resumed their line of questioning.

"Where was I?" asked Tom.

"She said . . ." chorused his parents.

"She said . . ."

He closed his eyes and took a deep breath. He was remembering Ethel's rebellious fingers escaping his own.

"She said yes," Tom lied. "Ethel told me that her answer is yes, but we've got to wait a bit before we announce it to her brother. He's very lonely, her brother. She doesn't want us to talk about it until then, not even with her."

The parents fell into each other's arms, moaning with joy. It was terrifying to witness. Without realizing it, each of them emptied the contents of their champagne glass behind the other's back. They let out little squeals of delight. They were all puffed up with pride. They didn't make a single gesture in their son's direction.

This was their victory.

Ethel had leaped from her box into the circle below before tearing down the stairs. Who could have cut the power with such split-second accuracy? She ran down corridors without knowing where she was headed and arrived at the main entrance, but Boris Petrovitch was already in front of the doors, giving orders to the men there. So she started running backward, bumping into the usherettes.

There was a door with a security guard at one end of the stretch of red carpet. Ethel made her clothes look respectable again and walked hastily toward that exit. It was the only way to the wings.

"I should like to see Romeo," she told the guard in her pretty accent.

"Not during intermission. You can come after the performance. That's when the actors receive visitors in their dressing rooms."

"I've come all the way from the Highlands of Scotland to see Romeo. I've brought him flowers."

"Yes, I can see you've had a bit of a journey!" He sniggered, looking at her wilted bouquet. "Like I said, come back at the end."

She heard a noise behind her in one of the circles. Her pursuers were hot on her heels. Ethel's heart was palpitating.

Just then, a mysterious voice from the wings said, "Let her in. I can vouch for her."

The porter stepped aside. She passed inside. There, with his shoulder pressed against the wall, was a short bald man.

"I'm sorry I'm not your Romeo, Mademoiselle."

She didn't know it, but this man was none other than the columnist Albert Desmaisons, who had been singing her praises in the press. She hesitated.

"Hurry up, little lady. You have someone to see. And the intermission is almost over."

Ethel gave him her bouquet and a peck on his left cheek.

"Thank you, Monsieur. Thank you."

Listening to the sound of her heels lightly heading off, the columnist stood there marveling. He was seeing stars and didn't even notice the three unleashed men who, having pushed the guard out of the way, rushed furiously past him, trampling his roses underfoot.

During the final acts, Boris and his acolytes turned the wings upside down and inside out. But they didn't find anything. A couple of hours later, once the performance was over, they accompanied Prokofiev back to the embassy on Rue de Grenelle.

Ethel was on the roof of the theater. Below her, all of Paris was bathed white by the moon.

Ethel was almost asleep now.

A fifteen-year-old girl who looked like an angel perched in the flies had whistled to her in the wings.

"Over here! Come on!"

The girl had made Ethel climb the rungs of the ladder two at a time, then slide into an invisible passageway. This girl had saved her life.

Now they were buried in each other's arms, between two zinc walls, beneath the summer sky.

"Who are you?" Ethel asked.

"I was the one who turned off the electricity."

"It was you?"

"I've been keeping an eye on the Russian for almost a year."

"What's your name?"

"The Cat."

22

THE TRAP

Paris, seven days later

Voloy Viktor was sitting on a steel seat that was fixed to the floor. His eyes were closed.

His hands and feet were attached to the chair by leather straps. A wide metal belt prevented his upper body from moving.

His face looked calm and confident. It was reasonably handsome and appeared almost indifferent to the light of the lamp that had been angled to shine down vertically onto him.

A projector was hanging from a wire just above his head. Voloy Viktor was breathing calmly. The projector swung gently at the end of the wire, casting disturbing shadows across his features. The rest of the room in the basement of the Quai des Orfèvres was in darkness.

In the shadows, behind a glass panel, Boulard was watching the scene. He had returned to Paris five days earlier. Standing on his short legs, he dipped a piece of buttered baguette into a cup of coffee the size of a chamber pot.

Boulard was waiting for Zefiro. He was fully aware of the danger to which he would be exposing the monk who had already worked so hard to secure Viktor's capture. And he knew that out on the street in front of the police headquarters, any passerby, any innocent ice-cream seller, might in fact be one of Voloy Viktor's men, waiting for Zefiro to emerge from his hole so they could spot him and give chase.

Boulard's team had offered the monk an armored van to transport him to Paris from the port of Marseille, but Zefiro had refused, letting it be known that he would arrive under his own auspices. No one knew the day or the hour: simply that he had agreed to turn up before the last day of July.

The month of July would be over in a matter of hours.

"No news of Z?" Boulard asked his second in command, who couldn't take his eyes off the man presumed to be Viktor.

"No," replied Avignon.

"If he doesn't come, I don't know what I'm going to do."

"You said that you trusted this Monsieur Z."

The superintendent nodded.

"We're not going to be able to keep Viktor much longer," said Boulard. "If Z doesn't come to identify him, the game's up. He'll be free tomorrow. There's already a huge amount of pressure to release him."

"There was another call from the minister's office."

"I know. They're all scared of Voloy Viktor."

"The minister's special adviser wanted to inform us that Gaston Balivert, a beaver-skin trader, had been arrested by mistake at a French border," Avignon added, "and the Canadian authorities are demanding that their man be released."

Boulard was so angry he nearly choked on his baguette.

"He's not Balivert! His name is Viktor! And Canada hasn't requested anything at all. I have the proof that his passport is a fake. The real Gaston Balivert died twelve years ago when he slipped in his bathroom. I am convinced that the man in front of us is Voloy Viktor. And the minister knows that as well as I do. But seeing as Viktor pays half the rulers of the world in emeralds and rubies from Anvers, they're all worried they won't be going on vacation next year. . . ."

Behind three thick layers of glass, Voloy Viktor couldn't hear any of this conversation. But he still had a smirk on his face and was staring directly at Boulard, who was shifting about uneasily in the gloom.

In the main waiting room of the police headquarters, Ethel was sitting with her hands on her knees.

There were a lot of people, and it was all fairly chaotic. As a result of Voloy Viktor's being kept in the building, there were all sorts of checks and controls in place. Tempers were being lost. And meetings were running late.

Ethel looked around her.

Among the shambles she could see: a mother with her three children, a lawyer sucking on a peach pit, a ticket puncher from the Métro, a redheaded man wearing earplugs so as not to be disturbed while he read, a builder's mate holding a pink summons and asking everybody to read it back to him, tourists who had lost their suitcases, a well-heeled couple who had been burgled, widows of men who had been murdered, elderly gentlemen who looked as if they had been waiting since the previous century and might in fact be stuffed, and a nice-looking man in a suit with, at his feet, a suitcase marked: DRAT THAT RAT!—PEST CONTROL AND RAT CATCHING.

Ethel glanced at the clock. Once again, she had told her hosts that she was off to see her elderly aunt in the Île de la Cité.

The Camerons had changed their tune since that

unforgettable night at the theater. They hadn't mentioned Ethel's sudden disappearance during the intermission of *Romeo and Juliet*. When she had explained to them that she'd felt slightly ill and had stepped outside to drink some homemade lemonade at the end of the street, the Cameron parents had winked at their son and said, "It's an emotional time!"

And Tom Cameron, looking very pale next to Ethel, had wished that the ground would swallow him up.

Ethel had reported to reception. She knew that Boulard was back. This had been confirmed by the police officer behind the counter.

The same man had just called out a name. And each time this happened, the red-haired man opposite her conscientiously removed his earplugs, stood up, put his book facedown so as to keep both his seat and his place, and headed over to the officer.

"Which name did you call?"

"Madame Poirette!"

"Ah. Not me, then. Thank you."

And back he went to sit down again, poking the wax earplugs into his ears with his thumbs.

The man with the pest-control suitcase was sitting right next to Ethel, and the pair of them smiled at this charade as if they were at a puppet show.

The man didn't really look like a rat catcher.

Another police officer entered and paced around the waiting room, looking for somebody. He stopped in front of Ethel's neighbor.

"Are you the gentleman from Drat That Rat!?"

"Yes, that's me."

"We'll come and get you in ten minutes. The superintendent isn't in a good mood. He says it's really not the day for it, plus nobody let him know. But I'm very glad you're here."

Then he lowered his head and whispered, "The place is crawling with them down there. All the rats of the Seine come to cool off here every summer. I promised the superintendent you wouldn't disturb him. I'll be taking care of you."

"Yes. It'll only take a few moments. I've got a stunning new product."

Ethel took the opportunity to tackle the police officer directly: "Do you know if Monsieur Boulard is seeing people today? I've asked someone to let him know I'm waiting. I haven't heard anything back."

"He's not in his office for the time being. We'll keep you posted."

Ethel had already been waiting for at least an hour. The police officer moved off.

"I'd be better off catching rats," she remarked to the pest-control expert.

"Yes, it looks as if I'll be let in ahead of you. I do apologize."

The man was charming. He had a natural poise. Only his peasant's hands were testimony to a life that hadn't been spent in high society: he must have seen the world a bit before moving into pest control.

One of the children belonging to the mother sitting in the corner near the window started playing with an old man's walking stick, mimicking a Charlie Chaplin film that had just come out.

"Don't be silly!"

Chaplin's mother grabbed him by the ear. He gave the walking stick back to its owner and returned to his mother's skirts, like a good little boy.

Ethel's neighbor had also watched this scene. They were disappointed when the show came to an untimely end.

Ethel nudged the man's suitcase with her foot.

"You're not really in the rat trade, are you?"

He started laughing and declared, as if confiding in her, "No, of course not, dear child. It's all a camouflage. . . . The truth of the matter is I'm a hermit monk on the trail of arms dealers!"

They laughed together. She was staring at him closely.

"I can tell you're not what you appear to be," whispered Ethel. "Who are you?"

The man seemed bothered by this.

"Who are you?" Ethel teased him again. "Who are you?"

He fell quiet.

Zefiro was paying attention to everything. He was trying not to let his curiosity get the better of him. It was all very disorienting. He was emerging from fifteen years on a lost rock in the middle of the Mediterranean.

But he had already said too much to this girl. He had to stay one step ahead. Invisible lives depended on him.

The best would have been to enter 36, Quai des Orfèvres accompanied by Vango. As a duo, the rat catcher and his assistant would have been less easy to spot. Viktor's spies were looking for a lone man.

But no matter how hard Zefiro had tried to explain at the entrance that he couldn't do without his assistant, the security officer had been adamant: the sidekick had to stay outside.

In the end, Zefiro had told Vango to wait nearby, close to the bird market, in their van with DRAT THAT RAT! emblazoned in gold letters against a black background.

He was glad he'd brought the boy with him. He hadn't put up much of a fight when Vango had insisted, because this way they could warn the monastery if something went wrong. And if the padre was captured by Viktor, the monastery would instantly have to be dissolved.

"Who knows if they'll be able to make me talk?" Zefiro had confided in Vango on the boat coming over. "I've got no idea what my levels of resistance are like. I might end up revealing Arkudah's existence."

Which was why, in the waiting room at the Quai des Orfèvres, Zefiro couldn't afford to let his guard drop for a second.

He was keeping a particularly close eye on the reader with the earplugs. He didn't trust him. For all he knew, it might be the ideal way for this man to sit in the waiting room and focus on everything that was going on.

As for the girl to his right, he refused to believe that she could be with the enemy. Even a monk who'd been faithful to his vows for thirty years and who had resisted the charms of fifty nuns at the Abbey of La Blanche in Noirmoutier, couldn't help but find this young woman irresistible.

He felt her elbow nudging him.

"I think this time it's for you," she said.

But it was for her.

"You see, my child. You're going first after all."

From a distance, before she went through the door, she repeated her question: "Who are you?" mouthing the words without a sound escaping her lips. She smiled.

Zefiro had heard her first name being mispronounced in a French accent by the officer as "Heh-tel." It sounded like "Hey, tell!," which seemed to be just what Ethel was trying to make him do: blow his cover.

"I've got very little time," Boulard warned Ethel as soon as she sat down opposite him. "I'm expecting someone. I might be called away at any moment."

He appeared to be nervous.

"I've known you be more gentlemanly, Superintendent. Our housekeeper, Mary, asks to be remembered to you."

Boulard had no answer to that.

He was trying to find where to put his legs under the table.

Mary, the housekeeper he had met at Everland, kept writing him letters in English. He would read them at night with a magnifying glass and a dictionary before hiding them in the curtain lining so his mother wouldn't find them when tidying up his bedroom. Modesty prevented him from writing back.

Madame Boulard would stop the concierge, Madame Dussac, as she was bringing up the mail. They spent hours talking in the stairwell. When these letters arrived, with their British stamps and their scent of faded rose, Marie-Antoinette Boulard used to explain to the concierge that her son was corresponding with Scotland Yard, the flagship of the British police.

This was what Boulard himself had told her, to justify the frequency with which the letters kept coming.

And so his mother and the concierge would stare devotedly at the envelope, picturing the proud figure of Sherlock Holmes leaning over his table as he stamped his seal, in a cloud of pipe smoke.

"He's an important man, your son," Madame Dussac concluded.

And even when there was a little heart drawn on the back of the envelope, they put it down to the legendary sentimentalism of the English.

"Have you got any news for me?" Boulard asked Ethel.

"Yes, Mary is doing well, she's—"

"I'm talking about Vango Romano," interrupted the superintendent, blushing.

"What about you?" Ethel fired back. "Have you got any news?"

"Not really. I'm convinced he's far away by now."

Boulard couldn't have been further from the truth. Vango had never been closer. He had just leaped onto the roof, a few meters above them.

"Don't tell me that a yearlong investigation hasn't turned up any results," said Ethel.

Boulard rubbed a cheek.

"I have to confess, I'm dealing with some very big cases at the moment."

"And what about a nineteen-year-old kid who kills an elderly priest on the eve of being ordained himself and who then gets shot at in front of thousands of people in the center of Paris—doesn't that count as a big case?"

"No, Mademoiselle, not at all," the superintendent exploded

as he stood up. "That is not the heart of the matter! I care about that murder as much as my old hat. I'm sitting on that murder as I'm sitting on three quarters of all the crimes in Paris. The real issue here is to find out where that boy comes from, when no one has the first clue about him despite the fact that he seems to know everybody."

Boulard was pacing from one end of his office to the other, waving his arms and banging into files and pieces of furniture.

"The real issue is Vango Romano's true identity. That's the mystery that interests me. And that mystery is the only reason I'm not giving up on this whole wretched inquiry. When it comes to murder, there are enough murders in this city every day to keep thirty-six Superintendent Boulards busy! Do you understand, my little lady? Thirty-six Superintendent Boulards! But I've never met a single Vango Romano before."

"I'm not your little lady," said Ethel, on the verge of tears.

"I'm sorry, I . . ."

Boulard collapsed into his chair and in so doing flattened his hat.

"I'm a bit overworked," he went on. "I didn't mean to. . . ."

The superintendent was looking at her. There were tears forming in the corners of her eyes. Ethel really was crying.

"If there were thirty-six Superintendent Boulards, I would throw myself straight out of the window," she said, sobbing.

The two of them fell silent.

Boulard opened a drawer and took out a large white cotton handkerchief, which was perfectly clean. He always had these at the ready, ironed on Sunday afternoons by his mother, for those who dropped by his office.

There had been so many tears in forty years in this room. Boulard's job depended on the grief of others.

Sometimes he felt as if he spent his life swimming lengths in a great lake of tears. And the worst thing was that without the dramas, the people in mourning, the destinies felled, Boulard's life would be dry, and he would find himself all alone trying to swim backstroke on the parquet.

Ethel took the handkerchief.

Just then, they heard something that sounded like an explosion. Boulard's door sprang open as a result of an almighty kick.

23

DRAT THAT RAT!

Lieutenant Avignon came flying into the office.

When he saw Ethel, he tried to pull himself together. He turned to Boulard.

"Superintendent . . . Superintendent, he's downstairs. . . ."

"Who is?"

"The . . . the . . . the rat catcher. . . ."

Ethel sat bolt upright.

Boulard was trying to decode what was being said. He screwed up his eyes.

"The rat catcher?"

"The one . . . the one you've been expecting. . . ."

Avignon stared at the superintendent. Was the penny ever going to drop?

"Yes, the one you've been expecting . . . the man you asked us to . . ."

"My God!" exclaimed Boulard, leaping to his feet. "I'm coming."

He rushed over to the door. Ethel was stunned. So she wasn't the only person on whom that rat catcher had made such a big impression.

"This is an emergency. I do apologize, Mademoiselle. Good-bye."

He told Avignon to follow him. And disappeared.

Once outside, Ethel walked along the river as far as the Pont Neuf, stopping in the middle of the bridge under a street lamp. She climbed over the handrail and got onto the small ledge that jutted out over the eddying Seine.

She crouched down.

Ethel could feel how low her spirits were as she watched the water flowing beneath her. In the distance, near to the Pont des Arts, people were swimming.

"Tell me about it," said the Cat, who'd been waiting for her.

"There's nothing to tell."

In the basement of the Quai des Orfèvres, the rat catcher had been taken to a small room where the daylight entered via a tiny basement window.

Boulard walked in, closing the door behind him.

They stared at each other.

"Thank you for coming, Padre Zefiro."

"I'm not doing this for you."

"I know."

"Where is he?"

"At the end of the corridor; follow me."

"Wait. I want everything to be absolutely clear. Only one man here, apart from you, knows who I am?"

"Augustin Avignon. He has my complete trust."

"That's already one man too many."

Boulard glanced at the suitcase with DRAT THAT RAT! stamped on it.

"You're not going to get rid of my Avignon?" he ventured.

"No. But I don't want a single other witness. Nobody. To everybody else, I must remain the rat catcher."

"Of course."

"Is it dark where we're going?"

"Yes."

"Voloy Viktor mustn't know that I'm alive."

"The suspect is blinded by a projector. We're taking no risks. This is my responsibility."

"No. It's mine. I have the lives of dozens of men in my hands. If I'm seen, my monastery will be condemned."

"You won't be seen."

"I will simply tell you if it's Viktor. Then I will make the sign of the cross, and I will leave the way I came."

"Through what?"

"Through the door, Superintendent. Do rat catchers often fly out windows?"

"You're quite right, yes, of course, sorry."

"I want everything to be normal and in order as regards this business. You should even have the payment for my pest-control services delivered to the company address, Drat That Rat!, Maison Aurouze, Rue des Halles. You never know. The people we're fighting against know everything, they watch over everything, and they'll examine all documents with a fine-tooth comb."

"Agreed."

Zefiro grabbed Boulard by the jacket and said very earnestly, "Listen to me, Superintendent. Father Zefiro never came here, all right? He never came here because he's dead and buried with an ocean view, under the green oak trees of the Abbey of La Blanche. There are even bones in my grave bought from the Museum of Mankind to prove it. I don't leave anything to chance."

"Understood," said Boulard, who was beginning to realize the full gravity of the situation.

He had never imagined that being dead could be so complicated.

The padre opened his suitcase and spread a pungent powder along the walls.

"What are you doing?" asked Boulard.

"I am getting rid of your rats, Superintendent. You clearly don't understand anything!"

"Yes, of course, sorry."

Zefiro gathered up his belongings.

"Let's go. Make sure the corridor is empty. Then check the booth we'll be in. Come back and get me."

Zefiro was on his own for a moment. He took a deep breath. He was remembering those meetings with Voloy Viktor. Zefiro had managed to deceive him for six months. But each time, when he found himself in the small confessional box, in a chapel in the Dolomites or in Brittany, waiting for his dreadful penitent, he half expected to feel an arrow going through his heart, shot from behind the grille. His life hung in the balance from one second to the next.

He had believed he wouldn't have to relive that experience, that the only darts that posed any threat to him now were those of his bees on Arkudah.

"Come this way; the coast is clear," said Boulard, pushing open the door.

Zefiro picked up his suitcase and followed the superintendent. When he passed behind the window, he immediately saw the man attached to his seat. A chilling shudder ran down his spine.

He had been expecting someone as bait, a man trying to pass himself off as Viktor in order to reel in Zefiro.

In the darkness, Auguste Boulard couldn't make out the padre's reactions.

"Is it him?" whispered Boulard.

There on his seat, Viktor still had that uncanny smirk.

"It's him," Zefiro answered.

They remained there, without moving, for seven or eight seconds. Zefiro would always regret those few seconds. If he had turned around right away, if he had left, it would all have been so different.

But before the monk and the superintendent had time to move at all, Voloy Viktor tensed his entire body, thrust his neck backward, and, with a head butt of almost inhuman violence, struck the projector lamp shade that was brushing against his hair. The beam of light shot away from him in a vertical line, like a swing, and swept the darkness at random. It spun around and in a second sway of the pendulum the bulb lit up Zefiro's face with the precision of flash photography.

The image of that face blinded by the light was etched on Voloy Viktor's eyes.

He sat frozen to the spot. A trickle of blood ran down the beginning of his hairline.

Viktor's lips moved. And if the projector had been on him, it would have been possible to read on his lips the lyrics of a song that Nina Bienvenue sang in Montmartre and that everybody was singing that year:

Welcome to Paris . . .
Glad to know you're alive . . .

It was a song about a soldier returning to his loved one after the war, but in Viktor's mouth, it was a death sentence for Zefiro.

Father Zefiro let out a cry, grabbed Boulard by the collar, and dragged him into the corridor.

He pinned him to the brick wall and spluttered, "You swore to me—you swore you wouldn't make me take any risks. . . ."

Boulard had turned deathly white.

"I don't understand what happened. I mean that. Avignon checked everything."

Zefiro let go of him.

"Leave," panted Boulard. "Don't worry. We've got him. And we won't let him go. Nobody will be able to communicate with him. Nobody will know that you're alive."

"That's what you say."

"He'll rot in a cell for the rest of his days—"

A shrill ringing noise started up.

"What's that?" demanded Zefiro.

"The alarm signal. I—I simply don't understand any of this. Somebody unauthorized must have entered police headquarters. They'll block all the doors."

Beside himself with fury, Zefiro kicked his Drat That Rat! suitcase before telling Boulard, "I'm warning you not to let Viktor get away. Or you'll spend the rest of your life paying for it."

And he ran off. He was no longer the dignified tradesman

expecting to exit via the main entrance; he was Zefiro the clandestine.

He would have to leave the premises like a rat.

As they strolled past the bird market, Ethel and the Cat stopped. Ethel had just seen the small black van advertising DRAT THAT RAT!, ESTABLISHED 1872 She went over and peered inside through the closed window. Nobody there.

She'd have liked to see the man from the waiting room again.

"What are you doing?" asked the Cat.

"I wanted to say hello to a friend."

The small van was blocking people's access. With nobody to shout at, the market deliverymen had left a string of insults scrawled on the windshield. This was an old Paris tradition that dated back to the invention of the wheel.

Ethel snatched a piece of paper, drew a line through what was written on it, and, smiling again, she wrote down the same question three times: *Who are you?*

Then she signed it: *Ethel.*

The Cat watched her tuck the piece of paper back under the windscreen wiper.

She had finally met someone more unpredictable than she was. Ethel never stopped surprising her. Compared with this intense Scottish character, the Cat felt entirely reasonable. And that did her a world of good. The Cat felt she was the more sensible one in this team. And she was thriving on it.

She'd even told Ethel that she had a boyfriend named André. She hadn't said any more so as not to let on that he didn't actually know about the Cat's existence or that his real name was Andrei and that he received his orders from one Boris Petrovitch.

The two young women had decided to pool their efforts in order to find the person responsible for making their paths cross: Vango.

Lieutenant Avignon discovered his boss on the verge of a nervous breakdown.

Boulard was fuming as he crossed the courtyard.

"Who set off that alarm?"

The visitors in the waiting room had been herded into a secured room for further checks. Nobody had the right to leave now. Even the trash collectors who'd been taking out the garbage from the cafeteria found themselves stuck. A rotting smell was spreading across the cobblestones and seeping into the offices. It was some stench.

"I asked who set off the alarm!"

"It wath me," said Avignon.

"You? Avignon?"

"There wath someone in your offith," the lieutenant went on, holding his nose. "Badeboiselle Darbon spotted them."

"Who?"

"Badeboiselle Darbon."

"Stop pinching your nostrils, you stupid oaf!"

"Mademoiselle Darmon."

"Did they make off with anything?"

Ten days earlier, a file of no interest relating to the Vango Romano case had inexplicably disappeared. It was the file for the witness known as the Cat.

"I don't think so."

"What, they didn't even make off with Darmon?"

"Not even," said Avignon, who didn't dare smile.

"That's a shame. Tell Mademoiselle Darmon I'm expecting her in my office."

Mademoiselle Darmon was three months away from retiring. She had been secretary to the superintendent for forty-four years, and in all that time, he had gotten on perfectly well without her. Truth be told, he'd never known what to do with her. And so she had spent forty-four years doing crosswords and reading slushy romances and advice columns, and that's exactly what she would continue doing for a few weeks more.

Darmon walked into the office with her four-tiered chignon and her never-ending heels.

She sat down opposite the superintendent.

"What was he like?" he barked.

"Very good-looking," she replied, batting her eyelashes. "And very young."

"What else?"

"Very well brought up."

"He didn't do anything to you?"

"No," she said, sounding rather regretful.

"How did he leave?"

"Through there."

She pointed at a window. It was a small horizontal window that gave onto a tiny courtyard, which in turn served as a light well for the glass roof below. Boulard's office window was the only one set into the four walls of the courtyard. The walls offered no footholds whatsoever.

"Did he have a rope?" asked the superintendent.

"No. He jumped onto the wall opposite and climbed it."

Avignon and Boulard glanced at the wall in question, which was as smooth as a bar of soap, three or four meters from the window and fifteen from the ground.

Avignon closed the window, disgusted by the smell of rubbish that was spreading everywhere.

"Right, right, right, right . . ." Boulard muttered softly.

He exchanged looks with Avignon. Mademoiselle Darmon had a very active imagination. One day, she had informed them all that the actor Clark Gable had come over to her little garden in Bagnolet for cocktails and a game of croquet.

Boulard paced the office. None of his files had been moved. Everything appeared to be in order. He inquired of his second in command in a falsely sweet voice, "So Monsieur Avignon makes the whole building jump because Mademoiselle has a gallant encounter in my office with a young Apollo who has special powers when it comes to sticking to walls. Is that it?"

"I thought that . . ."

"Get out!" he thundered. "Get out of here right now!"

Avignon and Darmon were about to leave the room when Boulard muttered, "Mademoiselle, do keep me in the loop if your cat burglar writes you letters during your retirement in Bagnolet. . . ."

Mademoiselle Darmon stopped.

"Oh, yes, I almost forgot. I have something for you."

She reached into her blouse and reluctantly took out a piece of paper folded in eighths.

"He left this for you."

Boulard pounced on the scrap of paper and unfolded it.

The letter was signed Vango Romano.

Vango's clothes were hardly crumpled at all.

He had just escaped via the roof of the Palais de Justice and dropped down again from the top of the Sainte-Chapelle.

A young magistrate had seen him passing vertically by his window; another even got an apologetic wave from Vango for disturbing him. Ashamed of their hallucinations, neither of them breathed a word about what they had seen.

Vango emerged from the bird market a second after Ethel had turned the corner at the end of the street.

In an ideal world, we might have dreamed of a benevolent hand intervening so that one of them tarried a little longer while the other hurried up, and that they would have found themselves at precisely the same moment in front of the black van with DRAT THAT RAT! stamped across it. In an ideal world, there would have been music playing in the distance and a ray of sunshine would have lit up the scene.

But, even in an ideal world, would it have been worth changing the course of these two lives, treating them like pawns to be pushed one square ahead or one behind, just for us to enjoy a reunion scene played out in slow motion?

So Vango got into the van alone.

Events hadn't gone according to plan. Vango had lied to Zefiro. Since their departure from the Aeolian Islands, he had had a secret scheme. He wanted to speak with Boulard, at last, to tell him everything he knew and get him to follow up other leads than his own trail. In Zefiro's presence, he had nothing to fear. Superintendent Boulard would listen to him.

They had turned him away at the entrance. He had pretended to accept this. He had entered the premises via the walls and the roof instead.

But Boulard and Zefiro weren't in the office.

He had ended up having to write a letter in great haste, which he gave to a secretary who batted her eyelashes at him before shrieking for help.

Vango started up the van.

If things went wrong, his instructions were not to wait for Zefiro. They would meet up later at the station.

A piece of paper was spread on the windshield. Vango got out to remove it. Sitting at the steering wheel, with the engine roaring, he scanned it.

It had the effect of sixteen hydrogen balloons from the *Graf Zeppelin* popping out of his chest one by one.

Vango read three words repeated several times and a first name. Those words would change his life. That first name had been haunting him ever since he was fourteen. Those words and that name had one chance in a billion of ending up on this piece of paper in this spot at this moment.

Who are you?
Who are you?
Who are you?
Ethel.

Later on that same night, in a dump at Saint-Escobille, outside the gates of Paris, the contents of a garbageman's cart was being tipped onto a mountain of trash. A site worker pushed out what remained with a fork.

"You're the last ones," he told the old man in the hat, who was pulling the cart.

"They kept us for four hours at the police station. They'd blocked all the doors. I had no idea what was going on. I'm off to bed."

The worker helped him park his cart alongside the others.

"Good night."

"'Night."

Silence was restored.

The only sound was the scurrying of rats.

A moment later, the stinking mound started moving. A man got out and stood up. He gave one of the rodents a good kick and wiped his hand across his greasy face.

"My God," he said.

A few hours earlier, he had been carrying a case with PEST CONTROL AND RAT-CATCHING on it: Zefiro had managed to escape.

He fumbled for his watch in his jacket pocket. It was time to join Vango at the Gare d'Austerlitz.

Once he was outside and hugging the wall of the dump, he didn't have the faintest inkling that twenty-five meters behind him, the old man in the hat was following him in the shadows.

PART THREE

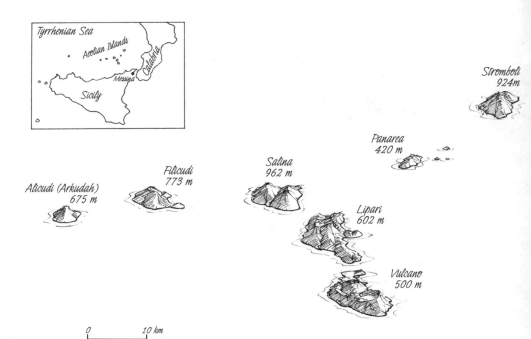

Tyrrhenian Sea

Aeolian Islands

Calabria

Messina

Sicily

Stromboli
924 m

Panarea
420 m

Salina
962 m

Filicudi
773 m

Lipari
602 m

Alicudi (Arkudah)
675 m

Vulcano
500 m

0   10 km

Aeolian Islands

24

THE SURVIVOR

Sochi, a few days later, August 1935

"Setanka! I don't want to play anymore."

Setanka didn't answer. She was hidden in the long grass on a dune, just above the others. The little boy had been trying to find her for the best part of an hour. He was close to tears.

"Tell me where you are!"

Why didn't Setanka enjoy these picnics on the shores of the Black Sea so much anymore? During their never-ending games of hide-and-seek, she would let her little cousin brush past without seeing her.

"Setanka, Setanotchka . . ."

As she lay there, daydreaming, she could feel the grass-hoppers climbing over her skin. She was watching the clusters of people sitting in the sun.

There were so many of them, just like in the old days. Grandfather, Grandmother, Uncle Pavloucha, the Redens and their children, Uncle Aliocha Svanidzé and Aunt Maroussia, who could sing opera arias. If Setanka turned slightly, she had a view of her father, half propped against a dead tree, talking to a man she didn't recognize. Surrounding them, standing in the rushes or in the water, a handful of guards watched over this gathering.

Until she was six, when her mother was still with them, these picnic lunches were sheer bliss for Setanka. The songs were merrier, the sun more radiant, and the tender words her uncle Pavloucha whispered in her ear as he knelt down in front of her weren't tinged with sadness as they were today. When August came to a close, and they had to return to Moscow for the start of school, it used to be a wrench to leave their dacha in Sochi.

These days, despite everybody hooting with laughter at her grandparents' eternal quarreling, despite Aunt Maroussia's serenades, there was a sense of fear in the summer air that nothing could assuage.

At only nine years old, Setanka had no idea where this fear came from, but she could feel it everywhere, clinging to her even more closely than the dress on her sweaty shoulders.

Sometimes she thought about all those people who had suddenly stopped coming to the house and who were never mentioned again. Where had handsome Kirov and all the others gone? Where?

Not even in her wildest nightmares could she have imagined that her father, Joseph Stalin, was a man who ruled his country with terror, that he had just organized the famine in the Ukraine, and that in the future, he wouldn't even spare his own family. A few months later, Aliocha and Maroussia would be arrested, Uncle Pavloucha would die in his office of a strange heart attack, and then there would be Uncle Redens, shot the following year, his wife deported . . .

"Why didn't you give me a clue? I've been looking for you for an hour!"

The little boy had finally found Setanka. He was trying to hide the tearstains on his cheeks.

Setanka held out her hand and pulled him up onto the dune. He crouched down next to her.

"Are you brave?" she whispered.

"Yes," he replied, sounding rather worried.

"Then follow me," instructed Setanka.

They started crawling through the grass. Setanka was in front. She was the elder of the two. Nobody paid any attention to this pair of snakes advancing over the dune. The boy's knees and elbows were turning green as he dragged himself along.

"Don't go so fast," he begged her.

"Shhh, be quiet. . . . We're nearly there."

The children slid behind a fallen tree trunk. They could hear voices on the other side. On reaching the dead tree that Setanka's father was leaning against, they strained their ears.

Somebody referred to a piece of "good news," and not long afterward, Setanka heard the words she was always listening for: "The Bird . . ."

Her heart leaped.

"The Bird has shown his face in Paris," a man said. "He left a letter with the police."

Setanka put her head to the ground. She could hear her father saying words she didn't understand.

"No," the man replied. "They didn't catch him."

A heavy silence followed.

"Is that your good news, Comrade?"

"In his message, the fugitive explained to the police that he is being pursued, but he doesn't know why or by whom. . . ."

A fresh silence. Over by the water's edge, Aunt Maroussia was singing.

Registering her father's cold anger, Setanka tried to flatten herself even more.

"And you're going to let him make fools of you again?"

"C-Comrade," the other man stammered, "I was able to read the whole letter. . . ."

"The letter tells lies, you idiot!"

"But . . ."

"Good-bye."

When Setanka heard the rustle of clothes, she curled herself into a ball and pushed her cousin's face into the grass.

"Find him!"

The visitor had just stood up.

"My apologies for disturbing you, Comrade."

Stalin let the man head off before summoning him back with a whistle.

"You mentioned the woman who brought him up. What do you call her again?"

"The Bird Seller. She poses no danger. Over there in Italy, everyone says she can't remember anything. . . ."

"Put her in a place where she'll no longer be a risk for us."

"You want me to . . . ?"

"Yes, I do."

"You . . . ?"

"Bring her here. And keep your eyes peeled. It may well be an occasion for the Bird to show himself. People become very attached to that kind of woman."

Setanka thought of her own nanny, Alexandra Andreyevena, who had looked after her with infinite kindness ever since she was born. After her mother had died, Setanka had been saved by her nanny's tenderness.

"An operation like that, abroad . . ." the man objected timidly.

"Act cleanly."

"I thought that . . ."

"Deal with that woman, and don't disturb me again on a Sunday."

Setanka and her cousin stayed there, crouching silently in the grass, for several minutes. They had almost drifted off to sleep, their eyelids growing heavy, when they sensed a shadow of giant proportions hovering over them and heard the terrifying roar of a bear. They rolled over to one side, shrieking.

The bear smelled of tobacco. It had Uncle Pavloucha's brown eyes. It had his long legs too, not to mention his melancholic laugh and his sand-colored jacket cut by a reputable tailor from Berlin.

The two children jumped on their uncle, who had given them such a fright.

But the game didn't last long. It was a halfhearted attempt by Pavloucha to remind the little ones of bygone summers, when Grandfather would pretend to be the bear or when he would gleefully throw Setanka's mother into the water.

On the other side of the dead tree, Comrade Stalin was staring at Pavloucha and the children, sprawled on the ground.

In a few hours, the order would be communicated to remove Vango's caretaker and to put her in a secure place. Forever.

Salina, Aeolian Islands, at the same time

The moment she walked through her front door, Mademoiselle knew that someone had been in the house before her. When you live alone, objects assume a huge importance. Your eye grows accustomed to them. They stay in their allotted place, and the tiniest change is as astounding as a footprint on a deserted beach.

The cup on the table had shifted position. Not only had it moved a finger's width, but it had also been turned halfway around. And that half turn was what startled Mademoiselle the most. This tiny nudging of a teacup was as startling for her as a horn blasting its warning through the silence of the island.

The most striking factor of all was that the cup's handle had been turned to the right. Now, to anyone else, that might have seemed like a small detail, but for Mademoiselle it was an earthquake. She was left-handed and she always used the handle when picking up her cup, so it was impossible for this cup to be in that position without the intervention of a stranger. A right-handed stranger or, in the worst-case scenario, a left-handed stranger so badly brought up that they didn't pick up a teacup by its handle.

Careful not to betray her surprise, she made her way over to the stone sink with her basket of fresh capers.

Mademoiselle had suspected that they'd be back one day. The last time, they hadn't found what they were looking for. This time, they wouldn't give her a second chance.

She started sorting the capers. She preferred eating the big juicy ones, which she put to one side, while the little ones would fetch a good price.

Capers are the buds of the caper-bush flower. Mademoiselle made two piles on a board whitened with salt. It was the end of the harvest. She always left a row of unpicked shrubs up on the hill, and that way she got to see their white flowers bursting into bloom. The flowers lasted only a single day. And right now she was wearing one in her hair.

Mademoiselle had her back to the room. She had no desire to run away.

On her way home, she'd noticed that Mazzetta wasn't in his cave.

She had even picked up the pace to avoid him catching her with this flirtatious flower in her hair.

The doctor had frequently suggested that she move into his place if she was afraid of getting another nasty visit. She wasn't frightened of anything, she had replied.

This was true: the only fear she had ever experienced had been for Vango's sake. And now that he had gone away, Mademoiselle felt a painful sense of peace.

The mystery of Vango's absence, and his silence, sometimes kept her awake at night. She would talk to him a bit, as if he were still there in his little bed, in the corner of the bedroom. She would regale him with stories. She would tell him about a dazzling big white boat that sailed across the seas, with dozens of dolphins following in its wake.

Her voice would break at the ends of her sentences. Often, she couldn't finish her tales.

But once a year, Vango let her know that he was alive and well. One letter, the day after Easter. A few loops in that clumsy handwriting she was so familiar with. That was all she asked for.

Mademoiselle slid her hand under the sink.

She wasn't mistaken. She had just seen a reflection in the white ceramic tiles. Somebody was behind her. A shadowy shape had emerged from the bedroom and entered the kitchen.

There was a small shepherd's knife hidden under the stone sink. She had it in her hand now. The blade was slim and cut like wild grass.

Mademoiselle mustered all her courage. Her right hand continued sorting capers while the left one gripped the knife.

The man didn't move. Mademoiselle was singing. The reflection in the tiles was blurry, but she could see that he wasn't very tall.

His silhouette was like a brush-and-ink drawing, with narrow shoulders. Perhaps he was young, or else standing sideways.

She would be able to overpower him.

She had no choice. Or her life would be over before the flower in her hair had wilted.

Mademoiselle was waiting. She needed him to get a bit closer.

She decided to talk to him without turning around, to let him come to her.

"You won't get him. I know what he's been through," she called out in Russian before adding enigmatically, "He has the strength of a survivor."

Behind her, the figure moved slightly and pinned itself to the wall, as if it couldn't quite make up its mind.

"You won't get him!" she shouted.

With one leap, the man rushed over.

She released her left hand and turned around forcefully as the white flower flew out of her hair. The blade of her knife ripped through the air, but it didn't touch the visitor, who managed to dodge.

"Mademoiselle!" he shouted.

The nurse's fingers relaxed. The knife landed in the thick wood of the tabletop, chopping the caper flower in half.

She opened her eyes again.

It was him. The survivor.

"Vango! Evangelisto! Vango!"

He fell to his knees before her.

"Mademoiselle."

He wrapped his arms around her waist.

A LIGHT ON THE WAVES

She was crying so hard that everything was a blur. She clasped Vango's head and stroked his face to make sure it really was him.

"Evangelisto, you're here," whispered Mademoiselle.

Vango was getting used to the sound of her voice again and to his name, Evangelisto, which he'd almost forgotten. She had always called him Vango, but on important occasions the full version of his first name would put in an appearance, as if she needed more letters to express everything she wanted to say.

"Leave, Vango."

"Who were you expecting, Mademoiselle? Who were you talking to?"

"They're looking for you."

"Who?"

"I don't know. Leave."

"I'm not going to stay for long. I came to ask you something."

In his pocket, Vango could feel the piece of paper from Ethel. The message had landed in his hands, transported by an invisible force. And it asked the question that would haunt him from now on: "Who are you?"

Vango was reviewing his life and its mysteries.

There are some closed doors we're so frightened of opening that we don't see them anymore. We've pushed furniture in front of them; we've jammed the lock. Children are the only ones who might crouch down on all fours to stare at that red glow coming from under the door as they wonder what lies behind it. But Vango had always been afraid of the glow. He preferred to soak up the sunlight outside.

Today, this secret was all that he could see. In barely five days, he had rushed from Paris to get an answer out of his caretaker.

"Mademoiselle, tell me everything you know. Tell me who I am."

She looked up.

"What?"

She had understood perfectly, of course.

"Tell me who I am."

"My little one," she whispered into Vango's hair, "you are my little one."

Vango stood up and gazed deep into her eyes.

"Tell me," he begged.

This time she felt her resolve weakening.

They stayed like that for several minutes, staring at each other. Mademoiselle had gone to sit down. Her face was unrecognizable. So many memories were flickering across it, one after another. Not a word in all of this. Her face was a flag in the wind, stretched, rippling, supported by the power of recall.

The winds of memory were bringing an entire other life back with them. There was no time for the sobbing and the laughter to stop. They were like grains of sand whipped up by that Mediterranean wind known as the sirocco.

Mademoiselle still hadn't uttered a word, but Vango could already recognize his own life being played out silently across her face.

"I won't be able to tell you everything today. These days, I can't always distinguish between what really happened and what I've dreamed. I'll need a little time."

"I haven't got time!" exclaimed Vango.

With her finger, Mademoiselle nudged the empty cup that had betrayed the news of Vango's arrival.

"I'd like to begin at the end," she declared. "With the last night. Let me start with the last night."

From his belt, Vango took out the silk handkerchief that had never left him: the blue square with the capital *V* and his surname. And those crumpled words: *How many kingdoms know us not.*

Mademoiselle stood up and took the handkerchief. She held it very close to her mouth and began to speak.

"We'd had fine weather all day."

She repeated herself, as if she needed those words to act as a springboard: "We'd had fine weather all day. And when the weather was good, the boat was a little piece of paradise. There was some shade provided by the rattan parasols, making circles on the deck. The three masts swayed gently. The oriental carpets were spread out up on the bridge. The crew shut down the steam engine. It was hot. They were diving off the roof of the boat."

Her voice sounded mellifluous; she was smiling.

"I can see you, Vango. You're on a deck chair made out of a wood that's almost black. There are splashes of sunlight around you. I remember a voice singing."

She sang the first few notes of a Greek lullaby, as poignant as a siren's song.

"Who was singing?" Vango interrupted her with tears in his eyes.

Mademoiselle continued as if she hadn't heard him: "We'd had fine weather all day. That evening, you were sleeping on the deck chair in your blue pajamas."

"Who was singing?"

"Give me time, please, Vango."

She put her hands together on the table.

"That night, the boat was gleaming like a gold coin. There were garlands of lights strung between the mast cables, and flares along the bridge. It was a big boat, nearly sixty meters long, with only six sailors. When night fell, the wind picked up. We were enjoying the breeze after the heat of the day. But it began to whip the sea into motion. The rain came down on the carpets on the bridge. We took shelter inside the cabin."

"Who took shelter, Mademoiselle?"

"You, me, . . ."

She closed her eyes and hummed the sirens' song to summon the strength.

"And your mother . . ." she said at last.

A sort of gentle shifting noise could be heard coming from Vango's direction. A breeze sent a piece of dried grass gliding to the floor.

"And your father . . ." Mademoiselle added in a whisper.

Her pupils shone as she spoke these last words. She carried on with her storytelling.

"We were in the small cabin belowdeck. The storm was taking its hold on the sea. We weren't afraid. There wasn't a more reliable boat in the world. It had sailed over wild seas to Denmark. A more reliable boat did not exist. That's what your father always used to say."

She smiled again.

"And I'm sure he was right. Your mother sang again, to help lull you to sleep. Your father was sleeping too, his head on his wife's knees. He loved her. He'd had the boat's previous name removed from the prow, and he had a star painted with five points, because your mother's name—and the boat's—was Stella. I admired your father. He spoke to me as if I were a lady, even though I was just a French nanny, while he was every inch a prince."

Night fell over the house at Pollara. Vango was barely present inside those walls. Instead, he was rediscovering a past he had forgotten all about. In his stomach he could feel the rolling motion of that October night in 1918.

"The sailors came in to dry off. We heard them talking in their cabin at the front of the boat. That's why it happened. Your mother didn't want them to stay outside in the rain. She told them to go into their cabin. She took them some hot water."

Vango thought of those hands carrying the kettle. His mother. How sweet to hear that forbidden word. His mother was named Stella. The star. Vango's eyes were shut now.

"I was sitting near one of the portholes," Mademoiselle

explained. "I was the only one to realize that something strange was going on. At one point I said, 'There's a light out there, on the waves.' Your father went outside for a moment. He came back in and reassured me. He hadn't seen anything. He said there was very little risk of a stray boat crashing into us in the storm on this stretch of sea. He pointed to a dot on the map. He said, 'We're here.' I can remember that very clearly."

She put her finger on the blue handkerchief that lay unfolded in front of her.

Vango could sense the impending catastrophe, but he was clinging to the picture of those fingers on the map, the heat of the cabin, his mother's singing. *A little while longer,* he thought. *A bit more tenderness before the end of the world. . . .*

"You fell asleep at the same time as your mother. Through the porthole, I was watching the rain lashing the waves as the white foam flew up. Then came the first explosion."

Vango opened his eyes.

"Your father stood up. I think he understood right away. There hadn't been any jolt. Just an explosion at the front of the boat. Another followed. Then several more. Your mother got up and asked, 'Is it a rock? A boat?' Your father didn't answer. He went over to a drawer and rummaged around in it. Your mother asked him what he was looking for. He said, 'A weapon. I'm looking for a weapon.' There wasn't one. You were still in my arms. You were sleeping. Your mother wanted to hold you again, but that was when the door opened."

And, seventeen years later, she began to describe the men as if they were still standing there in front of her.

"There were three of them, armed with hunting guns.

Three jittery men. They spoke a mix of Sicilian and Italian, and they wanted to know where the money was. I translated for your parents. The first intruder was behaving like a madman. Another was trying to calm him down. And the third kept quiet. Your father told them there wasn't any money. So he offered them his watch and the gold chain around his neck, and took off the four rings he was wearing. The madman snatched them and cast them to the floor with a derisory laugh. And then . . ."

Mademoiselle started sobbing.

"Yes?" Vango prompted her.

"He . . ."

"What did he do?" whispered Vango.

"He fired."

She was still sobbing.

"The madman fired his gun. He knew what he was doing. He didn't want to kill your father before getting what he wanted. And since I was carrying you in my arms, he didn't shoot at me either. . . . No . . . He fired . . . and your mother fell to the floor."

Vango went over to Mademoiselle, squatted down, and pressed his cheek to hers.

"You didn't even wake up," she said. "You stayed asleep in my arms. It was because of me. If you'd been in your mother's arms, she might have survived. A child should be in his mother's arms. Why didn't she take you in her arms? Why?"

"But then you wouldn't be here."

She had folded the blue handkerchief on the table. She couldn't take her eyes off it. She was reeling.

Vango took Mademoiselle's hand.

"They tore your father away from his wife's body. They made all three of us go outside. . . ."

She fainted.

Aeolian Islands, October 1918

They shoved them toward the bow of the boat.

A salty rain was pounding down.

None of the three pirates knew what they were doing. None of them, the day before, would ever have imagined that they'd be mixed up in this madness. They were peasants and fishermen. One of them had a wife and three daughters in Santa Marina. Another had an elderly father waiting for him back on dry land, on the other side of Salina.

Who would have thought they would dare to attack a boat with their blackened hunting guns, to wreak carnage, to murder the crew in cold blood and strip the passengers of their possessions?

They had no idea whether there was a single silver coin in the hold.

Only Gio, the leader of the group, had discovered his true nature. The smell of gunpowder was going to his head. He acted the part, spoke overexcitedly, and fired in every direction.

The other two had lost all control of the situation. Egged on by Gio, they were chancing this desperate act in order to seize what they needed to leave their lost island and reach America, like all the others, except by force. America! They had received the letters and the photos. It was real life over there. But the first shot had started a nightmare from which they would never wake up.

"Show us where your money is!" shouted Gio.

As he spoke, he held the flare up to his victim's face. The rain hissed as it came into contact with the flame.

The little boy's father was still wearing indoor clothing. Barefoot, he had an old red Cossack scarf around his neck, his hair was sopping wet, and he held his sleeping son in his arms.

It was as if a magic spell had been cast over the child, keeping him sheltered in his citadel of sleep. He was smiling, and his hand clutched a blue handkerchief.

The father said a few words.

The nanny translated for Gio.

"He'll take you to it provided you don't touch a single one of the three of us. Swear you won't."

The pirates looked at one another.

"Swear," she insisted.

Gio was the first to swear, touching his medallion. His eyes were bloodshot.

The father thought for a moment. What was it worth, the word of a man possessed?

The two others made the sign of the cross.

Delicately, the father finally entrusted his child to the nanny.

He kissed his son's hair. He walked backward so that he would keep seeing him for as long as possible. His hand was gently held out toward him. His soaked waistcoat, embroidered with gold thread, gleamed in the lamplight. He kept mouthing the words "I'll be right back" over and over again.

Then he vanished into the darkness, beyond the stern, followed by Gio and one of the others.

They had left the nurse and child with the pirate who hadn't spoken a word since the beginning. He was a tall, thickset man in a crude pigskin jacket that still had traces of black bristles on it. Slung over his shoulder was the rope he'd used to board the boat.

Just then the child woke up. He looked at the man, who averted his gaze.

"Sleep a little longer," the nanny kept saying to her charge. "Sleep, my angel."

The minutes ticked by.

They were sitting on a bundle of oars and planks tied together.

Every now and then, the nanny would glance at the tall fellow with the shoulder-length hair. Their lives were in his hands.

He was their only hope.

"Your friend will kill us," she said. "You know that your friend's going to kill us."

The man pointed his gun at the woman. She spoke Italian the way they speak it in the northern towns.

"He swore," he barked.

"He swore on the Madonna," she replied, "but he had a mother's blood still fresh on his hands."

The man was petrified.

"When he's got what he wants," she went on, "he will kill the father of this child. You'll hear the sound of the shot to the rear, and it will already be too late. It'll be our turn next."

"Be quiet—that's enough!"

"That's what's going to happen."

"Shut up!"

The child was listening to what they were saying. He was sitting bolt upright. He kept his lips tightly shut so they couldn't see his teeth chattering.

The man in front of him looked like an ogre. It was hard to know where his sweat stopped and the rain began. He was straining his ears.

"Listen," the nanny said.

The wind started to drop.

After a long pause, they heard the gunshot.

The pirate leaped to his feet with a roar.

He pushed the woman and the child aside, bent down to the deck, managed to lift up the bundle of wooden planks, went over to the edge of the bridge, and hurled the raft into the water. The timber clattered against the hull.

The ogre made the woman lower herself down with the rope. He took the little boy in his arms and threw him toward the waves. The nanny caught him before he plunged into the black water. With the other arm, she was clinging to the wooden raft for dear life.

The ogre was watching them.

A wave carried them off.

Just then, the others appeared with a haunted look in their eyes. Gio was carrying a duffel bag that was almost full. His body kept going into spasms. He was laughing. The two pirates seemed roaringly drunk, despite not having had a drop to drink. They couldn't even speak.

Gio held on to the ogre's clothes to stop himself from falling over.

"Look!"

Trembling, he opened the bag and held his flare over it.

"Look!" he boomed again.

All three of them stepped back.

The whole bag was gleaming with gold and precious stones. The rain added fiery pearls to the mix.

"Look! Look!"

Treasure. Treasure just like in the storybooks.

Gio was whooping at this spectacle.

He plunged his hand in, all the way up to his shoulder.

"And the man?" asked the ogre. "Where's the man?"

Gio simply flashed the Cossack scarf he'd tied around his neck, a crimson scarf with silver tassels.

"He didn't need it anymore," he said, shaking his head like a demon.

Gio burst out laughing and made for his boat, ranting, staggering, without even asking where the two hostages were. He had the bag slung over his shoulder, and he was defying the sky with his fist.

Gio's dreams were already drifting far from there.

He was muttering about building a diamond-encrusted bridge that would stretch from the port of Malfa all the way to Manhattan.

Once he was back in his small fishing boat and feeling a little calmer, Gio barked at the ogre, who had started to row next to him, "What's your problem? You don't even look happy!"

Then he hurled an oil lamp over onto the big boat, where it smashed over the piles of hemp rigging. He threw in his flare for good measure.

The fire gained hold of the stern bridge.

Gio gave his blessing by tossing a handful of gold toward the fire, as if bidding farewell to a departing ocean liner.

"Buon viaggio!"

His two fellow pirates, who were facing the other way, were horrified.

Only one end of the boat had time to burn. The hull was soon springing leaks. The painted star on the prow was the last thing to disappear. The sea and the storm took pity, engulfing the glimmering flames and memories before it was too late.

Gio couldn't stop laughing. One last time, before everything turned dark on the sea, he called out to the man rowing, "What's your problem, eh? Why aren't you happy? You and your donkey have a whole new life ahead of you!"

26

BEELZEBUB'S TITTLE-TATTLE

Arkudah, September 20, 1935

One day, when it was flying over the jungle that plunged into the sea at Rio de Janeiro, in Brazil, the zeppelin had gotten very close to the treetops. So close, in fact, that Vango had brought on board one of the small monkeys with sideburns that had been staring at the airship, completely mystified.

Hauled up by its tail into this gray cloud, the monkey wondered where it was. It had taken refuge in the saucepans of Otto the chef. For a few hours, it had been the spoiled child of the crew and the passengers.

On their return leg, as they passed over Rio once again, Vango had released his simian friend into the creeper-entangled branches on the sugarloaf mountain dominating the bay.

Marco, the cook at the invisible monastery, was the spitting image of that monkey. He was hopping from one oven to another with a mock-scared look in his eye that was a cover for mischievousness. It was eleven o'clock.

Marco was talking to Vango in the monastery kitchens.

Brother Marco's apron was cut from the same waxed cloth that covered the tables at his father's trattoria in Mantua. He was wearing pink dancing slippers suited to the flurry of kitchens. His fingers were always stained with spices. He wore his sleeves rolled up and held in place by teaspoons bent in half, like tongs.

On his forehead was a pair of glasses in the final stages of life, covered with string and sticky tape, glasses that had been ground down, washed out, worn out, as patched up as a bicycle attempting the Tour de France with a dairy cow on the back rack.

"So, Zefiro didn't show up when you were supposed to meet at the Gare d'Austerlitz?" he asked, rolling his eyes at Vango.

Marco never spoke with empty hands. This time, despite the gravity of the situation, he was pummeling a fish.

"No, Zefiro did come to the train station as planned," Vango confirmed.

"Well, then, where is he? Where is he?"

Brother Marco sounded traumatized. He had taken on responsibility for the invisible monastery since Zefiro's departure. He was itching to return the keys to its founder.

"Where did he go?" Marco insisted.

The poor fish was being subjected to a rough quarter of an hour.

Vango had just arrived at the monastery. He had left Mademoiselle at her house in Pollara. She had collapsed before finishing her account of the final night. He had carried her to her bed. She had appealed to Vango for forgiveness, promising to finish the story the next day.

"I'm begging you, dear Vango. I'll tell you everything I know."

"But what about my father? Just tell me. . . . Did he . . . as well?"

She had closed her tear-soaked eyes and nodded. Vango had stayed there for a long time with his forehead pressed against the pillow before being able to get up. Now he knew. He had finally pushed open the gates to the past. They opened onto a mixture of relief and pain. For him, any kind of grief was better than not knowing. Vango had a slightly better idea of the world he came from.

He still had to find out the basic facts: the days and years that had preceded those events. His parents' story before that stormy night. Where had they traveled from? Where were they going? Mademoiselle must know all that.

She hadn't told him anything about the three pirates, those men who had surely grown up in this very archipelago. What did they gain from their crime? Was there anything worth stealing from that boat? Seventeen years had gone by. They might be dead by now. Or not.

Do not foster a desire for revenge.

From now on, as far as Vango was concerned, that monastic rule no longer meant anything.

Before leaving the hamlet of Pollara, a shaken Vango had promised Mademoiselle that he would return the following night. He had to break some painful news to the invisible monastery.

"I'm going to tell you the truth, Brother Marco. I saw Zefiro at the Gare d'Austerlitz, but we didn't leave together."

"Why?" Marco wanted to know as he opened the wood oven. "Why were you both so stupid?"

A huge basket of freshly cut herbs scented the room.

Brother Marco picked up the fish with his monkeylike hands.

Vango had noticed the way he always stared his dishes in the eye before popping them in the oven. This was Marco's furtive homage to his fellow creatures—whether they had scales, fur, or feathers—before he cooked them with a vengeance.

"Something odd happened," Vango went on.

"Pass me the salt."

Vango did as he was told. Catching his eye, Brother Marco exclaimed, "What's the matter? I know you think I always add too much salt! Well, so what? I'm no culinary genius. I just turn out tasty home cooking!"

"I didn't say anything, Brother Marco."

"In that case, you think too loudly. Where is he, our padre? Where is he?"

And, knowing full well that Vango always cooked swordfish over a gentle heat, the monk deliberately put two more logs on the fire to show just how exasperated he was.

"I've got no idea where he is," Vango explained. "When I saw Zefiro . . . he didn't recognize me."

The cook shrieked. He had burned himself.

"What did you just say?"

"Zefiro . . . Zefiro didn't recognize me."

Marco turned deathly white.

"My God."

A few hundred meters from the kitchens, Brother Mulligan couldn't believe what he had just seen. This Sunday, just like every Sunday, John Mulligan was the Cardinal of the South.

There were four cardinals at all times on the island. The monks alternated in filling these posts. They took it in turns to wear the red skullcap. They held these titles because they were responsible for overseeing the cardinal points: north, south, east, and west.

Each one had his day and would look forward with a degree of impatience to that period of solitude spent facing the vastness of the sea and sky. Some of the cardinals were dreamers, some mystics, and some just drowsy. But Mulligan was a fisherman.

Perched on a rock, his breviary and fishing rod between his feet, John Mulligan had taken up his post at daybreak. Every thirty seconds, almost as a refrain to the psalms he was reciting, he would scan the horizon and move the cork on his fishing line.

He first saw it with his naked eye: a black line passing at high speed on the open sea, trailing a white foamy wake.

Reaching for his telescope, he couldn't help exclaiming out loud.

It was a motorboat with three cockpits. A speedboat as fast as the Hacker-Craft he had seen in New England, where he used to keep company with Al Capone and the Mafia when they were vacationing on the beaches of Cape Cod and Nantucket. The speedboat glided over the water, steering a perfect course.

In Europe, such boats could be found only in the Venice Lagoon, or on the great lakes of Switzerland or Lombardy. You would always see elegant women aboard, sitting on leather banquettes, their hair billowing in the wind, and gentlemen with their hair slicked back, dressed in white trousers and sleeveless tops.

But the four men on board this speedboat didn't look like luxury yachtsmen. They each carried a Thompson submachine gun with a drum magazine that Brother Mulligan was familiar with, having glimpsed enough of them in the cupboards of his parishioners in Chicago at the time of Prohibition.

The four men also looked like the kind of cutthroats who'd have made Al Capone's worst cronies run in the opposite direction.

On seeing the boat speed by without slowing down at all as it steered around the long island of Filicudi before heading for Salina and the crater of Pollara, Brother Mulligan didn't worry anymore about this sudden apparition.

He had watched a sperm whale swim by the previous month, and a long time ago now, in the middle of the night, he had even caught sight of an airship.

Because he that is mighty hath done great things for me. . . .

John Mulligan returned to his breviary and to the cork on his line.

An hour later, after morning prayers, Brother Marco addressed the monks gathered before him.

He had to explain that Father Zefiro would be held up in France for a while. Marco gave them the sorts of excuses you would expect to hear from a stationmaster when the trains were running late. He talked about an unforeseen delay, about a regrettable incident. He was deliberately fudging it.

His announcement was met with a murmur of disappointment.

"He'll be among us again as soon as possible. He is think-ing of you. He embraces you with his fraternal love."

Marco fiddled with his cracked lenses as he uttered these words. They were misted up. He glanced at Vango. He wasn't ready to break the news that their padre might not even remember their faces, that he had lost his mind, and that he was cast adrift somewhere in the big wide world.

Afterward, Marco sought refuge in Zefiro's cell and asked not to be disturbed. He leaned against the wall and slowly took off his glasses.

Brother Marco couldn't muster the strength to welcome this new assignment. He cast his eye around the room. Three books. A mattress. That was all that remained of Zefiro. How were they going to cope without him?

Marco noticed the clapper for the big monastery bell hanging from a hook. The bell was set in a hollowed-out rock above the chapel, but its tongue, this lump of bronze in the shape of a water drop, stayed in the abbot's cell. No one was allowed to touch it.

Every day, from matins to compline, a silent bell was rung so as not to attract the attention of the neighboring islands.

Marco pushed the bronze object, which had become the symbol of this silent and invisible monastery.

Thirty-nine monks, thought the cook.

He didn't feel his shoulders were broad enough to cope with the weight of such a responsibility.

He remembered a stormy night when Zefiro had entrusted him with the clapper for a few hours. That evening, Marco had just learned of the death of his little sister Giulia, whom he hadn't seen in ten years. He couldn't even go to the funeral. Back in Mantua, Marco's family thought he had disappeared forever.

And so Zefiro had deliberately paid him a visit in a storm. He had held out the instrument to Marco.

"Go on. Ring the bells. Let them hear you all the way to your hometown."

All the monks had heard tell that this was what Padre Zefiro did if the storm was growling loud enough to cover the sound of the bells and one of the brothers was having a hard time of it.

That night, Marco had hung up the clapper inside the enormous bell. And for two hours in the middle of all those flashes of lightning and the roaring of the wind, he had rung that bell fit to bring down the monastery. Hanging from the rope, he rose up two or three meters with every swing. The bell was crying for him.

It was something he would never forget.

Marco put his glasses back on. He missed Zefiro as he would a father, but he had to attempt the impossible: to play the part of the responsible family man at a time when he felt like an orphan himself. He exited the cell and headed toward the kitchens.

Leaving the chapel after Marco's announcement, Vango followed Pippo Troisi toward the hutches.

Troisi was complaining about his lot.

In Zefiro's absence, he had been made responsible for the rabbits. This was too much of a cross to bear. He had always loathed them, and now he had to look after twenty-four wild rabbits. He was visibly losing weight. He even had nightmares about it. He was like an asthmatic who had been parachuted into a henhouse.

"Wretched rodents," he moaned, opening the first cage. "Now look—even more of them have been born! Why didn't they entrust me with the hives instead? I'm not afraid of bees!"

Vango helped him take out the newborn bunnies and put them all onto the grass.

Two young rabbits tried to slide down Pippo's trouser legs.

"It looks like they're very fond of you!" Vango smiled.

Pippo growled something incomprehensible as he tried to unfasten the rabbit's grip on his thigh.

Vango was right. This was true love.

The rabbits always sensed Pippo coming from a long way off. They threw themselves at him as soon as he got there. Large bucks could be seen fighting over who got to greet him first. Violent duels had taken place. The rabbits clustered around him. The little ones mistook him for their mothers and rubbed themselves passionately against his ankles.

His kicks had no effect. They loved him!

The two men closed the caging again. They headed down in search of the buckets of water that were leaning against a stone.

Pippo started washing his hands.

Vango was watching him. He sensed the time had come.

"Pippo, weren't you there the day I was found on Scario beach, in Malfa, when I was three?" he asked, trying to sound as offhand as possible.

Pippo drew himself up to his full height.

"It's not just that I was there, little one: I was the one who found you."

He thrust his chin boastfully and wiped his hands on his sleeves. He wasn't thinking about the rabbits anymore.

"Yes, me, Pippo Troisi!" he declared, beating his chest. "The first person I found was your nanny. I alerted the others. And we got you out from the rocks a bit later."

Vango nodded. Ever since his return to Arkudah, he'd been wanting to question Pippo Troisi.

He needed to find out more before going back to Mademoiselle.

"I never did find out where you appeared from," Pippo added softly. "But since we've been here, I've got this feeling you came to me from above: before I even knew how to say Arkudah! I swear that's all I know."

"Didn't anything happen on the island just before or after?" asked Vango, refusing to give up. "You didn't notice anything?"

"Nothing."

"Try to remember, please."

"What kind of thing do you have in mind?"

"Something, I don't know . . ."

"But what?'

"A change . . . an accident . . ."

"An invasion of rabbits?" joked Pippo.

"I was wondering . . ."

"Nothing, I'm telling you. I don't know anything. Do you understand?"

His tone was too curt to be honest. They returned to the enclosure.

Pippo got back to work, emptying one of the buckets of water in order to sluice down a rabbit hutch.

"Back then, nothing ever happened in my life," he added, by way of an apology.

He gave the bunny rabbits back to their mother. Pippo insulted one poor animal that was licking his fingers, and another that wanted to be left in his pocket. In a corner, he piled up the peelings that had come from the kitchen. When it was time to leave, Pippo froze and said, as if for his own benefit, "One thing, perhaps. I think it was the same autumn that Bartolomeo died."

"Sorry?"

"When you arrived . . ."

"Who died?"

"Bartolomeo. He was a lad with a very pretty wife and three little girls in Santa Maria. He died from a gunshot wound at home. My wife used to have a thing or two to say about that."

The exact phrase escaped him. He made the sign of the cross as if he were talking about Beelzebub himself. He became very superstitious whenever he mentioned his wife.

"What did she say?"

"She said things."

He made the sign again.

"She had something to say about everybody."

Pippo headed off toward the monastery.

"But about Bartolomeo, what did she have to say about him?"

"She said that he'd played a dirty trick."

He was reluctant to dig up his wife's old gossip. It might bring bad luck.

"Tell me about it."

Pippo sighed.

"A dirty trick with a gang. She maintained that one of his accomplices attacked him to steal his share."

Vango shaded his eyes with his hand so that he could see his friend against the sun.

"A gang?"

"Yes, a gang. Three fellows. I'm not sure about their names now. They wanted to emigrate but didn't have the means to. Perhaps they staged a holdup in a grocer's shop on the mainland. It wasn't a fortune, in any case. . . ."

"Did they leave the island?"

"Bartolomeo died, poor man. But at least one of them set off for America, before the others could so much as say Arkudah! I don't know what he was called. And the last one stayed, that tall one you know."

"Who?"

"The one who's like an animal, tall, you know who I mean. . . ."

"Who?"

"The big fellow who gave up his house."

"Who?" insisted Vango, unable to believe his ears.

"The big chap with the donkey."

"Mazzetta?"

"Yes, that's it, Mazzetta."

Vango stopped. Pippo Troisi was watching him.

"I need your gun" was all that Vango could say.

27

REVENGE

The crater of Pollara, Salina, the next night

Vango was hiding in a scrubby bush with the gun pressed tightly to his chest. Mazzetta's lair was fifty meters away. Not even the donkey had noticed him approaching. It was a dark night. No clouds, no wind, no moon.

Time had come to a standstill on this last night of summer.

Vango didn't want to pay Mademoiselle a visit beforehand, just to hear her confirming what Pippo Troisi had already told him. He would see her later on.

She had known everything from the very beginning. She had never revealed a single name. She wasn't responsible for what he was about to do.

This was his story. His revenge.

He had been taught to show the left cheek if the right one was hit. But this wasn't a case of a slapped cheek. Two innocent hearts had been riddled with bullets.

This was a matter of life and death. It boiled down to the law of mechanics: *To every action there is an equal and opposite reaction.* Vango believed that by acting in this way, he would breathe life back into his parents.

Afterward, his final task would be to track down the last remaining guilty man.

But for now it was all about Mazzetta. The man who had been present in Vango's most distant childhood memories.

That silhouette on the crater, that shadow in his den, that cold lava creature who lived a few paces from their home. Never a word exchanged in all those years. But Vango knew that Mazzetta had watched over them every day of their life in Pollara.

Each new moon, the small silver coin they lived off appearing on their doorstep—that was him. The vine arbor miraculously re-erected after the storm—that was him. The scorpion killed ten centimeters from Vango's face when he was five years old and having a siesta under a prickly-pear tree—that was him. The only vines on the island not to fall prey to disease—that was him. Even the straw in Mademoiselle's hat that always came back as good as new when she left it outside of an evening. Mazzetta never owned up to these acts. The coin, the scorpion, the vine arbor, the rejuvenated hat, and everything else. Guardian angels leave no traces.

But Vango had always recognized Mazzetta's shadow.

And, in three minutes, he would stand before him with his gun.

Crouched down, Vango made his way over to the stone wall blocking off the cave where Mazzetta had lived for nearly twenty years. A lamp was on. The old man must have led his donkey inside, just like he did in winter.

"Come out, Mazzetta."

Vango didn't want to take him by surprise.

"It's me, Vango. Come out, Mazzetta!"

He heard something move in the shadows.

"I know you're there. Come out. I know about everything else as well. It's time to show yourself."

Several minutes went by.

There was still some low-level noise in the cave. Scratching sounds on the floor, and sighs.

"I know what you did, Mazzetta!"

Vango decided to go in. He made it as far as the entrance, bent down, and peered into the gloom.

The first thing he saw was the donkey's carcass on the floor. Its huge leather collar was blackened with blood. Then he saw Mazzetta with his arms outspread and his head on the beast's rump. The old man was writhing about in the final throes of death. Vango threw himself down onto the floor next to him.

"Ma'az . . ." The dying man was trying to stammer something for Vango's benefit.

"She . . . Ma'az . . . elle . . ."

Vango put his ear closer to the dying man.

"Ma'azelle."

He rushed outside with his gun.

Mademoiselle.

He ran toward the house.

Thorns were tearing at his legs. But he didn't feel a thing.

Vango approached from the west side, where there were two windows. The first gave onto the main living area. Without hesitating for a second, he loaded his gun and jumped headfirst through the glass pane. Inside, he rolled onto the blue floor, instantly got up again, and turned full circle, still pointing his gun.

The silence and emptiness were dreadful.

A night-light was about to go out near to the fire. That cup she always used, on the table, had been smashed to pieces, and all that was left was a tiny heap of snow.

Vango rushed into the bedroom. Nothing.

"Mademoiselle!" he called out.

He went outside onto the terrace, where everything was pitch-black.

"Mademoiselle!"

His voice came echoing back to him, all the way from the bottom of the crater. He quickly searched the neighboring deserted house, behind the olive tree, before setting off running again in the direction of Mazzetta, who was still breathing.

Vango put the gun to the dying man's forehead.

"Where is she?"

"Or . . . men . . ."

Mazzetta moved his hand and tucked his thumb into his palm to indicate the number four.

"Four?" asked Vango. "Four men?"

Mazzetta's eyes answered yes with all their might.

"Did they kill her?"

"No."

"Carry her off?"

Mazzetta's eyes acquiesced, and then his whole body was wracked by a convulsion. He was suffocating. He stretched out his arm to hold on to the donkey's collar. Vango released the old man's grip from the leather yoke.

"Where? Where did they take her?"

This time, Mazzetta could only move his lips. Vango pulled

his gun away and put his ear to the fading man's mouth. He made him repeat it three times.

My donkey. He had definitely said, "My donkey."

A second later, Mazzetta died on Vango's knees, and the boy began to weep.

A few hours earlier, while it was still light, Brother John Mulligan, who was about to remove his skullcap as Cardinal of the South, had seen the speedboat going past in the opposite direction. But this time, through his telescope, he could make out a woman standing at the stern, who kept turning to face Salina. From observing the woman's face with her white hair stuck to it, and the weapons pointed at her, it was clear to Mulligan that something was afoot.

Before the night was over, Vango had dug two deep holes at the top of the cliff.

He buried Mazzetta in the first and the donkey in the second.

He couldn't manage to undo the donkey's collar, so he buried it with him.

He made two crosses on the ground with wild fennel flowers.

Vango lingered on the cliff top, in front of the mounds of fresh earth. He knew that Mazzetta had died defending Mademoiselle.

But this didn't assuage the hatred raging inside Vango.

What he did feel, however, was an instinctive sense of respect before these two corpses, the strange respect that

VANGO

all civilizations show toward human beings once they have stopped breathing.

In the old days, in the Carmelite seminary, Father Jean used to remark to Vango how, in the history of humanity, if a land had existed, a single one, where the living were afforded the same respect as the dead, it would have been sweet to live in such a place!

At dawn, Vango passed by Mademoiselle's house again.

Helped by the early light, he searched the premises for traces of the kidnappers. He couldn't find any. Higher up, in Mazzetta's lair, even the bullets that had killed the donkey and his master had vanished. It was a perfect job.

Vango closed up the house as if its owners were going away on vacation. The lock was a bit stiff. They'd never had any need of it. He hid the key in the hollow of the olive tree and thrust his hand into the foliage to feel how firm the olives were.

Suddenly, down on the ground against the roots, he caught sight of the little ball of blue silk. He picked it up. And the handkerchief of his childhood spread out between his fingers. The blue handkerchief that knew everything but said nothing, while hinting at tales of inscrutable kingdoms.

Vango noticed the star. It had been embroidered just above the sloping bar of the capital *V*. But it hadn't been there the day before. The handiwork looked unfinished. The fifth point of the star hadn't been completed. The saffron-colored thread was still hanging loose.

Mademoiselle had wanted to embroider the memory of Vango's mother, Stella, in that silk.

She had been interrupted by the men arriving. The handkerchief had fallen to the ground, between the snaking roots.

Vango climbed the winding path and crossed over to the other side of the crater, where he was surrounded by Malfa's oldest vines. He could see the black smoke of Stromboli on the horizon, as well as the island of Panarea, the outline of Filicudi and, even farther off, the top of a huge stone that marked the invisible presence of his monastery. He wasn't ready to return there yet.

He reached the port at the hour when the fishermen return. He slipped through outstretched nets, onlookers, and sailors. He made straight for a small, rusty, corrugated-iron hut.

Vango knocked on a sheet of metal as if he were knocking at the door of a cottage.

A woman in rags was busy crushing an eggshell.

"It thickens up the grub, gives me something to chew on," she said. "And that's a start. It means you've got something between the teeth."

"Are you Signora Giuseppina?"

"Signora Pippo Troisi," she corrected him.

"I knew your husband a long time ago. He was a good man."

"Yes," she replied with great tenderness, before asking, "And do I know you?"

"No," Vango answered hastily, because he didn't want her to remember. "I've just got here and I'm leaving with the next boat."

"In four minutes!" declared Giuseppina, who knew the timetables of all the boats that might bring her love back to her by heart.

When Vango greeted this information with silence, she updated it: "In three minutes and forty-five seconds."

Around her neck she wore the handsome watch the doctor had given her.

"I want to talk to you about a very old story," said Vango.

"You've landed on the right person."

"Why?"

"I only like old stories."

"Do you remember the beginning of the autumn of 1918?"

"Yes. There were a few big storms."

"A man was killed back then."

"Bartolomeo Viaggi, twenty-nine years old. Three daughters. Only one of them's still with us. And his wife died too, very soon afterward."

"That's sad."

"Yes. It's sad when people leave."

"People say you know something about Bartolomeo."

"Who? Who told you that?"

Giuseppina's eyes shone. She had never spoken about this to a single person.

"I want to know who killed him," said Vango.

"Who told you about this?"

"Answer my question, please."

She was staring at Vango very attentively.

"I can tell you about Bartolomeo. It wasn't Mazzetta who killed him, even if he was involved in the business. It was the other one, the third one."

"His name?"

"Who told you about me? I recognize you. I . . ."

"Tell me the name of the third man."

"His name was Cafarello, Giovanni Cafarello. He left for America, for New York. He abandoned his father up there between the mountains. A father who died alone last spring, at the age of a hundred."

Giovanni Cafarello. That name was now etched in Vango's mind forever.

He looked at the woman leaning toward him. He thanked her.

"Don't go," she said. "Tell me who you are. Tell me you saw Pippo Troisi not long ago."

Vango moved off. The boat was there. The crowd was squeezed along the dockside. Giuseppina had knelt down on the ground, like a woman from the deserts in front of her tent.

"Please," she begged him. "Tell me. Is Pippo alive? I recognize you now. I know who you are. Vango!"

Vango stopped. He went back over to her and said softly, "He's alive."

There were tears of genuine joy on her cheeks.

Vango jumped into the boat.

A man helped the woman stand up again.

"Lean on me, Pina. Calm down. . . ."

He had just stepped off the same boat, having sailed from the island of Lipari.

He was smiling.

It was Monday. What bliss. The best day of the week. He had dressed up with his red tie. He was dancing.

Dr. Basilio was going to have lunch with Mademoiselle.

"Tell me . . . Is something wrong, Pina?"

"Pippo is alive," she whispered.

The doctor smiled. This woman, Pina Troisi, was the only person he truly understood. Both of them had chosen an inaccessible love. She loved someone who had disappeared. He loved someone who was a mystery.

"Who told you that your husband is alive?"

"Vango, the wild boy of Pollara."

"Where is he?" asked the doctor, suddenly standing up straight.

"He's leaving."

The good doctor Basilio ran across the black stone jetty. But the boat was already some distance from the dock. He saw Vango. And Vango spotted him.

Neither of them waved.

A little later, the doctor discovered the locked door at Mademoiselle's house.

Hope had flown away.

28

THE HORSE THIEF

Everland, Scotland, October 1935

The small plane flew by a second time, close to the tower. But this time, the pilot had a clear view of the man running toward the stables. A woman was chasing him. She was wearing a white nightshirt hitched up to her thighs.

"Tell me I'm dreaming," muttered the pilot.

But he wasn't dreaming. It was Mary the housekeeper, down below.

Paul increased the altitude and began a wider loop to make it look as if he was heading off.

The plane was a Sirius, the single-engine aircraft with which Lindbergh had broken records over the Pacific. Paul owned one of only fifteen models in existence.

Slowing down, he headed toward the waters of Loch Ness. He could see the edge of a forest already turning an autumnal yellow, as well as some remote sheepfolds in the hills.

Paul was both amused and perplexed.

"Mary! Mary!" He kept saying her name over and over again, his eyes as wide as saucers.

There were various explanations competing in his mind for the scene he had just stumbled on. He started to fantasize about a double, a triple, and even a quadruple life for Mary, who, for all that she looked like an elderly spinster straight out of a storybook, was perhaps the most brazen woman in the Highlands.

Mary had started working at the castle when Paul was born, twenty-six years earlier. He was finding it hard to imagine that she had hidden her libertine lifestyle for so long behind her blushing cheeks, behind her maternal tenderness and her thick woolen stockings.

"No . . . it's just not possible."

He swerved sharply, putting the wing of his little seaplane into the vertical position. He was heading for the castle once more. It only took him a few seconds to fly over fields crisscrossed with low stone walls and arrive above the main driveway.

Mary was now alone in front of the stables. Her arms were spread wide, and she was signaling crazily at the plane.

Just before he rose up to fly over the castle's black roof, Paul saw the stable door burst open and a black horse gallop out of it. Its rider hadn't taken the time to saddle it up. He was riding bareback, holding on to the halter strap and kicking his mount vigorously in the flanks.

The aviator and the horseman passed each other.

A few meters farther off, as he turned around, Paul saw the rider jumping over a first wall.

This man was unlikely to be one of Mary's lovers. And, most pressingly, he had just stolen a horse.

Paul nosed his plane up over the castle. He had decided to give chase.

Overcome with admiration, Mary fell to her knees, which were somewhere in the midst of the folds of her nightshirt, and gazed on at her hero's derring-do.

He began by climbing vertically, high in the sky. All that was visible was a black dot surrounded by smoke. The roar of the engine became inaudible. Continuing with his loop, Paul let his machine rest on its back before putting on a burst of speed as it headed for the ground, tracing a perfect circle. The plane slowly corrected its position as it approached land.

Mary held her breath. She was pretending to shield her eyes as she shrieked in fright, but in fact she was spying proudly on the virtuoso skills of the young fighter pilot.

The plane completed its looping when it was level with the heather, which it sheared in a purple haze. It was now very close to the ground and heading directly for the horse-man, who was in turn galloping toward the plane. Neither of them deviated at all.

At the last moment, Paul put his foot down on the accelerator, and the horse passed between the plane's two floats.

Confronted by the castle for a second time, Paul realized there was no sense in what was he was doing.

He had no intention of sacrificing a horse he loved, or of decapitating a man he knew nothing about, still less of landing his seaplane on the ground when the only surface it tolerated was water.

And so Paul had to concede that his aim had been to dazzle a seventy-year-old woman who was sitting in the grass, waving admiringly up at him and the sky.

Aside from his elusive sister, Ethel, who was so often absent, Mary was the only person he had left to impress. Even on the day when he had become the youngest wing commander in the Royal Air Force, Paul had dined alone in his big castle.

The horseman disappeared into the forest.

The plane performed a final circuit to impress the public.

When he landed on the loch, a small boat came to meet him. Mary was in the bow.

Her comfortable arms hugged Paul. She wasn't wearing her nightshirt anymore. She was wearing what she called her Sunday best, which consisted of the black outfit and apron she had donned every day since her thirtieth birthday, almost half a century ago. But, as a special treat, she was also wearing a sort of white choker that gave her a special Sunday look, according to the reflection in her tiny bedroom mirror.

"You were magnificent. I was scared stiff."

You'd have thought she was talking to a trapeze artist after a night out at the circus. She kissed him.

"Bravo . . . bravo . . ."

"Tell me," said Paul.

Suddenly, she recalled her own adventures.

"Oh, it's dreadful," she said.

"Tell me all about it."

"I came in search of you instead of Peter. We're very wary now. He's busy mounting guard with his son."

It was difficult to find anybody on the property on a Sunday. Paul insisted that everybody take the day off. The staff played at hide-and-seek in the castle in order not to show their faces. And Mary enjoyed sleeping late.

"Well? Who was he?" Paul still wanted to know.

"He got in through the window when I was up on the second-floor landing. If you only knew what a fright it gave me. I was hardly wearing a stitch. I mean, I was just about to go to the——"

"But what did he want?" interrupted Paul, who wasn't eager to hear about Mary's calls of nature in any more detail.

She leaned toward him and whispered in his ear, "He's a common thief."

She was speaking in hushed tones in the middle of the lake, as if the old carp or even the Loch Ness monster might overhear her secrets.

"So tell me what he stole. . . ."

She glanced to the left, then to the right, then took a deep breath before whispering even more quietly, "Nothing."

Things were calm that night. Paul had gone on the prowl in the forest at dusk. He had found the hoofprints, but they disappeared into the bushes.

The next morning, just as everyone was getting up, there was the black horse, grazing on the castle's lawn.

"Look," Mary urged, opening Paul's curtains.

So the horse thief hadn't even stolen the horse.

Mary felt rather deflated.

"But what if it's a fake?" she suggested.

"The thief?" inquired Paul, stretching his arms in front of the large window.

"No, the horse."

"The horse?"

"Yes. It could be a fake."

Paul scratched his head.

"A fake horse?"

"If he swapped your horse for another one."

"Why?"

"To steal yours."

Paul peered out the window. He was trying to keep a straight face.

"Well, it's a very good job. For a fake."

All day, Mary kept an eye on the animal that was tethered near the steps. She even kept guard for the night shift. She was convinced it was the Trojan horse and that it would open up in the middle of the night to release the intruder.

The suspense was dreadful. But the next day, she had to admit that all the horse had off-loaded was one or two shovel-fuls of fresh manure.

The story had almost been forgotten by the following week, when Paul caught the thief.

"That's him," declared Mary in a state of great excitement.

Paul had discovered him snooping around in the castle cellars. He was a very young man who barely spoke any English. Paul took him up to the dining room, where he locked them both in.

A dozen people passed by the door that morning, curious to see in what state Master Paul was going to hand over the thief who hadn't stolen anything.

Mary already felt sorry for the young man.

"I do hope Paul won't be too hard on him. The child's a vagabond. He didn't know what he was doing. And Paul's become very strict, now that he's an officer."

But she was almost vexed when the master of the castle came out alone, clearing a path through the little crowd gathered on the landing to say to Mary, "Give him some work clothes. We'll keep him on to look after the horses."

"But . . . Paul . . ."

"And feed him, Mary. He's been sleeping rough in the woods for weeks."

Paul headed off.

Mary soon found herself face-to-face with the thief. The crowd had dispersed.

"What's your name?" she asked fiercely.

His answer comprised two syllables, which she translated into a good Scottish name that was more familiar to her ears.

"Andrew. Good. Well come on then, Andrew. And watch your step."

She stopped to feel the young man's shoulders.

"There's not a lot of you. Some of Paul's old clothes should fit you, but I'll need to take up the sleeves. Take those shoes off for me. You're making my wooden floors mucky."

The boy was quick to obey her. She took his muddy shoes without making a disgusted face, like the washerwomen who spend their whole lives dealing with the grime of others. She was less bothered about clean hands than she was about maintaining a glistening waxed parquet floor.

They walked down an endless corridor, the young man padding behind her in his socks.

"Where do you come from?"

"From the East."

She looked out the window in an easterly direction. He must have come from Nethy Bridge or Grantown, over that way. She felt sorry for anyone who had grown up beyond the grounds of the estate.

"Ah, from the east."

"Yes, the East," the boy repeated.

"And do they like roast beef over that way?"

A delicious smell was assailing their nostrils. Mary pushed open the kitchen door.

When someone had sad eyes and dirty shoes, it didn't take long to win her over.

Ethel turned up two weeks later, in the middle of the night.

Her headlights slowly swept over the driveway leading up to the sleeping castle. An owl was flying low ahead of her.

Since her trip to Paris back in the summer, she had spent only a few days at Everland. Paul had given up remonstrating with her about how often she was away. The time they spent together was too short; they had to make the most of every second.

She parked in the garage, next to the stable. She had driven very slowly so as not to make any noise.

The car came to a halt.

At the back of the garage, in the glare of the headlights, Ethel had seen someone.

The young man was shading his eyes. He had come down from the manger that doubled as his bed. What was referred to as the garage was in fact part of the old stables, converted at the beginning of the century to accommodate cars.

Ethel switched off the engine but kept the headlights on. She opened the door.

"Good evening," she said.

"Good evening."

"What are you doing here?"

"My name is Andrew. I look after the horses."

Andrei had ventured the only two sentences he could manage without an accent.

"You're Russian."

"Yes. From Moscow."

He was covering his eyes with his forearm now. He was as dazzled as a rabbit in the headlights.

"Lift your arm, so I can see you."

He did as he was told.

"Did Paul ask you to look after the cars?"

"No. The horses."

Andrei hadn't yet been able to glimpse the young woman's face, but he could tell it was her.

Ethel. He had been expecting her for a month.

"If you're looking after the horses, why are your hands in that state?"

He looked at his fingers, which were covered in grease. She switched off the headlamps.

He didn't answer.

She took a few steps over the flagstones and turned on an electric bulb that hung over a workbench.

At last, he could see her.

She was wearing a navy-blue suit with white stripes, a short jacket, trousers that were too big for her, and, tucked under one arm, she was carrying a leather-lined gabardine bag.

Her hair was tied back. She looked very tired.

Ethel had driven for twelve hours from London, having spent the last three nights in places where people were more interested in dancing than sleeping.

She was watching Andrei with her eyes half closed

while keeping her finger on the timer switch that operated the light.

"Well? Why are your fingers in that state?"

Andrei was alarmed. This girl saw everything.

She suspected something. He was sure of that.

"I enjoy mechanics," he said.

"Why did he hire you?"

"I stole a horse."

Mary had made him repeat this sentence as well, like a primary-school teacher making a child write out his mistake again and again. I stole a horse. I stole a horse. Andrew stole a horse.

"Do you think that's a good reason?" demanded Ethel.

He didn't know what to say. She went over to a bulky shape that was covered in a black cloth. Andrei was trembling, but this didn't show in Paul's clothes, which were too big on him and had been patched up by Mary.

Ethel tugged at the black shroud like a magician revealing what lay beneath.

"I hope you're not messing around with my father's car."

"I enjoy mechanics," Andrei repeated.

The car that had belonged to Ethel's father was a white Silver Ghost Rolls-Royce, dated 1907. The best-looking automobile in the world. This particular car had been gathering dust for the last ten years. And Andrei had spent his nights restoring it to as good as new. He had cleaned each piece of the engine. It started up on the first try now.

"Who asked you to do that?"

"No one."

"Does it work?"

"Yes."

Andrei took a step toward the vehicle. He wanted to show off his handiwork. He had done everything with this aim in mind. Mary had told him how attached Ethel was to the car. So Andrei had set to work.

As instructed by Boris Petrovitch, he was keeping an eye on Everland, in the hope that one day Vango would pay a visit.

To succeed in his mission, he needed to win Ethel's confidence. Andrei put his hand on the hood of the car.

"Stop!" Ethel shouted. "Take your hand away from there."

Her eyes were half shut. There was a lump in her throat.

"I'm warning you. If you so much as touch that car again, I'll throw you out!"

Ethel went into Paul's bedroom and revived the fire by putting a log on it. He was asleep.

She sat in an armchair.

One day, she would no longer have the right to open the door to this bedroom in the middle of the night. She knew that. In fact, she was almost impatient for the day. Paul would have his own family. Doors would have to be knocked on, private apartments would be designated in the castle, the rules of the game would be rewritten.

At last something would change around here.

Ethel stretched her legs close to the flames.

For the two of them, the world had frozen on the day when their parents had died.

There were people growing old around them, but they wouldn't let anything or anyone else in. A dark shroud had been placed over their world, just as it had over the Silver Ghost Rolls-Royce. And no one had the right to touch it.

Nothing had moved on. Paul's airplane was a copy of the miniature one he used to play with as a child. And little Ethel had already learned how to drive, all that time ago, on her father's knees.

There was nothing new on earth.

A single meteor had punctuated this long period, as far as Ethel was concerned. And that was Vango. She loved him. She loved him with all her heart.

When she stayed in smoky cafés until daylight, when the faces, the music, the fast life made her feel intoxicated, she knew she was running away from something that was missing.

It had all happened too quickly for her to catch him, for the world around her to warm up for good.

Paul found Ethel asleep in the armchair when he woke up. Delicately, he lifted her feet and put them on a footstool.

Soon she opened her eyes.

He smiled at her. He had put on some music in the little study next door.

"I didn't want to wake you," he said.

"Me neither."

She stroked his forehead.

"I saw your aviator friends in London."

"They're very lucky to see you so often, Ethel."

"They've been wondering what you're up to."

"Nothing, as you can see. I don't do anything. And you?"

"I'm trying to live."

"You look sad, Ethel. Are you thinking about him?"

"Who?"

They were silent for a while, and then she said, "Your aviator friends say you don't like partying."

The music stopped. He shrugged.

"Each to his own party," said Paul.

He got up to turn over the record in the study.

Flying with wild ducks, steering his plane under the natural arch formations in the cliffs near to Duncansby Head lighthouse, crossing deep rivers on horseback. These were all parties in his eyes.

He could hear Ethel's voice coming from the bedroom: "Who's the Russian looking after the horses?"

"A vagabond," he replied, coming back out of the study.

"A vagabond?"

"A vagabond who was looking for work."

"Don't you find it surprising that a Russian vagabond would stray this far?"

They started laughing.

"Here you go again. Perhaps he's a spy! A seventeen-year-old spy come in from the cold to watch over two orphans."

Ethel had been harboring these kinds of suspicions for a month now. She claimed that someone had searched her hotel bedroom at night while she was out, in Edinburgh. All she needed to do was be in her room at night, her brother had retorted.

"You see people who don't exist, Ethel, and you can't even see the ones who are here. Take Tom Cameron, who's always circling around you!"

"He should stop circling," she whispered, "because he's getting dizzy."

Sure enough, the most recent visits from the Camerons had resulted in some surreal scenes. Tom's parents had arrived in a fever pitch of excitement. They always looked dressed up. And they sounded muddled as they waffled on about "what we're not supposed to know" and "having to feign ignorance." The more the parents spun out of control, the more their son turned green, shrank from sight, and hid behind his hat.

Most of the time, Ethel wasn't there. Paul had to handle the situation alone. When they arrived for an impromptu visit, John the butler had gotten into the habit of announcing, loudly and clearly, "The asylum opposite!"

They would troop in.

Each time, Paul found a good explanation for his sister's whereabouts. And Lady Cameron always answered with "Yes, yes, of course! Let her make the most of it while she can!" Which is what you might say about a hen that's still prancing around when it's got a date with the saucepan. Beth Cameron took the paintings off the walls to examine the signatures closely; she counted the crystal chandeliers and weighed the silverware.

Ethel stretched in her armchair in front of the fire.

"Are you honestly saying you don't have anything to tell me about Tom?" asked Paul, taking his sister's hand. "You haven't spoken?"

Ethel smiled.

"No. I promise."

"Well, in that case, I think there must be a misunderstanding. Poor Tom!"

"Don't worry about him."

There was a knock at the door.

Mary brought in a pot of tea. Ethel got up to give her a kiss and then wanted to dance a waltz with the housekeeper. Paul opened the study doors wide so they could all hear the music from the gramophone.

John, the venerable butler, entered and viewed the scene with some consternation.

Mary hadn't even had time to put her tray down. She was spinning around the room, letting out little squeals of delight. Ethel wouldn't let go of her. They were twirling around together. Paul caught the first cup as it flew through the air, then a second, then the teapot. John caught Ethel's shoes.

The sugar bowl ended up in the fireplace, and a smell of caramel wafted through the room.

The music was making everyone feel giddy.

Ethel eventually let go of Mary.

"You're all mad," the housekeeper sighed ecstatically as she fell into Paul's arms.

MADAME VICTORIA

Somewhere in France, a month later,
November 1935

A ribbon of white steam was winding its way through the gorges between the mountains. The train was hurtling through black pine forests, straddling streams and escarpments of scree.

Voloy Viktor was squinting through the narrowest of openings at the landscape as it flashed past him.

There were five armored train cars. It was impossible to tell which one held the prisoner.

Troops occupied the rest of the train.

Identical trains had left Paris a few minutes apart, with the same number of soldiers on board, but without the prisoner.

The mastermind behind this operation was Superintendent Boulard.

The prisoner would arrive at one of the three fortresses that had been made ready for him. One in the Alps, high up on a mountainside; one off the Île de Ré, on the Atlantic coast by La Rochelle; and the last one in the marshes of central France. Only Boulard knew which one had been chosen at the last moment.

The plan was to rule out any possibility of escape.

Voloy Viktor was breathing in the fresh mountain air. He approved of cold air. It was a fine day, and Viktor hardly noticed the numbness in his limbs.

His hands were bound together on a cast-iron block, and his feet were soldered into the floor of his cage. This cage, with its heavy bars, had been placed inside one of the armored cars borrowed from the Bank of France. The train had been built to withstand attack from a tank or an air fleet.

Boulard was standing on the platform of La Rochelle Station, accompanied by his faithful Avignon, two penitentiary divisions, and a blacksmith, who would cut Viktor out.

The station was surrounded by military troops.

So far so good. Boulard kept his hands in his coat pockets. He was wearing a dapper new hat from Mossant's.

The train was due to arrive in a few minutes. It had been reported at a level crossing outside Marans.

"Have you received any news about the other two?" asked an anxious Avignon.

Boulard gestured toward the stationmaster, passing the question on to him.

"Yes," came the reply. "And there's nothing to report. The trains are due to arrive into their respective stations at exactly the same time. Their speeds were calculated with this in mind."

Boulard gave a satisfied smile.

He had been organizing this day for some time. He owed this much at least to Zefiro. He had sworn to put Voloy Viktor in prison for the rest of his days. It was the only way of reducing the threat to the padre and his monks.

The whistle of an incoming train could be heard. Boulard's eyes lit up.

"Here it comes," announced Avignon.

The locomotive pulled smoothly into the station. The five cars were lined up alongside the platform, which was briefly empty. Foot soldiers immediately surrounded them.

"Time to play the guessing game," joked Boulard. "Car four!"

The small army moved toward the rear of the train. Avignon was sweating.

"Here it is," he called out.

"Open up for me!" shouted Boulard.

Two men emerged from the ranks with a set of keys. They opened several locks. Boulard gave them a five-letter code to release the final padlock, before declaring, "You can go in now, Avignon."

The blacksmith was getting his blowtorch ready.

Avignon pushed open the sliding door with the help of three guards. He glanced feverishly at Boulard.

"In you go," coaxed the superintendent.

Avignon disappeared inside. A cry was heard. Then he reappeared at the door.

"There's nobody in here!"

"Search the whole train, you bunch of idiots!" boomed Boulard.

They searched the four remaining cars. All they found were the soldiers who had been posted there.

Avignon walked back toward Boulard, his knees gone weak.

"He's not here."

Boulard glanced up at the station clock.

"Well, he should have arrived by now."

The superintendent put his hand on Avignon's shoulder.

"My dear fellow, you didn't really think I was going to wait with my welcoming committee at the appointed station? What do you take me for? Call Lieutenant Rémi, at Bourges Station."

Avignon rushed away to make the phone call.

"Excuse me, sir . . ."

Someone was hovering shyly around the superintendent, who was busy trying to prize open a tin of candy.

"Superintendent, sir . . ."

"Yes," said Boulard.

It was the blacksmith. He suddenly felt redundant.

"Can I go now?"

"What do you think?"

The poor man had no idea what he was supposed to say.

"Ah . . . can I?"

"Unless you care to redo my fillings for me?" roared Boulard.

The stationmaster signaled discreetly that yes, the blacksmith could leave.

Lieutenant Avignon swiftly reappeared, looking just as pale and washed out as he had earlier.

"No, Superintendent, he's not over there either. There's nobody in the train that's arrived at Bourges."

Boulard played at being astonished.

"What a surprise! Is that so? He's not at Bourges, you say?"

Then he adopted the pose of a tragic actress, exclaiming, "Well, in that case I'm done for!"

He pierced his heart with an imaginary dagger, before checking the station clock again.

"Call Chambéry."

Avignon set off for the second time, his tongue hanging out. The small army was staring at the superintendent in bewilderment.

This time, Boulard wasn't quite so relaxed. He sucked nervously on a candy.

He knew that nothing was in the bag yet, and he already regretted his little theatrical performance. Voloy Viktor was a subject for neither farce nor tragedy. He was a lunatic who could inveigle his way in anywhere, like those large flies that are found alive in the tombs of the pharaohs, despite the monuments' having been sealed up for three thousand years.

The engine had stopped spitting out steam.

Avignon still wasn't back.

The station was perfectly silent.

To pass the time, Boulard tried to set his watch by the station clock. The winder came off in his hand.

"Go and get him for me," he finally bellowed.

They located Avignon in the station office, where he had passed out in a cold faint.

Someone was trying to revive him by fanning him with a railroad timetable.

"Out of the way!" the superintendent ordered before sitting down next to Avignon and slapping him twice.

"Lieutenant!"

"Sugar, I think he needs sugar," proffered the manageress of the station's café, bringing over a bottle of fruit cordial.

"Thank you, Madame," Boulard accepted politely.

"Would you like a straw?"

"Thank you, no."

Boulard raised the bottle high and emptied the entire contents over Avignon's face.

The lieutenant finally opened his eyes.

"Hasn't the train reached Chambéry?" demanded his boss.

"Yes, of course. The train arrived bang on time."

"Well?"

"Viktor isn't in the Chambéry train."

Voloy Viktor was listening to all the noise outside. He couldn't work out where he was exactly. The train had stopped. His narrow window offered a view of a yellow wall. A bit of a kerfuffle could be heard, a few cries outside the car. A dog was barking.

He was thinking about Zefiro. He had always been suspicious of the monk's death.

"Died of natural causes"—that's what he'd been told. He didn't like natural deaths. He didn't believe in them.

Deaths by natural causes were an aberration for arms dealers, and Voloy Viktor was never taken in by them. For him to feel well, Viktor needed to hear the sound of weapons and see the lifeless bodies in front of him.

The dog started barking again, a bit closer this time.

"I insist that you tell me which train he boarded!"

Boulard was about to have an apoplectic fit. He was on the line to Paris.

"I don't know," came the voice on the other end. "I've got absolutely no idea. Your trains all look the same to me!"

"Now, look here! Did he board the first train? The one that went to Bourges?"

"The first train?" the man repeated. "Let me just ask my colleague. . . . No. He wasn't in the first one."

"Well, was he in the second, then? The one that was going to La Rochelle?"

"Hold on."

The man in Paris could be heard talking to someone again. The phone line was so bad that he sounded like a chirruping cricket.

"Well?" Boulard snapped after several seconds. "Was he in the second train?"

"The second?"

"Yes, you heap of dehydrated remains!" the superintendent erupted. "In the second! I asked about the second. Two! Two! Two!"

"Oh, no, certainly not, not in the second."

"Well, then he must have been in the third!" shouted an exasperated Boulard. "Can you confirm for me that he boarded the train bound for Chambéry?"

"Sorry?"

"In the third! Three! Three! Two plus one!"

"No, Chambéry, the third train was for Chambéry!"

"Yes," groaned Boulard. "The third going to Chambéry."

"In the third? Let me just ask my colleague. . . ."

"Pass him over, that colleague of yours, you pile of toenail clippings! Pass him over or I'll have you sent to a penal colony for the rest of your days."

"Hello?"

"Hello? Are you the colleague of Toenail Clippings?"

"No, it's still me."

Boulard nearly hanged himself with the telephone cable.

Lieutenant Avignon gently took the receiver out of his hands.

"We would simply like to know whether he was put on the third train," he stated as calmly as possible.

Boulard was watching him like a snarling dog ready to bite.

"You are joking?" said Avignon after listening for a short while. "Are you . . . Are you quite sure about that? Right. We'll call you back."

He hung up and turned to face Boulard.

"They're saying that Viktor was in the fourth train."

Superintendent Boulard's eyes had glazed over. With the end of his tongue between his lips, he looked like a five-year-old child.

"The . . . fourth. All wight, Lieutenant. Thank you. You may go. Tha'th all I wanted to know."

He clutched at the bar and asked for a cold drink.

"Any particular preference?"

"Yes. Those . . ."

With a sweep of his hand, he indicated the entire shelf of liquor.

There was no fourth train.

Through his narrow window, Voloy Viktor caught sight of a glistening waterfall cascading over a rock face. The train had been on its way again for some while.

The Pyrenees. They were almost there.

The fourth train had just passed the French-Spanish border between Cerbère and Portbou, close to the Mediterranean.

It hadn't been made to stop at any station or by any barrier. It had simply filled up on coal and water somewhere in the open country. But it had instantly set off again because a dog was barking.

Someone must have been lurking in the vicinity.

Viktor finally felt the train braking as they passed beneath a very high bridge that dominated a wild valley. It was gliding silently over the rails now as it entered a tunnel where it switched tracks and entered another tunnel. Finally, it pulled up to a giant concourse carved out of the mountain and lit by powerful projectors.

The train stopped on a platform where ten men were waiting for it.

The door opened.

Two figures appeared, their faces encased in welder's masks. They didn't say a word to Voloy Viktor. In a matter of minutes and by the glimmer of a blue flame, they had liberated him. Viktor stood up and walked toward the light.

"Here we are!" he declared.

Dazzled, he stepped down onto the platform and had a good stretch.

"Is everything all right?" a man asked the arms dealer.

"Have you got our padre?"

"No."

Victor shot him a murderous look. He had just been ushered into a chair in the middle of the platform, where three people were bustling around him.

"In that case, everything is most definitely not all right, Dorgeles. How did you let him get away?"

"We followed him from the police station as far as the Gare d'Austerlitz."

"How very admirable. Fifteen minutes by Métro! You really are geniuses when it comes to trailing people. And then?"

"We saw him go into the Jardin des Plantes."

Victor started to clap.

"Congratulations, Dorgeles. Following a man into the Botanical Gardens: you've clearly got an eye for this line of work!"

The men and women around Voloy Viktor smiled on cue. They looked like the devil's courtiers. Their hands were full of pencils and hairpieces. They were busy applying his makeup. He was already unrecognizable.

"The trail for Zefiro went cold in the Natural History Museum," explained Dorgeles.

"What a pity."

The irony had dropped out of Viktor's voice.

"He was very familiar with the premises, Mr. Viktor; he knew them like the back of his hand. He shook us off."

"He could only shake you off if he knew you were following him in the first place. How did he know that, eh, Dorgeles?"

"Zefiro is very cautious."

"And you're not cautious enough."

Dorgeles was single-handedly responsible for devising Viktor's escape. He had prepared the fourth train, disguised and armed an entire regiment, bribed the pointsmen, and corrupted ten other people, but Viktor showed no sign of gratitude.

"Don't you have something else to say to me?" demanded Voloy Viktor.

The makeup team was working frantically on his face. Even his voice was changing.

"Don't you have something else to say, Dorgeles?"

"I've got an important lead. A photo taken at Gare d'Austerlitz."

Snatching the photo out of his hands, Viktor repeated, "I'm asking if you haven't forgotten something, Dorgeles!"

Voloy Viktor pushed aside the people who'd been fussing over him. He was no longer the same man.

Dorgeles took a step backward.

Before him stood a forty-five-year-old blond woman who looked like she was hardly wearing any makeup at all.

"I asked you something, Dorgeles."

Dorgeles finally understood what Viktor was expecting from him.

"Yes. I'm sorry. Please accept my apologies . . . Madame."

Viktor didn't answer.

Dorgeles moved off. He knew that time was running out for him.

"What about this photo?" Viktor wanted to know.

"It's someone who was trying to speak with him, at Gare d'Austerlitz. Zefiro pushed him away. But I'm convinced he knew him."

"And have you got him? This somebody?"

"We've just picked up his trail in London. He had disappeared for a few weeks, but we won't lose him again."

"Who is he?"

"A criminal wanted by your old friend Boulard for the murder of a priest. He claims to be innocent but is pursued by hit men."

"Get to him before the others do, and make him talk about Zefiro. Don't let me down. It's your only chance of redeeming yourself, Dorgeles."

"I've already got ten men on the case."

Voloy Viktor stood there alone on the platform. From now on he would be called Madame Victoria. As a character, she suited him. No one had ever recognized him under this identity.

It was cold in the depths of the earth. Madame Victoria was wearing a silk coat over her shoulders. She was holding her high heels in one hand and in the other a photograph, which she brought closer to those long-lashed eyes of hers.

The photo had been taken in a smoke-filled train station.

Padre Zefiro could be seen on one side of the shot, staring straight at the camera. And on the other, a young man was walking toward Zefiro. Smiling.

HOW TO WATCH SNOWFLAKES

London, the following night

It was raining. Vango was running along the bridge. There were still three men behind him. He could see them in the light of the oncoming train. They had been on his heels since the beginning of the night.

Dozens of intersecting railroad tracks covered the bridge. Vango had got off the train just before Cannon Street station, and his pursuers hadn't wasted any time in jumping after him. Now he was running between the rails over the Thames. In the distance, he could make out the halo of light from the docks.

Three times, Vango thought he had escaped them.

The first time he saw them was when they entered the pub where he had just started working.

He had traveled across Europe, from south to north, like a stray animal, only coming alive at night. He had long since run out of money, so had taken to feeding himself in the back alleys behind buildings. It was on the outskirts of London, while Vango was picking through some leftover vegetables, that the proprietor of the Blue Fisherman had offered to hire him as a kitchen porter.

"Can you wash up?"

"Yes."

"Come by tomorrow, then."

Vango had accepted. On a few coins a day, he would eventually be able to buy the train ticket he needed to continue his journey up north.

On the third evening, they came for him in the restaurant. They must have followed Vango in the street and spotted the place where he was working. Five or six customers were sitting at various tables. The visitors made straight for the kitchen.

The landlord tried to stop them at the door.

"It's no-entry here, thank you."

He received a punch in the forehead and collapsed to the floor.

When the intruders burst in, the cook put his arms in the air, a carrot sticking out of each hand.

"I surrender! I surrender!"

"Shut up."

"Are you looking for me?"

"No. The other one."

"Take him. I don't know him!"

They stuffed an enormous turnip into the cook's mouth to make him pipe down.

Here we go, thought Vango.

He was trapped at the back of the long kitchen, with no exit. There were four of them. One by one, he hurled the dirty plates and cast-iron pots that were piled up next to him. The cook had tucked himself under the meat safe.

With no weapons left to halt their advance, Vango poured the greasy, hot dishwater over the floor.

He managed to shut himself in the storeroom by upturning

a table. Vango could hear them skating around on the tiled kitchen floor as he climbed on top of a cupboard, smashed through a skylight with his elbow, and emerged into the back alley.

In a few movements, he had scaled the facade of the building, aiming for the window on the next floor up. The shutters were closed. He scaled another floor, and then another. All the windows looked rotten. The building had been left to rack and ruin.

Wiping his face with his arm, Vango felt something hot and wet trickling down his neck. The elbow he had used to smash the skylight was bleeding heavily. He couldn't really move his right hand anymore. He stuffed it into the bottom of his pocket and didn't take it out again.

Noises rose up from the kitchens. Vango completed his ascent like a maimed spider, but with astonishing speed.

He hung on to one of the wide shutters on the top floor. He wanted to reach the roof.

Two voices rang out below him. He froze.

"He must be up there. He couldn't have got out of the alley."

"Where are our English friends?"

The two men were speaking in French, unlike those who had burst into the kitchen.

"They're searching all the floors; they'll find him, you mark my words."

Just then, Vango felt his shutter swiveling around.

"Hey!" came a voice very close to him.

The two men looked up at the man who had just flung open both shutters of the top window.

"We're heading back down. There's no one up here."

"Little brat! He's going to pay for this."

Vango was pinned behind the left shutter, invisible.

Four hours later, when there hadn't been another noise for a long time, Vango finally dared to venture slowly back down toward the courtyard.

He had heard the police turning up in the middle of the night to record the attack on the restaurant.

The pub owner was already in the hospital. From behind his shutter, Vango had heard the cook's heroic tale of how he had defended the young kitchen boy with the aid of a skewer and a butcher's knife.

"I didn't give up until they were down on their knees, begging for forgiveness. Then they left."

A little before dawn, Vango slipped down into the street. Everything looked calm. The rain was freezing cold. There was no light at all. Just the sound of a few coins clinking in his pocket and the splat of his poor shoes in the puddles.

But as he was about to turn the corner of the next building, a car started up and began to give chase.

Would this never stop?

Almost at breaking point, Vango ran through the night, down unpaved roads. The rain was making the gutters even wider, so the streets were awash.

He was up to his ankles in water. The car was growling behind him.

Suddenly, a crashing din drowned out the noise of the engine. Vango thought it must be a shoot-out. Glancing backward, he realized where the noise was coming from. There was a railroad line behind the fence, on the right-hand side.

A train was approaching.

Vango stopped in his tracks, making the tires of the car behind him screech. He took a deep breath and pounced like a lion toward the high fencing, which, as if by magic, he managed to scale.

"Don't shoot him!" one of his pursuers called out. "Don't shoot!"

Vango had already leaped into the train.

It was the first train of the morning, and it was headed for the city. A few passengers were dozing on the wooden benches. They didn't even notice the boy who had appeared without the train stopping.

Except for an old lady, who smiled at him as if she knew. Vango didn't acknowledge her. Everything frightened him at that moment.

He moved closer to the door. He couldn't trust anyone or anything. He would even have been suspicious of a newborn baby.

Vango allowed himself to collapse in a corner, against a window. His arm was hurting.

It wasn't rain that was falling now, but snow. Gray, fleeting snow.

What was this deep footprint he seemed to leave behind wherever he went, whether on cobblestones or sand, that meant he could always be found?

How had they spotted his tracks when there was nothing solid to tie him to this earth anymore?

Nothing. His parents, Father Jean, Mademoiselle, Zefiro . . .

they had all disappeared. It was as if Vango were floating above everything.

Ethel, perhaps. Ethel still held him by a silk thread.

He watched the snow falling. His eyelids were starting to grow heavy. Tall factories were belching out smoke over wastelands. There were people walking along the platform. He saw them pass by in a flash. He was also revisiting the long downward spiral of his life.

It can be boring to watch snowflakes falling with your eyes fixed in one place, but when you follow a single snowflake from up high, when you follow its aerobatics, you embark on an intoxicating adventure.

Vango woke up at the first station. He had slept for only a few minutes. As he opened his eyes, the train was setting off again. Just then, he saw the men running onto the platform and climbing aboard.

"No."

He got up. His pursuers' car had been quicker than him.

The old lady was still there.

Vango opened the window and stuck his head outside. The snow was wet and almost warm. He reached out with his left hand to find a grip-hold on the roof. He heaved himself up with his only functioning arm.

The old lady watched him disappear, as if the great outdoors had swept him away, just as the men entered. She didn't say a word. They were panting as they bent down to search under the benches.

One of them rushed over to the open window and looked outside.

"That window's stuck, sir," the old lady pointed out. "If you were able to close it, we'd all be much obliged."

The man pushed it with one finger, and it closed perfectly.

"Thank you very much."

The old lady nodded and closed her eyes for a moment.

"Why did you say that window was stuck?"

She opened her eyes again. The man was very close to her face now, and he looked menacing.

"Eh? I hope you don't have anything to hide. . . ."

The other passengers were pretending to be asleep.

A minute later, as he lay on his front on the roof of the train heading for the bridge at Cannon Street station, Vango saw a man appear, buffeted about by the wind. He had climbed out the same window.

"Come here!"

"Who are you?"

"Come here, my boy. Now, I want you to make your way calmly toward me."

The man was threatening him with a pistol.

Vango started to head over, as requested. The train was passing between two pylons.

The man followed his every movement. Vango was barely a meter away now. He was crawling slowly. The man would soon be able to reach out and touch him. As the train went under a footbridge, Vango stood up and suddenly jumped, catching hold of a metal arch. He vanished into the darkness.

A shot was fired into the air. This was the signal for some of the men to jump off the train.

Which was how Vango found himself running along a bridge above the Thames, on rail tracks leading to Cannon Street station. At first, his pursuers had gone under the arch, where they hadn't spotted anything. But another train had tooted loudly on sighting the boy on the tracks. The men had retraced their steps and resumed their hunt.

Vango wanted to reach Cannon Street station itself, which would be full of commuters even at that time in the morning. He could melt into the crowd.

He was gaining ground. He might just escape them.

Snow had given way to rain again.

Vango came to an abrupt halt. He had just seen shadows moving in front of him. They were coming at him from both sides.

He recognized the Frenchmen and two other nasty pieces of work who must have got out at the next station.

Vango was caught in a vise.

The lamentations of the Scriptures rang out inside his head:

Thou renewest thy witnesses against me,
and increase thine indignation upon me;
changes and war are against me.

The men were closing in on him. They were all around him. The different factions were even talking to each other.

"We're not going to hurt you," the French were saying.

Trains were passing through, indifferent to the drama. Faces could be seen lit up in the windows.

My brethren have dealt deceitfully as a brook,
and as the stream of brooks they pass away. . . .

Vango leaned against a parapet, allowing himself to be slowly trapped.

He removed his aching hand from his pocket and placed it gingerly in his other hand.

He was very focused.

"Don't move," the Frenchman kept repeating.

The enemy was only two paces away.

And then, with both hands gripped together, Vango raised them toward the sky, arched his back, and jumped. He flew over the parapet and dived into the river.

Friedrichshafen, Lake Constance, the same evening

Captain Lehmann entered the map room of the *Graf Zeppelin*. Eckener was working in there, peering through his pince-nez.

The airship was in its hangar.

"Your good friend Paolo Marini has just arrived."

"Sorry?"

"Someone named Paolo Marini. He claims to be your best friend."

Eckener folded up his pince-nez. He hesitated for a moment before exclaiming, "Paolo! That old Boy Scout! Tell him I'll be with him in a jiffy!"

"He hasn't got a ticket, Commander. He's busy explaining himself to the SS officer."

"What about me?" asked Eckener, losing his temper as he stood up behind the table. "Have I got a ticket? Paolo is no different from me, he's my friend, my brother, Paolo Murini . . ."

"Marini. He said Marini."

"Marini, yes, that's what I said. My old friend from the Scouts. Is it snowing, Captain?"

"No. Not yet."

Captain Lehmann headed off. He was getting used to all these friends the commander suddenly seemed to have, none of whom he ever disowned.

Eckener returned to his desk and cast his eye over the map.

He had no idea who this Paolo could be.

All he knew was that for some time, friends he had never met before had started coming to him from all sorts of countries. He was a refuge, a land of welcome for those the Nazis were hunting down. They were former soldiers, artists, and, increasingly these days, Jews. The laws against them were multiplying all the time. They were banned from practicing many professions. They couldn't be lawyers or civil servants. And for two months now, marriage or any kind of relationship between Jews and non-Jews had been forbidden.

Eckener was trying to use his influence. He was doing all he could.

The bulky and untouchable figure of Hugo Eckener meant that in his shadow he could still provide shelter for many of those who needed it.

Eckener walked through the zeppelin.

Night had fallen. In two hours, they would take off.

This would perhaps be the *Graf*'s last moment of glory.

It was going to make a short voyage to New York before

returning to spend the depths of winter on the shores of Lake Constance. The following spring, the world would only have eyes for the *Hindenburg,* the biggest zeppelin ever built. That monster was already champing at the bit in the hangar right next to them. Two hundred and fifty meters long, twenty-five cabins, fifty passengers. This was Hugo Eckener's greatest victory.

But as he exited the *Graf* and turned back to glance at its elegant shape, the commander felt a twinge in his heart. He sighed.

A few flakes of snow had been forecast. He hoped the forecast would be right. One day, a long time ago, from one of these windows, just there, he had taught Vango how to watch the snow falling.

If Captain Lehmann had any doubts about the link between Hugo Eckener and Paolo Marini, these were immediately dispelled as he watched the two men being reunited.

Their exclamations and tears were genuine. They stayed there, hugging each other, for a long time.

Standing at the hangar door, Eckener had been thrilled to recognize his great friend.

"How are you doing, ah . . . Paolo? What have you been up to, old friend?"

"I've come to fly for a while in your arms, Commander, old pal!"

A little group had formed around them, including several soldiers, a few German travelers, and the SS officer in charge of checking the passengers.

"You're insane. They'll require umpteen authorizations," Eckener whispered into his friend's ear. "Go away, Zefiro."

Zefiro—for it was indeed him—stepped away and made all those around him witnesses.

"Do you know what my friend Hugo Eckener has just said to me?"

Eckener froze.

"He told me I was insane! Do you hear? He says I won't be allowed to embark."

The officer in uniform smirked.

Zefiro put his hand on the commander's shoulder in response to his look of alarm.

"I'm joking. . . . It's my fault. I'm not good at keeping you up to date with my news, and I don't suppose you read the newspapers." He signaled to the officer. "Show him the letter."

Eckener took the letter, which he proceeded to read.

It was written in German and Italian. It came from the president of the Council of Ministers of Rome. It entrusted Signor Paolo Marini, holder of the Fusillini Military Cross and Commander of the Minestrone, with a special mission in the name of the friendship between the Reich and the great power of fascist Italy, by way of a voyage on board the *Graf Zeppelin,* symbol of the power of national socialism. The letter also contained expressions such as "the glorious alliance of our two countries," "hope never-ending," and the "undying purity of our children," which would have been laughable were it not for the fact that they were a faithful copy of the rhetoric of the day.

The letter had been signed in a convoluted ink scrawl, where "Bibi" was the only decipherable word. But the block capitals just above spelled out the name Benito Mussolini.

Eckener folded the letter.

He shook Zefiro's hand.

"In that case you are most welcome, Paolo Marini. And as it so happens, we've got a free cabin for you. We're leaving in an hour."

They headed off together toward the commander's study. Marini could be heard marveling at how handsome the balloon was.

When Eckener closed the door behind them and they were alone at last, Zefiro asked the commander to forgive him. He put down his small suitcase and punched him in the face.

Eckener reeled slightly before punching the monk in the stomach. Zefiro bent over but soon retaliated. They started fighting like kids on a playground.

Eckener was the first down on the floor, spluttering and writhing. Zefiro watched him, foaming at the mouth and out of breath.

"What have I done to you?" gasped Eckener.

"You know full well."

"No, I don't."

"You revealed the location of the monastery to the police."

"I revealed it to Esquirol and Joseph so that you'd be able to identify Viktor."

"Viktor escaped last night."

Eckener was shell-shocked.

"I have to leave Europe," said Zefiro. "That monastery is my whole life. I can't put it in danger."

"I don't feel at home anywhere either, Padre. I no longer recognize my own country."

Zefiro crouched down to help his friend up again.

"I'm doing what I can," Eckener went on. "If you ask me, Germany is already at war with herself. Yesterday morning, the police went to strike out the name of our friend Werner Mann from the war memorial in his village, near Munich. The name of Mann, do you understand? Hitler gave the order three days ago. No Jewish names on the war memorials of 1918."

Werner Mann, the hero who had died in battle, and who had signed the pact for Project Violette with Zefiro and his friends, had just been erased from history.

The two friends helped each other dust off their clothes.

Zefiro wiped a bit of blood from Eckener's lip with his handkerchief.

"I won't be a burden to you for long, Hugo. I'll spend the winter in New York. It's impossible to return to the monastery for the time being. But I've got a few projects to be getting on with."

"We need to leave as quickly as possible," Eckener remarked. "Your fake letter is pretty farcical. I don't know how the SS were taken in by it. It probably won't last."

Zefiro finally cracked a smile.

"But I put a lot of effort into it. As you saw in line seven, I had myself decorated with the medal of my favorite ham!"

They burst out laughing and held on to each other's hands again.

"What about Vango?" inquired Eckener after a pause.

Zefiro remained silent.

"Has something happened to him?" Eckener insisted.

"I'm worried I've got him tangled up in a nasty business," admitted Zefiro, trying to restore his hat to its original shape as he explained to Eckener what had happened. "At precisely the moment when I was supposed to meet Vango, I discovered that I was being followed. It was in a train station in Paris. I spotted the photographer in the crowd, one of Viktor's men. He was hiding a gun behind the curtain of his camera."

"You left?"

"Too late. I saw Vango coming toward me. I had to act as if I didn't recognize him."

"Nobody could have known he was with you."

"Yes, they could. Vango wanted to talk to me. He came right up to me. He was happy to see me."

"They won't find him," declared Eckener.

"I saw the flash from the camera. They've got a photograph."

Half an hour later, the zeppelin had taken off. The SS officer called the Italian embassy to inform them that the famous Paolo Marini had left his overcoat behind in the air terminal at Friedrichshafen.

As far as the embassy was concerned, that particular name didn't appear to be famous at all. Nobody recognized it. But when the officer read out the list of Marini's decorations, he could hear people roaring with laughter on the other end of the line. Among those medals were all the necessary ingredients for a substantial Italian dinner, from the salami appetizers to the panna cotta for dessert.

A BLOODY TRAIL

Moscow, a month later, December 1935

The little boy was rolling around in the snow. He looked about seven.

"Kostia! Kostia!"

The woman who had called out to him was sitting on a bench on the other side of the path. She had a girl on her lap who looked the elder of the two children.

"Do you think they're going to come, Tioten'ka?"

"Don't worry. They always come," the woman replied.

She was such a gentle *tioten'ka*. The little girl was already very fond of the mysterious woman who had appeared in their apartment only five or six weeks ago.

Where had she come from? A man had brought her to them one October day. She had a funny accent when she spoke Russian. The girl's parents had been told that she would live with them from now on and that they should call her Tioten'ka, which means little aunt, so as not to arouse any suspicion from the neighbors.

Her parents had offered her their double bed, but Tioten'ka had turned it down, making herself comfortable in a little storeroom off the entrance hall, where their big brother used to sleep when he was still with them.

The whole family had given up on treating her as a guest of honor. She insisted on undertaking more than her share of the household tasks. It was hard to stop her. As well as her tiny bedroom, Tioten'ka had inherited two winter coats from the big brother. It was emotional for the family to see them hanging from the hook on the back of the door, like in the old days.

Kostia headed back toward the bench, soaking wet.

"I'm cold," he said.

"Me too," piped up his sister, Zoya.

Their nurse opened her coat and tucked them both inside it.

"Will you bake us the white cake again this evening?" requested Kostia, already dreaming of a crystallized violet on top of the whipped cream.

Tioten'ka was such a magical cook, she was straight out of a fairy tale.

On her excursions to Sokolniki Park, twice a week, Mademoiselle wore both the coats, which were too big for her. Those layers of fur kept her warm in the freezing wind. One was turned inside out, with the furry side against her skin, while the one with the fur on the outside became white with frost. She would stroll around the park with Konstantin and Zoya.

Mademoiselle knew that every step she took outside was being watched. She always wondered which of the passersby were her shadows.

When they had abducted her from Salina, she had been worried they would send her to a gulag in the Arctic Circle, but instead she found herself in the heart of Moscow. She was in captivity in the middle of a family in a tiny apartment, between the coal bucket and the icons hanging on the walls.

"Here they are!" chirped Zoya, emerging from her furry nest.

She ran toward a little girl who had just let go of her nanny's hand.

The children and the nannies kissed each other and huddled up on the bench.

This scene had been played out twice a week for the past month. It was a Wednesday and Sunday friendship between two little girls and two women, under the friendly gaze of Kostia.

The little girl was named Svetlana, but her nickname was Setanka.

Her nanny never mentioned Setanka's family. She preferred to talk about times gone by, when she belonged to the great houses of Saint Petersburg, before the Revolution. She had served princesses and people in the theatrical world. Once, she had almost gone to Paris!

Mademoiselle barely said a word. She listened. Sometimes there were tears in her eyes. She enjoyed these stories from the past.

Zoya and Setanka, for their part, talked in hushed whispers. One spoke about her brother, who had gone away, and the other about a boy she called the Bird, someone she had never set eyes on.

"What are they telling each other, those two?" Setanka's nanny would sometimes whisper with a sidelong glance.

But the girls didn't hear. Each was listening fervently to the other's tale. In the course of those Wednesdays and Sundays, almost without their noticing it, their secrets were changing hands. Setanka was falling a little bit in love with Zoya's big brother, as was Zoya with Setanka's Bird.

When it was turning dark, they went their separate ways at the park gates. There was always a black car waiting there for Setanka and her nanny. The others went down into the subway at Sokolniki Station. They loved the subway. The first line had opened the previous spring.

"Look at me, Tioten'ka. Look!"

Kostia was running through the station as if through a gray marble palace.

That evening, when they got back to their apartment, which smelled of melted candle wax and incense, the children's mother seemed very emotional.

"There's a letter from your brother," she announced in a flat voice. "He sends you lots of love."

"Can I read it?" asked Zoya.

"It's supper time now!"

She wouldn't let her children read it later on either.

This was the first letter. It had come via the neighbors so that the political police wouldn't seize it. The family was under house arrest.

Oddly, the letter had a stamp from Great Britain.

In the middle of the night, when the father returned from his working day, Mademoiselle, who had already gone to bed in her little room, heard the mother rushing to the front door.

"There's a letter from our son, my darling. A letter from Andrei."

A silence followed, as if she was about to burst into tears.

"Our Andrei isn't doing well. . . ."

Mademoiselle looked up at the three small violins hanging from the wall above her bed.

Paris, the same night

It happened in a café at the foot of Montmartre, a little before dawn. The customers had been drinking heavily. The Cat was the only person ordering a fruit cordial.

Next to her, Boris Petrovitch Antonov took off his wire glasses. He wiped his hand over his waxen face and rubbed his small yellow eyes. His other hand was placed affectionately on top of the Cat's. He didn't want to let go.

It had all started two hours earlier.

The Cat had been waiting in the gutter above the Russian cabaret on the Rue de Liège. The bright lights on the sign for SHERAZADE had just been switched off. It was four o'clock in the morning, but the man she was waiting for hadn't come out yet.

The Cat was following Boris Petrovitch Antonov, in the hope that he would lead her to either Andrei or Vango.

Thanks to a surprise visit, she had lost all trace of Andrei for several weeks now. The Cat's parents had dropped by to spend a few hours with her, and this had interfered with trailing Andrei.

The Cat had found her father a changed and anxious man. He had sat down in front of her. He had even taken off his coat and hat. He talked about selling his businesses and moving to America. He said he was just back from Frankfurt. His name had been removed from the brick walls of his factories and replaced by another name that chimed better with the times.

He had lost everything in Germany.

"You've still got France! And the factories in Belgium," his wife called out from the bathroom.

He frowned. It wasn't so easy in France now either.

And so, exceptionally, he had spent several minutes talking to his daughter. He was looking at her in astonishment, as if seeing her for the first time.

"And what about you, Emilie? Are you all right?"

The Cat didn't utter a word. It would take more than calling her by her first name, winking at her three times, and asking her a couple of questions to win her back.

"If they strip me of everything," her father was saying, "the three of us will set off together."

His wife was laughing loudly in front of her mirror and calling him a scaredy-cat. She emerged smelling of rose and jasmine. She hadn't even taken off her woolen hat and promptly reminded her husband that they were expected for dinner in town.

She ran her powdered glove over her daughter's cheek.

"We'll see you soon, my angel."

An hour later, the Cat observed that Andrei hadn't returned to his bedroom in the boardinghouse on the Rue du Val-de-Grâce.

Nobody else was coming out of Cabaret Sherazade, so where had that dreadful Boris Petrovitch Antonov gotten to? She'd certainly seen him go in there, just after midnight.

The Cat could remember a time when the word *loneliness* meant nothing to her. A time when she had lived suspended above the city and its people, when she hadn't suffered in any way. That time was long since gone.

Now Vango had disappeared, Ethel had gone back to Scotland, and, particularly in Andrei's absence, the Cat had become an expert in loneliness, a world champion. She felt as if a part of her was permanently missing.

But she picked herself up again. Bonds don't break just because the people themselves have gone away. She still felt connected to the others, and it did her a world of good to feel these bonds. It was as if she was awake at last, after being asleep for the longest time.

She was very fond of Ethel, and Vango. And she cared deeply about Andrei, even if he didn't know she existed.

The Cat slid down a zinc pipe: it was time to take a look, close-up.

The street was deserted. She reached the ground and took a few steps through the snow toward the cabaret. Just as she'd made it to the middle of the street, the door was flung open. Now they were face-to-face. And Boris Petrovitch Antonov was with another man. They stopped talking when they saw her.

The Cat was at precisely that age when half the men she met asked her, "Have you lost your parents, little girl?" and the other half asked, "Can I buy you a glass of something, you pretty young thing?" All she needed to do was change her posture or the smile on her lips ever so slightly.

With one hand on her hip, she made sure the two men belonged to the latter category.

Boris Petrovitch Antonov swayed as he watched the young girl.

The snow was pocked with black footprints.

Cold or fear? Boris couldn't tell which was making his shoulders tremble. The man behind him had a loaded pistol in his pocket. He was called Vlad. Boris was fully aware that, when it came to human relationships, Vlad was about as refined as a vulture in mid carve-up.

Vlad was there to bump Boris off the job.

For months now, Boris Petrovitch Antonov had unearthed nothing in his search for Vango. He knew that, given half a chance, Vlad the Vulture would take him out in cold blood on some street corner to make this mission his own.

For two hours, in a corner of Cabaret Sherazade, Vlad had tried to piece together the file. He wanted access to all of Boris's leads before disposing of him. But Boris wasn't in a chatty mood. He knew what lay in store for him at the end of their conversation.

The cabaret lights had been switched off, and when the last of the dancers had put their coats on over their red boleros glinting with precious stones, the remaining customers were asked to leave.

Now all three of them were standing under the street lamp on the sidewalk. Who was this girl?

"Won't you join us for one last drink, you pretty young thing?"

It was Boris's only chance of survival. Vlad the Vulture wouldn't kill him in front of a witness. He would almost certainly have been ordered to act with complete discretion. If the girl agreed, she'd become his accidental bodyguard until daybreak.

"Leave her alone," said the Vulture.

He spoke only in Russian.

"We're in Paris," replied Boris. "We can't leave a pretty young girl all by herself. . . ."

"Shut up. Tell her to be on her way!"

The girl looked starry-eyed.

"Just a glass, then. I'm tired, but I don't like walking alone at night."

Vlad didn't have time to intervene. The Cat gave Boris her arm, which he clung to for dear life.

"You're quite right," he said. "These streets aren't safe."

They spent a long time looking for a bistro that was open at that hour. In the end, they found one on the slopes of the Sacré-Coeur.

As she sat down, the Cat felt dizzy. The room was small and smoky. The customers were talking loudly. She could feel her claustrophobia getting the better of her again.

"I've got to go outside," she declared, standing up.

"What?"

She looked at the two men and, in that same glance, she saw Boris's terror and Vlad's satisfaction. Her eyes half closed, she breathed out slowly through her mouth.

"A double grenadine, please."

Bravely, the Cat fell back into her seat.

Only the Vulture's look of glee had made her change her mind.

An angry Vlad was trying to obtain the final missing pieces of information. Next, he had to locate Andrei. That boy was useless, but he knew too much.

Vlad had orders to eliminate both of them.

"What happened to that young boy you hired, the violinist? I'll need to speak with him too."

"Andrei?"

The two men were talking in Russian, but the Cat recognized Andrei's name. She stopped drinking her grenadine. She had even forgotten her claustrophobia. Recalling Andrei's gray eyes was enough to turn the roof above her to glass.

Boris responded with a few words, including one that the Cat could pick out: *meeting.*

He must just have told the Vulture where and when he would be able to meet up with the boy with the violin. This was why she had followed Boris in the first place. The Cat could sense how much danger Andrei was now in.

The Vulture had understood that he wouldn't get anything more out of Boris. He stood up and used a sign language of sorts to ask where the phone was. A small staircase leading to the basement was pointed out to him.

A moment later, the Cat noticed that Boris Petrovitch's waxen face had broken out into beads of sweat.

"I'll be back."

She saw him heading off in turn. He went down the spiral staircase, grabbing a butcher's knife on his way past the kitchen.

The Cat held her breath.

People at the bar were laughing. They were coming in from the local nightspots in Pigalle. From the Boule Noire and the accordion dance hall, L'Ange Rouge, which had just opened on Rue Fontaine. The Cat knew these places only by their rooftops, from where she watched the fights between warring gangs in the surrounding streets. Two years earlier, she had witnessed the battle of the Corsicans against the Parisians.

The smell of coffee wafted through the room. In one corner sat a chimney sweep, who was still perfectly clean at this time of day, chatting with a laundress. It looked like any other early morning in Paris.

Had she dreamed everything? Had she fallen asleep?

All of a sudden, the Vulture appeared at the top of the stairs, grimacing. He was clutching his belly as if he'd been wounded. He didn't even glance in the Cat's direction but rushed out into the street.

Some customers starting screaming.

A dead man had been found in the basement.

Panic spread through the bar.

Outside, the Cat was already running over the snow, guided by the thin trail of blood the Vulture had left behind.

SCOTTISH HUNTING SCENE

The Highlands, Scotland,
Christmas Eve 1935

Bare highlands gave way to forests, but the rain, mud, and fog made everything blurry. The hounds were braying for death. Horns were being sounded on one side and then the other, giving contradictory orders.

The hunt had started seven hours earlier. And for seven hours, the pack had been after one beast. A diabolical animal, fiendishly difficult to catch, and on the verge of making thirty riders and fifty hounds lose their minds.

Ethel, who was looking for a stray ewe that had abandoned its lamb for the past three days, found herself caught up in all of this.

Mary had turned up in Ethel's bedroom that morning with the three-month-old lamb in her arms and bleated at her mistress to find its mother again.

Ethel was guiding her horse through the fog toward the boundaries of the Everland estate. Not a single hunter paid her any attention.

Occasionally, she would spot a horsewoman riding side-saddle between the trees, a few birds flying scared, or hounds splashing through the water. Nobody seemed to hear her or see her.

At one point she was galloping alongside a man who could barely sit anymore. He let out a howl of pain every time he came into contact with the saddle.

"You haven't found a sheep, by any chance?" Ethel asked him.

The man stared at her as if she were a lunatic before deigning to answer.

"I can assure you there are no sheep here, young lady! Unless flying, tree-climbing sheep that play havoc with our nerves and wreak mayhem on . . . *ouch* . . . my bottom!"

Ethel thanked him and left him to his pain, letting her horse pick up pace before riding through a small copse. The barking of the hounds to the right was getting closer. Two hunters emerged on the left without seeing her. Her horse jumped nervously over a series of dead trees. It wasn't used to the thunder of hounds and horns.

The horse and its rider felt their hearts beating together as one, as if they were the game in this hunt. But Ethel didn't want to abandon her search.

She galloped over bog land toward the braying pack. Where was this beast? Ethel was intrigued by the wild creature that had outwitted the entire hunt since dawn.

A yapping noise prompted her to slow down. They had arrived at a mound of rocks, in the middle of the trees, known as Chaos. Ethel had heard tales of strange things happening there at night.

She could see a lone hound with a piece of black cloth in its mouth. It was sniffing the ground frenetically, then howling up at the sky. She dismounted from her horse.

"Come here. Give that to me," she ordered, walking toward the hound.

Ethel led her horse by the reins and took the piece of cloth from the dog's mouth.

On taking a closer look at the wet, panting, slathering hound, she sent up a prayer that Lily the doe hadn't wandered off from the tame copses surrounding the castle.

The hound raised its muzzle. A faraway whistle summoned it back to join the rest of the pack. It disappeared. Ethel slipped the scrap of torn cloth into her pocket. A bird flew overhead. She mounted her horse again and headed away from the chaos.

The hunt was going around in circles now. Trails led nowhere. The pack was scattered. At one point, Ethel found herself elbow to elbow with a huntsman on a black mare. They were flanking a thorny hedge.

"I simply can't understand it," the huntsman confided in Ethel. "Never seen anything like it. I've been hunting for forty-five years, and I've never known a hunt this hard."

"I suppose the stag has to win from time to time," muttered Ethel.

The rider, who had his horn slung across his shoulders, was riding jockey-style.

"This isn't a stag," he said.

"Then what is it?"

"That's what I'd like to know."

Using the crop on his mare, he straddled the thorny hedge and parted company with Ethel.

She decided to go around one last time before heading home. Her curiosity was still keen, but her horse was flagging. It was not fit enough to gallop for this long. Since Andrew had left, on Saint Nicholas's day, there was nobody to ride out the horses at Everland on a regular basis.

Andrew had announced he would be back in April, and Paul had absurdly accepted his departure, even though Ethel had pointed out that a groom was useful only during the winter months. As soon as spring arrived, the horses lived outdoors. Ethel didn't trust the Russian vagrant: he was too gentle, too handsome; he went away for five months of the year, and he played the violin in the garage like a child prodigy.

Suddenly, jumping over a ditch, she landed on the sand and sawdust of a felling area. The horn of a vehicle tooted as her horse reared up high. A car had nearly mown them down. It braked shortly afterward and the driver could be heard letting out a torrent of swearwords. It was pouring rain. And the car was open topped.

Ethel calmed her horse by stroking its neck. This track was completely unsuitable for motor vehicles. There was no reason for a car to be driving around here.

A woman started insulting them from the passenger seat.

Ethel and her horse trotted over to the car.

The driver was holding an open umbrella and examining a scratch on the metal bodywork through a magnifying glass.

"Damn and blast . . ." the driver muttered.

Then the woman in the passenger seat cried, "Vandal! Vandal!"

"Your horse scratched my car!" said the driver.

"Heavens above!" exclaimed the woman. "Look, Ronald, it's Ethel."

Ethel had just recognized the entire Cameron family. They resembled a bunch of sopping-wet floorcloths. Lady

Cameron's hairdo had collapsed under a makeshift paper rain hat, and her husband's ankle boots made dubious *glug-glug* noises with every step he took.

In the back, Tom had turned as pale as the beige car upholstery. This was his favorite form of camouflage.

"Hello," said Ethel. "Out for a spin?"

"No, my dear," Ronald Cameron corrected her. "We're hunting."

"You're hunting?" Ethel smiled in amazement, staring at the two picnic hampers swimming on the backseat.

"Yes, we're the guests of the Earl of Galich. He's a friend of ours. I'm lending him a field for his horses this evening."

"He's a close personal friend," Beth Cameron was quick to point out.

"We're hunting by car. It's more sporty," boasted her husband.

"I'm very happy to see you, Ethel," declared Beth Cameron, taking up the baton. "I've been wanting to talk to you about your plans. This whole story has been rather trying for us."

"Now is hardly the time or the place," her husband protested.

"Be quiet, coward!" snapped Beth Cameron.

Tom, who hadn't said a word up until this point, stood up.

"And you can pipe down too," shouted his mother before he could even get a word out.

"Th-there! Look!" Tom managed to stammer, pointing at the horizon.

Ethel turned around to see a mud cloud rising up at the

end of the path. Thirty riders and fifty hounds were galloping at top speed in their direction.

"Heavens above!" gasped Lady Cameron.

"I . . . I'd better pull over to the side, perhaps," said Lord Cameron.

"Perhaps you had, yes," his wife agreed.

The thunder of hooves on the wet path was already audible.

Ronald Cameron started up the engine and clung to the steering wheel. He pressed his foot down on the accelerator. The wheels were spinning on the spot, sending up huge amounts of sawdust and sand.

"Heavens above!" repeated Lady Cameron.

The stampede of dogs and horses was getting ever closer.

Cameron pressed down on the pedal one more time. His wife was bouncing about in the passenger seat.

"You can't do this to me, Ronald! You simply can't do this to me!"

"I'm sorry to interrupt," ventured Ethel, "but I suggest you leave your car and make your way over to the edge. I'll help you."

"Never!" boomed Sir Ronald. "I won't give in!"

"Never!" echoed his wife, who was soaked to the skin and trembling like jellied beef.

"Please, Tom!" cajoled Ethel. "Come with me over to the side."

Tom glanced at his parents.

"Tom, if you desert us, I shall never speak to you again," declared his mother.

"Lady Cameron," shouted Ethel, "they're almost here!"

"We Camerons don't behave like that."

"In any case we'll be out of here in a flash. This is a brand-new car!"

Tom didn't budge.

At the last moment, Ethel ordered her horse to ride on.

Fifty hounds and thirty hunters rode straight over the Cameron family and their new automobile. It didn't take long. At the end of it, there weren't many spare parts in the car worth saving.

The Cameron family itself, on the other hand, emerged from this experience sufficiently unscathed to continue hunting on foot.

An hour later, just as the hunt was about to disband for the day, a rumor went around that they had found the animal at last.

Hunters and hounds gathered around a small oxbow lake with a bulky gray shape moving in it. Tom and his mother were standing on the shore in a pitiful state.

"He's got it! He's caught it!" crowed Beth Cameron, approaching a man who was dismounting from his horse.

In the middle of the braying pack, Ethel recognized the man she had spoken with by the thorny hedge, the rider on the black mare.

"Earl, my dear Earl!" simpered Beth Cameron.

"And who are you?"

"I am Lady Cameron."

"I don't believe we've met," said the Earl of Galich, without much regret. He was sure he'd never encountered this muddy specimen before.

"We've lent our field for your horses."

"The field . . . ah, of course. Yes, they did tell me about that. Thank you very much."

"Look! Sound the horn. It's my husband. He's caught the stag with his bare hands."

A second later, a bulky shape rose up triumphantly out of the lake, and under the beating rain, Ethel could just make out that Ronald Cameron was indeed holding a live animal in his arms.

"A sheep," murmured the earl, scrunching his eyes.

"Heavens above!" said Lady Cameron. "It's a sheep."

My ewe! thought Ethel.

The ewe had a broken leg. She had gotten stuck in the bog two days earlier. So it hadn't been the sheep that had kept the hunters on the run.

"A strange day," the earl concluded.

Galich had politely turned away to spare the Camerons. Even the hounds thought it was a sorry scene. They stopped barking.

They tied the legs of the quavering animal together, and Ethel wedged it in front of the saddle on her horse and rode off.

The hunt vanished into the fog.

Tom Cameron had never felt so embarrassed.

It was the first time that Paul wouldn't be there for Christmas. His squadron had been posted to India until the rainy season.

So Ethel went down to the village church with Mary, who dragged her along for the celebrations. She also went to please the minister, for whom she had developed a soft spot.

This dated back to the time she had caught him picking mush-rooms in the Camerons' woods and hiding them in haversacks beneath his cassock.

The church was full. And hot. The Christmas carols rang out to the far end of the village. The minister noticed Ethel sitting in the pew at the back and even put in a word for stray ewes in his sermon.

Ethel sometimes took the minister out for a spin in her Railton. She would set him a metaphysical question or two while driving at ninety miles an hour downhill:

"Didn't you ever want to wear trousers?"

The minister would burst out laughing, and Ethel would smile. Nothing she said could shock him.

"Don't you wonder what you'll say, if none of it really exists after all?" she had asked him on one occasion.

"None of what?" asked the young minister, cupping his hands close to his ear.

"None of it, none of your stories, none of what you believe in. Heaven and all the rest . . . If it doesn't really exist?"

The minister started laughing again and shrugged.

"Don't tell anyone, but it wouldn't much matter to me!"

"Why?" Ethel had grilled him, narrowly avoiding going off the road.

"I'd ask myself, would I have preferred not to believe?"

She gave him a quizzical look.

"What matters," he declared midjolt, "is that I can answer this question: Would I have been happier for not believing?"

Ethel frowned. She drove in silence for a while to mull over this response. Then, with a mounting sense of indignation,

she shouted above the roaring engine, "What about my parents, then? What about them?"

The minister fell quiet. But Ethel wouldn't let it drop.

"Answer me! Give me an answer!"

He turned toward the rearview mirror. She had hoisted
her pilot's goggles up off her face. The minister was watching
the tears on Ethel's cheeks being erased by the wind and the
speed. But he couldn't say anything to make the tears go away.

As the parishioners trooped out of the church to greet one
another in the cold, Mary exchanged a few words with the
mother of a girl she had taken on as third linen maid at
Everland. She turned to Ethel to explain that she had just been
invited to her protégée's family for Christmas Eve dinner.

"You don't mind being on your own?" asked Mary
excitedly.

Ethel smiled and shook her head.

"Why don't you invite yourself to join in Justin's party?"
Mary suggested. "He'll be with his family."

"Don't worry about me."

"Are you sure? Are you quite sure?" asked Mary, who was
already in the festive spirit.

"Happy Christmas!" Ethel called out as she headed back to
the castle. Her footsteps made crunching noises up the drive.

The kitchen was lit up, and there were strains of songs
coming from it.

The entire family of Justin Scott, the cook, had traveled
up from Glasgow, having requested permission to celebrate
Christmas in the servants' hall. There were forty-two of them.

Ethel didn't show her face. She climbed the stairs to her bedroom, got undressed, and went to bed. The rain was lashing against the windowpanes. Laughter could be heard coming from the other wing of the castle.

She found herself staring at the canopy above her four-poster bed.

She was alone. She had never felt so alone. She turned over and plunged her face into her pillow. The overstarched linen squeaked against her forehead.

Ethel had been hoping for a Christmas fairy tale tonight. She had requested it silently, and with a certain sense of embarrassment, in front of the church candles. A Christmas fairy tale. Nothing else. It was ridiculous, she knew. Part of her was laughing in her funny, disillusioned way. But her hands and sheets were drenched with tears.

Even the lost ewe had been returned to its mother in the shed. But Ethel was alone.

When she finally got to sleep, she had a dreadful nightmare. The pounding heart of the hunted prey was coming back to her in flashes. She could dimly hear the sound of cries. It felt as if she were struggling in the undergrowth. She thought she could hear her horse whinnying and stamping its hooves in the stable. Suddenly, a steaming hound dragged a man's body over to her.

Gasping for air, Ethel opened her eyes.

She got up and tiptoed over to her jacket, which was hanging in the corner.

She felt in her pocket and took out the scrap of black material that had been torn by the hound. She stared at it for a long while, and sniffed it too. Then she opened her ward-robe and took out a hunting gun.

Five minutes later, she was back on her horse. She had put her clothes on over her nightshirt. She had no idea what she was doing anymore. Her horse was galloping over the moor. The rain had stopped.

She rode through woods, over streams and hills, and reached the edge of the rocks of Chaos. It was almost pitch-black. A few openings in the treetops let in a glimmer of light from the sky. She dismounted, tethering her horse to a branch. Birds flew overhead, following the heartbeat of the night.

Ethel started to walk between the trees.

She reached out to touch the trunks, one after another. The gun was slung across her shoulders. She went over to the rocks. The branches were swaying gently above her as if a breeze had picked up, but she couldn't feel any air moving on her face.

She realized that the glimmer had to be a fire in the hollow of the rocks. She was sure of it.

She slid her hand over her shoulder to grab the gun and held it in front of her as she advanced, step by step. The branches kept on swaying above her. She approached the cave. No one. He couldn't be far. She knew he could see her.

Ethel hadn't been mistaken. The animal pursued all day by the hunt was in fact a man. She had seen him in her nightmare.

She skirted the mound of rocks in the midst of the trees as she felt her boots sinking into the mud. She stopped, retraced her steps, and shivered. Her legs felt heavy.

At that moment, she heard a loud cracking in the branches.

She looked up. A shadow was moving quickly in the tree above her. Ethel started running. The shadow moved at the same time. The forest was increasingly dense. Ethel couldn't see where she was putting her feet. She kept bumping into tree trunks. Then she fell to the ground.

Her hand began to tremble on the gun. She aimed it into the night sky and fired the first shot. The shadow stopped and flung itself into the void just above her.

"No!" screamed Ethel.

She fired her second shot at random.

The shadow let out a cry and came crashing down, half crushing her.

Ethel was panting, groaning, trying to push the heavy body off her chest. Her arms had gone numb. She heard an exhausted voice whisper in her ear:

"Ethel."

I must be dead, she thought, *and in another world, because that voice belongs to Vango.*

"Are they here, Ethel?"

"Vango?"

"Are they still here?"

"It's just me, Vango."

She put her arms around him, kissing his forehead and his eyes.

"Who fired?" asked Vango.

"It was me. Just me."

Ethel was sobbing and smiling at the same time. She hugged him very tightly.

"Where have you come from, my Vango? There isn't even any moon to see by."

"They'll be back," he said.

"No. You're staying with me."

"They're after me. They'll never stop coming after me."

"They won't find you here."

"They've got hounds. I'm tired."

"Don't be afraid."

"You've hurt me," said Vango.

"You're the one who hurt me. I've been waiting for you for six whole years."

"I was on my way to you, Ethel. I've come on foot from London. And from much farther than that too. . . ."

"Come here."

"They won't leave me alone. There are so many of them. They've got hounds."

"Stay with me."

"I'm not mad, Ethel. But they're closing in on all sides."

"I know you're not mad. I know they're after you."

"Ethel . . ."

"You promised me, Vango. In the balloon, you promised me. . . ."

"You've hurt me, Ethel."

"I'm the one who's been suffering. I love you. I'm here. I love you."

"You've shot me through the arm," sighed Vango.

Ethel let out a shriek. She could feel the blood on her hands.

"Vango!"

The first bullet had gone in just above where he'd been injured in London, and he had felt the second one skim his hairline.

She had to leave him lying on the ground to go and find her horse: she felt as if they were being torn apart.

But nothing could separate them, not even the darkness and the forest. After gently helping Vango to climb up, she thought she must be dreaming when she felt him behind her, his arm around her waist. Then she gave her horse a sharp kick in the flanks.

A WORLD ENGULFED

At three o'clock in the morning, the horse walked into the kitchen.

The Scott family's Christmas Eve party was in full swing.

Justin had just put four spit-roasted chickens on the table, their grilled skins swimming in a pool of boiling grease.

When the horse appeared, everyone gathered in the kitchen rose to their feet in a clamor of surprise.

"Bandages and a doctor!" Ethel called out without dismounting. "Justin, bring water and alcohol up to my bedroom."

Vango had fainted against her back. Ethel guided her horse down the corridor, then coaxed it to climb the grand staircase to her bedroom.

Mary arrived back at the castle a little later. People were running everywhere. One by one, the lights were going on in dozens of the castle's windows.

"Should I untie the horse from the piano on the second floor?" Peter the gardener inquired of the housekeeper without batting an eye.

Realizing something was most definitely up, Mary began to take charge of operations. She didn't ask who the boy lying on Ethel's bed was, but she put herself at the doctor's disposal.

The doctor had arrived by car, together with his small red-haired dog. He had winced on discovering the state of Vango's arm.

He began by removing a bandage that Vango had tied around his own arm. The wound was infected. Vango had swum in the Thames, traveled the length of the country, slept in barns and cattle wagons. There were still pieces of glass in his skin. And the gunshot hadn't helped matters.

Ethel threw the bandage into a basin. As the blood spread through the warm water, she recognized the blue handkerchief. The embroidered writing was slowly being reborn. The star was shining above the *V* of Vango.

How many kingdoms know us not.

Before getting down to work, the doctor pushed Ethel out of the door and ordered his dog to stand guard. She no longer had the right to be in her own bedroom.

Ethel lay down on a rug on the landing outside. She was still unable to sleep. She was overwhelmed by the emotion of it all. The effect was like that of rain on a mountain stream: at first, you don't notice the rain falling on the swirling waters, but slowly it makes the water levels rise until, one fine day, the stream overflows its banks and floods everything.

The doctor looked quite a sight when he emerged from the bedroom in the morning light. He was disheveled, his forehead was terribly pale, and his eyes were surrounded by dark circles that looked like lunar eclipses.

Ethel rushed over to him.

"If you want to keep him alive . . ." began the doctor, sounding very serious. He was busy unbuttoning his blood-spattered shirt on the landing. Ethel watched him pacing about half naked in front of her.

"If you really want to keep him alive, young lady . . ."

He took a clean shirt out of its package and put it on.

"You'd better stop firing at him!"

Ethel broke into a smile.

"Is he doing better?"

The doctor nodded as he tightened his tie. Beaming, Ethel put her hand on the door handle. The dog growled.

"No," said the doctor. "You've got to let him sleep for twenty-four hours. I don't trust you, Miss Ethel. Don't go in there before he's able to defend himself."

At that moment, Mary appeared.

"I'll keep an eye on him," the housekeeper reassured him.

"It's this young lady you should be keeping an eye on, ma'am!"

The doctor whistled to his dog and headed downstairs.

"I'll be back tomorrow."

Vango didn't sleep for twenty-four hours. He slept for twenty-four days and twenty-four nights. He might even have slept for a hundred years, just like in a fairy tale, if he hadn't found Ethel sitting next to him or standing in front of the window each time he half opened an eye.

He had also sensed someone breathing above his face while he was asleep.

At night, when the night-light was dimmed, to begin with he couldn't see her kneeling close to his bed. He thought he was alone, but little by little he was able to make out the ivory white of her eyes staring up at him through the darkness.

Vango would eat a small amount and try to take a few steps, his arm wrapped in a sheet. Then he would lie down again.

So he woke up the following year, in the third week of January 1936.

And then they started talking.

It started slowly, shyly, with long pauses. When they were able to walk as far as the window together, and later to the steps leading outside, and then as far as the trees, their words increased with the number of steps they took.

Week after week, they filled the years of silence with words.

Ethel told him about how it had been for her, six years earlier, after their grand round-the-world trip in the zeppelin, to experience his sudden disappearance. Icy voiced, she told him about the ensuing years with her brother at Everland. Then about the times she had spent in Edinburgh and London, from the age of fifteen, dancing, twirling, and trying to stay awake in order to forget. Then her despair, on the day she had received a note that she'd mistaken for an invitation to a wedding at Notre Dame, and her surprise on arriving in Paris for the marriage ceremony to discover Vango lying on the cobbled square in front of the cathedral. She told him about spotting the marksman who had been standing in ambush, about the investigation, about the visits she had paid to Eckener and Boulard, about her encounter with the Cat.

Vango, for his part, told her about his headlong flight, about all those who had fallen or disappeared around him:

Father Jean, Mademoiselle, Zefiro, even Mazzetta and his donkey. He told her about his childhood, about the cliffs, about the monastery, and the fragile secret he had finally discovered: the big boat marked with a star, his mother singing, the pirates, the murder, the shipwreck. He told her about the questions that still remained, about Mazzetta's guilty involvement, the death of the second pirate, the departure of the third for America, and the plunder that he might have taken with him.

"Treasure!" exclaimed Ethel.

"Why did Cafarello kill his friend? It makes me think perhaps there was something to share."

Vango also told her about the message signed by Ethel, containing the words "Who are you?," which had proved such a wake-up call for him. And the shadows always there behind him that would inevitably find his trail, making him chase after zeppelins and trains and jump into rivers.

Together, they began trying to piece together some answers to this string of mysteries.

Toward mid-March, when Paul had just announced his imminent return from India, the occasional silence was allowed to occur between them. These silences spoke volumes. Sometimes they led the two of them all the way to the other side of Loch Ness.

What now? That's what those silences were saying. What now? They would look at each other, then avert their gaze.

Ethel wasn't wearing her heart on her sleeve. She hadn't said "I love you" again since that Christmas Eve. They were waiting.

* * *

One morning, sitting on a flat stone down by the loch, Ethel said to Vango, "What was the name of that donkey again?"

"What donkey?"

"Mazzetta's donkey."

He didn't even need to reply. He clenched his fists. Vango had just understood.

They set off the following day.

Salina, Aeolian Islands, first day of spring, 1936

Dr. Basilio saw the little airplane landing on the sea by the pebble beach. A girl and a boy got out and waded to shore. From the old harbor, they headed for the cliffs and climbed as far as the crater of Pollara. The plane had already set off again after being waved off by the boy and the girl. They passed in front of the house with the olive tree and the barricaded shutters. In the setting sun, the doctor couldn't make out their faces with the light behind them. He just saw them take the path between the broom and the wild fennel. Then they disappeared from sight.

Dr. Basilio sat in the little driftwood armchair. He shut himself in this house every morning and every evening. He was waiting for Mademoiselle.

Paris, first day of spring, 1936

The bell in the clock tower of Saint-Germain struck eight in the evening. Superintendent Boulard blew on the bubbles in his bath to create little islands.

Two pigeons were watching him through the window.

Someone knocked at the bathroom door.

"What is it, Mother?"

Superintendent Boulard hadn't been able to take a bath in peace since he had turned twelve, back in 1878. At the age of seventy, he was starting to feel rather fed up.

"There's someone who wants to talk to you."

"I'm having my bath, Mother."

"It's rather urgent. The gentleman is in the sitting room. He doesn't look happy."

"Who is it?"

"Would you mind saying your name again for me?" Madame Boulard asked breezily. Boulard heard four letters being uttered by a voice that came from the steppes.

"VLAD."

Behind the door, with a metal bar in his hand, was Vlad the Vulture.

New York, first night of spring, 1936

Zefiro looked up.

He was at the foot of the Empire State Building.

The tallest skyscraper in the world stood at three hundred and eighty meters.

The top had been completed in 1931 with the intention of mooring airships there, but then the financial crisis had hit and the project had been put on hold. That said, despite everything, an embarkation lounge did exist on the one hundred and second floor, with customs and the abandoned air terminal lower down.

The rest of the tower was occupied by offices and a luxury hotel.

Zefiro walked into the lobby of the Plaza Hotel with his suitcase. He had refused to entrust it to the porter. He made his way over to reception and asked for Madame Victoria's room. The receptionist smiled at him in a knowing kind of a way.

"Who should I say is here?"

"Mr. Dorgeles," Zefiro replied.

"I believe Madame Victoria already has company."

The receptionist unhooked the receiver, mumbled a few words, and waited.

Above the counter, five clocks told the time in the major cities of the world. Los Angeles, Rome, London, Paris, and Tokyo. It seemed a very long wait to Zefiro. A young beggar had stopped in the street on the other side of the glass. He was staring straight at the padre, flattening both hands against the window. From one hand to the other, three words were written: *God bless you.*

A doorman in a purple tailcoat promptly shooed the beggar away.

"Filthy kid," commented the receptionist, who had been following the scene with the telephone glued to his ear.

It was clear that he was appealing to Zefiro for approval.

But the visitor didn't respond. The wait was becoming worrying. Zefiro was thinking of the real Dorgeles, whom he'd bound hand and foot and put in the trunk of his car, two streets away from Central Park.

Suddenly, the receptionist hung up the receiver. He looked at Zefiro.

"She's expecting you, Mr. Dorgeles. Nineteenth floor."

Father Zefiro glided inside the elevator and pressed the button for his floor before the attendants had even noticed. The door slid shut. He was alone.

The elevator started to rise. Zefiro opened his suitcase and took out a hook, which he poked through the elevator's wire caging. The elevator came to an abrupt halt. He unwrapped two objects from a piece of cloth. They were automatic pistols. He pushed the suitcase under the velvet banquette, checked his weapons, added a round to each of them, and put two more rounds in his pockets. He held his watch in his hand and waited.

As Zefiro took the time to catch his breath, he pictured the clearing at Falbas, near Verdun, and Werner Mann's plane that had crashed in the tree, as well as the green oak trees of La Blanche, his fellow monks, Vango, and the bees at his monastery. Finally, his mind turned to Voloy Viktor, a few dozen meters above him. The end was so close. When the second hand of his watch returned to the vertical position, he pulled out the metal hook. The elevator continued on its way.

In forty seconds, the doors would open in the middle of Voloy Viktor's reception room.

Salina, Aeolian Islands, first day of spring, 1936

The swallows were flying in arabesques around Vango. They swooped in close to him. He had to shield his eyes with his hand.

Ethel had gone to perch on the cliff top. The sun was setting behind the islands. Vango had started digging up the earth.

The swallows, which had arrived at the same time as these two young people on the island, had come from the Sahara and were overjoyed to be rediscovering warmth.

Ethel, Vango, and Paul had made several stopovers to reach the island, filling up three times on fuel at Orléans, Salon-de-Provence, and Cagliari in Sardinia: the opposite direction from that which the swallows would take the next day, to reach Notre Dame.

The plane had disappeared on the horizon now. Paul couldn't stay with them. He was expected in Spain, where his Republican friends, only recently elected, were beginning to fear a coup d'état.

The scrubland was covered in flowers. Ethel was breathing in the smells that had been such a part of Vango's childhood. She was thinking about Salina, and Everland, and all the different lost paradises where people live and grow up.

Vango didn't have a shovel. His nails had broken on a very hard object. Right away, he spotted the steel rivets on the donkey's collar. The animal had decomposed, leaving a skeleton that was almost clean. Vango had just managed to release the enormous collar.

Mazzetta's last words had been for his donkey.

Vango dragged the collar over to a small rock.

The circle of swallows was bunching up. Higher still, the falcons had also recognized Vango. They let themselves drop like stones and then set off again, hovering by the cliff tops.

With all the strength he could muster, Vango raised the harness above his head. He hurled it against the rock. The leather casing split open, and diamonds poured out in the middle of all the flowers.

"Ethel! Come and see!"

She ran over.

Together they stared at the ground, now studded with precious stones.

Mazzetta had named his donkey Tesoro. The value of this treasure was unimaginable.

In their light-filled boat, a man and a woman had lain murdered. And the man guilty of this crime possessed twice as much treasure again somewhere.

Twice this for a murderer.

Vango turned to face the great drop below him. Where was that man?

Who were his parents, who had traveled the seas with such a fortune on board?

Who was it that wanted Vango dead?

For the first time, he sensed that the origins of his mad urge always to be on the run lay in the beginnings of the century, and in history.

Vango was no ordinary orphan. He was heir to a world that had been engulfed.

He moved closer to Ethel.

A swallow swooped down toward them before rising up again.

If it had wanted to fly between them, it wouldn't have found any space between their two bodies.